Rules to Catch a Devilish Duke

SUZANNE ENOCH

St. Martin's Paperbacks

This is a work of fiction. All of the characters, organizations, and events portrayed in this novel are either products of the author's imagination or are used fictitiously.

RULES TO CATCH A DEVILISH DUKE

Copyright © 2012 by Suzanne Enoch.

For information address St. Martin's Press, 175 Fifth Avenue, New York, NY 10010.

ISBN: 978-0-312-53453-0

Printed in the United States of America

St. Martin's Paperbacks edition / October 2012

St. Martin's Paperbacks are published by St. Martin's Press, 175 Fifth Avenue, New York, NY 10010.

10 9 8 7 6 5 4 3 2 1

ONE

There were some pieces of advice, Sophia White reflected as she clung to the overturned coach's wheel in the middle of the half-frozen river Aire, that one should simply not ignore. Heaven knew she'd been warned that this particular journey was a poor idea, and at the moment she could certainly attest to the fact that her friends had been correct about that.

Above her on the partly submerged left-hand side and now roof of the mail coach, the driver seemed far more interested in retrieving satchels of correspondence than in the dozen people splashing about around him. "Stop that and give me your hand," she ordered, the rush of the cold water leaving her breathless.

"I already lost the horses and the Christmas turkeys," the driver grunted, his voice thready through the wind and blowing snow. "If I lose the mail, it'll be my job."

"But you can lose your passengers?"

"If I was you, miss, I'd stop arguing and swim to shore like the others. It ain't that deep."

Shivering, Sophia opened her mouth to protest that the top—or side—of the coach was much closer than the shore, but a whipped-up wave of water poured into her lungs. Coughing, she decided that the coachman's advice fell into the "should be followed" category. And since she'd missed her chance to listen to her employer and all her friends who'd told her not to journey to Yorkshire in the middle of December when she already had an obligation in Cornwall in mid-January, this time she needed to pay attention.

Her legs were numb, but with a deep breath she pushed off from the coach and began a half-swimming walk to the nearest shore. Chunks of ice dislodged by the coach's demise and the swift current pushed at her, sending her flailing toward the solid section of ice beyond. Most of the men were already on shore; evidently chivalry didn't include fishing freezing women out of chest-deep water during a snowstorm.

Abruptly beginning to worry that the water would shove her under the jagged-edged ice and drown her, Sophia clenched her chattering teeth, hiked her dragging, tangled skirts up around her hips, and pushed forward. A drowned turkey bumped into her bare thighs, making her lose her footing. Her shoe lodged into a pile of tumbled rocks, and with a curse she stepped out of it. Her next footstep, though, found the bottom missing, and she went down.

Icy water closed over her head. The slight amusement she'd felt earlier at the pure absurdity of the moment vanished along with her air. Oh, she should have stayed in London. She should have listened to Lady Haybury when that wise woman had told her she would find more trouble than welcome in York. She knew that the Duke of Greaves had only invited her to a holiday party because he liked to make a stir; asking to have the Duke of Hennessy's bastard daughter in attendance wasn't an act of kindness. But a chance to see an old friend, to experience one last, magnificent holiday, would have been worth it—though her plans would hardly matter if she drowned.

Someone grabbed her shoulder and hauled her upright. Sophia gasped air into her lungs, her drenched hair draping across her face. She seized onto the arm that had caught her and squeezed it while she fought to get her feet back under her.

"Steady," a deep voice ordered. "I have you."

Even through the shock of the icy water she recognized the voice. "Your Grace?" she gasped, shoving her drenched, twisted red hair out of one eye.

The lean, handsome face just inches above hers looked at least as astounded as she felt. "Sophia? Miss White, I mean. Are you injured?"

"No, Your Grace. Thank you for inviting me to Christmas." With her standing chest deep in rushing water, the howling snowstorm blowing all around them, it seemed a ridiculous thing to say, but being saved from certain death seemed to have rattled her brain loose.

He flashed a brief grin at her. "Thank me later. For now, hold on to me."

"You'll have to pry me loose," she stated, attempting a return smile and instead inhaling more water. Coughing, she decided it would be wiser to be brave in silence, at least until they were out of the river.

Adam Baswich had jumped into the water to rescue her, though he hadn't known who she was. For someone as famously controlled as the Duke of Greaves, the act itself was rather surprising. And certainly fortuitous. But at the moment, she just wanted to be out of the freezing cold water. Sophia held on to his back, her shaking fingers dug into his shoulders, as the group of men on shore hauled in the rope he had tied around his waist. Greaves was as wet as she was, but when she tucked her frozen face into his spine he felt warm, and his large frame stopped the wind from blowing snow into her eyes.

"We have to climb up onto the ice to reach the shore," Greaves said, his voice strained. "Move around in front of me."

It took several attempts to get her fingers to uncurl. "I'm trying."

"Try harder. This isn't healthy for either of us."

"I'm aware of that, Your Grace." She clenched her jaw. "Unlike you, I didn't dive in on purpose."

With her water-laden skirts tangling at her legs and trying to drag her under water again, Sophia couldn't do much but not fight him as the duke simply hauled her around in front of him. "I could never resist a damsel in distress," he panted in her ear.

The fatigue and panic beginning to press at her faded a little. "Yes, I'm certain I look quite irresistible at the moment."

She was certain she felt his breathless chuckle against the back of her neck. "You have no idea. And I apologize," he said, then before she could ask what he was apologizing for, he placed both of his large hands under her rump and heaved her up onto the ice.

With a surprised *wumpf* she sprawled onto the hard, frozen surface. She'd once seen drawings of the seals on the beaches of the Orkney Islands, and Sophia was certain she very much looked like one as she flopped on the ice, gasping for air. A moment later the Duke of Greaves hauled himself up beside her.

"I apologize again," he panted, and reached over to tug at her dress.

Wet material slapped against the back of her knees, and she realized the gown must have been hiked up her bare backside in a very unbecoming manner. "Oh, dear," she coughed out, pushing herself into a sitting position. "If I were less frozen, I would likely be mortified. As it is, thank you."

A swift, surprised grin touched his mouth and then was gone again as he stood to offer her both of his hands. Disheveled midnight hair obscured the eyes she knew to be a deep, ocean-colored gray, but he didn't seem to notice either that or her scrutiny as he pulled her to her feet. Her legs felt wobbly as a newborn's, and she sagged against him. And to think, she generally scoffed at females who pretended weakness or light-headedness in order to enlist the aid of a big, strong man.

"I'm so sorry," she muttered, belatedly righting herself again. "But truthfully, if I'd fallen on you intentionally, I would have fixed my hair first."

"Your hair is quite . . . spectacular," he returned, wrapping an arm around her waist and half lifting her as with the assistance of the rope he plowed up the snowy bank. "It's your lips turning blue that has me more concerned."

Immediately someone threw a heavy blanket over her shoulders, and she wrapped it close around her. Sophia shivered, certain the cold wind must be turning the water that drenched her clothes and hair and skin to ice. A snow-encrusted turkey scampered by squawking loudly, the coachman's assistant close on its heels.

"Poor thing," she muttered, "learned how to swim just to escape drowning, and it's still to be someone's Christmas dinner." It seemed a great deal of effort for very little reward. In a sense, she was in the same predicament. She only hoped a holiday at Greaves Park would be worth her efforts. The memories would have to last her a lifetime, after all.

"I rank you freezing to death over a half-drowned fowl. Evans!" The duke gestured at one of the dozen dry men interspersed with blanket-wrapped ones along the bank. "Get Miss White into a wagon and escort her to the house. I need to see the rest of the passengers to the inn."

A tall fellow in a heavy coat, his floppy-brimmed hat secured to his head by a thick woolen scarf, took her by the shoulders. "Can you walk, miss?" he asked.

Sophia watched as the Duke of Greaves vanished

into the blowing snow, becoming just another of the bulky dark shapes hurrying around the growing cluster of horses and vehicles. Undoubtedly there were other foundering passengers waiting for heroic rescue. She blinked. "Yes. I've thrown a shoe, but I can walk. Thank you."

Evans guided her to a wagon and without warning lifted her into the back of the old vehicle. From somewhere he produced an additional blanket which he tucked around her legs and feet before he clambered up beside the driver. In a moment they were bumping along the same road she'd traveled before the collapse of the old stone bridge had interrupted the journey in a rather spectacular manner.

"How far is it to Greaves Park?" she called, ducking her nose beneath the edge of the blanket. Originally she'd meant to leave the mail coach at the close-by village of Hanlith and then hire a cart or a hack to take her to the estate. The ride now hadn't cost her the expected shilling, but she would rather have been warm and dry.

"We're nearly to the carriage road now," Evans returned, twisting in his seat to look at her. "Not ten minutes past that."

"How in the world did His Grace happen to be out here? And with all of you?"

"His Grace rides nearly every day, whatever the weather. We were in the village for onions and potatoes and heard the commotion. It's a lucky thing, miss."

Oh, she agreed with that. And considering she hadn't had much expectation of kindness or even polite conversation once she arrived at Greaves Park, her hopes hardly felt dashed by a dunking in the river. She'd journeyed from London to Yorkshire for only one reason—or two, she supposed—and that hadn't changed. "Do you know if Keating and Camille Black-wood have arrived yet?"

"You'd have to ask Udgell about that, miss. I don't have much to do with the house."

Even with the blankets, now that she was still and not fighting for breath, the cold began to seep into her bones. She needed to get out of her wet clothes, but that would have to wait until they reached Greaves Park. Resolutely she tucked her feet closer to her body and concentrated on thoughts of how grand it would be to see Camille Pryce—or rather Blackwood, now—after six months.

Whether Greaves had invited her as a favor to his good friend Keating Blackwood or because he thought she would be a good way to stir up a bit of scandal for his friends, she was supremely grateful to have been asked to the Christmas holiday. After years of being bounced from place to place, of simply waiting for her fellow boarding school residents or supposed friends to discover that she was the Duke of Hennessy's ille-gitimate daughter, she'd finally found a true friend in Camille.

The fact that she and Camille had both been forced into employment at The Tantalus Club only meant that they had a connection neither of them would have other-wise expected. Yes, the club was scandalous because it only employed lovely young ladies—some of very good birth and all of them well educated—but that had been Lady Haybury's point when she'd opened the club. Scandal drew customers, or members, or whatever they chose to call themselves. They came, and they gambled and ate and spent their money, and ruined women like Camille and her had a place they could call a home. And an income, and freedom enough to live however they chose.

The club also granted them protection from the outside world—to a point. Or so she'd believed until just under a fortnight ago. She shook herself. *No thinking about that now.* It wouldn't do her any good, and she meant to enjoy herself while she could.

On the tail of her thought the wagon crested a small rise and the valley beyond came into view. Peripherally through the blowing snow she noted where wilderness softened into a large formal garden, now heavily dusted with white and fronted by a small frozen lake. On the far side of that lay a substantial wood of oak and elm, twisted and knotted by Yorkshire's harsh weather despite the relative shelter of the shallow valley. At the center of it all, catching and holding her gaze as it emerged from the murky gloom of snow and twilight, stood a light-colored, sprawling behemoth.

Dozen and dozens of windows gazed out from the huge rectangular center section of Greaves Park and the narrower east and west wings that rose from the snow at either end, forming a tremendous, chimney-dotted H. She'd driven past Blenheim Palace in Oxfordshire once, and Greaves Park made that magnificent building look like a cottage.

The white and gray stone made the estate house seem almost part of the snowstorm around it, emerging and vanishing again in the changing light of dusk. In fact, it reminded her of those silly gothic tales her friend Emily Portsman kept in her room at The Tantalus Club. A shiver only half from the cold ran down her spine.

"Don't you fret, miss," Evans abruptly commented. "Mrs. Brooks, the head housekeeper, 'll have you inside and warm and dry in no time."

Perhaps Evans could read minds, or perhaps he was merely accustomed to the overwhelmed awe of first-time, half-drowned visitors to the estate. Either way, the conversation drew her away from her own overwrought imaginings. "How many servants does His Grace employ?" she asked, her teeth chattering so badly she wasn't certain she made any sense at all.

"More than enough to see to everything you could ever need, Miss White. We may be out in the wilds of Yorkshire, but don't you worry about that."

Drat it all. She must have sounded like some pointy-nosed, spoiled prima donna. Which might have been fun, except that she doubted her performance could compare to the actual noblewomen who'd already arrived there. "I only meant that it must take a small army to keep up such a grand house."

Evans faced her again, his bundled-up expression quizzical. "Near fifty then, I think. Udgell or Mrs. Brooks'll know better than me."

She nodded, much preferring to be a curiosity over some easily deciphered chit—even one who'd evidently just displayed her bare, frozen arse to half of Yorkshire. Finally the wagon stopped at the head of the wide, semi-circular drive, and Evans hopped to the snowy ground with enviable ease. Sophia couldn't even feel her legs any longer. That hardly mattered, though, because the servant lifted her out of the back of the cart before she could do any more than gasp her surprise. Evans carried her up the trio of shallow granite steps to the massive front door. Under other circumstances, with two other people, this would have been terribly romantic, she was certain.

The heavy oak door opened just as they reached it. "Evans," a reedy male voice intoned, "what have you there? We are not a charitable estab—"

"This is Miss White, one of His Grace's guests," the groom returned breathlessly, shifting his grip a little around her knees. "The bridge finally let loose and tossed the entire mail coach into the river. Drowned nearly a dozen turkeys, and—"

"Stop talking and follow me," the absurdly tall, thin butler interrupted, turning his back and heading for the curved, mahogany-railed staircase at the rear of the foyer. "Roger, find Mrs. Brooks immediately."

A footman scampered off into the depths of the house. Sophia nearly began a protest that she could manage on her own, but she closed her lips before she uttered a sound. It was a very grand, very tall staircase, and at the moment she doubted she would have been able to drag herself up to the first landing.

More servants fell in around them, and she began to feel as though she were leading a parade of hot water buckets, pillows, coal-filled bed pans, and what looked like someone's oversized night rail. The bed pan looked especially blissful, and she could almost imagine how the warm metal would feel against her chilled feet.

They reached a large bedchamber, and after a brief conversation a short, rotund woman chased the male servants and all but one other maid out and closed the door behind them. "There we are," she said in a warm voice that didn't much feel like it belonged in the large, cold house, stripping the wet blanket from Sophia's shoulders and handing it to the second maid. "They might at least have sent for the coach and kept you out of that dreadful howling wind."

With the blanket gone, cold air rushed in around Sophia, and her already stiff muscles tightened so much she creaked. She shuddered, then nearly fell to the floor as Mrs. Brooks and the other woman began pulling at buttons and untying ribbons. She was too cold even to care when her gown fell into an icy puddle on the hardwood. Now the remainder of Yorkshire had seen her bare arse. Together the two servants half dragged her to the large, cast-iron bathtub and plunked her down into the steaming water.

"Oh! Oh . . . goodness that's nice," she chattered,

sinking chin deep into the water. "And I didn't mind the cart. I'm only grateful His Grace arrived before I ended like the poor Christmas turkeys."

"Don't you even try to talk, Miss White. We'll have you warm and dry and tucked into bed in no time."

"Actually, I think I'd like to stay in the bath for a bit," Sophia countered, all the attention beginning to make her uneasy now that she didn't feel in imminent danger of freezing to death. "And I can tuck myself into bed. Truly. Thank you so much for your help."

Mrs. Brooks opened and closed her mouth again, then nodded. "As you wish then, Miss White. If you require any assistance, pull the bell. Gilly or I will see to you."

The other maid, a petite blonde with a dash of freckles across her nose, dipped a curtsy. "I'll set your gown out by the fire to dry, miss."

"Thank you. And please. It's just Sophia." Even without these odd circumstances, she and servants had a bond that none of Society's proper misses would ever dare to claim. Her mother had been a duchess's maid, after all.

She closed her eyes, and in a moment the bustling and rustling ceased, closely followed by the click and thud of the bedchamber door closing. Ah, warm, steamy bliss. With the surprise and brief terror as the coach pitched headlong into the river, everything had been so busy she'd barely had time to breathe. Chaos and turkeys and shouting men and the heavy, thick crack of ice, the shock when she'd found herself submerged as the coach slowly rolled onto its side—they were all quite lucky that no one had been dragged under the ice and drowned. *She'd* nearly drowned.

And who would even have noticed? Camille, of course, would have missed seeing her for Christmas, but the new Mrs. Blackwood had a husband and a new

life now. The other girls at The Tantalus Club—until
the next scandalous chit came along looking for sanc-
tuary and employment. Her aunt and uncle didn't even
know where she might be, as far as she knew, and they
would care even less. To them she was just a nuisance
dropped on their doorstep to eat their food, an unre-
markable girl with no prospects and a supremely troublesome parentage.

For once her father would have noticed, and he would
likely have been extremely annoyed that his twenty-
three-year-old mistake had managed at the last moment
to evade his reach now that he'd suddenly decided to
notice her. Or perhaps the Duke of Hennessy would only
regret that she hadn't perished, after all. Her drowning
would have saved him the trouble of following through
on his threats to either remove her from The Tantalus
Club or to remove the Tantalus from London, the awful,
arrogant man.

The door thudded and clicked again. Grateful for
the interruption of her unaccustomed morose thoughts,
Sophia opened her eyes again. And then she yelped.
The Duke of Greaves stood in the doorway, gazing at
her with steel-gray eyes.

Adam Baswich, the Duke of Greaves, stood looking
down at the naked young lady in the cast-iron bathtub.
Steam rose from the water to straighten the damp strands
of unusual scarlet hair that tangled deep red and lush at
the top of her head. If she hadn't been wearing the remains of a bonnet earlier he would have recognized her
even in the middle of the river Aire; he'd never encountered anyone with hair of quite that color.

Realizing that Mrs. Brooks wasn't present, he hesitated for a brief moment, then moved forward anyway,
stopping halfway into the guest bedchamber. Saving a

chit's life should grant him some license to speak with her. "Miss White. You're unhurt, I hope?"

She nodded, sinking still lower in the tub so that her lips were only a fraction above the rippling line of water. If they hadn't been chattering, he might have considered them kissable, but that was neither here nor there.

"Bumped and bruised, I think, now that I can feel my arms and legs again. But yes. This is much better than being drowned." She offered a smile that only improved the enticement of her mouth. "And as you're the reason I didn't drown, I think you should call me Sophia."

"Considering that the coachman was saving the mail and the turkeys, aiding you seemed the least I could do," he returned. "I hate when my guests expire while answering my invitations. It puts people off."

"I can see where that might happen."

This seemed an odd and rather amusing conversation to have with someone—a chit in particular—who'd nearly drowned, but on the other hand she would have need of her good humor. "I'm afraid that this was all we were able to recover of your luggage." Putting a sympathetic expression on his face, Adam lifted up the wet, misshapen hat box that dangled by its fraying handle. "I'm sorry. We did search, Sophia."

Sophia White looked at him, then at the box. Then she laughed, her mouth upturning and eyes squinting at the corners in genuine amusement. The sound, her entire reaction, in fact, was completely unexpected, and he frowned, even more intrigued now. Although he didn't have much experience with half-drowned women, he doubted most of them would laugh at additional misfortune.

"I enjoy a good joke," he said. "Is this one?"

Choking a little, Miss White lifted one hand out of

the water and pointed at the hat box. "I detest that hat. I only purchased it on a dare and meant to wear it to shock Cammy and your other guests." She chuckled again. "Oh, it's dreadful. I daresay it only survived because Poseidon refused to have it in his river and cast it back upon the shore."

If there was one thing Adam insisted on, it was having his curiosity satisfied. For the moment he put aside the information that she meant to shock his guests. That had been one of the reasons he'd invited her to his party in the first place, actually. With all the misery he meant to inflict on himself this holiday, he deserved a bit of amusement.

Keeping half his attention on Miss White, he set the box down on a chair and with his boot knife cut the string holding it closed when the wet knot wouldn't budge. Once he'd removed the lid, he reached in and pulled the sopping wet thing out into view. It was blue, with what looked like the remains of two bright blue ostrich feathers arching over the top of it and shading two concentric rings of red and yellow flowers. A faux bird—either a sparrow or a bullfinch—nested in the center of the yellow, inner ring. "Good God." She was absolutely correct. The hat was hideous.

Even considering the ugly hat, her reaction wasn't anything he'd anticipated. After all, he'd just informed her that everything she'd brought with her to Yorkshire was gone. Perhaps she hadn't understood that. Or perhaps that had been hysterical laughter, though he abruptly doubted that. Previously acquainted with her or not, he was beginning to suspect that Sophia White had rather more facets to her than he'd expected.

Adam took a breath. "Well, it's not a disaster yet. I'm certain we'll be able to find something for you to wear." Setting aside the hat, he noted that if he took a step or two closer he would be able to see her bare legs beneath the water. He had no objection to seeing them again, actually, but it seemed a bit like taking advantage.

"Camille is nearly my size," she commented, sending a glance at the towel across the foot of the bathtub. "I know she would lend me a gown."

"Mrs. Blackwood isn't here."

Her pretty green eyes blinked. "That complicates things somewhat, doesn't it?" She sighed, her mostly submerged shoulders rising and falling beneath the thinning curtain of steam. "Perhaps one of your other guests could be persuaded to lend me a castoff, then, until Cammy arrives. Or I'd be happy to purchase something from one of the maids."

So in the space of a very few minutes she'd lost her clothes and the presence of her dearest friend, but Sophia White didn't seem overly concerned by any of it. Adam almost hesitated to tell her the rest, but he had the distinct feeling that the news was more of a tragedy for him than for her. Aside from that, Miss White didn't seem to overset easily. But then again, her entire future didn't hinge on the next few weeks. He wasn't so lucky, himself.

"You are my first guest, Sophia," he said aloud. "And until the storm stops and the bridge can be repaired, you shall be my only guest."

This time uncertainty crossed her expression, and he could practically hear her thoughts. Was she trapped at Greaves Park for the winter? Was there anywhere she could go to escape her situation? He could answer all those questions, of course, but he wanted to hear her ask them aloud, first. Sophia White might be a child of unacknowledged parentage, and one who worked in a profession most of his peers considered highly unacceptable, but there were times a few months ago when he'd actually found her amusing. And interesting. Had it been a façade, or was she actually as good-humored and practical as she pretended?

She spent a moment gazing at him, then wrinkled her nose in a thoughtful scowl. "Well. Unless I'm to remain submerged in the bath until spring thaw, I shall have to hope that Mrs. Brooks liked me well enough to allow me to alter one of her old dresses. Unless you have a supply of onion or potato sacks to hand, of course."

Considering how rarely anyone accomplished the perturbing feat of surprising him, Adam couldn't quite believe that she'd done so unintentionally—though under the circumstances, unless she'd taken a powder keg to the bridge, she'd had no idea what awaited her on the road to Greaves Park. "You mean to tell me that as long as someone has enough charity to lend you a gown, you have no other concerns over your situation?" he asked, unable to keep the well-honed skepticism from creeping into his voice.

"I *am* somewhat concerned that you've barged into my bath without so much as knocking," she returned promptly. "But I'm also aware of precisely what sort of female everyone thinks me." She tilted her head, a straying strand of her autumn-colored hair dipping into the water as she assessed him. "Is that why you came in here? I'm still dreadfully cold, you know."

Hm. Perhaps it had crossed his mind, but he wasn't about to admit to it. "You are the friend of my friend's wife, Sophia. I wasn't aware that you would be naked."

"Fair enough. And considering that you pulled me out of a river, even if I were prone to be otherwise offended, I certainly wouldn't be now."

Was that an invitation? He hoped so, but he had a few questions he wanted answered, first. Of course if he'd been a true gentleman, now that he did know she was naked, he likely should have left the room. Instead he hooked his ankle around a chair, dragged it closer, and sat. "You're well educated."

She nodded, looking up at him from beneath long lashes. "I am quite well educated."

"And yet I recall one evening at The Tantalus Club when you complained to Lord Effington that if that Cleopatra chit ever showed her face in London, she would regret attempting to steal the Nile from us."

Her mouth lifted at the corners. "And Lord Effington laughed so hard at me that he didn't even notice he'd lost seven hundred pounds at faro to the club." She lowered her gaze briefly before her green eyes met his squarely again. "Should I dissemble, then? It gives me an aching head after a while, but I can pretend stupidity if it benefits me."

In the company of Keating Blackwood and Camille, Adam had once escorted Sophia to the Tower of London and had even untangled a lion cub's claws from her hem. He couldn't recall that she'd said anything ridiculous, or if he'd been lured into saying anything haughty or condescending in return. The fact that he was attempting to recall several brief conversations with her, however, spoke volumes. She'd just elevated herself from mildly interesting to intriguing. "I prefer that my guests be themselves," he said aloud. "So I suppose I shall converse with whichever face you choose to show me."

"I just showed you my actual face, so that will have to do, I'm afraid."

All of the ladies of The Tantalus Club were beauties; the owner, Lady Haybury, only hired the most tempting of chits. The fact that they were untouchable except by their own choice made them even more attractive to most of the lordlings of Mayfair. Some of the young ladies came from good homes and bad circumstances, and all of them were well spoken and charming.

He'd noted months ago that Sophia White was an attractive young lady, just as he'd noted that she had a very unattractive parentage. In the same way, he noted now that she didn't blush and hide when a man disrupted her bath, and that she'd looked him over from head to toe at the same time she'd stated that she wasn't offended by his presence, but was simply too chilled to leave the bathtub.

A living, breathing conundrum, when he'd expected—at least for the time being—a tiresome, fluttery, complaining headache. As for tomorrow, well, that remained to be seen.

"So I am your only guest."

"You are. For the moment, anyway." He drew a breath, wondering if she realized just how . . . vital that made her to him at the moment. "But you are not the only female in residence. My sister arrived a week ago. As I am unmarried, Lady Wallace hosts my Christmas gatherings. I don't invite guests in order to deliberately ruin their reputations." Not this year, at least. He had particular need for a female of sterling reputation.

Color had begun to touch her cheeks again, though the amusement in her eyes faded a little. "I suppose the proper thing for me to do would be to volunteer to leave Greaves Park for Hanlith, since your large house party is now a small family gathering."

"That's not necessary." In fact, under no circumstances did he wish her to leave him alone with his sister. A week had more than sufficed to provide him with all the family interaction he could tolerate. Before he could tell her that, however, that compelling smile of hers made him pause.

"Good," she returned, "because I think the holiday will be much more enjoyable here."

"I would have to agree with that." Belatedly Adam shook himself. Whatever seductions he might have had in mind, they could wait until the chit with the stunning red hair and unexpected wit had a chance to dry off and warm up. After that . . . well, Christmas was for opening gifts, after all. He stood. "I will see to it that you have a suitable wardrobe."

"I will see to my own wardrobe. If you begin dressing me, I'll feel . . . obligated to you. Even more than I already do."

People rarely turned down his offers of generosity. He didn't make them very often. And while it annoyed him, he had to respect her wishes. And her. "As you will, then. I'll send Mrs. Brooks back in to tend to you. Work your wiles on her if you wish a gown. I'll have Mrs. Beasel the cook save a potato sack, just in case."

Sophia snorted, then belatedly attempted to cover the sound with a cough. "Thank you, Your Grace."

In the doorway, he stopped again. "You are quite welcome, Sophia."

TWO

"I must have been mad to think that just once you wouldn't attempt to mar our holiday by bringing one of your bloody mistresses here."

Adam looked up from his correspondence. "Good morning, Eustace. I could tell from your tone that you were saying something accusatory, but I didn't quite catch it."

Eustace Landen, the Marchioness of Wallace, remained in the doorway of his office. Her dark hair was, as always, immaculately fashioned atop her head, and a deep gray morning gown set her light gray eyes off to perfection. Adam had always found it ironic that his older sister looked more like a warmhearted confidante than an ice-cold shrew, but he'd certainly known her long enough to see past her pretty skin.

"I had thought that this year, at least, you would manage something respectable—or at least your interpretation of the word. I'm not surprised, but I am disappointed. You know how important this holiday is, Adam, and yet you invite a Tantalus girl? I thought you'd make some effort, even knowing the . . . regard you have for your only family. There is at least one person you will need to impress this Christmas."

"Beg pardon, but are you crediting me with destroying the Aire bridge? Or conjuring the storm? Or perhaps causing the mail coach to run three hours behind schedule? I assure you, while I have my methods, I'm not a god."

"You invited an unacceptable female."

"Yes, I did. I also invited Keating Blackwood, who once killed a man. And Keating's new wife, Camille, who abandoned the same man at the altar twice. And Lord Lassiter, who's been through four wives. And Haymes, who won his butler in a wager. And—"

"Don't remind me," she retorted. "I've seen your guest list. But you've also invited a dozen highborn ladies here, for you to . . . evaluate, I presume. Or is it merely for a laugh with your disreputable friends? Is it still all a jest to you? Because I can promise that I've had several solicitors review the contents of Father's will. It can't be contested, or amended. Even by you. And you are very nearly out of time."

"Enough." Setting aside the letter he'd been writing to Keating, Adam gave his full attention to his sister. Most people didn't care to receive his full attention, and even Eustace wandered over to fiddle with the potted ivy on an end table. "I've had solicitors engaged, as well, and I know why you were so eager to volunteer your services this year. You're a vulture, Eustace."

"I'm concerned over this family's reputation. And I will be prepared to step in when you fail."

"The Christmas party will go on," he stated, "and my parade of would-be brides will arrive, even if I have to swim across the river and carry them back. I'm sending instructions for everyone to be put up at Etherton, at my expense, until I have the bridge repaired, also at my expense. So I'm afraid that you and your grasping son will not be assuming any more of my dukedom than I choose to give you. Which is not a penny more than you already receive."

His sister shook her head, the curls at either temple swaying. "I didn't make any of these stipulations," she retorted, "and I'm not the one who's put off marriage long enough to endanger my own inheritance. For your own sake, send your whore to Hanlith at least, so no one has to look at her."

"She is a guest." And the one bit of fun he'd been looking forward to having. "You are an unpleasant necessity."

"I know that . . . thing is Hennessy's bastard, Adam. Gotten on a maid, of all things."

"I'm aware of her parentage. She is a friend."

"'A friend,'" Eustace repeated, her lips thinning. "Like that actress Sarah Nichols was a friend, and Rebecca Reynolds was a fr—"

"I had no idea you kept such a close eye on me," Adam interrupted, his voice low and even. If she wanted an argument, he was certainly in the mood to oblige her with one. A damned holiday party with no guests, a wedding to arrange with no potential brides to speak of. If he had to put his head in the noose, he meant to make it as painless as possible. Therefore, Sophia White wasn't going anywhere if he had anything to say about it. Which he did.

"Someone has to keep an eye on you. Mother always said you were just like Father, but since you can't even live up to his diminished expectations of you, I'm beginning to think you're even worse. And if you don't marry by the first of February, I will see to it that Father's will is enforced, and you will lose every unentailed bit of property and wealth to my son."

"Your twelve-year-old son."

"Yes. Which means that you will soon be doing as *I* say. And that will be the end of your overbearing arrogance."

They'd had this conversation before, and especially over the past two years, when Eustace had begun to hope that he would fail. He still didn't like it any more than he had the first time he'd heard it. "It's a pity you're my sister," he returned, "or I could marry a self-righteous shrew and be just like Father."

"If you *were* married, I could spend the holiday with my family and friends and have nothing further to do with you."

"That's the best reason for me to marry that I've yet heard." Standing, he strode up to his sister. "Sophia White is to be treated as any guest, Eustace. Better, because she expects less. Is that clear?"

His sister took a step backward, but only clucked her tongue at him.

Taking Eustace's chin in his hand, he forced her to meet his gaze. "Tell me if you think I'm jesting."

She did meet his gaze then, her light gray eyes widening almost imperceptibly. "Very well, Adam. Have your amusement. At least no one is here to witness it, thank God. Just remember that no one is here to save you, either."

"I haven't forgotten anything."

Once Eustace glided back down the hallway to her own rooms, Adam sat again to gaze out his window. Soft white covered the garden below and weighted the branches of the nearest trees. The lake and forest beyond were obscured by the low clouds and the heavy falling snow. In the near silence it almost felt as though Greaves Park had been removed from the world to sit on the edge of an endless, empty sky.

Generally Adam didn't like the illusion. He spent his life acquiring information and using it to influence people and events, and that couldn't be done in isolation. During the Season he rarely spent as much as a single night in only his own company. Parliament, dinners, soirees, the theater, clubs—those were the times he enjoyed. Everyone knew something, whether they realized it or not. And he'd made an art of uncovering even the most well-hidden bits and bobs.

Evidently he enjoyed the pursuit of information so greatly that he'd neglected tending his own garden, as it were—that idiotic clause in his father's will which stipulated that the disappointing heir he'd produced with his disappointing wife prove himself at least half a man by marrying before his thirtieth year, and by becoming a father by his thirty-first. Back when he'd inherited the title—God, had it truly been eleven years now?—the paragraph had seemed ridiculous. By now he'd expected to have overcome his . . . reluctance to be a husband, for the memories of his own parents and their so-called marriage to have faded away. And now with an almost absurd abruptness, he'd run out of time.

It wasn't that he disliked women. Far from it. In fact, the list of his former mistresses was nearly as long as that of his business and social appointments. Mistresses served two purposes as far as he was concerned. They frequently knew a selection of unexpected gossip, but it was equally important that they simply be . . . available, and whenever he decided to call. But a wife, someone who never actually went away when he'd tired of her, that was a completely different tangle.

He'd parted company from his last mistress, Lady Helena Brennan, some six weeks ago. While he hadn't engaged her for her wit, he had expected honesty about any other entanglements. Unfortunately, dishonesty had proven to be the quality she had in most abundance. And so he'd arrived in Yorkshire alone. He wondered what Helena would have thought if she'd known how close she'd come to becoming the Duchess of Greaves, simply to save him the effort of looking elsewhere. Now he could only be thankful that she'd disappointed him *before* he could ask the bloody question rather than after he'd donned his shackles.

The timing of this damned storm and the subsequent collapse of the old stone bridge yesterday couldn't have been worse. A week later and all his guests would have been safely to Greaves Park, warm and well provisioned until spring thaw, if necessary. Now, however, not even Eustace's husband, Phillip Landen, had arrived, though Adam hardly counted anyone who would willingly marry into the Baswich family as someone with whom he would care to converse, much less call a friend or an ally. As this holiday had become about something other than a gathering of friends, anyway, what he required was marriageable females. What he had at the moment was one potential mistress—which, although more pleasant to contemplate, simply wouldn't suffice.

He'd instructed that ropes and pulleys be strung across the Aire at the bridge, so at least mail could travel back and forth. And now he needed to find an engineer, an architect, and a quantity of stonemasons. In the meantime, he went to work finishing with sending word to any guests who might be traveling to Yorkshire that they were not to turn around and go home. For those who might have already reached Etherton on the far side of the river, he would pay for their accommodations if they would wait for the bridge to be repaired, or they could risk an additional four days of travel through the rugged, snow-covered Yorkshire countryside and go around.

"Damnation."

"Shall I take that as a signal that I shouldn't disturb you?"

Adam looked up again from his desk. And choked back a completely inappropriate grin. "Sophia. I see you found something other than onion sacks to wear."

She brushed a hand down a very yellow, very over-sized muslin gown. It appeared to be held up by hair ribbons knotted around the waist and shoulder straps sewn into the existing sleeves. "I'm afraid Mrs. Brooks is a fraction larger than I am."

"I would agree with that assessment." Eustace was much nearer to Sophia's height and weight, but he wouldn't trust his sister not to poison any gown she was forced to lend his sole houseguest. "I have several other females on staff. Surely one of them owns attire that doesn't make it look as though you're wearing a Bedouin's tent."

Sophia snorted. "Mrs. Brooks has promised to inquire. I won't take anything that someone needs, however. At church on Christmas they will wish to wear their Sunday best, and I doubt they'll appreciate me wearing it beforehand."

He shook himself free of the abrupt thought that her Sunday best would be wearing nothing at all. "Have you had a tour of the house?"

"I have not."

"Well, I happen to be momentarily available." Rising, he walked around the desk. "At the risk of repeating myself, I could purchase you a gown or two," he added, deciding her mother must have been Irish. Hennessy certainly wasn't, and he couldn't conjure another reason for her deep red, curling hair. "I believe there's at least one seamstress in Hanlith."

"Thank you for the offer, Your Grace, but you know I cannot accept. If you purchased me a single gown, by the time I returned to London everyone would know it. While that might make me the envy of some of the other girls at the Tantalus, the . . . penalty would be more than I am willing to pay."

"A penalty? For being seen as my mistress."

She nodded. "Precisely."

"And you don't wish to be my mistress? You did accept my invitation, after all."

Color touched her fair cheeks. "I thought you invited me here so I could spend Christmas with Cammy. Was I in error?"

Adam stifled a frown. He hadn't expected a gentlemen's club employee with standards. Several things he'd taken for granted about Sophia White had evidently been wrong. She certainly wasn't dull-witted or grasping, for one thing. And while he wouldn't say that she embraced her scandalous birth, she didn't seem overly troubled by it, either. And then there was the fact that she was employed at quite possibly the most scandalous establishment in Town with the exception of an actual bawdy house. And yet she hadn't considered becoming some wealthy gentleman's mistress. "I doubt my failure to provide you with clothing will prevent any rumors."

"True enough," she conceded, "but I'm accustomed to rumors. A gown from you would be proof."

"You are an unusual woman."

Amusement touched her meadow-colored eyes. "Thank you, Your Grace."

"That wasn't a compliment."

Sophia lowered her gaze briefly. "Well, then." With a breath she visibly shook herself. "Camille told me that you always have a large house party at Christmas. Is it a family tradition?"

He left his office and gestured for her to join him. "It was a tradition of my father's. After his death, my mother stopped it. When she died eight years ago, I began it again."

"She didn't like the gatherings, then?"

"No, she didn't." Generally hearing of his mother's death, no matter how long ago it occurred, the listener expressed his or her unfelt condolences. Not so Sophia White, though her own mother had expired at approximately the same time, he knew. Curious, that. Perhaps they each held the same level of affection for their maternal figurehead.

"So *did* you invite me here simply to create a stir? I've noticed that you seem to . . . enjoy being surrounded by scandal."

"Do I? How so?"

"You allowed Keating Blackwood to reside at your house in London," she returned promptly. "Bloody Blackwood, himself. And then you went to his cousin's wedding when you knew Keating would never allow the ceremony to take place."

"You have me deciphered, then."

"Not even a little." She grinned briefly, her green eyes dancing. "But I do think you enjoy a ruckus."

Adam wondered if Sophia had any idea how few people jested with him. As long as she was his only distraction from winter and from solitude and from his sister, he hoped she wouldn't realize it. "I'm a duke," he said aloud. "It would be very easy for my life to become unbearably dull and dusty. So yes, I suppose I do have a certain appreciation for people who thumb their noses at Society."

"That's good for me, since I was born with my proverbial thumb attached to my proverbial nose."

"I'm glad it's proverbial, or you would look rather odd," he returned, reflecting that he'd been lucky. If Francis Henning had been the only guest to make it across the bridge, for example, Adam would have locked himself—or Henning—in a storage room by now.

His circumstances could definitely have been even worse than that. One of the marriageable chits he'd invited for inspection might just as easily have been tossed into the river, and he would have been forced either to court her or to dance about in avoidance to prevent becoming leg-shackled before he managed a look at the rest of the dress-wearing herd.

Together they descended a side staircase, and he pushed open the door to the orangerie. Three dozen fruit-bearing plants in large pots had been arranged in a quaint indoor garden complete with benches and caged songbirds. He stood back as Sophia swirled in a circle at the center of the room.

"This is lovely," she exclaimed, her overlong skirts billowing out around her ankles.

The sight was unexpectedly . . . charming, and for a moment he lost the track of the conversation. "It's the only way to keep the weather from killing the orange and peach trees. I've been told this is a pleasant place to sit and read, if you've a mind to do so."

"How many guests were you expecting?"

"I still am expecting," he amended, "somewhere between thirty and forty." He pushed back at the urge to straighten the sliding sleeve of her oversized gown. "Do you ride?"

Sophia blinked. "I've sat on a pony a few times, at boarding school. I don't believe that makes me a horsewoman. Why?"

"I ride nearly every day." He gestured her back through the door and down the rear hallway. "I have several ponies. We'll go out once the weather clears."

"You don't need to keep me entertained, Your Grace," she said, stopping. "Simply being here is a gift."

"You need more gifts, then. I saved your life. You owe me an outing."

"But—"

"And you may trust that I generally do as I please," he interrupted. "Now. Through here is the Baswich family portrait gall . . ." He trailed off as he realized that she hadn't followed him. "Is something amiss?"

For a long moment she stood in silence, meeting his gaze. That in itself surprised him; most chits gazed demurely at his feet while conversing with him. Then she sighed. "I have noticed that you didn't answer my question earlier. Are you going to attempt to make me your mistress?"

A laugh pushed its way out of his chest. Attempting to ignore the fact that firstly, more than a few women would have given a great deal to become his mistress, and secondly, that he rarely attempted something without succeeding, and thirdly, that this holiday had him looking for a wife, whatever he might prefer, he lifted an eyebrow. "Well, if I meant to attempt a subtle seduction you've certainly foiled me."

She frowned. "I believe I mentioned that I'm not as foolish as many people think, Your Grace."

"I recall. Why?"

"I have several requirements for my life, some of them very recent and . . . unexpected. My best interests are not served by being any man's mistress. And however close your friendship with Keating might be, I have to ask myself—and you—why I'm here."

Adam dropped into one of the gilded chairs set in the hallway just outside the portrait gallery. "I rarely explain myself, Sophia. That said, while I might appreciate the stir your presence would cause, you are not here for anything more nefarious than that. For God's sake, at the moment it's either you or my sister with whom I'll be spending time, and Eustace is remarkably unlikable."

Sophia decided that if the Duke of Greaves *had* meant to offer her the position of mistress, or even force her into it, he wasn't the sort to dissemble about it. As he'd commented before, he generally got what he wanted. He did have a reputation for enjoying the company of ladies, but the majority of them—at least the ones she knew of—were wealthy, independent, and either highborn or so popular that their birth didn't matter. While she was independent for the moment, she was only highborn on her father's side, and she certainly wasn't wealthy. Or popular.

She shook out her thoughts. Why she felt the need to tally her qualifications for being a mistress, she had no idea. Until two weeks ago she'd thought that the rules of Society didn't apply to her at all. Then she'd discovered that she'd been very, very wrong. And now, while a night or two of pleasurable scandal was one thing, becoming even a duke's pampered mistress would make matters even worse.

"You're being quiet," he observed. "Do you require more assurances of your safety?"

Sophia forced a chuckle as she hiked up her sleeve and approached his chair. "I've survived ice and turkeys. Do your worst, Your Grace."

"For God's sake, call me Adam. Or Greaves, at least. As you said, we've faced fair and fowl—both spellings, mind you—together."

Adam. It was an honest, forthright name for a man with a reputation for subterfuge and subtle skill, but it suited him, nonetheless. But now those gray eyes were gazing at her again, as if he could hear her thoughts. She cleared her throat, hoping he couldn't hear all of them. "Adam, then. I expected to see Lady Helena Brennan here already," she ventured, as he led her into the portrait gallery.

She felt his gaze on her. "Did you, then?" They strolled in silence for a moment. "Evidently you aren't aware that Helena recently wed Lord Crandell and moved to Surrey."

"Oh." No, she hadn't known that. Once the Season

ended, most of the good gossip left London along with the regular members of The Tantalus Club. "Am I happy for her?"

If she was being too bold or speaking out of turn, she had little doubt that Greaves would tell her to mind her own damned business. Best to know now, however, precisely where she stood. Or if she needed to make her way to Hanlith before nightfall, after all.

A muscle in his lean cheek jumped. "*I* am marginally put out, but somewhat admiring of a devious intelligence I hadn't thought she possessed. Crandell is a lump, but he'll provide for her."

She nodded, secretly wondering why anyone would choose to marry a lump if given any chance at all to do otherwise. She certainly wouldn't—but then, sometimes a person didn't have the chance to choose. "Then I am happy for her."

The glance he sent her this time was even sharper. "Yes, thank heavens she's escaped the clutches of a fine town house and pin money some kingdoms would envy."

So now he'd decided to be offended. *Splendid*. "I didn't mean it that way. Lady Helena—Lady Crandell—sought a certain thing and she was able to find it." Sophia sighed. "I admit to a weakness for happy endings."

"You don't like working at The Tantalus Club?"

"Oh, I love being there," she returned, meaning it with every fiber of her being and pushing back at the tears which threatened when she thought of leaving the club. "Diane—Lady Haybury—saved a great many of us from disaster. That may not have been her aim in opening that club, but she's inconvenienced herself enough now on occasion that she does realize how vital the Tantalus is to her employees." Realizing she sounded overly vehement, she paused, looking up at the wall of portraits. Then she stopped close to the center of the long hallway and stared.

The portrait there, though not the largest or the most elaborately framed, was quite simply the most . . . compelling piece in the room. An unsmiling man in his early twenties stood in what looked like a drawing room. He leaned one elbow along a mantel of dark mahogany with a roaring fire behind him, and at his feet coiled a pair of sleek, dark brown hunting dogs. Eyes of a gray so light they seemed almost colorless gazed straight at her, deep inside them not amusement, but a clever intelligence leaving her feeling mesmerized and uncomfortable all at the same time.

"Michael Arthur Baswich, the ninth Duke of Greaves," the tenth duke's low voice whispered into her right ear, from close enough to touch. "My late father."

"Who painted him?" she asked, noting that her own voice had become hushed.

"Some say otherwise, but I say Gainsborough."

"It's disputed?"

"There are those who say only the devil could paint something that disconcerting. But they've missed the point. The devil is the subject. Not the artist." He blew out his breath. "Dead for eleven years, and he still manages to plague me."

That last part didn't seem to be particularly for her benefit. Sophia blinked, tearing herself free from that gaze. Beside her, the duke wasn't looking at the portrait, but rather at her. "It's finely crafted," she admitted, facing him directly and pushing back against the unhelpful curiosity that wanted to know why he seemed to feel about his father the same way she felt about her own. "Where's *your* portrait?" she asked instead.

"As I'm not dead, it's in the main drawing room."

"So you won't forget you're the duke?" Sophia returned, hoping he would appreciate hearing sarcasm as much as he seemed to enjoy speaking it.

"So no one else does." He sent a swift glance past

her shoulder, toward the wall and the portrait. "My private rooms are at the southeast corner, and Eustace's are at the southwest corner. Other than avoiding her, feel free to go wherever you wish. There's no one else here to frown or look askance at you, so there's no need for you to confine yourself to your bedchamber. Not that I imagine anyone else's opinion would trouble you overmuch, anyway."

Opinions didn't matter, unless they could enforce them with something more substantial. "No, frowning faces don't trouble me," she said aloud. "I'm quite accustomed to them. In fact, I'm fairly certain I wouldn't recognize half of Mayfair if they actually smiled in my direction."

A brief smile touched his own mouth. It drew light to his countenance, made him even more handsome than he had been previously. She wondered whether he'd smiled for his portrait; if he had, his likeness had to be even more compelling than his father's.

"Do you always say precisely what you're thinking?" he asked.

"You said you'd already figured me out," she returned, "so I decided I might as well. Unless you object." She'd learned how to comport herself properly; years at boarding schools had ensured that, whether she'd ever thought to make use of the lessons or not. She wanted to stay, to enjoy one grand Christmas before . . . before everything changed. If he required more propriety, she would make an attempt.

"I absolutely do not object."

She blinked, surprised. He *liked* when she spoke without thinking? That was the last thing she expected to hear from an aristocrat. "Then do you ever say what you're thinking?"

A faint scowl furrowed his fine brow. "Occasionally.

I will admit that you just caught me flat-footed, for instance."

Sophia grinned, absurdly pleased with herself. "And now you shall see me take advantage of that by asking if my run of the house includes the billiards room."

"Is that a challenge?"

"I don't know. Are you a challenge?"

"I suppose we'll find that out. Give me an hour to finish my correspondence."

That seemed like the end of the tour, but Greaves didn't move. It was the first time in their admittedly brief acquaintance that she'd ever seen even a whisper of hesitation. Then he nodded almost imperceptibly, as though he'd made a decision about something. It seemed vitally important that she find out what, precisely, that something was, but before she could make the attempt he took her hand and brushed his lips against her knuckles.

"We'll dine at seven tonight, in the small dining room," he said. "Since you're seeking out your own wardrobe, I'll only suggest that you speak with Mrs. Beasel, my cook. Her daughter is married to a solicitor in Hanlith; I imagine Susan Simmons will have something appropriate for you to borrow. The girl does like to dress well."

With that he inclined his head and turned away to vanish through the door at the far end of the hallway. Sophia stood where she was for a moment. Feeling the gaze of the former duke on her back, though, she shook herself and left through the nearest doorway. How odd, that a painting of a former duke left her more unsettled than the presence of the current duke.

In fact, despite his wealth, power, and reputation, he'd never been anything but polite to her. And he was turning out to be more good-humored than she'd expected. She rolled her shoulders. Despite being dumped into the river and despite Cammy's absence she found herself enjoying Greaves Park. It remained an adventure, with a bounty—so far, anyway—of interesting and amusing twists and turns. And a very handsome duke who'd been paying her more attention than she would ever have expected. Whatever might happen, she wanted to stay. Because this was also her last adventure.

"Mrs. Beasel."

The cook jumped, spinning away from the stove and dropping what looked like a very promising meat pie onto the stone floor. "Oh, dear. Your Grace. I do apologize. You startled me."

"Clearly," Adam said dryly. "Your daughter, Susan. She still resides in Hanlith, yes?"

"Yes, Your Grace," the cook said, her expression becoming dubious. "She's married these four years to John Simmons, esquire."

As if he would pursue the daughter of his very fine cook for any reason. There were some things that one simply did not risk. "Good. I require your assistance. And hers. Send her a note asking that she have a . . . dark green evening gown made to her size. Send ten pounds along with the letter. The gown is to be finished by four o'clock this evening."

"But Your Grace, you—"

"At four o'clock, Susan will receive a request from my guest, Miss Sophia White, to borrow an appropriate evening gown. Susan will send her the green dress." He pulled a ten-pound note from his pocket and set in on a cutting board. "Get to it."

"I—right away, Your Grace."

That done, Adam found Udgell overseeing the polishing of the silver. At least the butler still thought Greaves Park would be full of guests for Christmas. "Miss White will very likely request that you send a note to Susan

Simmons in Hanlith. Agree to her request, but do not send that note on until four o'clock this afternoon."

"Very good, Your Grace."

The entire house was too damned quiet, and the blanketing snow outside only made him feel more like he was locked into a tomb. Of course when the bride parade arrived he would likely find that he preferred the solitude. Or relative solitude, anyway. Adam made his way into the upstairs billiards room. It stood empty. Shrugging off his unexpected disappointment, he walked forward and yanked open the half-closed curtains.

Though only half a mile distant, he couldn't make out the line of ragged cliffs that cut Greaves Park off from the rest of Yorkshire, but he knew they were there. He had the paths, the best fishing spots, the few places where someone could climb up to the moors beyond, all memorized. Trees with branches bent and twisted into claws by the wind leaned off the clifftops, reaching for the boy he'd been to drag him off into the faerie realms. There were times he wished they'd done so.

And there were times now he wished he could be that naïve again. But someone of his position, with his wealth and power, couldn't afford to be naïve. He couldn't afford to trust more than three or four people in the entire world. The trade-off for that had been to have a large circle of acquaintances, people with whom he could share a meal or a house over the holidays, but never allow close enough to learn anything that could be used against him.

Large parties were grand for avoiding people when he wished, and finding companionship when he preferred. No guests at all meant being left to his own thoughts and devices, which he didn't like but supposed he could tolerate. This year, however, the guests were a necessity. His father clearly hadn't had any more faith in his ability to be a man than his mother had—which would have been amusing, considering the contempt in which he held his father, except for the damned matter of the will.

His thirtieth birthday would fall on February first. And if he hadn't married by then, most of his properties and a great portion of his wealth would go to twelve-year-old Jonathan Landen, Eustace's son. That was unacceptable. If he hadn't disliked the idea of being forced onto a particular path, he would have seen to his matrimonial state long before now. If he hadn't stayed awake nights wondering whether he truly wished to allow another Baswich, even his own heir, to be born and roam the streets of Mayfair, he certainly hadn't lacked for the opportunities to produce one. But now he'd very simply run out of time, and he had only this holiday to make his decision. It was ridiculous. It would be laughable, if it didn't fall so far onto the side of tragedy.

And then there was Eustace. She wasn't an ally; while she did have a fanatically strong interest in preserving the Baswich family reputation, her own version of what that reputation should be was the only one that mattered to her. He did not fall between the margins of her expectations, and generally that was intentional. The price of being someone of whom she approved was one he utterly refused to pay, whatever the consequences.

Which left his sole guest. Previous to yesterday he hadn't known Sophia White well enough to classify her as other than pretty, good-natured, and an already obvious thorn in Eustace's side. That had been enough to make her a welcome counter to his not-quite solitude. What he hadn't expected was to find her interesting. And witty. And surprisingly, refreshingly forthright—with a dash of absurdity thrown in for flavor.

"Your Grace? Adam, I mean."

He turned from his gaze out the window. The yellow muslin Miss White wore hadn't improved its proportions, but she didn't seem to note that any more than she had earlier. "Sophia."

"I spoke with Mrs. Beasel as you suggested, and we sent a note to her daughter. I'm still perfectly content to wear this, or to take dinner in my room if my present attire is unacceptable for the dining room."

"I happen to appreciate your yellow tent, but I refuse to give Eustace a reason to pick at either of us." He sent another glance at the bleak view outside. "You don't actually play billiards, do you?"

"I'm better at faro and whist, but I've played a game or two." She grinned, the expression lighting the room. "That isn't at all proper to say, is it?"

"Not in the middle of a ballroom, I suppose, or in front of the queen, but we happen to be in my billiards room. And you're to speak your mind, if you'll recall."

Her smile resumed. "Excellent. I should ask if your sense of self-worth will be flattened if I should win, then."

"Hm." Striding over to the racked billiards cues, he took two down and tossed one to her, noting that she caught it without a single flutter of her pretty eyelashes. "I suppose we'll discover that together. How about a small wager?"

Green eyes danced. "I have three pounds, eight pence, to hand at the moment, Your Grace. And a garish hat. I'm willing to put any or all of it to the test."

And she was more gracious about her present circumstances than the very well dressed Eustace. It was damned charming. "Not for money. If I win," he said slowly, considering, "you will owe me . . . a kiss, at the time of my choosing." It seemed rather juvenile, especially for a duke of his reputation. But at the same time it seemed important that he give her the opportunity to refuse him. Now. Because otherwise he had the distinct feeling that he would be kissing her, regardless.

She eyed him for a moment, her lips pursing thoughtfully. "And if I win?"

Hm. He hadn't thought about that. "If you w—"

"If I win," she interrupted, "you will owe me a kiss at the time of *my* choosing."

"Then you may break, Sophia."

"Thank you, Adam."

THREE

"Mrs. Brooks, you truly don't need to help me dress," Sophia commented, frowning. "I've seen to myself since I was six years old."

"His Grace said that you're to have a maid. And I'm the one who'll be assisting you. Stop squirming now, dear."

With a sigh, Sophia stopped wiggling and instead faced the tall dressing mirror in her large private bedchamber. The deep green silk gown looked completely impractical for the cold weather of Yorkshire, but then she imagined the assemblies here were as stuffy and close as they were anywhere else. And actually she didn't much care if the gown might be inappropriate for cold weather. It was lovely.

Dark green lace turned the round neck into a pretty V-shape, while more lace flared out from the half-length sleeves. "I feel like Juliet Capulet in this gown," she said. "I had no idea the assemblies here were so fancy."

"It's a bit much for a solicitor's wife, isn't it?" Mrs. Brooks agreed. "But it fits almost like it was made for you. Lady Wallace won't be able to say anything against your attire, that's for certain."

"Just the rest of me." The general disdain with which the world at large viewed her had truly never troubled her—until the moment a fortnight ago that the Duke of Hennessy had arrived at The Tantalus Club to deliver

his terms for her surrender. And so tonight she would
pretend to be proper and regal, because it amused her to
do so. She might have agreed to her father's demands—
he'd left her no alternative—but before January fifteenth
she meant to do as she pleased. And that had seen her to
a grand holiday in Yorkshire.

"Don't you mind that. I'm a housekeeper, Sophia. If
the master of the house comes calling, there isn't much
a girl can do against it. And none of it's the babe's fault,
for heaven's sake."

Evidently the story of her birth had traveled as far as
the servants in Yorkshire households. Turning around,
she gave the housekeeper a hug. "Thank you, Mrs.
Brooks. I never expected to hear that here."

"I'm just thankful that if only one guest is to be at
Greaves Park, it's someone pleasant, and not one of
those fribbery females Udgell said would be descend-
ing on us. And us having to be so pleasant to all of
them, as one of them will be His Grace's choice for his
duchess."

That sounded like the beginning of a very interesting tale. "What do you mean?"

"Oh, we're not to discuss it." The housekeeper leaned
closer. "But His Grace needs to marry, or he'll lose
most of his properties. He made a list of females he
thought might suffice, and invited them all to holiday at
Greaves Park. He means to choose one of them to be his
bride."

Sophia's heart thudded in abrupt, surprised, hope,
until reality crashed back around her ears. He'd invited
her to Greaves Park as a kindness to a friend. She was
not a marriageable female. Not to a duke. No amount
of cursing or wishing would alter her circumstances.

Interesting as this conversation was, though, whatever effect the lovely gown was meant to have on her
host's reportedly frowny sister would be negated if she

was late to dinner. "Wish me luck," she said, giving a sleeve one last fluff and heading out of her bedchamber.

"I fear you'll need it, my dear."

Squaring her shoulders, Sophia descended the main staircase and made her way to the so-called small dining room. The duke had said seven o'clock, and so she walked through the open doorway at one minute before the hour. And found the room occupied only by a single footman who was bent over the table with a ruler and moving the silver utensils by minuscule amounts. "Does anyone ever check the measurements?" she asked, grinning.

The bony-cheeked young man straightened with a smothered yelp. "I beg your pardon, miss," he gasped.

"I apologize. I didn't mean to startle you." She took another step forward. "I simply had no idea there was such precision involved at the dinner table."

"I— Excuse me." Grabbing up the ruler, he fled the room.

Well, that was rude. But at the same time it wasn't difficult to imagine that the servants here had very limited conversation with the guests of the house. At The Tantalus Club the employees ate at four large tables in the attic common room. Since they all had varying duties and schedules, the food was set out on a sideboard and everyone served him or herself for every meal. Dealers, hostesses, servers, the Helpful Men who saw to it that none of the male membership took liberties they shouldn't—rank and salary didn't matter at the Tantalus. Each of them was a misfit, which made all of them a very odd family.

Clearly none of the diners at Greaves Park would be serving themselves this evening. She would have known that even without a man measuring how far each spoon was from the edge of the table. The room—the entire house that she'd spent nearly four hours exploring, in fact—spoke of formality and rules and . . . nobility, she supposed it was. And despite the generous fire in the hearth, that left the room feeling very cold, indeed.

Yes, she'd become accustomed to making the best of whatever situation in which she found herself, and yes, what she needed from this holiday was an adventure. But as she looked at the immaculate settings and the blemish-free soup tureen and the curtains hemmed with gold thread, it was difficult to believe that she wouldn't have been better off remaining in London.

She'd originally accepted the duke's invitation because she missed her friend. Well, Camille Pryce—no, Blackwood—wasn't here. But all staying in London would have given her was a last holiday at the Tantalus, because one way or the other she wouldn't be able to return. *Stupid arrogant dukes and their overblown pride.* With a sigh Sophia nudged a knife with her fingertip, setting it just slightly askew. There. That felt better.

"So you're the sort of female who enjoys destroying other peoples' nice things. I'm hardly surprised."

Jumping, Sophia spun to face the doorway. *Damnation.* "Lady Wallace, I presume."

She wouldn't have described the marchioness as simply a female version of her brother, but there were definite similarities. The very dark hair, the gray eyes, the attractive features, and the distinct air of confidence. Without a doubt Lady Wallace was someone who'd never had to go without, or even ask twice for anything.

Her face was rounder and softer than Adam's, her build much more delicate, her stature much more petite. Like her brother, though, she was lovely. Not quite as compelling, perhaps, but Sophia reflected that that might have been because the Duke of Greaves was very, very male. Lip-wetting, fingers-tinglingly male.

"I debated whether to sit down to dinner with you or

not," Lady Wallace continued, strolling into the room. Her soft blue silk gown sparkled at the waist and shoulders as she moved in the candlelight. "My brother insists that I be civil to you, but that task would be much easier if I simply kept my distance."

Facing the table again, Sophia straightened the knife. Evidently they weren't going to be friends. Best, then, to let the marchioness know that she wasn't anyone to be trifled with or dismissed, either. "But you felt the need to first tell me of your disdain, I assume?"

"My, aren't you bold for such a little nothing?"

Once Lady Wallace took a seat at the head of the table, Sophia likewise sat—though she decided that the chair nearest the door made the most sense strategically. "I'm sorry to tell you that you are far from the first person to insult me for being born, my lady. In fact, I've been insulted by people whose opinion I hold in much higher regard than yours."

"Your birth was an unfortunate mistake, but I was insulting you for working at that club. And for then having the presumption to accept an invitation made either as a jest, or in a misguided attempt at charity."

"I rarely jest, and I didn't invite Miss White here out of any kind of charity."

The Duke of Greaves walked into the room, Udgell and two footmen on his heels. And however regal his sister might be, Sophia knew without hesitation to whom this house, this room, this life, belonged. "Good evening, Adam," she said deliberately.

A smile touched his lips, then vanished again. "And to you, Sophia." He walked around the table, not to take Lady Wallace's place at the head, but to sit directly opposite Sophia. "If you wish to rule the dinner table, Eustace, then call for the soup. I'm hungry."

Her own expression much less amused, the marchioness waved her fingers at the butler. "You've ordered me to be polite, but evidently you don't require that your own sister be treated with any respect at all."

"I heard you being a viper before I reached the door. Mind your manners, and I imagine that Miss White will do the same."

She felt rather than saw his glance at her, but she nodded. "Of course." When she did look over at him, his gray eyes were lowered, sweeping down to her bosom and back again. Her insides heated. She owed this man a kiss, at the time of his choosing. Losing a game of billiards had abruptly become more interesting than she'd ever expected.

"Susan Simmons, I presume?" he asked after a moment.

Belatedly she remembered the borrowed dress. "Yes. This gown must have cost her a fortune. She's very generous to lend it to me. Thank you for mentioning her."

"I thought you and she might be the same size."

She almost asked if he noticed everyone's dimensions with such accuracy, but considering how lovely the dress was and how short on allies she happened to be, she decided that now might not be the best moment to jest with him. "I'll attempt not to spill anything on it."

A deeper grin flashed across his mouth, attractive and infectious. "I'm certain Mrs. Simmons would appreciate that," he returned.

"That is a borrowed gown?" Lady Wallace put in. "How gauche."

Ha. The marchioness should have seen her in the yellow morning dress. "My things were lost in the river," she said aloud. "I am making do."

"A shame you weren't lost, as well."

"Eustace. You may dine in your rooms. Now."

Her gray eyes narrowed, Lady Wallace stood and flung her napkin onto the table. "Conduct yourself as you will then, Adam. I'm certain no one could be surprised to see you following in Father's footsteps. A redhead, even."

"That's enough."

"I'm very nearly ready to stop wishing you well, Adam, and to be thankful that bridge fell and this won't go on for much longer."

Sophia watched her out of the room. As she turned back to commiserate with the duke, however, the deeply angry expression on his face stopped her. His sister's parting words had seemed a minor insult, but she'd also seen the painting of the former duke in the portrait gallery. And she'd felt the heaviness in the air when she looked at it.

As she was casting about for something to say that wouldn't cause him to suggest that she also take dinner elsewhere, the two footmen reappeared. The lovely scent of onions and warm bread accompanied them, and she took a deep breath. In addition to having a generous daughter with a fine taste in dresses, Mrs. Beasel also clearly knew how to cook.

"That smells delicious," she said, hoping the duke couldn't hear her stomach rumbling in anticipation. Sophia dipped her spoon into the beef and onion soup before her, brushed the bottom against the rim of the bowl, and slipped it into her mouth. "And it tastes delicious."

"Udgell will see that your compliments are passed on to Mrs. Beasel." Adam tore off a piece of bread and spread rich yellow butter across it.

"Please do so, Udgell."

"Very good, Miss Sophia."

"I gave an order," the duke said shortly. "There's no need to supplement it with your own."

Oh, splendid. "So now you're going to be sullen and cross?" she said aloud.

Gray eyes held hers. "I am neither of those things. Stop trying to pick a fight with me simply because my sister bested you."

Sophia blinked. "Your sister did not best me," she retorted.

The shadow of a smile touched his mouth before he lifted another spoonful of soup. "I stand corrected."

"Oh, stop it. You were hoping we would fight."

Adam gestured for Udgell to bring in the main course. The scarlet-headed chit seated three feet in front of him continued to be a surprise. Very few people of his acquaintance contradicted him, and much less intentionally began arguments with him. And yet there she sat with a pretty grin on her pretty face, baiting him.

"I'll admit to a certain curiosity to witness your first meeting," he admitted, finishing off the soup and sitting back as one of his footmen removed the bowl, "but that is all."

"So you weren't secretly wishing for fisticuffs?"

"Not at all."

"Mm-hm. And I suppose you think I didn't *let* you win at billiards."

"If you were allowing me to win, you would have said so."

She shrugged. "I just did."

Just when this holiday had gone from necessary rout to disaster, he knew to the second. But when disaster had become . . . interesting, he had more difficulty pinpointing. All the same, the annoyance and stark disappointment with which he'd been viewing this holiday since well before the collapse of the bridge had, in the last few hours, fled.

"In the future, then, I shall see to it that I *earn* any victories," he said aloud.

Her cheeks dimpled in a rather fetching manner. "I do hope so. I'm generally rather competitive, you see." She sat forward, her green eyes dancing. "But I was curious about the wager."

And so was he. "Were you, then? And its collection?"

Her gaze lowered to his mouth. "Yes. That was quite generous of me, I thought."

Sweet Lucifer, she was charming. He would have said so aloud, but Sophia White seemed utterly unaware of precisely how irrepressible and appealing she truly was. If he pointed it out, he could very well ruin it. And that would be a shame. "We'll see if you say that after I collect what's due me," he said instead, then set down his utensils. "No doubt you're wondering what my sister's parting words meant," he went on, torn between being mindful of how many times Sophia must have been left out of conversations and wanting to continue the long-held custom of keeping his own counsel.

"You mean the part about the bridge and something not continuing? It did seem rather . . . cryptic."

"Yes. Likely everyone else will know within minutes of their arrival here, if they haven't already realized, so you might as well hear it. I invited a great many eligible females to Christmas, as my father's will stipulates that I be married by my thirtieth year. And that I father an heir by my thirty-first."

She lifted an eyebrow. "You're looking for a bride? A parade doesn't seem very subtle. And I've seen you be *very* subtle."

That reminded him—as if he needed a reminder—that she noticed far more than he'd realized. Considering some of the machinations in which he'd been involved over the past Season and her own part in them, she *had* seen him being subtle. And not so subtle. And she'd kept her mouth closed about it. "The time for subtlety seems to have passed," he returned, attempting to sound witty rather than annoyed by the entire damned situation.

Sophia cocked her head at him, a lock of her scarlet hair drifting across one green eye. "I'm assuming you selected ladies of the most impeccable bloodline, an appropriate age, and . . . a modicum of attractiveness, because, well, why wouldn't you? Any number of single women would cut off their own legs to marry you."

"That *would* prevent any stampedes, at least," he noted, reflecting that this was closer to a conversation he'd expected to be having with his good friend Keating Blackwood—if Keating hadn't been on the far side of the river Aire at the moment—and not with a pretty young chit with whom he had a wish to sin. "But yes, I take your meaning, and yes, I did do some research into each of the chits."

"Then why am I here, again? Surely you don't consider *me* eligible to join the marriageable parade."

She spoke briskly enough, but from the swift glance at him then away, his sole guest had some pride resting on his answer. *Damn.* He hadn't meant to insult her, but neither did he intend to go to the effort of spinning a lie that neither of them would believe. Adam picked up his fork and knife again, mostly to give himself another moment to think. "You are here because firstly you're a friend to one of the few married women I've invited, and secondly, because I find that I enjoy having a conversation with a chit without her assuming that every other damned thing I say is a promise of betrothal."

"You didn't know that when you first asked me here. You only thought I was shocking and relatively harmless."

Adam laughed. He couldn't help himself. "Very well. You've stunned me by having a wit and the gall to use it as you please." Lifting his glass of wine, he tilted it in her direction. "A pleasant surprise, to be certain."

She smiled back at him, her warm countenance half a league away from Eustace's calculating use of the same expression. "Thank you, then," she returned. "But when the remainder of your guests *do* arrive, I ask that you keep in mind the fact that I do have some pride, and a heart that yearns for love as much as any better-born lady's. Please attempt not to stab too deeply when you begin your comparisons."

For a bare, mad moment he opened his mouth to comment that she was likely to be the most interesting of any female he'd asked to Greaves Park, and that she had nothing to worry about when he began making his lists of flaws and attributes. At the last second it occurred to him that not only would that be an inappropriate thing about which to commiserate with her, but that it would also be rather cruel. After all, Sophia White *was* interesting and pretty and charming, and most of that seemed to be despite the efforts of the world at large to grind her spirit into dust. But she was also the daughter of a lady's maid—a fact that neither of them was likely to forget.

"I shall do my utmost," he said aloud, "if in turn you will refrain from gossiping that I nearly lost a game of billiards to you."

"Agreed."

Just as they were finishing a very fine roast venison and a rather interesting conversation about the perils of wagering and drink, the dining room doors burst open. Two large, dark brown streaks lunged into the room. "Damnation," Adam said, shooting to his feet. "Brutus! Caesar! Down!"

The two huge mastiffs halted, one on either side of Sophia's chair and their heads an inch below her shoulders. Adam rounded the table, prepared to offer his guest any necessary assurances that she wasn't about to be eaten.

"I apologize," he said tightly, cursing whoever might have released them. And he had a very good idea who that must have been. "Despite app—"

"Which one is which?" she asked, offering a hand to the beast on her left.

"That one's Caesar. He has that spot of white above one eye there," Adam returned, beginning to wonder if anything frightened this chit.

"The pair in your father's portrait are hounds. These seem closer to horses, I have to say." The hand sniffing finished, she scratched Caesar between the eyes. He began pounding a rear paw against the floor in response.

"Half horse. Mastiffs, actually. An acquaintance of mine purchased them for me as pups two years ago. I don't believe she had any idea what they were, other than dogs and dark brown." In fact, nothing seemed to arise in Constance Biery's mind at all. Her general obliviousness served her well as a mistress, but it hadn't made her particularly interesting, otherwise. The arrangement had been mercifully short-lived as a consequence. "I believe they were in honor of that damned painting."

"They're darlings! Or will I be devoured if I turn my back?"

"You may be killed with affection, but you're completely safe otherwise."

Sophia rose from her chair and knelt on the floor. Adam watched as she divided her attention and her scratches between the two pony-sized dogs.

"I should have guessed that your spirit would match your hair," he murmured under his breath.

"What was that? I had a dog snout in my ear," she said with a chuckle.

"I'd forgotten," he said in a more conversational tone, bending down to ruffle Brutus's fur, "that you spent a morning petting lion cubs at the Tower Menagerie. These two must pale in comparison to that."

"No, they don't," she cooed. "You're such handsome boys, aren't you?"

"Perhaps they should join us in the morning, then. For our ride."

After another few minutes she straightened, and Adam held down a hand to help her to her feet. Her fingers were warm in his. Just her presence seemed to warm and brighten the entire room, in fact.

This estate in York had been a cold place for as long as he could remember. Even the annual influx of guests and festivities only made him forget for a short time how Greaves Park remained chill all year long. He'd thought it reflected the cold, calculating part of his character that had thus far served him and his purse exceedingly well. But the warmth—her warmth—had a very definite appeal.

"Do these big lads travel with you?" Sophia pursued, retrieving her fingers from his. "I don't remember Keating speaking of them when he stayed with you in London, and they do seem rather memorable."

"They're a bit large for Baswich House. And many of my guests find them intimidating." Even Constance had shrieked and fled the room when she'd set eyes on the dogs once they'd reached their full size.

She glanced sideways at him. "Perhaps you should use them as a test for your potential bride." Her soft-looking lips curved in another slow smile. "I'm glad to have met your faithful companions. Dogs aren't precisely welcome at boarding schools. Or in The Tantalus Club, for that matter."

"I had them closed up in an upstairs sitting room. If it pleases you, though, I'll give them the run of the house. Until my potential brides arrive, of course."

Udgell made an irritated sound from the corner, but Sophia's grin only deepened. "I would very much like that."

For a moment he felt the distinct sensation that time had slowed, that the room had darkened except for the emerald-garbed woman smiling at him. He wanted to collect on that kiss, whether he'd meant the wager as a tease or not. He wanted to taste that smiling mouth of hers. He wanted to inhale the scent of her, feel her bare skin beneath his hands.

Realizing he was staring, Adam took a breath. Yes, she seemed to be the sole saving grace in what had become a very grim holiday even before the bridge's collapse, but generally he had a firmer grip on cynicism. "I have a few more letters to write to innkeepers across the river," he said, inclining his head. "If you require anything further this evening or wish to be rid of these monsters, Udgell will see to it. Good evening, Sophia."

"Good evening, Adam."

On his way to his private quarters, Adam detoured to the large sitting room that connected to his sister's bedchamber. With a cursory knock he pushed open the door. "You let my dogs out."

Eustace looked up at him over the rim of her cup of tea. "Beg pardon?"

If he hadn't known her as well as he did, he would almost have believed that she had no idea what he was talking about. "Rather petty and infantile of you, don't you think?"

"I am not the one insisting on keeping an ill-mannered light-skirt about simply to annoy a member of my own family."

"I'm beginning to lose patience with this argument, Eustace. Especially when I only stopped in to thank you."

"Thank me? For what?" She sat forward, setting her cup of tea aside. "That thing wasn't frightened away by those brutes of yours, was she?"

"Far from it. She likes Brutus and Caesar. I'm letting them roam the house now, by the way, so don't be startled if they wander in here at all hours. And I'm considering using them as a test of any potential bride's mettle. I can't have a chit about who's afraid of my dogs. Good night."

Leaving the room again, he shut the door behind him. Nearly, anyway. If a large mastiff should find a way in, well, it was no more than Eustace deserved. He'd even warned her about it. A moment later, porcelain smashed against the far side of the heavy oak. With a grin, Adam continued on to his own bedchamber. This could very well turn out to be an exemplary Christmas, after all. Even if it did mean he would have to rush his selection of a bride when the parade did finally arrive.

Sophia awoke to the sound of heavy curtains being pulled open. "Lucille, it's too early," she groaned, turning over and pulling the covers up under her chin. "And close the blasted window. It's freezing."

"That would be the fine Yorkshire winter saying good morning," the lilting voice of Mrs. Brooks announced.

Shaking free of the cobwebs of her dreams, Sophia opened her eyes and sat up. "Mrs. Brooks. I apologize. I was dreaming I was in my room at The Tantalus Club. I share quarters with Lucille Hampton, and she is always far too cheery in the morning." In her dream all her friends had been safe and happy, and the club hadn't been threatened with ruination simply for taking her in when she had nowhere else to go. And the Duke of Greaves had been sitting at her faro table, and for some reason no one else had noticed the way he kept flirting with her and touching her hand. Sophia rubbed her fingers.

The housekeeper chuckled, but continued pulling back curtains. "My late husband Charles was just the same; he always awoke with a song on his lips. Ah, there were times I wanted to hit that man with a shovel, fine as he was." She leaned down to push a footstool out of the way—then shrieked as the furniture stretched and came to its feet. "God have mercy!"

Sternly stifling a grin, Sophia scooted to the edge of the bed and stood. "Have no fear, Mrs. Brooks. It's only Caesar."

Putting a hand to her ample chest, Mrs. Brooks sagged against the back of a chair. "Good heavens. You'd think I'd be accustomed to those beasts by now, but they always spend the night in His Grace's rooms."

Did they? That was interesting. "After they escaped last night, Adam said he would let them wander. I don't know where Bru—"

Her door burst open. "What's wrong?" the Duke of Greaves demanded, striding into the room.

His jacket was missing, his cravat only half tied and baring his throat to her view. The effect was startlingly sensual and masculine all at the same time. A low flutter began in her stomach. Previously she'd noted that Adam Baswich was tall and lean and attractive—after all, it was so obvious that only a blind woman wouldn't notice him.

But back in London she'd thought of him first as a duke, a powerful, wealthy aristocrat who for some reason had deigned to help Keating win Camille. He'd been one of a number of unexpected acquaintances she'd made over the years. And then he'd invited her to Christmas the day after her father had delivered his ultimatum. And now she owed him a kiss. And—

"Sophia," he barked. "Is something amiss?"

Heavens. "No. No. We're quite well. Caesar startled Mrs. Brooks, is all."

"I thought him a footstool, Your Grace," the housekeeper said, curtsying. "I apologize for disturbing you."

He sent a cool gray glance at the servant, then returned his gaze to Sophia. Because she was looking back at him, she couldn't help noting his eyes lowering to sweep down and then up the length of her in a rather leisurely manner. Belatedly she remembered that she wore nothing but a hopelessly oversized night rail that drooped from one shoulder. She pulled her sleeve back into place, that odd heat shivering through her again. A kiss from that man would be very nice, indeed. When, though, would he collect on the wager?

"Very well, then." His gaze returned to her face. "I recommend you borrow something warm, Sophia. The snow's stopped, so you'll go riding with me after you eat something."

It sounded more like an order than an invitation, but she nodded. "I'd love to see the countryside. As long as you keep in mind that I've ridden only rarely before."

He inclined his head. "If you fall from the saddle, the snow will be soft. And the dogs can drag you home."

Sophia snorted before she could stop herself. "Perhaps I should begin by riding Caesar."

A laugh, deep and merry, rumbled from his chest. "I would pay good money to see that."

Grinning back at him, for a moment she wondered what he would do if she simply walked up and kissed his smiling mouth. She did owe him just that, after all. Her heart skittered. What did she have to lose? She'd been ruined since birth, and whatever remnants of respectability might have existed had vanished the moment she found employment at The Tantalus Club. And after this holiday she would be so far from the eyes of Society she might as well be dead. She'd almost rather *be* dead, actually, then walk into what lay in wait for her.

His gaze met hers. Abruptly he cleared his throat and took a step back toward the door. "Since no one has been murdered, I'll leave you to dress. I'll see you at the stable."

"Thank you for coming to my rescue."

"You're welcome. Unnecessary or not, I appreciate receiving credit for the effort."

Once he'd closed her door behind him, Sophia walked over to survey the three gowns the servants had been kind enough to lend her. None of them would do for horseback, particularly not in the snow. She pursed her lips, then turned to Mrs. Brooks. "I don't suppose anyone owns a riding habit," she mused.

"Only Lady Wallace. I could inquire of her maid, Grace."

"Oh, please don't. She'll only insult both of us."

Mrs. Brooks looked relieved. "Perhaps I could borrow a heavy coat from one of the grooms, then. It wouldn't be very fine, but it would be warm."

That would suit. And however necessary borrowing garments was at the moment, she'd also noticed that the duke seemed to . . . appreciate her unconventional wardrobe. It was rather odd to realize that he shared her enjoyment of the absurd. "You know, Milly, your suggestion of the warm coat gives me something of an idea."

Adam kicked a heel against the outside wall of the stable as he waited for Zeus to be saddled. The weather and the waiting for his other guests was setting him off kilter, he decided. Otherwise he couldn't explain why he—a man of nine and twenty who had a great deal of experience with women—would be thinking still of a single bared shoulder. Its creamy paleness against a caress of fiery red hair, the twitch of his fingers as he'd wanted to peel the night rail from her skin.

And why the devil shouldn't he? Sophia wasn't anyone's wife, and she wasn't some chit whose

eputation . . . mattered. They were both adults, thrown
ogether by circumstance, and she was damned attrac-
ive. And much wittier than he'd realized. That in itself
aised her several steps above the majority of his mis-
resses. And she'd agreed to the wager of a kiss, and
ost. It was hardly his fault if he knew the table better
han she did.

"Good morning officially," her lilting voice came
rom the stable yard, and he looked up. And choked.

"What—what are you wearing?" he managed.

She smoothed her palms down her thighs. "It's a
ootman's uniform."

"Yes, I can see that."

He could see it, indeed. She'd donned a man's shirt
nd waistcoat with a scarf rather than a cravat at the
hroat, knee-length black pantaloons and white stock-
ngs, and a pair of plain, black shoes. Sophia had even
ied her long, curling scarlet hair back with a black rib-
on. The effect was amusing and . . . arousing all at the
ame time. The carnal edge to his thoughts deepened.
A chit in trousers. Good God.

"I thought this would be warmer than a muslin
gown." She sent a smiling glance at Evans as the groom
ppeared with Zeus and a small chestnut mare in tow.
Evans. Might I borrow a coat and a spare pair of
oots?" she asked brightly. "I don't think footman's
hoes are appropriate for riding."

Sophia knew how to be proper, but mostly didn't
eem to bother with it. And those glimpses of humor and
awdiness peeked through her demeanor like rays of
unshine. That raised the question of how he'd missed it
n their previous encounters. Yes, she'd been amusing
nd pretty, but the warmth and wittiness of her had com-
letely eluded him. Or was it that she shone brighter in
ight of his own isolation?

"Certainly, Miss Sophia. I'll go fetch 'em." The groom tied off the horses and trotted back into the stable without a backward glance at his employer.

Hm. "I thought we might ride into Hanlith," Adam decided. "There's a seamstress there, and you could order some additional clothes if you wished."

Sophia nodded. "I could afford two muslins," she agreed. "But as I lost one of my shoes in the river, I think that should be my priority. I can wear my gown home again, but I can't very well ride in the mail coach barefoot." She flashed her infectious grin. "It would be very cold."

That wasn't what he wanted to hear. She'd come to his home because of his invitation and lost her things as a direct consequence of that. He had the power to replace her wardrobe with an even prettier one, and she wouldn't allow it. Her, saying no to him. And he already knew he would give in to her wishes—at least as far as she was aware. The seamstress in Hanlith was going to be very busy, regardless. As to how to get the gowns to Sophia in a manner she would find acceptable—well, he would manage that, as well.

FOUR

In front of them the riding trail undulated like a narrow white ribbon, disturbed at the edges by the shrubs and trees and rocks that stood taller than the recent snowfall.

Sophia turned her head to look behind them. There the pathway was absolute carnage. She knew that only two horses and two pony-sized dogs had torn up the snow, but it might as well have been an entire brigade. "We wouldn't be difficult to track, would we?" she said aloud.

Beside her on a massive black thoroughbred named Zeus, Adam followed her gaze. "I daresay even blind old Homer would be able to find us," he agreed. When he looked back at her, he lifted an eyebrow. "You aren't a fugitive, are you?"

Not yet. After all, in what her father had actually called a "generous gesture," he'd given her until the middle of January to say her good-byes. Or rather, he'd given her until just before the nobility was set to return to London for the little Season. She knew that was what mattered to him, that she be gone before his cronies could resume carrying tales about her and The Tantalus Club.

And so she had seven weeks. Seven weeks before she was whisked off to Cornwall and the marital clutches of the Reverend Loines. She was the one who'd decided that venturing to Yorkshire was the best way to spend her remaining time.

The Duke of Hennessy had said that the vicar of Gulval had agreed to marry her to save her soul from the choices she'd made in life. As if she'd done poorly for herself. The difficulty was that she had a very good idea of how the vicar would save her. No dancing, no chatting with other females—much less men—no music, no reading any book but the Bible. She didn't wish to be saved. She only wished to be left alone.

Adam was looking at her, so she summoned a smile. "I'm only a fugitive from Milly Brooks smothering me to death with helpfulness." Abruptly she frowned, worried that she'd just caused trouble for the head-housekeeper-turned-ladies'-maid. "Though she does it well; I'm simply not accustomed to being coddled."

"You're on holiday. Enjoy yourself."

"Oh, I am. Definitely." Her sigh fogged the air in front of her, and she experimented with blowing out a circle as she'd seen men do with cigar smoke. Hm. Her effort looked more like a dented cloud that dissipated before she could examine it too closely.

"What are you doing?" the duke asked, his gaze on her rounded mouth, and his expression . . . intrigued.

"I'm attempting to make a fog circle."

"Ah. Of course you are."

Bending forward, Sophia patted her mount on the side of the neck. A few random bits of snow kicked up by the pretty chestnut mare's hooves fell back to the ground. "Whose horse is this?" she asked.

"Copper? She's yours."

Clearly he'd misunderstood. "I mean, who generally rides her? She's very calm and gentle. You ride that beast, so who does the mare belong to?"

"Many of my guests enjoy riding, and not all bring their own mounts. I keep twenty or more horses here."

He reached over, adjusting her right hand on the reins. "Copper likes you, and you like her. Therefore, she's now yours."

Sophia scowled. "You can't simply give me a horse."

"I just did."

Risking holding the reins with one hand, she jabbed a finger into his very solid shoulder. "That would be just as bad as purchasing me clothes. Even worse, because a horse is more expensive."

For a moment he gazed across the glinting white landscape. "You said you have three pounds, eight pence, with you, yes?" he commented.

"Yes. Why?"

"You're purchasing Copper from me. The price is three pence, and I'm providing boarding in London because you're such a damned fine bargainer."

The fact that she truly didn't need a horse in London evidently didn't matter. And she hadn't yet gathered the nerve to tell him that she wouldn't even be returning to London. She'd said her good-byes to her friends at the Tantalus. And she doubted the Duke of Greaves would care to listen to her tale when he had pressing concerns of his own, anyway. "Clearly I am a formidable negotiator, since all I said was 'no.'"

Adam chuckled. "Exactly."

"But why are you being so generous?"

"I do very few good deeds," he responded promptly, "so I may not be very proficient at it. I like you, and I can certainly afford it. Does there have to be an additional reason?"

Her mind seized on the middle part of his statement. He liked her. Other than her fellow employees at The Tantalus Club, she hadn't given a fig in a very long time what other people thought of her. But she couldn't deny that it was very nice to hear him say such a thing, unprompted. "I don't suppose there does," she conceded.

"Then you owe me three pence."

Sophia shook herself free of her future miseries and grinned. This was today, and today was turning out to be quite grand. "I'm good for it."

"We'll see about that." With a smile of his own, he gestured at a rise to their right, just off the main trail. "Let's stop over there."

She allowed herself a happy sigh at the thought of stopping and climbing down from the horse for a few minutes. Her bottom would certainly appreciate it. "How close are we to Hanlith?"

"It's just over the hill." Swinging down from the saddle, Adam stepped into the knee-deep snow. With it crunching beneath his steps, he made his way around to her side and lifted his arms.

"I am wearing trousers," she said. "I think I can manage."

"You're still seated sidesaddle," he returned. "Lean forward, and I'll catch you."

She certainly hoped so; otherwise she'd end up buried headfirst in the snow. With the dogs bounding around them, Sophia released the reins and held her hands down, leaning toward him until she could catch his shoulders. His hands swept around her waist, and then he rather effortlessly lifted her down to the snow.

Her boots sank into the soft powder. The sensation was quite odd, as if the ground itself was shifting and giving beneath her feet. But that was secondary to the thrill running up her spine as Adam kept his loose grip around her waist. She lifted her head to look up at him.

Light gray eyes met hers, his amused expression fading as his gaze lowered to her mouth. "I'm going to kiss you now," he murmured.

Sophia nodded, abrupt tingling excitement running down her scalp to her fingertips. "Oh, good. I was beginning to think you'd changed your mind about the wager."

"Stop talking." He took a half step closer, then leaned down and touched his mouth to hers.

For a moment everything was absolute silence. Silence and the warmth of his lips driving off the cold, sinking into her. She had no idea whether she was supposed to be bashful or brazen, but she very much wanted to kiss him back. Swiftly she slid her gloved hands up over his shoulders, pulling herself closer against his wool-coated chest.

Finally he lifted his head to look down at her. "I think I might wish to seduce you," he said in a low voice. One of his gloved fingers brushed along her lower lip.

"As long as you don't think you can purchase my affections, I think I might be amenable to that," she returned, not quite steadily.

Men at The Tantalus Club had offered her things, gifts or money, and for the most part she'd refused— not out of prudery or some last hope of salvation, but because she liked the way her life had finally shaped. And frankly, because none of her would-be lovers had seemed all that interested in anything other than her appearance and her notoriety. As for their own appeal . . . well, she'd successfully resisted all but two of them. Those two had both been very brief mistakes.

His gray eyes assessed her. "Have I mentioned before that you're a very unique female?"

"Yes, I believe you have." She grinned again. "Feel free to continue complimenting me, however."

Adam returned her smile; the chit's good humor was damned infectious. He enjoyed things—people, conversation, a well-written book—but Sophia White had an indescribable way of finding . . . delight in nearly everything. For someone of her background, that was remarkable. And exceedingly arousing.

Belatedly he lowered the hand that still gripped her

waist. "This way," he said, offering his arm to escort her to the top of the shallow rise.

She was amenable, he was definitely amenable, and he wasn't entirely certain why he didn't immediately put her back on Copper and return them to the manor house. God knew he'd had lovers before, and ones he'd felt less attracted to than he did to Sophia. But at the same time and for lack of a better word, this was ... different.

For one thing, neither of them had any immediate escape if an intimate relationship went poorly. For another, she'd already mentioned that she valued the freedom The Tantalus Club allowed her. Saying the word "mistress" would, therefore, be quite unwise.

Aside from all that, in his mind a mistress was for sex. And he'd already discovered that he enjoyed chatting with Sophia White. He might even go so far as to say that he enjoyed her company. It was all exceedingly odd, and he wasn't ready to put any kind of place card on whatever this was.

She stopped, her fingers tightening on the arm he'd offered her. "Hanlith?"

Adam turned his gaze forward. At the edge of the frozen river Aire, and tucked into a shallow hollow between two low hills, lay a cluster of half a hundred shops, houses, inns, a church, and two large public stables. "Hanlith."

"It's so lovely!" she exclaimed, an already familiar grin touching her mouth and lighting her green eyes. "Someone should paint it."

"Blake did, actually," he replied. "In summer, though. The painting's at Baswich House in London."

"I'd love to see it. I can't imagine the scene could possibly be prettier than this. Snowy roofs, smoke rising from the chimneys, light shining from the church windows. It's ... perfect."

At the last second he refrained from pointing out that

the snow at least covered the horse shit on the streets. It *was* pretty, he supposed, in a way he hadn't before considered. Previously his first thought about Hanlith had been that it lay on the northwest edge of his property, and therefore belonged to him. He was the landlord, and all the citizens his tenants.

"Milliner, cobbler, or dressmaker?" he asked aloud, turning them back to collect the horses and the rollicking dogs.

"Cobbler," she returned, refusing to be swayed from her decision that a pair of walking shoes would be eminently more practical than a new gown. "And Mrs. Simmons, if you have time. I would very much like to thank her for the loan of that lovely gown."

Damnation. He might have considered that of course generous-hearted Sophia would wish to thank her benefactor—even if she didn't actually know who that might be. "I don't know her address, but we can inquire."

"Thank you."

Taking her waist in his hands again, Adam lifted her back into the sidesaddle. Those trousers she wore continued to fascinate him, as did the notion of stripping her out of them. Thank Lucifer they were so close to the village, because the remainder of the ride was going to be damned uncomfortable.

Luckily the cobbler had a large wooden boot hung outside his shop, or Adam would have had no idea where to find him. Perhaps he needed to begin spending more time in Hanlith. The tall, narrow man who emerged from the back of the shop and immediately began dipping in an oddly birdlike combination of a bow and a curtsy had likely resided in Hanlith for his entire life, and Adam didn't even know his name. It was an odd, uncomfortable sensation, to not know all the facts of the situation at hand.

"Oh, Your Grace," the cobbler was warbling. "You honor me. I—my wife is at the butcher's, but—do you wish a cup of tea? Or—no, we ate all the eggs for breakfast, but I can go to the bakery and fetch some biscuits, if you'd like. Or—"

"If everyone in Hanlith is so kind," Sophia interrupted with a warm smile, "I shall never wish to leave. I would welcome a hot cup of tea. Adam?"

Tea with a cobbler. Him. "That would be grand."

Sophia glanced sideways at him, then stepped forward to offer her hand to the cobbler. "How should I address you, sir?"

"Oh. Jenkins, my lady. Robert Jenkins."

So she'd realized he had no idea to whom they were speaking. Taking a breath, Adam joined her. "Mr. Jenkins, this is Miss White, a dear friend of mine. She was in the mail coach yesterday, and lost her shoes in the river."

"And you've come to me," the cobbler breathed. "I am doubly honored." For the first time Jenkins seemed to notice Sophia's very unusual attire. "Lost all your luggage, did you, miss? My wife's a bit—quite a bit— larger than you, but she's a good hand with a needle and thread. If you n—"

She took both of the cobbler's hands in hers. "I am very grateful, Mr. Jenkins, but that isn't necessary. The people of Greaves Park and Hanlith are so generous, my heart can't quite believe it."

Because Adam watched so closely, he saw the rapid blink of her eyes, the color flushing her cheeks. Not only was she utterly sincere in her gratitude, but she was near genuine tears. The realization of just how . . . unfriendly life had truly been to Sophia White struck him like a punch to the gut. Her only sin had been to be born to a maid and a duke. And she'd paid for that mistake, someone else's mistake, for the ensuing twenty-three years of her life.

"Perhaps we could have that cup of tea?" Adam suggested.

"Oh, aye, Your Grace. My pleasure." With that the tall fellow practically jumped over the shop's counter and disappeared in the direction of the back stairs.

As soon as the cobbler left, Sophia walked toward the near wall and stood there with her back to him, ostensibly to examine a shelf of shoe sizers. Adam stayed where he was, giving her a moment to compose herself. Instead he turned his attention to the pairs of shoes tucked into wooden display boxes tacked to the nearest wall. And scowled. "Yorkshire residents evidently have very practical taste in shoes," he said in a low voice, moving closer to her.

Though she kept her back to him, she nodded. "They look very solid," she agreed, in the same quiet murmur. "And somewhat furry."

"I imagine most of his customers don't spend much time in London."

She faced him. "Oh, I hope they don't."

He understood what she meant. She hoped none of the other residents of Hanlith had any more idea who she was than Mr. Jenkins did. "Do you see anything you like?"

Her gaze remained steadily on him. "Yes, I believe I do."

By the time they left Mr. Jenkins's cobbler shop, Sophia had a very sturdy pair of walking shoes and had been measured for an additional pair of what the cobbler had termed "shoes more appropriate for such a lovely, gracious lady." Adam keenly wanted to see what such a miraculous pair of shoes would look like.

"I'm sorry that took so long," Sophia said, as he tied

the shoes to his saddle. "I know you must have better things to do than watch someone measure my feet."

That had actually been a rather . . . invigorating experience, considering that she'd had to remove her borrowed groom's boots. For a moment Adam had wished he'd become a cobbler, so he could have been the one wrapping the measuring tape about her bare ankle and across her absurdly dainty foot.

Luckily logic broke in before he could tell her that he would happily spend the remainder of the day following her into shops. If he said that he had no other plans, their next stop would be Mrs. Simmons's house, and his gift of her green dress would be discovered.

"It was . . . interesting," he said aloud. "I do need to see to some things at home, however. I apologize for cutting your trip short. We can return tomorrow, if you'd l—"

"You don't need to grant my every wish and whim, you know," she broke in, stopping beside Copper.

"I'm a duke, Sophia; as I believe I've already mentioned, I generally do as I please." He finished tying off the sack and joined her. "Would you like to return tomorrow?"

"I would like to visit Mrs. Simmons and the bakery tomorrow. That bread smells heavenly."

"Very well, then." Adam slid his hands around her waist, pausing for a long moment before he lifted her into the sidesaddle once more. If they hadn't been standing in the street with a dozen windows facing them, he would have kissed her again.

"If you're not busy this evening," she said as she gathered the reins in her hands, "I hereby challenge you to a game of piquet." She regarded him for a moment. "The same wager as before."

She was thinking of another kiss as well, then. He

grinned. "You haven't a chance." And more than likely, neither did he.

"I can understand why you would learn to play faro or vingt-et-un," Adam said, dealing them each twelve cards and setting the other eight into a pile beside the discarded ones. "Those games require a dealer or a banker. But no one plays piquet against a bank. It's two opponents. And I've played it a great many times."

"Is this where you attempt to rattle me, to force me to lose my concentration?" Sophia arranged her cards by suit to take a look at them.

"It's a fair warning. I rarely give those."

"Before the Tantalus opened, Lord Haybury taught us the rules and play of nearly every card or dice game imaginable."

She thought his jaw tightened at the mention of the Marquis of Haybury's name, but she couldn't be certain. Everyone at the club knew the rumors of a falling-out between the two men, but it had evidently happened better than five years ago—well before the club opened. But if he was attempting to rattle her, it was only fair that she do the same to him.

"So you know the rules," he said after a moment, glancing at her over the fan of his cards. "That doesn't mean you can play."

"Well, I've played it nearly every morning and on my days off for a year. As you know, there aren't many places outside The Tantalus Club where I'm welcome. I therefore stay inside. And my friend Emily Portsman is an inveterate gambler." They played for pennies, but he didn't need to know that. Nor did he need to know that Emily Portsman wasn't even her friend's true name. No one at the club knew who she might actually be, but she was pretty, well educated, and had been in desperate need of employment. That was all that had mattered.

His mouth curved in that rare, attractive smile of his. "Please don't tell me what you chits do when you aren't working. You'll destroy my imaginings of you all walking about upstairs naked and hitting each other with pillows."

Sophia snorted. "That's only on Thursdays."

He laughed, a low rumble that tickled through her like fine champagne. "My new favorite day of the week."

"What would you be doing tonight if Greaves Park were packed to the rafters with guests?" she asked, selecting five cards from her hand and setting them aside in exchange for five of the cards in the talon.

"Likely roasting chestnuts and singing carols." Casting aside three of his own cards, he collected the talon's remaining trio.

"Truly?"

Adam lifted an eyebrow. "Why? Does it sound too dull and domestic?"

"It sounds rather wonderful. But I can't quite imagine you singing 'God Rest Ye Merry, Gentlemen.'" Lowering her gaze to her cards, she pursed her lips. "Point of six."

"Good."

Silently she wrote down her score of six. "What else do you do for your holiday gatherings?"

"First of all, I sound very grand singing 'God Rest Ye Merry, Gentlemen.' Second of all, are you bored with playing cards and billiards?"

His tone seemed a bit . . . hard, as if she'd offended him. *Drat.* Sophia met the steel gray of his eyes. "I think the merits of domesticity aren't appreciated enough by those who are accustomed to it. This is the best Christmas holiday I've ever spent." And she was very glad of that, since the memories would have to last her a life-time.

"Are you including the bit where you nearly drowned and lost all your luggage?"

"I put that in a separate category, which also makes this my most harrowing holiday." Freeing one of her hands from her cards, she leaned across the table and tapped him on one knuckle. "I don't want this to be *your* worst holiday ever."

For a moment he gazed at her. "You may rest assured that this is not my worst holiday ever. Far from it, though that may change when the remainder of my guests arrive. Now. Are you going to continue trouncing me, or was that end of your attack?"

Well, he hadn't directly answered her question, but what he *had* said was rather nice. "Ha. Prepare to be devastated. Sixième."

"What? Damnation. Good."

Chuckling, she added sixteen points to her total. "Oh, and tierce." Still grinning, she added in three more points.

"Mm-hm."

She shifted the three jacks in her hand. This was the point where he was likely to best her, but she did have quite a good lead at the moment. "Trio."

"Equal."

"Blast it. Jacks."

"Not good."

Sophia sighed. "Fine. What do you have?"

"Kings. Oh, and queens." As she watched, he gave himself six points. Then he looked up at her again. "Finished declaring?"

"Yes, damn it all."

"Quatorze," he said.

"Take your blasted points."

By the time they'd played the tricks and totaled the score, he was behind her by only two points. "What score are we playing to?" he asked, shuffling the cards for the next hand. "Or should we settle our wager hand by hand?"

She glanced toward the closed door of the drawing room. However little use she had for propriety, she did know that an unmarried woman did not spend any time unchaperoned in a man's company without an extreme risk of ruination. Adam Baswich knew that, too. And neither of them had so much as batted an eye over playing billiards together or going riding together or playing cards together with only his two great dogs in the room with them, sleeping in front of the fire.

"Do you think I'm being absurd, refusing to allow you to purchase me things and yet sitting here alone with you?" she asked.

"I think you have found that there's a difference between being seduced and being . . . kept," he returned promptly. "I don't think it's about propriety, but I do recognize that it's important to you. And no, I don't find it—or you—absurd in the least."

She watched the graceful flick of his long-fingered hands for a moment. Hands she'd occasionally daydreamed about back in London, and hands that she very much wanted touching her now. "I suggest a new wager."

"I'm all atingle."

So was she. "The loser of each hand removes an article of clothing." She gestured from his very fine gray and black suit of clothes to her own footman's attire. "We are dressed in a nearly identical fashion, after all."

Setting the deck of thirty-two cards aside, he reached up and briskly unknotted his cravat. Then he slid it slowly from around his neck and dropped it to the floor. "Agreed."

* * *

An hour later, she wondered if the Duke of Greaves knew what he'd agreed to. She sat, a small, delicious shiver of excitement running down her spine, as Adam took his shirt by the bottom hem and pulled it off over his head. *Oh, my.*

As he'd lifted her in and out of the saddle and, even more tellingly, hauled her out of the river, she'd known he was strong and fit. He had the body of a born athlete, lean and muscular and just . . . perfect. A dark dusting of hair across his chest narrowed as it traveled downward to vanish beneath the waistband of his buckskin trousers, which she found at least as intriguing as the parts of him that she could see.

Once he'd discarded his white superfine shirt, he sat back in his chair and crossed his arms over his chest. In response, Sophia stifled a scowl. She wasn't finished with gazing at him, yet. As she returned her attention to his face, he was contemplating her coolly.

"Are you cheating?" he asked.

"I am not cheating. I warned you that I've played nearly daily for a year."

"Yes, but I've played piquet since I was sixteen. That's nearly *fourteen* years." Momentarily straightening one arm, he brushed a finger across the paper he'd been using to tally his points. "You haven't lost a single hand."

Deciding it would be both poor form and dangerous to laugh, Sophia settled for nodding. "You've come quite close several times."

"Don't placate me, chit."

She stifled a reluctant sigh. "Well, I suppose we can end the game, if you wish."

"So you can call me a poor loser?"

"I'm not the one complaining." She stacked the cards and cut them. "It's your deal. I certainly don't wish to cause an argument. That wasn't the point of . . .

this." In fact, she was quite happy with the way events had unfolded, so to speak, but evidently he'd expected to see her removing clothes. Another thrill stirred through her.

"You suggested the wager," he said, sitting forward to take the deck.

"I did."

"You have no objection to being naked, then."

Heat touched her cheeks as she realized that once again, this was not a conversation a gentleman had with a proper lady. At the moment, however, she didn't care. "Your argument has a logical bent to it."

For a moment he gazed at her. "Then I propose we change the game."

Her breath quickened. "To what?"

Eyes still on her, he reached over to the edge of the table for the twenty cards they'd discarded before the beginning of the game. Without looking down, he shuffled them into the deck. "We cut the cards. High card wins."

"There's no skill at all in that," she protested.

"I've been suffering here for a damned hour." He slammed the deck onto the table between them. "Cut the cards."

Even the Duke of Greaves could run out of patience, apparently. Fingers not quite steady, she reached out, lifted a section of the cards, and turned them faceup. Finally she glanced down. "Queen of spades," she declared, utterly unable to help the twitch of her mouth.

He cursed. "Bloody hell." The moment she set the cards back, he leaned in to grab the top card and flip it over. "Seven of clubs. For God's sake."

A laugh escaped her lips before she could pull it back. "Oh, dear. Perhaps we should try a diff—"

"Don't you dare." Shoving his chair back, he reached

down, yanked off his left boot, and tossed it aside. "Cut the cards again."

As he wore stockings, she reckoned he had four more articles of clothing to remove before he would be completely naked. And she still hadn't even removed her scarf. The odds that he would be naked before she was even nearly so seemed very much in her favor. "Very well," she said with an exaggerated sigh. And then she turned over the four of hearts.

"Aha! I have you now."

She set the cards back. "This evening has tilted so far away from your favor that I have to caution you against premature celebration, Your Grace," she said, attempting to keep a straight face.

"We'll see about that." Cutting deeply into the deck, he turned his wrist so only he could see the card he'd uncovered. And then, a self-satisfied and rather predatory grin playing attractively about his mouth, he showed the card to her.

The nine of hearts. "Very well, then," she said as evenly as she could, and with great ceremony untied her scarf's loose knot and cast the pretty thing aside.

Adam glared at the scarf as if it had offended him. "Insufferable."

"What? Did you think I would begin with something else?" she commented. "Or did you just realize which of us the odds favor to be rendered naked?" Deliberately, attempting to disguise the rapid hum of her pulse, she looked him up and down. "And what do we do once you've lost?"

From his expression, he'd had something in mind from the moment the original game began, if not before that, even. He gave her the same languid inspection with which she'd just favored him. "I'm prepared to find that out, Sophia. Are you?"

"Hm." In response she shuffled the cards and cut the

deck again. A low flutter ran through her. The three of diamonds.

After he showed her the jack of spades, she bent down to remove her left boot. Handily there were no rules about the order in which garments were to be removed. And she wasn't precisely wearing proper women's attire, anyway. If she had been, she would have been much closer to being naked already.

She lost the next two hands, and removed her other boot and her jacket. And then she turned over an ace and a queen, leaving Adam with but one stocking and his trousers. As he straightened from removing his boot, he continued to his feet. While she watched him, quietly mesmerized by the play of his muscles beneath his skin, he walked to the door and turned the key, locking them in. Locking everyone else out.

"Another glass of wine?" he asked, continuing on to the generously stocked liquor cabinet and pulling out a decanter of brandy. "Or something stronger?"

She licked abruptly dry lips. "You know, demonstrating how composed you are might serve to distract me in a game of skill," she informed him, "but cutting cards is pure chance. And I would like brandy, if you please."

He pulled down two snifters and poured the amber liquid. "You're wrong. It's a matter of luck as much as it is of chance. Considering the outcome I'm anticipating, I'm feeling quite lucky." Adam returned to the card table, a snifter held elegantly beneath the bowl in either hand. "Unless you mean this as a tease, that is. If you do, you should tell me now. And then you should run."

Sophia lifted the snifter to her face and inhaled deeply of the heady, smooth fragrance. "This is a very fine brandy."

"Of course it is."

She eyed him over the rim, warmth cascading and crashing through her. It had never occurred to her from the moment she'd suggested altering their wager that this was only a tease. Even now, when he'd offered her an unexpected escape, all she felt was deepening excitement and arousal. "You're an exceedingly handsome, witty, and interesting man," she commented after a moment, the rush of her blood making her voice and her hands shake just a little. "You've been kind and generous on every occasion we've ever met, and three days ago you saved my life. I—"

"Is this gratitude, then?" An abrupt frown furrowed his brow.

"No. For heaven's sake, I didn't mean to prick your manly pride. All I'm saying is that you've never given me a reason to think ill of you. Quite the opposite, and I'm very . . . amenable to letting this evening play out as it will."

"Good."

Sophia took a sip of brandy, savoring the warm roll of it down her throat. "But I'm still willing to continue this game. Are you?"

He tilted his head, eyeing her. Then he set aside his brandy and picked up the cards. She expected him to shuffle, but instead he turned them faceup before he silently picked out three aces and slid them toward her. "I just won the next three hands," he finally said, looking up again.

"You're cheating!"

"I'm leveling the playing field. Three things. Remove them."

Goodness, she thought, then grinned at the thought. This seemed to be the exact opposite of goodness. "Very well."

Once she'd removed both stockings, she paused. Clearly he meant for the third garment to be her waistcoat, so that her next legitimate loss would mean removing either her shirt or her trousers. But he still had on one stocking.

"Well?" he prompted, taking a sip of brandy.

"I'm thinking."

"Too late for that."

"Ha. It's never too late for thinking." Offering him a slow smile, she reached up to undo the top button of her waistcoat. Adam Baswich actually sat forward, his gaze on her hands. "Oh, wait a moment. I nearly forgot," she continued, and reached up to untie the ribbon holding her hair in its long ponytail. "Now the field is level."

Brief surprise and appreciation crossed his expression. "Well done, chit."

"Thank you, Your Grace."

"Shake out your hair."

Deeper arousal spread through her, down to her most intimate place. She slowly shook out her hair, drawing her fingers through the red waves to settle the mass down her back and across her shoulders. "Like that?"

"Yes. Very like that."

Her hands shaking even more noticeably, she gathered the aces and shuffled them back into the deck. "You first," she said, placing the cards back on the table.

Adam reached out, brushing a finger across her knuckle, and turned over the two of clubs. "Don't even bother," he said as she went to pick up a card of her own, and he bent down to pull off his last stocking. Straightening, he dropped it to the polished floor.

"Next hand?" she asked.

When he gave a brusque nod, Sophia took a breath and cut the deck. This time she turned over the four of clubs.

"Thank Lucifer," he muttered, and quickly reached over to select his card. "Eight," he said, at the same time showing her the eight of diamonds. "The waistcoat."

The low, intimate rumble made her damp. Her mouth abruptly dry, she took a large swallow of brandy and then went to work on the quintet of buttons running down her front.

"Slower."

Evidently he'd lost the ability to speak in full sentences. Then again, so had she. Slowing her fumbling with the wrong-sided buttons, Sophia kept her gaze on Adam's face, watching his expression as intense gray eyes followed every motion of her fingers. It made her feel . . . powerful. In some things, it didn't matter if a man was a duke or a groom. Desire was desire, and it was all intoxicating. She could practically feel the heat and weight of him on her already, his warm breath in her ear, the pounding of their hearts.

Finally the last button came free, and she shrugged out of the garment, letting it fall behind her in the chair. The buds of her nipples showed plainly through the thin white shirt covering them, and she heard his intake of breath.

"Pick a card," he said, his tone making it more an order than a suggestion.

Not bothering to shuffle first, she went into the middle of the deck and selected a card. Lowering her gaze from his, she looked at the card. *Good heavens.* Someone had a sense of humor, she decided as she showed it to him. The eight of clubs. Right in the middle. Even odds as to whether he or she was about to remove a very important piece of clothing. "Well, this is interesting," he murmured, clearly making the same assessment she had. Then he turned the top card remaining on the deck and flipped it faceup so they could both see it at the same time.

The king of hearts gazed up at her.

FIVE

As a gambling man Adam reckoned the odds favored Sophia pulling off that damned shirt, but she'd already surprised him so many times over the course of the evening that he couldn't be certain. Likely some witty comment was called for, but all the blood had left his brain half an hour ago. "Well?" was the best he could manage.

Women didn't discomfit him like this. They didn't arouse him to the degree that he wasn't entirely certain he could shift in his chair without ruining both his trousers and very likely the evening. He was the definition of jaded, and had even had a female or two tell him that to his face. Yes, he enjoyed sex, and he engaged in the act frequently. But he didn't lose all cognitive abilities while the chit still had her clothes on.

He could admit that this was a slightly different experience, in that Sophia White was neither an actress or opera singer who relied on the good graces of her gentleman admirers for survival, nor a highborn lady who needed to maintain a proper reputation in public whatever she might prefer in the bedchamber. No, Sophia made her own way in the world, and didn't seem to care a fig what anyone else thought of her. Not even *he* could say that and be entirely truthful.

The lady in question wet her lips, then untucked the white shirt from her trousers. Keeping his seat by sheer force of will, Adam lifted his gaze from her hands to her face. Either garment would be perfectly fine with him, though he had to admit that he'd been imagining her breasts in his hands since before he'd kissed her that morning.

Sending him an amused, aroused glance, Sophia wrapped her hands around the hem of her shirt. In one motion she lifted the material off over her head and dropped it onto the dark blue carpet.

Adam blew out the breath he hadn't realized he'd been holding. She was smooth, pale, and utterly perfect, and she mesmerized him. Her creamy skin made the deep scarlet of her hair even more striking, and his fingers curled as his cock jumped.

"Shall we go again?" she suggested, her breathy voice uneven.

"I think I've had enough card play for this evening," he returned, downing the rest of his brandy in a manner very unfitting for such a fine vintage. "What about you?"

"I agree, as long as we say that I won."

Things seemed to be going rather well for him, as well, but he nodded. "As a gentleman, I could do no less."

When she began stacking the cards into a neat pile, though, he decided that he'd had enough with waiting. Standing, Adam leaned across the table to cup the nape of her neck and draw her in for a deep, plundering kiss. Her hands swept over his bare shoulders, and he shoved the table out of the way to close on her.

He cupped her palm-sized breasts in his hands, tilting her face up to continue kissing her. She smelled of lemons, of summer even in the cold winter of Yorkshire. And she wore damned trousers.

The dogs had settled on the thick rug before the hearth, so Adam swept an arm beneath her knees and carried her over to the deep couch. He knelt on the cushions between her legs to unbutton those trousers. As he did so, Sophia sat up and leaned in, licking his left nipple. The contact jolted into him like lightning.

This was the difference, he decided as he opened the last button and tugged the trousers down her hips, between a lover and a mistress. There was no formal arrangement, no promise of exclusivity or even discretion. He wanted her, and she wanted him. Nothing else signified. And considering the path he needed to take this holiday, Sophia White might well be the last lover he ever had. A married man, if he cheated on his wife, did so with a mistress. He'd be a fool to risk a lover with no rules or indebtedness to him, and he was not a fool.

"Don't rip them," she said, grinning breathlessly as she lifted her hips. "I have to give them back."

"I think you should keep them."

Finally he got the trousers down to her thighs and shifted backward to pull them off past her knees and over her feet. Moving over her again, he took one of her breasts in his mouth, flicking across her nipple with his tongue.

She moaned, digging her fingers into his hair and arching her back and rendering his own trousers entirely too tight. Clearly Sophia was no virginal miss, but he hadn't expected her to be one. And that didn't matter. Of far more interest was the way she pulled him up to kiss him again, and then reached between them to begin unfastening his trousers.

"So tell me," she said, shoving down his buckskins and then stroking a forefinger lightly down the length of him, "would you have stripped if you'd lost that last hand?"

His eyes practically rolled back in his head at her touch. For a moment he fought for control, refusing to give in before he'd had her. "I was ready to strip regardless," he returned in a voice that sounded like a growl even to him. "I may never be able to play piquet again."

Sophia laughed, the merry sound traveling from her and on into his chest. "I'd like to see you attempting to explain that at The Tantalus Club."

"I think that'll remain our secret."

With another kiss he made his way slowly down the length of her body, kissing and nipping at her breasts, her stomach, then down to her ankles and up the insides of her thighs. With her pale skin and bright hair she reminded him of fire and ice, except that she wasn't at all cold. Just the opposite.

Beneath him she moaned and wriggled and yanked at his hair, which made keeping his own composure that much more difficult. This was entirely more pleasurable than singing Christmas carols. In fact, if any of his missing guests had arrived at that moment, he would have closed the front door on them, regardless of the consequences to his purse and his power. With a half-smile he lowered his head, tasting her.

"Oh. Oh." She sat up on her elbows, watching as he parted her with his fingers and moved in again with his mouth.

She was certainly no shy, retiring miss. In fact, she'd been the one to suggest they strip. For a moment he wondered just who had seduced whom, but immediately on the tail of that thought he decided it didn't matter. They were both where they wanted to be.

"Stop teasing, you horrid man," she gasped.

"Horrid?" he repeated with a grin, straightening. "Me?"

Momentarily leaving the couch, he retrieved his jacket and removed the French condom from one pocket. He'd put it there after dinner, on the chance that this very thing might happen. And he insisted on using one; he was not one of those fools who littered the countryside with bastards, as her own father had done.

"Allow me," she said, sitting more upright and taking the thing from his fingers.

"Just don't strangle me," he cautioned, clenching his jaw as she slid the sheath over his throbbing cock and tied the delicate ribbon around the base.

Sophia grinned. "Think of it as a first-place award."

Her humor was infectious, and he smiled back at her, reaching between them to adjust the fit just a bit. "I hope you're saying that you're impressed."

She lowered her gaze to his cock again. "Oh, yes." Sinking back again, she beckoned with one finger. "Come up here."

He didn't wait for a second request. Pausing again at her soft breasts on his way, he favored her with a deep, openmouthed kiss as he settled his weight on her. Sophia wrapped her ankles around his thighs and lifted her hips in as plain an invitation as he'd ever received.

Settling himself a little, he canted his hips forward and entered her tight, welcoming heat. Beneath him Sophia groaned, digging her fingers into his shoulders. The world seemed to narrow to the places they touched, hips and hands and tangled legs.

He began slowly, sinking into her as deeply as he could, studying her aroused, excited expression, her wild scarlet hair against the gold of the couch. Adam lowered his head to take her mouth in another heart-pounding kiss. God, she was lovely.

"Mm, that feels good," she moaned.

"How does this feel, then?" he breathed, increasing his pace.

"Good." Sophia pulled his face down for another kiss. "Very . . . Oh, very good."

Harder, faster, then slow and deep again. Adam felt

her clench and break, her keening moan of pleasure nearly pulling him over the edge with her. It was too soon to let go, too soon to stop this, however badly his body wanted the release. Taking a deep breath he rolled them, putting himself on his back and her straddling his hips.

She looked down at him, surprise and then delight crossing her mobile expression. So her previous lovers had never done this with her before. Good to know. "Come here," he rumbled, sweeping his palms over her breasts before he sat up to kiss her.

In a moment she was bouncing on him enthusiastically, her hair wild across her face and shoulders. He imagined she looked very like an Amazon warrior woman of legend. Except that she was warm and alive and moving on him exquisitely.

He surged up into her, his hands on her hips to keep her close against him. Again and again, until with a soaring rush he found his own release.

Sophia collapsed against his chest. Even breathing as hard as she was, she could feel the fast beat of his heart beneath her ear. Good heavens, that had been nice. Much, much better than nice.

"Do you play whist?" she asked.

His responding chuckle reverberated through her, and he stroked his fingers deliciously through her hair. "I challenge you to billiards tomorrow night," he returned. "Same terms of victory."

"I accept."

This was the difference between being a proper lady, a proper and legitimate daughter of a duke, and being a female who made her own way in the world and consequently had no one to answer to but herself. If the Duke of Hennessy hadn't finally visited The Tantalus Club and taken away every bit of satisfaction she'd ever felt in finding her independence, she would have ended up in this exact same place, enjoying the intimate company of this very handsome, very compelling man. The only difference was that she wouldn't have abruptly wondered if one duke would stand against another. Possibly, but not over the dispensation of the illegitimate daughter of one of them.

"Have you ever met your father?" he asked into the silence of crackling logs and snoring dogs.

The question startled her. Surely not even a duke could read minds. Sophia rose up to look down at him, her palms on his hard chest and his penis still inside her. "Why?"

Dark gray eyes glanced down her bare front, then returned to her face. "Curiosity."

For a moment she debated whether to dissemble, but she truly didn't see the point of lying. "Yes," she answered. "A fortnight ago."

"In London? I thought him at Hennessy House."

"So did I." Reluctantly she moved off him and went to collect her footman's shirt. "Until then, the only connection I'd ever had with him was that he reportedly sent money to my aunt and uncle to pay for my education. I wouldn't have known him if he walked up and asked me to dance."

"What happened, then, to bring you together?" He sat up, naked and likely completely unaware of how . . . delectable he looked.

"It's a very sad and sordid tale, at least from my perspective. Are you certain you want to be troubled with it?" She hoped he would decline. It would sound too pitiful to say how much this holiday, his invitation, had meant to her.

"You'd be surprised by how many sad and sordid tales I know. Some of them are even about me. Tell me."

Drat. "Very well." She took a deep breath, shrugging

into her footman's shirt. "As you know, Hennessy has never acknowledged me. I daresay that hasn't prevented everyone in England from knowing that he is my father."

"Yes, it is one of the worst kept secrets in the history of the kingdom."

"Evidently he could tolerate this, as long as I was a . . . a nobody. A barely visible speck on his résumé. But then I went to work at the Tantalus."

Narrowing his eyes, Adam stood as well, using his cravat to clean himself off before he tossed the ruined thing into the fire. "A man who doesn't provide for his daughter doesn't precisely have the right to dictate how she makes her way in the world."

Sophia belatedly realized that what she knew of Adam Baswich could fit into a teacup. And what she'd taken for granted about him—his reported ruthlessness in business, his affection for scandal—didn't include such a keen insight into desperation. "I agree," she commented, her voice not entirely level. "But according to him, my idiotic and scandalous way of conducting my life in so public a manner is adversely affecting his reputation and that of his son and daughter. The legitimate ones."

"Shit-breeched toad," Greaves muttered, so quietly she almost couldn't hear him. "Did he have a solution to this difficulty, or did he just wish to shout at you?"

"He had a solution," she returned, swallowing. "He's arranged for me to marry. A vicar. The Reverend Loines, in a very small parish in Cornwall."

Coughing, Adam took a moment to shrug into his trousers and button them. "A vicar?"

"I know. It sounds ridiculous, doesn't it? Evidently Mr. Loines, for an undisclosed donation to the parish, has agreed to wed me and to . . . save my damned soul."

"That's ridiculous," he stated. "Why in the world

would he think you would agree to such a thing? You would be . . . you would be miserable. I hope you told him to go shit himself."

Sophia buttoned her own trousers, then sat heavily in the chair by the disabused piquet table. "I did."

"Good for you, Sophia."

"And then he told me that if I refused, he would use all of his wealth, power, and influence to see that The Tantalus Club ceased to exist. One way or another, he was apparently very determined to be rid of me and my scandal."

Adam looked at her for a long moment. She could practically see the words traveling through his mind, the scenarios he conjured and discarded as he mentally followed the various trails she'd spent a fortnight exploring. Then he slowly walked over and righted the gaming table. "In his eyes, it's undoubtedly the perfect solution," he mused, taking the seat opposite her. "He's provided for your future, and he's rid himself of the constant reminder your presence at the club elicits for him."

"Yes. Perfect. Thank you very much."

"Have you parted from the Tantalus, then? Run away? Is that why you're here?"

If only that would suffice. "Hennessy made it very clear that my running away wouldn't save the club. I have to do as he says, or he'll see Diane and Oliver and all my friends ruined all over again. And some of them—most of them—have nowhere else to go." A warm tear ran down her cheek, and she impatiently wiped it away. Tears wouldn't do anything but make her seem weak, and she'd already shed her share of them over this.

"Why are you here, then?"

"You invited me, if you'll recall," she retorted with

more heat than she intended. Sophia rolled her shoulders. At the moment he was an ally; if she annoyed him, she'd have nothing to do but return to the Tantalus and wait for the clock to spin. "I suppose I wanted to spend one grand holiday as I pleased," she continued in a more civil tone. "I wanted to see Camille and laugh and enjoy myself before the Reverend Loines locks me away to do penance."

Abruptly Adam stood and walked over to lean against the deep fireplace mantel. "Evidently we're both to be saddled with something we don't want."

"You don't want to marry?"

"I didn't want to have to fill a pot with politically advantageous potatoes and select the least offensive spud. But that's my own damned fault, for waiting so long to see to my responsibilities."

"Why *did* you wait so long, then?" she pursued. She could tell herself that any insight into his predicament could help hers, but Adam Baswich was a wealthy, attractive man. He *could* have married a decade ago, if he'd wanted to. Why, then, *had* he put off matrimony until the last possible moment?

A brief smile crossed his face. "It's a sad, sordid tale."

Standing, she strolled over toward him, stepping over the snoring dogs to lean her own shoulder against the marble mantel. "I told you mine."

He shook his head. "Another time."

Despite the mildness of his words, an awkwardness now hung in the air between them. It was the first time she'd felt less than entirely comfortable in his company, and she didn't like the sensation. With a sigh she put one hand on the marble mantel and lifted up on her toes to kiss him.

There was a chance, she supposed, that Adam Baswich had merely been curious about her in general. That once he'd had her, he would bundle her off to Hanlith and be done with her. But as his warm mouth met hers, teasing and exciting, that dismal thought crumbled.

He slid his arms up under her shirt to circle her waist and pull her close against him. "No more idle chitchat?" he commented, and she felt his smile.

"I like idle chitchat. Just not about our mutual troubles." She brushed a strand of raven hair from his eyes, then pulled out of his loose grip before he could seize on her use of the word "mutual." A duke wouldn't like having his troubles compared to a scandalous chit like her. "Do you still want to accompany me back to Hanlith tomorrow? Because if you lend me a groom, I can g—"

"Be ready by eleven o'clock," he interrupted. "We'll have luncheon at the White Horse Inn."

"Then I shall bid you good night," she said with a smile, "because I need to find something to wear tomorrow."

"I rather like what you're wearing right now," he returned, tugging at the hem of her shirt.

"And I like what you're wearing," she commented, using the opportunity to run her gaze once more down his very fine form, "but I think you might get cold."

"Mm-hm. Join me for breakfast at nine o'clock."

She gathered up her borrowed boots and the remainder of her man's clothes. "Good night, then."

"Good night, Sophia."

As she opened the drawing room door to glance out at the empty hallway, both large brown dogs rose to follow her. She liked having them about; nonjudgmental friends were, in her experience, fairly rare.

Her large bedchamber was empty, the fire lit and the sheets turned down. With a sigh she pulled off her shirt again and shrugged into her absurdly oversized night rail. She supposed she could have spent the remainder of the evening either in Adam's rooms or with him in hers, but this was better. Not more pleasant, but better.

She liked Adam, and physically having had him once, she wanted him even more. But clinging or somehow giving him the impression that she expected or wanted more than he was willing to give—that wasn't what she wanted.

She didn't want to ruin this unexpected friendship, if that was what this was. With a sigh she lay down and pulled the soft covers up to her chin. So far this holiday had exceeded her expectations—as had the Duke of Greaves, himself.

"What do you think of this?"

Sophia turned around from cleaning her teeth as Milly Brooks entered her bedchamber. In her arms the housekeeper-maid held a heavy velvet riding habit of burgundy and forest green. "It's lovely!" she exclaimed, standing to run her fingers over the soft, lush material. "You didn't go to Lady Wallace, did you?"

"I think her ladyship would rather go naked herself than lend you a button," Mrs. Brooks declared.

"I agree. Where did you get such a fine dress then, Milly?" It looked warm and lush and absolutely beautiful. She could hardly wait to pull it on.

"Agnes Smith had it in her trunk upstairs."

Sophia frowned. "Agnes? The cook's helper?"

Milly nodded.

"But she's . . . she's very tiny. I can't wear a gown of hers."

The maid shook it out. "She said it never fit her well, and that you should try it on."

It seemed a waste of time, but if the servants of Greaves Park were going to bother to be so kind, she had no intention of turning up her nose at anything they offered. Aside from that, it didn't *look* overly short. It was certainly worth an attempt, anyway.

"Very well." With a wistful sigh she pulled off her night rail and lifted her arms so Milly could fit it over her.

She half expected it to get stuck at her shoulders. Instead, it sank down to hug her hips and flare around her legs. Frowning, Sophia faced away from Milly so the servant could fasten the long row of buttons running up her spine.

"Oh, Sophia, it's perfect," the maid cooed, finishing the buttons and moving around in front of her.

"I don't understand," Sophia returned. "This is a very fine habit for a cook's helper. Does she—did she—even ride?"

"Well, as Agnes told me, she used to be quite a bit rounder, which might account for the extra length. As to the how she would have it, I don't know. But she said it's an old dress that hasn't fit her in ages, and that you're welcome to it."

Finally Sophia looked at her burgundy and green reflection in the mirror. The riding habit and the fit were exquisite, as if it had been made to her exact measurements. She gave an experimental twirl. "I need to thank Agnes," she said, giving in to the urge to smile.

Of course she'd worn fine gowns before; they were required at The Tantalus Club, the darker and more daring, the better. But she purchased them herself. No one gave her clothes. Particularly not fine, warm ones perfect both for riding and for a Yorkshire winter.

Once she'd stomped into her borrowed men's riding boots and with Milly's help finished pinning up her hair, she headed downstairs and to the rear of the mansion. The kitchen seemed quiet, which wasn't all that surprising considering the duke had only two guests in residence.

Agnes Smith stood at the stove, a pot of boiling eggs before her. Sophia smoothed the skirt of her lovely riding gown and stepped forward to hug the tiny woman.

"Thank you so much, Agnes!" she exclaimed, bending to kiss the older woman on the cheek. "It's lovely."

"Oh, bless me!" the cook's helper squeaked. "You nearly startled the heart out of my chest, child!"

With a chuckle, Sophia released the servant and stood back. "You must let me pay you something for the dress."

The servant, her cheeks already flushed from the heat of the kitchen, reddened further. "Oh, no, Miss Sophia. I can't wear it, and someone should have use of it. I'm happy to give it to you."

Sophia hugged her again. Never would she have expected the residents of Greaves Park, of all places, to be as kind and open as they were proving to be. "Then I thank you doubly," she said.

When she turned around, she nearly ran headlong into Milly, the housekeeper stood so close behind her. "You forgot your cloak, Sophia," the servant said, holding out a black, fur-lined cape. "It was Agnes's, too."

"Oh, this is too much." For heaven's sake, the two garments together must have cost the cook's helper better than a month's salary.

"Nonsense," Agnes said briskly. "You can see they go together."

They did, at that. And whether it was too generous or not, Sophia couldn't help anticipating what Adam would say. No doubt he expected her to appear at breakfast wearing trousers again. He'd certainly seemed to like seeing her in them. And she'd liked when he removed them.

With a last hug she left the kitchen and walked back up the long hallway to the breakfast room at the front of the house. The quickest route was through the portrait gallery, but the thought of seeing the father's unsettling likeness the morning after she'd so enjoyed the company of the son made her doubly uncomfortable. Instead she detoured through the orangerie, greeting the myriad servants as they went about their morning duties.

When she strolled through the breakfast room door, Adam was already present, sitting at the table with a cup of steaming coffee at his elbow and an open newspaper in his hands. Warmth swept through her at the sight of him, tingling and alive and very welcome on such a chill morning. However much trouble she might be, he hadn't sent her away. In fact, he was someone whom she could imagine calling a friend.

He wore blue and gray today, as impeccably perfect as always. And so very handsome, with a strand of dark hair slanting across his temple in a way that made her fingers twitch with the desire to brush it back into place.

And then she noticed Udgell the butler looking at her expectantly, and realized she was staring at the duke. *Silly girl.* "Good morning," she said lightly, moving forward to the sideboard.

Adam looked up. "Good . . ." He pushed to his feet, his gaze widening almost imperceptibly as he took her in from head to toe and back again. "You look quite . . . nice. Where did you get it?"

She grinned, a shiver of satisfaction strongly mingled with lust running through her. "From Agnes Smith, your cook's helper."

"Ag—Really?"

"Hush. It's grand, isn't it?" She hefted the heavy skirt an inch or two and stuck out the tip of one toe. "I am still wearing your groom's boots, though. I can't wear your second footman's best shoes on horseback."

"Of course not." He gestured at the table. "Udgell, a cup of tea for Miss White."

"Right away, Your Grace."

Once Sophia had selected her breakfast, she sat down opposite him. "Is that the London newspaper?"

"It is. They towed it across the river along with the mail. I'm sorry to tell you, but the weather in London has been exceedingly mild."

"I prefer Yorkshire weather. It's unpredictable."

"Not really. It's either snowing, or about to be snowing." With a half grin of his own he produced a folded note from his pocket and handed it over to her.

Their fingers brushed, and she took a deep breath. He was quite distracting. She'd had lovers before, and while she'd enjoyed the interlude, it had stayed in the bedchamber. This intoxication, however, seemed determined to linger. And it was such a pleasant feeling that she was loath to discard it.

Oh, and now she was staring at him again. Deliberately she lowered her gaze to the folded paper he'd handed her. "What's this?"

"Open it."

She did so, skimming her eyes down the dark, hasty scrawl to the signature at the bottom. "It's from Keating," she exclaimed.

"Read it aloud. I haven't looked at it, other than to see the address."

That had been supremely thoughtful of him. With a grateful glance up, she smoothed out the note and cleared her throat. " 'Adam,' " she read, then lowered it again. "I'm accustomed to . . . rough language, but I do try to avoid using it. The members at the club don't appreciate it from dainty females, and I imagine the vicar would make his displeasure . . . unpleasant for me." She shook herself, attempting to banish the thought and very aware that her host was still looking at her. "Keating can be somewhat liberal with the profanity, so I shall substitute the word 'albatross' where necessary, and you may read that part privately later."

He laughed. "Well, now I don't know whether I hope to hear you say 'albatross' or not. Read the damned—albatross, I mean—letter, will you?"

"Very well. 'Adam,'" she resumed, looking a few words ahead as she read, "'I should have known you would have an albatross old bridge here in the middle of albatross Yorkshire. I received your note this morning. Cammy and I are staying at the King George Inn in albatross Etherton. Given that Sophia is there with you already, we have resolved to remain here for at least a fortnight, on the chance that you will actually repair the albatross bridge.'" She looked up. "Keating does have a way with words, doesn't he?"

"Yes, he does. Anything else?"

"Let's see. Yes. 'You should see the gaggle of females milling about here, waiting to see you. Are you starting an albatross finishing school there? Give our love to Sophia, and for God's sake, don't scowl at her. We hope to see you soon.' And then some more cursing about you repairing the bridge."

She handed the letter back, and he read through it, his lips twitching as he no doubt reached the "albatross" bits. The obvious affection and humor in the letter, toward both Adam and her, touched her deeply. For the past five days she'd been having such a good time that she'd almost managed to forget both her troubles and her friends at the Tantalus, and the two people that she'd traveled all the way to Yorkshire to see. Abrupt guilt made her scowl.

"Would you wait on the far side of a river for a fortnight to see Camille and Keating?" Adam asked into the silence as he tucked the missive back into his pocket.

"Of course I would."

"Then stop frowning because they chose to do the same. You didn't make the bridge fall. And the King

George is a very nice inn. I'm paying for their stay, along with that of all my other displaced guests."

She sighed. "Very well. It's just touching to know they're thinking of me."

"How could they not?" he returned in an amused drawl. "You're rather memorable."

"I will assume that is a compliment." She cocked her head at him. "Keating doesn't know you're hunting for a wife?"

"He's aware of my father's stipulations, though he's probably paid it less mind than I have. He'll undoubtedly figure it out. He's clever that way."

"Perhaps you should write and tell him. While he and Cammy are waiting, they could be reviewing your potential brides."

"It's more likely that Keating would frighten them away with his albatross reputation."

Sophia laughed. With renewed enthusiasm she dug into her substantial breakfast. The activities of last night seemed to have left her with quite an appetite. She spared a moment to look up at Adam again, to find steel-gray eyes gazing at her. Her appetite wasn't just for food.

Adam had several things to attend to this morning, not the least of which was an appointment at noon to meet again with the Jones brothers, who'd sent word this morning that they had put a plan together to repair the bridge. And still he sat, pretending to read as he watched his one houseguest devouring a large slice of hot mutton pie and two soft-boiled eggs.

Mrs. Orling, the seamstress in Hanlith, was something of a miracle worker, it would seem. And Sophia had believed whatever it was Mrs. Brooks had decided to tell her about the riding habit—though he wouldn't have selected the pixie-statured Agnes Smith as the gown's previous owner. Small moments of unexpected magic seemed to abound at Greaves Park this holiday, so hopefully Sophia had simply accepted the dress as yet another improbable bit of luck.

"Have you ever gone ice fishing?" he asked, as much to distract himself from the increasing pressure in his groin as anything else. There were damned servants in the room. If there hadn't been, he would likely have been across the table and on her by now.

"That's how you caught me, isn't it?" she commented, offering him a sly smile.

"Generally a person doesn't fling himself bodily into the water to fish, but I suppose the basic principle is the same. Would you care to try the proper method?"

Sophia took a sip of tea. "I think that would be fun."

"Good. I'll make arrangements for this afternoon."

"Do you think we should include Lady Wallace?" she queried, her expression becoming serious. "She has been indoors for several days now."

He didn't know when they had become a "we," but it didn't bother him as much as he'd expected. The running of five estates and three houses in London had been *his* responsibility for better than a decade, and he relished it. No one was allowed to interfere with that, to counter his orders, or to attempt to press their own opinions regarding his duties. In order to keep all that, he needed to marry. This, however, wasn't the same as giving up power or control. This was a very kind-hearted young lady feeling empathy for a woman who despised her.

"Eustace would dislike both the activity and its ultimate goal," he stated.

"She doesn't like fish?"

"Eating them, yes. Seeing them alive and flopping about on the end of a rod, no."

With a final bite of pie, Sophia set down her fork and

dabbed delicately at her mouth with a napkin. "I look forward to catching more fish than you do."

Adam had no idea how she did that, being proper with one breath and then wagering with him the next. It was uniquely charming. "I accept your challenge." He glanced at the butler and pair of footmen lurking in the corner. "We'll decide the stakes later."

Soft rose touched her cheeks. "I'm certain they will be interesting."

Finally he set aside his own napkin and stood. "Let's be off, shall we? I have a meeting in a bit with my bridge engineers."

"Do you have time for a ride, then?" she asked, furrowing her fine brow.

"It just so happens that I have precisely enough time for a ride."

Her expression eased again. "That's very lucky, isn't it?"

"It is, indeed."

By now Adam had had time to send detailed instructions and bribes to his conspirators in Hanlith and to speak with all involved servants at Greaves Park, so he was fairly confident that Sophia could chat with whomever she wished without learning of his clothing deceptions. As they left the breakfast room to ride into Hanlith, he certainly hoped so, anyway.

"I think Caesar and Brutus were terribly hurt at being left behind," Sophia said from beside him, her breath briefly visible in the air.

"*I* think the villagers would riot at having a pair of wet, massive beasts trundling through their homes and businesses," he returned. "I have no wish to be stabbed with pitchforks."

She snorted. "Coward."

"Instigator."

As she laughed at that, he crowded Zeus into Copper,

took Sophia's shoulder, and leaned over to kiss her. Before she could react, he straightened and moved away again. The warmth of her mouth seemed to spread through him, heating his insides enough to keep all of winter at bay.

It seemed a very impulsive and boyish thing to do, and at nine and twenty years of age he was neither of those things. The last thing he cared to do was to give her the impression that he was besotted with a three and twenty-year-old card dealer. Because he wasn't. He merely enjoyed kissing her. And having sex with her, which he planned to do again that evening.

"May I ask you something?" she said after a moment, her green eyes assessing.

"Certainly."

"How old were you when you inherited the dukedom?"

He frowned. While he hadn't wanted to be asked about kissing or defining a relationship after five days, he *had* expected to be asked something about the two of them. "Why?"

"Because my second question is about whether you and Lady Wallace have always been so . . . adversarial."

Now it made more sense. "You're an only child."

Sophia squinted one eye. "I am my mother's only child."

"Ah. That's right. Hennessy has a son and daughter from his actual marriage."

"So I've heard."

Adam's scowl deepened. "I didn't mean to insult either your mother or the circumstance in which Hennessy has placed you."

When he looked over at her, she wasn't frowning, thank God. "I wasn't insulted," she returned. Sophia sighed, then glanced sideways at him. "And you didn't answer either of my questions."

"Seventeen, and yes."

"That's all you're going to say? I at least provided an entire sentence."

"I inherited the dukedom at age seventeen. My sister and I have been at loggerheads for as long as I can remember. And that's two complete sentences. Talk about something else. You didn't wish to discuss your family, and I'd prefer to not discuss mine."

They rounded the hill, and Hanlith came into view. She'd called it picturesque, and looking at the village through eyes that hadn't grown up knowing it far too well, he could admit that it was quite pretty.

"You know, before this holiday I thought of you as a stern, omnipotent duke who seemed to know everything about any given situation and who for some unknown reason had deigned to be kind. Or rather, had deigned to be kind to Keating and Camille, and in so doing was also kind to me."

That actually seemed a fairly accurate assessment, except perhaps for the knowing everything bit—though he had enough resources and spies in other households to at least make a decent attempt. "But your opinion has changed, I assume?" he asked aloud.

"Amended, I think. I didn't know you were witty, for example. Nor did I have any idea that you were being herded toward a marriage that you'd been avoiding. And I never expected to think of you as a . . . friend. Which I do, unless you're merely being kind to a stranded houseguest and I've overstepped and offended you." She kept her gaze on the nearing row of shops. "Have I?"

That was the word he'd been seeking to explain her to himself. "Friend." It wasn't quite encompassing enough, because he didn't wish to lick any of his other friends' naked skin, but it had a . . . a feeling to it of warmth and kindness and humor that fit her—them, together—quite well.

"I've never met a female I would call a friend. Un—"

"Oh. Well, that's fine, then. I didn't—"

"Shut up, will you? I was about to say 'until now.' I like the idea. As long as the kissing and sex is still allowed."

"Very much yes."

SIX

"You can maneuver those stones into place from a sled?" Adam asked dubiously, looking up from the large sketch spread across his desk to the trio of men standing across from him. The Jones brothers, stonemasons and—evidently—engineers.

"We can't sink supports into the riverbed like we could in summer," the largest of the three said, his heavy wool cap still clutched in his hands. "The ice would form around it and smash it to pieces."

"Don't ye worry, Your Grace," another of them, Tobias as he recalled, contributed, jabbing a stained finger at the drawing. "Our da' made the last repairs just the same way. All we need's a few days of good weather for the mortar to set. To be safe we'll reinforce the whole damned thing with timber till spring, when we can cement the bloody stones in place till Doomsday."

"That's quite a guarantee," Adam returned. "Get on with it, then. Put whatever supplies you need to my account. It's sixteen days until Christmas, gentlemen. I want that bridge repaired before then." It was bad enough, having to choose a wife based on a month's acquaintance. Doing so in less time was unthinkable.

After they left, Adam returned to the desk to sink into his chair. He'd sent for the Jones brothers an hour after he'd reached the bridge collapse, and they'd spent the subsequent five days coming up with what actually seemed a rather solid plan for repairs.

Five days ago he'd been furious that his holiday plans had collapsed just as strikingly as the bridge. A month trapped at Greaves Park with only his sister and a duke's bastard for company while he watched the clock tick toward the moment he lost half his holdings had seemed the worst torture Satan could devise. Even if this hadn't been the last few moments of his twenty-ninth year, he was a man who required social interaction, anything to . . . keep him from his own thoughts, he supposed.

Five days later, his frustration had faded considerably. It wasn't that he was smitten with his one houseguest or that he'd forgotten the need for the others, but he did enjoy Sophia's company. Greaves Park had never been a peaceful or a happy place for him, though it was certainly the grandest of the Baswich properties and the ancient family seat. The latter was why he came every year. And the former was why he tended to invite everyone he could convince to leave their own extended families and properties for the holiday and come join him.

He stirred his finger over the three pence Sophia had paid him for the mare Copper, as per their agreement. A smile touched his mouth. He'd been many things over the years—a rake, a manipulator, a villain, occasionally a friend—but he'd rarely been surprised. Sophia White surprised him. Almost constantly.

The door clicked open. "I assume those filthy men were here about the bridge," Eustace said, gliding into the room. "Thank goodness. How long until civilization returns?"

"A week to ten days, give or take," he returned, shuffling the coins into his hand and placing them in the top drawer of his desk. "I'm still uncertain why you're so eager to see my potential brides arrive. I thought you'd be happier having control of half a million pounds' worth of properties and a viscountcy and an earldom going to your son."

"Then you presume incorrectly. I am content to wait until you've proven whether you're able to live up to the one decent thing Father ever asked of any of us. You're seen as the head of this family, and I'd prefer to avoid any whispers or snickers as to why that might change in February." She straightened. "Especially if those tales are going to involve that . . . female. Which they're likely to, as what proper lady wants to see her prospective husband hanging about a Tantalus girl? Especially that one?"

"Considering how many of these so-called proper ladies are presently waiting across the river to begin the marital parade, I don't think Sophia will put any of them off." He snorted. "In fact, they could likely learn a thing or two from her." About being interesting, anyway.

"That creature has already taken over the household, conspired with all the servants, and seduced my brother so thoroughly he doesn't even realize he's being made into a fool. By Friday she'll be setting the dinner menus and changing the curtains. Something tawdry and red, I imagine."

Adam sat back in his chair. "Do you know what a breath of fresh air is?" he asked, meeting her angry gaze steadily. "Likely not, as you spend every moment in my company attempting to flatten me. Go away, Eustace, and spit your venom somewhere else."

"You're the one who's already been poisoned, twice over. And if you know what she's about, then you're a hundred times worse than she is. *He* preferred redheads, too, if you'll recall. I remember quite clearly the way he banished Mother to her rooms and paraded his women about, encouraging them to put on airs and squawk like the mindless parrots they were, until everyone looked foolish but him. And I know you remember it, too. You've even done it yourself."

To his surprise a tear ran down her cheek, though she faced away from him so swiftly that it might have been a trick of the light. He drew a breath, pulling back the vicious bite he'd been about to deliver. "Sophia is not a mindless parrot, nor is she after anything but her first pleasant holiday. And I am not our father."

"You are. You just don't see it yet, or you don't have the insight to admit it." She faced him again, her gray eyes snapping. "You're better at pretending propriety than he was, but we both know it's only a matter of time before you destroy our name and our reputation. If that is your intention, then I *do* wish you would simply decline to marry. Or better yet, die, so my Jonathan will have the dukedom, as well. At least then I'll be able to guide him to some semblance of propriety and without the most telling reminder of our father's . . . tyranny—you." With that, she stomped out of the room and slammed the door closed behind her.

Adam shoved to his feet. Eustace had peppered him with insults and criticisms for years, but for the first time he realized that she wasn't simply mimicking their mother; she actually meant what she said. She wished him dead. At once, so her twelve-year-old brat could take not just the majority of holdings when he failed to be a so-called proper gentleman, but the title and everything else, leaving her to rule the Baswich empire as she saw fit.

He was *not* his father. Every day he stopped in front of that portrait to remind himself of that fact. Yes, he remembered the endless queue of lovers and mistresses the duke had paraded in front of them, in front of his wife. Some of them he'd even had residing in the house with them. And yes, now that he thought about it, a majority of them in his recollection had been redheads.

But that didn't mean he'd become Michael Arthur Baswich, and it didn't mean Sophia bore any blame for anything. Growling, he yanked the bottle of Russian vodka from the liquor tantalus and poured himself a brimming glass. He could feel the black anger beginning to roil in his gut, fury at Eustace combined with the realization that she could very well be correct. About him.

It was only a coincidence, of course, that his one guest had been Sophia. And he would have found her warm and interesting whatever the color of her hair. Who wouldn't? And he wasn't married and intentionally insulting his wife and children with his affairs. Not yet, anyway. But was he insulting Eustace? He'd made an art of keeping mistresses, after all.

Their entire family had wanted their father gone. His mother had never said so openly, but he and Eustace both knew it. How could they not? And then there were the times, more and more frequent as Adam grew older, that the duchess had turned her anger and humiliation on him. He was male, after all, and the heir. The small-sized reflection of the duke.

On occasion, Adam had wished his own father dead, and then felt guilty for thinking such a thing. And then it had happened. For a week or two he'd felt relieved. The monster was dead. They could finally have some peace. But then his mother rose up from the cowering wretch that she'd been and had begun taking her years of pent-up bile out on him. And now Eustace said the very same thing to him that he'd always wanted to tell their father. *Or better yet, die.* And she'd meant it.

He refilled the glass, though he couldn't remember emptying it. Or if he'd done so more than once already. Judging from the empty bottle, the nearly drained twin beside it, and the slur of his thoughts, he had. *Damnation*. He'd let the monster slip past his hold before he'd realized it was even awake. And now it was too late to cage it.

The ugliness roared to life, filling him to the brim, shutting out sight and sound. Who in their right mind would want to continue this joke of a bloodline? Who but some title-hungry, grasping little leech would want to marry someone who could be utterly disgusted with his own father's behavior and yet had managed to trap himself into becoming just like the man?

He stumbled as he attempted to stand. Lurching upright again, he pulled open the door and strode down the hallway. Udgell appeared just as he reached the front door. "I'm going out," he growled at the butler.

"Very good, Your Grace. I'll have Evans saddle Z—"

"Move." Adam yanked open the door himself and stalked outside.

"Your Grace, your coat!"

Ignoring the servant, barely able to hear him anyway with the roaring in his ears, Adam kept walking. Cold air blasted against him, but only on the surface. Inside he felt boiling and molten, putrid and seething. He knew better than to drink so much, but that was likely why he'd done it. So he would feel the way he deserved to.

Once he'd left the ankle-deep snow of the much-shoveled drive, he began sinking to his knees. The going was harder, but the fight suited him and he continued on. Eventually either the heat inside him would burn him up, or his outside would freeze. If either outcome stopped him from thinking, he didn't care which happened first.

"I think trousers are better suited for ice fishing. Don't you?" Sophia asked, tucking her borrowed shirt into her borrowed pants.

"I think you'll freeze, regardless." Milly carefully brushed out and folded the riding habit, and put it into the very sparsely filled wardrobe. "There are things worth freezing for, but I wouldn't name fish as one of them."

Sophia grinned. "But I've never been ice fishing. And it's just out at the lake, so if I begin to freeze I'll still have time to return indoors."

"Unless you fall through the ice, as you've done once already."

Abruptly the conversation didn't seem quite so amusing. With a hard swallow, Sophia shrugged off her uneasiness and buttoned up her waistcoat. "I believe the odds are now in my favor. And I didn't fall through the ice; I fell into the river after the mail coach fell through the—"

"Oh, no," Milly interrupted.

The sharp edge to her voice made Sophia turn around. "What is it?" she asked, joining the housekeeper at the window.

A lone figure, stark black against the white of the ice and snow, stood halfway across the lake. Even from this distance, the elegant lines of his jacket bespoke a gentleman—and there was only one of those in residence. "That's Adam."

"He isn't even wearing a coat," Milly agreed, her tone worried.

As she watched, the figure sat down cross-legged on the snow-covered ice. "He isn't wearing gloves or a hat, either." Turning around, Sophia stomped into her boots.

"Sophia, you shouldn't," the housekeeper said, sending her an alarmed look. "He—His Grace—can be . . . unpleasant."

"Not if he's frozen to death." Shrugging into her jacket, she hurried for the door.

Downstairs she found Udgell pacing in the foyer, the

duke's heavy caped greatcoat in his hands and a frown on his usually impassive face. "Miss Sophia," he said, abruptly coming to attention.

"What happened?" she asked, noting that the usually busy front of the house seemed to be empty of servants.

"I . . . couldn't say, miss." He tucked the coat behind his back. "Do you require anything?"

"Oh, bother," she muttered, grabbing her heavy cloak and fastening it on, then reaching behind the butler for the duke's coat and folding it over her arm. "Give me his gloves," she instructed, pulling on the ones she'd borrowed from Evans the groom.

"But—"

"Don't argue, Udgell. And have a hot bath drawn in His Grace's rooms."

He handed over the gloves. "Very good, Miss Sophia. Shall I send anyone with you?"

"No. I'll wave at the house if I need assistance."

The butler nodded, then pulled open the front door. "He seemed very . . . unlike himself. It's happened once or twice before, and . . . it isn't pleasant." He blanched. "And you must please never repeat that."

"I won't." She had no idea what the butler or Milly meant by "unpleasant," but it couldn't be good. "Hurry with the bath," she returned, remembering how very good that had felt after her unexpected dunking in the river.

This was exceedingly odd. Everything she knew of Adam Baswich spoke of a very powerful, clever man who somehow in the chaos of London managed to stay several steps ahead of everyone else. People didn't cross him, because his vengeance was rumored to be devastating. The first time she'd seen him, when he'd first appeared at the newly opened Tantalus Club, he'd actually frightened her a little.

That night, when he'd arrived with people who'd

wanted to take over the ownership of the club, when he and the Marquis of Haybury had nearly come to blows over a friendship Haybury blamed Adam for destroying—he'd seemed dark and dangerous and very, very controlled. But then he'd actually aided their cause. And a year later he'd helped Keating Blackwood, stood by him even when most of London turned its back.

In the months since Keating and Camille's marriage she'd seen Adam only rarely, but nothing had alarmed her enough to keep her from traveling to Yorkshire for his holiday party, despite his reputation. Sophia frowned. Yes, Haybury had said that the duke couldn't be trusted, and Lady Haybury—Diane—had cautioned her about being so far from the haven of the club, but she'd already lost its protection. And until this moment, she'd been very pleasantly surprised.

She was out of breath from trudging through the snow by the time she crossed onto the lake. Adam hadn't moved, despite the fact that he must be frightfully cold. "Adam?"

Still nothing. Frowning, Sophia shook out his heavy coat. Then, holding her breath, she draped it over his broad shoulders. He didn't explode into motion or begin shrieking like a bedlamite, so she trudged around in front of him.

His head was bowed, his eyes closed. "Adam? Greaves. Your Grace!"

"You shouldn't be out here."

Oh, thank goodness. "Neither should you. I brought your gloves." She held them down to him. "Here." When he didn't move, she sank down on her knees in front of him. Immediately freezing wet dug through her trousers and into her skin, but for the moment she ignored it.

"Why are you here?" he asked, his voice low and very, very level.

"Because you went outside without your coat and sat down in the snow."

Gray eyes opened. Because she'd worked at The Tantalus Club for eighteen months, and even though he showed no outward sign other than a slight redness in his eyes, she recognized that he'd been drinking. A great deal. Considering that it was still early afternoon and she'd left his company only an hour earlier, the amount of and speed with which he must have imbibed were rather alarming.

"But why are you *here*?" he repeated, emphasizing the last word.

"Here on the lake? Because you're here, you're my friend, and you saved me from drowning and freezing. I'm having a bath drawn for you." Sophia blew out her breath. "Here in Yorkshire? Because my life is about to be destroyed, and I was lonely and I wanted to see Cammy again and be happy before I trudge off to my new, miserable life."

"I had nothing to do with it? With you coming to Yorkshire?"

She tilted her head, studying him as closely as he'd abruptly begun studying her. "Well, you invited me, and at a moment when I was feeling very sorry for myself. It was especially nice because Lucille Hampton—I share a room with her—was beginning to drive me mad with all her complaining about how dull and empty London becomes over Christmas. As if I didn't know that just as plainly as she did. At least she had plans to spend the holiday with her cousin, who's a solicitor, of all things. They will talk each other's ears off, I'm certain, which is better than her deafening me. I mean, I don't begrudge her having family, but that definitely makes me less sympathetic to her complaints."

She knew she was prattling, but his hard expression had eased a little, so she continued. "Before I received your invitation I'd thought to have a turkey and potato dinner with the rest of the employees remaining at the Tantalus, and then draw names and exchange gifts. Last year I gave a pretty faux pearl necklace and ear bobs, which went to Emily Portsman. I received a tin of Macassar oil, which was clearly meant for one of the Helpful Men. Mr. Jacobs traded me for a scarf, which I could at least use. Th—"

Adam reached forward, grabbed her by the lapel, and dragged her up against his chest. His eyes glinting, he closed his mouth over hers.

His lips were cold and tasted of vodka, but she kissed him back. That mouth of his was more intoxicating than any liquor. Anyone watching from the house would see they were kissing. So much for his blasted sister not having more reason to be venomous. As he yanked on her leg to pull her sideways into his lap, though, she decided that this was worth the additional trouble.

"You didn't come here to seduce me, did you?" he said after a long, delicious moment, making it more a statement than a question. "And you're Camille's dearest friend. That's why I invited you. Not because of your hair."

Her hair? Men said they liked her hair, but she'd always found it rather troublesome. "My mother said Hennessy hounded her because of her hair. As if that was her fault. As if it's my fault that mine is the same color." She pushed against his chest, giving herself a bit more space to look up at him. "Why are we talking about my hair?"

He took a deep breath, his expression hardening again, and for a moment she thought he wouldn't answer her. "My father favored women with red hair," he finally said, his voice flattening again.

"Well, I beg your pardon, but that's stupid. No one can tell a woman's character or intelligence by looking at her hair. You mean he didn't care who or what they were, as long as they had red hair?"

"Yes, that's fairly accurate." With an easier breath he ran his fingers through his own dusky hair. "My father was an unpleasant man."

"So is mine."

"Does anyone accuse you of being just like him?"

"None of his peers would dare do so," she answered, "and none of my peers know him. Or they didn't, until he stomped into the Tantalus a fortnight ago." If someone had made that accusation to Adam, it had to have been his sister. No one else would have dared. And no one else's opinion would have likely mattered to him, anyway. Her dislike of Lady Wallace deepened. Family wasn't supposed to be cruel. Whether that was ever actually so or not, didn't matter. "I have an idea," she ventured, handing him his gloves.

This time he took them and pulled them on. "I'm drunk; not softheaded. You caught me at a weak moment. I don't have many of them." He held her hand as she stood up. "Now. You said something about a bath."

When he pushed to his own feet he wasn't quite steady, but that might well have been because his legs had to be half frozen. When he refused the offer of her shoulder, she backed away a few steps.

Was she the enemy now, because she'd seen a crack in his armor? Damnation, that was not her fault. "I'm terrified of spiders," she announced.

He swung his head around to look at her. "Beg pardon?"

Sophia nodded. "Not merely shriek and climb onto a chair terrified. Vomit and faint terrified."

"Why the dev—"

"Now you know one of my weaknesses. So stop being so blasted stubborn and let me assist you."

"It's not the same th—"

"I'm not going to say anything to anyone," she cut in. "I certainly don't have enough friends to risk losing them by telling their secrets willy-nilly."

After a long moment spent gazing at her, Adam lifted his arm. "Come on, then."

She tucked herself up against his side, sliding an arm around his waist to help him keep his balance. Whatever had happened, she seemed to have passed the test. For the moment, at least. But then . . . "Was this about questioning *my* character, or yours?"

"I'm not a very nice man, Sophia," he commented, his tone, despite the slur of his words, much closer to its usual combination of jaded sarcasm and slight amusement. "I'm quite aware of that. Now you are, as well."

Sophia wasn't entirely certain that she'd gleaned the message he expected from this conversation. Because she very clearly saw a gentleman of wit and compassion who was attempting to be a better man than his father, who still felt trapped by the man, and who wasn't entirely certain he was succeeding.

Telling him that, however, would be a very poor idea. Clearly he saw his . . . struggle, she supposed it was, as a weakness. Sophia shifted, taking as much of his weight across her shoulders as she could. She liked being here. And so she would attempt to ignore that anything untoward had just happened. She liked Adam Baswich—not in spite of his faults, but because of them. And because he hadn't laughed when she'd suggested that they were friends.

The Jones brothers did indeed seem to know what they were about. After only three days, three sturdy, wide-bottomed sleds that looked more like river barges had been placed directly beneath the missing portion of the old bridge. From them rose a complex scaffolding of rope and timber, up which scampered a dozen men setting in large stones dragged up by two additional sets of workers on either side of the halved structure.

"Luckily she broke apart ragged, which makes fitting the new stones some easier," the middle Jones brother, Harvey, commented from the rise overlooking the construction. "We could use some iron bars braced in with it, as the mortar hardens slow in the cold. That'll be costly, though."

Adam nodded, patting Zeus beneath him. "See to it. I have guests waiting." And a shrinking amount of time for him to make a bridal selection.

"Aye, Yer Grace. I'll test her first meself, come Monday morning. Or Tuesday, if we have snow tonight. My creaking knee says we will."

Well, he wouldn't dispute the man's creaking knee, but he hoped it was wrong. Two or three more days, depending on the weather. Perhaps it was time for him to stop avoiding the house and enjoy the relative peace that still awaited him there. "Do your best."

Staying about any longer would make it look like he had nothing to do, which he certainly did. Sighing, Adam turned Zeus and kneed the big black toward the windswept road leading to the manor house.

At just about the halfway point he looked up to see a lone rider approaching on the same path. The horse gleamed red-orange in the clouding sunlight, the mare's hair dull in comparison to her rider's.

"What the devil are you doing out here alone?" he asked, stopping in front of her.

Sophia adjusted the floppy gray brim of her borrowed groom's hat. "My walking shoes are supposed to be finished today. Evans's boots are beginning to pinch my toes."

If she'd said a word about being worried that he'd lost his mind again, he would have ridden on without a word. But no mention of him at all—he hadn't expected that, either. "That doesn't explain why you're alone," he pressed, not believing her.

"I don't require an escort. And Copper isn't likely to run away with me if she has to plow through two feet of snow."

"You should at least have the dogs with you," he insisted, not certain why he wanted to argue, except that he felt disagreeable this morning, and she'd caught him unawares, and he still regretted that she'd seen him behaving like a lunatic out on the lake.

"I would have, but Udgell wouldn't let them leave the house without your permission, and I didn't feel like waiting for you to return. You have been away more than you've been present, you know."

Adam narrowed his eyes. "I'll speak to Udgell. He'll do as you ask from now on."

"Don't wallop him simply because you're in a foul mood."

That was enough of that. "You do not get to tell me what to do."

She actually rolled her eyes at him. "Likewise. Now I'm going into the village. Good morning."

He wheeled Zeus around to fall in beside her. "Then I'm going with you."

"I don't want you to come with me, Adam," she stated, starting Copper off again at a careful walk.

"Why the bloody hell not?" he demanded, keeping pace with her, daring her to comment further.

"Because you agreed that we were friends. But I've realized that you were either making fun of me, or lying, or . . . or I don't know what. But I don't want to be in your company right now. I can go several other places and be yelled at or taunted or insulted or ignored without my expectations being dashed."

"Your expectations of what, precisely?" he asked, ignoring the remainder of her argument.

"Of being treated like a . . . a regular, unblemished person, I suppose. The vicar will never see me that way, and I'm fairly certain he won't allow anyone else to, either. I'm accustomed to disappointment, but I don't like being angry. You're beginning to make me angry. So just go away."

Adam drew a hard breath in through his nose. "My sister said you came here with the intention of seducing me. That you're after money and power and protection." There. Criticizing her was better than looking at himself.

Sophia pulled Copper to a halt. For a moment she sat there, her head lowered. Finally her shoulders rose and fell. "Well. I suppose the game is up, then."

That stopped him, ice forming in the pit of his stomach. "What?"

"I admit; I did come here to seduce you. I wanted to have a big house in Knightsbridge, with servants and jewels. I wanted everyone to know I was your mistress so when I walked into a grand ballroom, they would . . ." She frowned. "No, I can't go to balls," she muttered. "I mean, I wanted to be your secret mistress, so I could . . . Hm. Oh, there is the way that my disobeying Hennessy will cause my only friends' livelihood to be destroyed. No, that's not it."

She awkwardly climbed out of the sidesaddle, falling on her arse in the snow before she stumbled to her feet again. "I just wanted jewels. And grand cloth . . . No, I have nice dresses. Not here, of course, but that's all part of my plan. Because being your mistress would mean I could do all sorts of things I can't do now."

The chill in his gut began to fade a little. "Things like what?" he asked, looking down at her.

"Things. Like . . . Copper. I have a horse, now. I can ride through Hyde Park." She jabbed a finger in his direction. "And if I had two horses and a carriage, I could drive through Hyde Park. For the next six weeks, anyway."

He turned his gaze across the snowy landscape. Sophia didn't have a fine life. Having money would gain her a measure of security, some hangers-on from the fringes of Society, the ability to more openly live the scandalous life she hadn't created for herself in the first place. But with Hennessy threatening the Tantalus if she didn't do as he said, being his—or anyone's—scandalous anything would do her no good. Just the opposite.

He at least knew her well enough to realize that she wouldn't allow anything to hurt her friends at The Tantalus Club. Even he could see that she'd adopted Lord and Lady Haybury and the rest of the employees there as her family. *That* was what she wanted, and that was what she was going to lose, regardless of her actions. She certainly didn't require anything from him to achieve failure.

Frowning, he looked back at her. "Sophia, I apo—"

A very large snowball splatted into his jaw and left shoulder.

"That was not funny," he growled, spitting out snow.

When he caught sight of her straightening, a second snowball packed in her gloved hands, her expression wasn't amused. In fact, she looked angry. Furious, even. Adam ducked out of the saddle, and the snowball whizzed over his head.

"Stop it," he ordered, stomping around Zeus to reach her.

"You are a stupid man!" she retorted, backpedaling and flinging loose snow at him as he approached.

He swiped the freezing stuff off his face. "I was attempting to apologize."

"I don't care! Your sister says awful things. The ones she says about you certainly aren't true, but you've decided what, that she must be telling the truth about me? You know she's only attempting to make trouble for you! Why would you listen to your sister about either of us?"

Three days ago he hadn't been all that certain Eustace hadn't been correct about him. He still wasn't. But the way Sophia simply dismissed his sister's words as being of no consequence at all—it made him feel . . . warm inside. Not bleeding and molten, but . . . alive. Soph—"

Another ball of snow smacked wetly into his front. Clearly logic had flown south for the winter. Bending down, he scooped up a handful of the white powder, patted it into a hasty ball, and threw it at her.

It caught her in the chest, and she blinked in surprise. "You hit me!"

"Likewise." He pelted her again.

In a moment the flurry of flying snow half obscured both of them. Snow caked his shoulders, knocked the hat from his head, and trickled coldly down the inside of his waistcoat. Adam grinned, and another one caught him in the teeth.

At her responding, breathless snort, he launched himself forward, tackling her around the waist. She thudded backward into the snow with him on top of her. "I agree," he panted, brushing snow and hair out of her face as he looked down at her.

"You agree with what?" she prompted, pelting him as best she could with her arms half pinned.

"At times I am a stupid man. Her accusations about you were—are—ridiculous."

Sophia nodded. "Yes, they are. And so are her accusations about you. I mean, I don't know precisely what she said to you, but an argument either makes sense or it doesn't. A person is either credible, or she isn't. And Lady Wallace isn't."

Adam wanted to kiss her, the desire surprising in its

sudden intensity. He held himself where he was, six inches above her face. "I agree."

"Good. Then stop trying to begin a fight with me. I don't like it. If you don't wish to call yourself my friend, then tell me so. My feelings will be wounded, but I'll certainly survive. And being hurt is much better than being lied to."

"I consider you my friend," he said. "And I won't abuse the honor again. I swear it."

A tear ran down the corner of her eye toward her ear, and he brushed it away before it could freeze there. Then he did kiss her, because he was *that* kind of friend, and he wanted her to know it.

She crushed a fistful of snow into the back of his head, because clearly *she* was *that* kind of friend. He'd never had one quite like her. Adam laughed against her mouth. He liked this kind of friend.

"Well, I can't go into Hanlith now," she said as he sat and pulled her up beside him. "I'm all wet." She eyed him speculatively. "And cold. I think I need a hot bath."

Luckily his servants were accustomed to carrying a ridiculous number of hot water buckets upstairs for a ridiculous number of people during the course of one of his holiday parties. "What a coincidence." Adam stood, brushing snow off himself as he did so, then took her hands and helped her to her feet. "So do I."

SEVEN

"Thank you, Udgell. That will be all."

The butler inclined his head. "Very good, Your Grace. I'll send in Felton."

"Not necessary. I'll manage." Adam followed the retreating servant to his bedchamber door. "And I'm not to be disturbed."

"Yes, Your Grace."

Once Adam had closed and latched the door, Sophia rose from her seat in the deep windowsill. "Who's Felton?" she asked.

"My valet." The duke shed his jacket, draping it across the back of one of the myriad comfortable-looking chairs that littered the large room. He continued forward, stopping in front of her to unknot the scarf from around her neck.

Arousal and anticipation skittered through her veins. Thank goodness they were friends again, so they could do this very thing. Three days of him avoiding her had been a very long time, after all. When he slowly slid the heavy material from around her throat, goose bumps rose on her arms. More complex and troubled than she'd realized or not, Adam Baswich was an exceptional lover.

He opened the top button of her waistcoat. "Lady Haybury should consider making this the official uniform of The Tantalus Club," he mused, his gaze lowering to her chest. "I can almost guarantee the club members would be more generous with their tipping, and less cautious with their wagering."

"I don't quite understand the allure," she admitted. "The members seem to prefer that we wear low-cut gowns. In a suit I'm dressed from my soles to my chin."

Adam finished with her waistcoat, but rather than pushing it off her shoulders, he merely pulled it open. Then he ran his palms from her waist up her stomach to cup both her breasts. "You're more covered," he returned, "but you're also more revealed. Your very long legs, for instance, and your slender waist and curved hips. In a gown little of that is visible except during the occasional twist or step."

She drew an uneven breath as he untucked her shirt and ran his hands up beneath it. His thumbs brushed across her nipples before he pinched them lightly, and she shivered. "I'll write to Diane and suggest it, then, shall I?"

"Yes. Pull off your waistcoat. My hands are full."

Oh, she'd noticed that. As she lifted her arms it altered the pressure of his hands on her breasts. Sophia half closed her eyes, savoring the sensation. Once she was free of her waistcoat, Adam wadded up the bottom of her shirt and then lifted it off over her head.

From the tented material at his crotch, he was enjoying undressing her as much as she was. She smiled, her hands going to the fastenings of her trousers until he pushed them away and did it himself. Then he squatted down and took one of her boots. Sophia braced her hands on his shoulders for balance as he pulled off one and then the other.

"You're being very quiet," he noted, drawing her trousers the rest of the way down so she could step out of them.

"Am I?" she returned as he straightened. "You distracted me, then."

Adam grinned. "Did I?" Abruptly he dipped and swung her up into his arms. While she clung to his neck a bit breathlessly, he carried her over to the iron-cast bathtub and lowered her into the steaming water.

At the sensation of warmth encircling and seeping into her, Sophia sighed and closed her eyes completely. Almost immediately she opened them again, however; she wasn't about to miss the sight of an aroused Duke of Greaves stripping off his clothes.

His arousal was even more impressive in daylight. She suspected that he would have been a popular lover even if he hadn't been a wealthy duke. When he paused at the side of the bath to drag a chair draped with cloths and towels closer, Sophia reached over to circle his cock with her fingers. Adam froze.

Grinning, her gaze on his face, she shifted closer to run her tongue along him from base to tip. Then she took the velvety head into her mouth. He dug his fingers into her pinned-up hair, his hips making an involuntary half-thrust forward.

For a long moment they stayed there, her gently sucking, and him with his head thrown back. With a shuddering breath, he pulled her face up again. "Stop that or you'll end me right here," he rumbled. "Warn a fellow before you do that, next time."

Somehow the idea that he assumed there would be a next time was very exciting. Shiver inducing, even. "Come in here, then."

Adam stepped into the bath and sank down into the water. The steaming liquid rose within an inch or two of the rim as he leaned forward and kissed her, hot and openmouthed. Their legs tangled, and she slid her arms around his shoulders.

She'd had more deliciously hot baths here in Yorkshire than she'd ever had at the club; tepid was the general temperature there, simply because the kitchen was too busy to allow for hot bathing water for the four dozen employees. And as pleasant as a hot bath in cold weather was, sharing one with Adam Baswich was even better.

Still kissing her, he fitted her legs around his hips and slowly drew her forward until he was fully inside her. She groaned at the fullness of the sensation, the tight, erotic slide of flesh against flesh. She moved, rocking back and forth on him as he surged into her.

Water cascaded onto the fine wood floor in waves that matched the rhythm of their motion. "We're making . . . a mess," she panted.

He kissed her deeply once more. "Don't care."

Tension drew through her, then let loose in a delirious rush. Sophia lowered her head against his shoulder as with a deep groan he sped his own pace. At the last moment he leaned back, pulling out of her, and grabbed a wash towel, releasing himself into it.

Sophia kissed his shoulders and his throat, working her way back up to his mouth. He felt even warmer against her, around her, than the heated water. With a low chuckle he tossed the cloth into a basket and wrapped his arms around her.

"What's so amusing?" she asked, though she rather felt like smiling, herself. Sex and heat and holiday—oh, yes, smiling was very appropriate.

It occurred to her, not for the first time, that even if her next Christmas was to be spent in the company of a man who wanted her only because he wanted to change her, this time, this moment was worth it. At least she would have memories of her very good friends at the Tantalus, and a very unexpected, arousing one of her time here at Greaves Park.

"Snowballs?"

Shaking herself, she slapped him lightly on the shoulder. "You made me angry."

"I'm glad we weren't near a rock quarry, then."

"You should be." She untangled her arms from his. "We should clean up the floor."

"That's why I have servants," he returned, offering a hand to help her step out of the bath.

She sighed. He said it so matter-of-factly. The air felt doubly cold now that she was bereft of both the bath and him, and she wrapped a blanket around her shoulders. She strolled over the wet floor to the window as Adam exited the bath and shrugged into a heavy dressing robe. "It's cloudy," she said, taking in the sight of a sky that seemed to begin just beneath the window and spread out forever in a blanket of uniform white.

"It'll be snowing by nightfall," he commented, moving up behind her. "Harvey Jones felt a twinge in his knee."

Sophia pursed her lips. "Is this Harvey Jones's knee very accurate in predicting the weather, then?"

"Evidently." Adam left the window again and walked over to place another log on the roaring fire in the hearth. "Should we make another attempt at ice fishing, or would you rather retrieve your new shoes? Or we could have a go at the sleigh the grooms just finished polishing."

A sleigh ride? She'd never even thought to do such a thing. But he'd mentioned fishing, first. And given the way their previous attempt at it had gone, perhaps he wanted to erase it from his memory, or at least bury it beneath more pleasant recollections.

"Ice fishing," she decided.

"Excellent choice. I've a taste for bream baked in lemon juice." He made his way over to the door and pulled it open. "Udgell!"

"Yes, Your Grace?" the butler's distant voice returned.

"We're going ice fishing. Have Mr. Daily find us a good spot on the lake and prepare it."

"I'll see to it at once, Your Grace."

When Adam turned around, Sophia had dropped the blanket to the floor and was pulling her man's shirt over her head. He'd told her how much he appreciated seeing her long legs in those trousers, but she looked almost even more delectable with the shirt hanging down to her thighs and her bare legs beneath. Lust stirred in him yet again.

He'd decided over the course of the last hour that the reason Eustace's theories and accusations had troubled him even more than they generally did was that he still couldn't quite figure out Sophia White. In his experience everyone wanted something, be it power or wealth or status or security. Sophia might have decided to venture to Yorkshire because she wanted to experience one grand Christmas before the inevitable chains of propriety dragged her away, but other than that, she didn't seem to want anything. And certainly nothing he could provide her.

Neither could he decide where she fit in the hierarchy of his friends, lovers, mistresses, and sundry acquaintances. She was a duke's daughter, placing her above most every other female he knew, but she was illegitimate and unacknowledged, which knocked her completely off the page. She chatted with servants and wore outlandish clothes, would sleep with him but didn't care to be called—or treated as—a mistress. She did as she pleased, which he found refreshing, but clearly she had her own unique compass which she followed regardless of whether it annoyed him or her or anyone else. And the Duke of Hennessy was a fool not to find her spirit and independence admirable, and instead to remove her from the life she'd made for herself.

"You're staring," she commented.

Adam shook himself. "I'm gazing admiringly at your legs."

"Well. Continue, then," she returned, grinning as she sat to pull her trousers on over them, "but they're getting a bit cold."

"You'll need a heavier coat if we're going to be on the ice," he decided, fastening up his own trousers and making his way into the dressing room that connected the sitting room to his bedchamber. "Most of mine are too broad across the shoulders, but they'll keep you warm."

Inside the sitting room he could hear her sifting through their clothes to find the ones that belonged to her. "Surely Milly or someone has a coat that'll fit me," her voice came. "Of course it won't match with what I'm wearing, but I won't feel like I'm dragging half of it across the ground."

A muscle in his cheek jumped. She wouldn't let him purchase gowns for her—which he was doing anyway, but that was neither here nor there—and she insisted on purchasing the horse he wanted to give her. And now she wouldn't even borrow one of his coats. What the devil was the point of being wealthy and powerful if he couldn't shower a female—a friend—with a few frivolous gifts?

He dug into the back of one shelf and pulled out a multicaped dark gray greatcoat. "Try this one," he insisted, returning to the sitting room. "I think I was fourteen the last time I wore it."

She took it from his hands and held it up. "You kept this?"

"Not so much kept it as forgot about it. I imagine if I looked hard enough, I could locate some of my old short pants and an infant's blanket."

Rather than smiling as he expected, Sophia took on

a thoughtful expression. "I forget that this has always been your home." With a sigh she put the coat over the back of a chair to finish dressing.

"When did you last have a home?" he asked, though from her wistful tone her idea of a home was much different from his experience in one.

"I lived with my mother above a dress shop in Surrey until I was nearly nine years old," she returned. "I suppose that was the last time, until the Tantalus, which isn't quite the same, but at least it feels—felt—safe."

"You stayed with your aunt and uncle after your mother's passing, did you not? I seem to recall you told me that, once."

This time she flashed a smile. "Yes, they took me in, until they realized that the solicitor who distributed my monthly stipend wouldn't allow them to spend the money on themselves. After that there was no point in keeping me there, so they sent me off to boarding school. Boarding schools." She rolled her shoulders. "Now, lest I find myself in dire need of strong drink, I think we should go fishing."

That was the closest he'd ever seen her come to being . . . unhappy with her past. For the most part she simply seemed to accept it as something that had occurred and no longer signified. Briefly he wondered how long it had taken her to learn how to do that. It was a lesson he could do with himself.

His old greatcoat fit her fairly well, and he complimented her on how very gentlemanly she looked. That elicited a grin and a bow, despite the fact that with that long, curling tail of hair and those very long eyelashes no one could be fooled by her clothing for as much as a second. He led the way outdoors, offering his arm to help her negotiate the low snowdrifts on the drive. Before they reached the edge of the lake, though, something occurred to him, and he stopped.

"Wait here for just a moment," he said, and strode back to the house.

Udgell pulled open the front door just as he reached it. "Your Grace?"

"Decorate for Christmas," he said.

The butler actually blinked. "You instructed that we were to dress the house during the night after all your guests had arr—"

"Yes, I recall. Bring it out now. Everything. I want fresh holly and ivy. And make certain we have a supply of chestnuts. And raisins."

"I— Yes, Your Grace."

"Don't dawdle. And begin in the drawing room. That bit, at least, is to be finished by the end of dinner."

Once he turned away, the butler shut the door rather firmly. Adam ignored that. A chit who hadn't had a proper home in fourteen years and who now lived above a gentlemen's club had never had a Christmas at a grand house. She'd already said this was her best Christmas. He meant to give her one to remember.

When he returned to her side, she wrapped her arms around his sleeve. "Is everything well?"

"Yes. Quite. So tell me, have you ever fished at all before?"

Sophia shook her head. "I once read Beakey's book about the subject; evidently, according to him anyway, fishing is very nearly a religious experience."

"Ah. I think you'll find that it's much more about worms and not sliding off your chair."

She laughed. "If that's the case, I shall master the sport in no time."

His gamekeeper, Jack Daily, had selected a promising location close to the forest side of the lake. By the time they reached the spot, the fellow had already finished sawing a two-foot hole in the ice and had placed a pair of wooden benches on either side. Several feet away, a brazier with a small fire sat atop a sled.

"With yer pardon, Yer Grace," the gamekeeper said, doffing his hat, "the worms is dug in too deep. I took the liberty of seizing a couple of chickens from the kitchen. The gizzards and necks and bits of feet, anyway."

"Well done, Daily. Miss White is a novice, so please aid her accordingly."

"Upon my honor, Yer Grace."

To his credit, the servant didn't even bat an eye as he took in Sophia and her unique wardrobe. Instead he helped her over to one of the benches, handed her a fishing pole, and placed a piece of a chicken's innards on the hook for her.

"Now, miss, you'll want to drop it into the hole. It's weighted so it'll sink, but ye have to flick it up and down. Pretend yer a bug that's fallen in and yer drownin', trying to get back out."

Sophia nodded. "May I be a grasshopper?"

"Aye. Breams likes 'em some juicy grasshoppers."

"I'll be a beetle," Adam supplied, baiting his own hook and dropping it into the water. "Hold the pole lightly, but be ready in case you get a nibble. Don't jerk it out of the water, or you'll lose the fish."

"Aye," the gamekeeper took up. "Tease it, like ye want to kiss it."

"Daily."

The servant blushed bright red. "I beg yer pardon, Miss White. That were—"

"It was fine," she interrupted, grinning. "A very good description. I knew precisely what you meant."

Adam lifted an eyebrow, gazing at her from across the hole in the ice. "Oh, you did, did you?"

"Certainly. A little forward, a little back, until you've drawn him to the surface and his doom."

She was laughing, but Adam decided it was a damned good thing she *hadn't* set out to seduce him. He seemed to have no ability at all to resist her charms. And the fact that he could relax around her precisely because she had nothing to gain by befriending him hadn't escaped him, either. Sophia White was unique in nearly every way he could imagine.

"Oh!" she exclaimed, jumping. "I felt a tug!"

"Be easy now," Daily instructed. "Lure him to his doom."

So the gamekeeper after three minutes liked her enough to adopt her choice of phrase. Adam shook his head, smiling. It seemed the only person Sophia couldn't charm was his sister, and as far as he was concerned that was Eustace's loss. He didn't intend to miss out on any of it, himself.

"I'm certain this is one of the fish *I* caught," Sophia said, motioning at her plate with her fork, "because it's delicious."

Adam sent her a mock glare from across the table. "You're not in some way intimating that you caught better fish than I did, are you?"

"Better fish and more fish than you did," she amended, grinning. She liked when he was at ease, relaxed and witty and amusing.

The oddness and awkwardness of three days ago seemed to have flown, thank goodness. She couldn't imagine how dreadful it must be to be constantly compared to a man he detested, and by his own sister, to the point that he'd actually come to believe it himself. In some ways she was glad she'd spent so much time on her own, if that had been the alternative.

A shiver ran down her spine. She wouldn't be on her own for much longer, and she was very likely to face a heavy daily dose of the same medicine that had poisoned Greaves. If Hennessy hadn't threatened the Tantalus if she fought him, she would be halfway to America by now. Like Adam, though, she'd found herself in a position where she simply would have to clench her jaw, bite her tongue, and endure it.

She looked up at him again, grateful for the distraction. "They have a term for your good fortune, you know," Adam countered.

"Skill?"

"Beginner's luck." He took another bite from his own plate. "And I instructed that you be served the fish I caught, to insure you the finer meal."

"Ha." Standing up, she leaned across the table to stab her fork into a piece of the baked bream on his plate. She popped it into her mouth. Then she made a face. "Oh, that one's definitely yours."

From the corner of her eye she thought she saw Udgell smile, but she pretended not to notice. Being caught with an expression on his face might cause the butler to expire. For a moment she wondered whether Lady Wallace would be dining on any of the fish she'd caught. Knowing the source of her meal would likely cause the marchioness to expire.

"Are you going to tell me why you kept me in the orangerie all afternoon and wouldn't let me go up to change for dinner?" she asked.

"No." His gray eyes practically sparkled as he answered her, so clearly something was afoot.

"Very well," she said aloud. "But you know I'll discover your plans eventually."

"Eventually," he agreed. He reached into his pocket and pulled out a folded piece of paper, which he handed to her. "This came for you with the afternoon mail. It arrived just before dinner, so don't bash me for keeping it from you."

"I know you wouldn't do that." She looked down at

it. "Oh! It's another letter from Cammy." Swiftly she opened it, skimming her eyes down the lines of neat handwriting. "She and Keating have read every book to be found at the inn, and Keating rode over to view the work on the bridge again today. He says he's surprised, but you may know what you're doing."

"I'm all aflutter with the compliment," Adam observed dryly.

Setting the letter aside for closer perusal later, she looked up at him. "How are the repairs going?" she asked, reflecting that she should have asked the question days ago. Of course she had an excuse, since Adam had been avoiding her, but someone could have told her. If she'd wanted to know. If she hadn't known this holiday would be less enjoyable once her host turned his attention to his parade of potential brides.

"Well. The snow tonight will set the schedule back by a day or so, but by Wednesday at the latest I should be able to send word to Keating and Camille to join us."

"That's grand!" she said, too forcefully.

When she'd received the Duke of Greaves's invitation so close on the heels of Hennessy's proclamation, she'd known immediately what she would do. She would have one grand adventure, at least, before she surrendered. Once here, of course, nothing had been as she'd expected. Over the last few days, even with the way she'd arrived, it had been . . . better than she'd imagined. Adam had made her feel special and wanted and even important. Would that change when his friends and his soon-to-be bride—whoever she might be—arrived?

Through the rest of dinner, even with his amusing banter, the question nagged at her. And then she felt selfish for wishing even for a moment that Cammy and Keating would have to remain at an inn over Christmas. That wasn't fair to any of them, most of all Adam.

He'd invited dozens of people to join him, after all, and she was the only one who'd managed to arrive. How did he truly feel about that, about having less and less time to choose a wife or lose nearly everything he valued and protected? This was just a pleasant diversion for her.

"Finished?" he asked on the tail end of that thought.

She set her napkin aside, and tried to do the same with all her worries about things she couldn't change. When there was nothing to be done, worry simply took up space she could use for making pleasant memories. "Yes. And *my* bream was clearly superior to yours."

"Mm-hm. Let's adjourn to the drawing room, shall we? I've a mind to test your luck at faro."

Sophia forced a smile. "I'm better at faro than I am at fishing. How many fish did you catch again? I've forgotten."

"I caught three, and you caught . . . four, was it?"

"Five," she supplied. "And the two largest."

He stood. "Faro. Now."

Her guilt easing at the sight of his genuine grin, Sophia joined him as they headed down the hallway. Adam pushed the drawing room door open and motioned for her to precede him. She did so, then stopped as soon as she entered the room. "Oh," she breathed, delight tickling through her.

Gold and silver and red ribbons hung from the trio of chandeliers, twisting and crisscrossing each other on their way to all four walls. Bunches of fresh holly and ivy hung from all the chandeliers and draped across the mantel, red and white candles rising from the masses of greenery. On the end tables, baskets of glass balls rested, more candles set into them and sending a rainbow of reflected color singing about the room.

"Do you like it?" he asked from directly behind her.

"You made Christmas."

"I had Udgell put Christmas out a bit early, but I'll accept credit if y—"

"I love it," she broke in. "It's . . . magical. Thank you so much."

"You're most welcome."

Sophia turned around, flung her arms around his neck, and kissed him. She couldn't not do so. The beautiful joy of the room demanded it. Even if there had been a hundred people present instead of just the two of them, she would have kissed him, anyway.

Adam kissed her back, putting his hands around her waist to pull her close against his hard, lean frame. "If I'd known it would please you this much, I would have done it earlier," he murmured, and touched her mouth with his again. "Though I don't think I knew you well enough until now to realize how . . . important it would be to do so."

"That's why I like it so much," she returned, turning her head to view the sparkling room again. "Because you *did* realize." She felt a warm tear run down her cheek. Until that moment she hadn't realized she was crying.

He lifted a hand and brushed the tear away with his fingers. "I probably could have told Udgell not to bother hanging the mistletoe," he mused, kissing her cheek where the tear had been. "It doesn't seem to be necessary."

She spied the plant with its deep green leaves, hanging off one of the ribbons that looped before the fireplace. "That shows what you know," she whispered, deeper excitement running like molten silver through her, and took his hand to lead him to the hearth and the thick rug before it.

Midnight had long passed when Adam opened his eyes. For a moment he wasn't certain where he was, until he caught sight of the bouquet of mistletoe twisting lazily some twelve feet above his head. The drawing room.

Memory returned languidly, and he turned his head. Sophia lay against him, her head on his shoulder and his arm draped loosely about her hip. The fire behind them was nearly out, the glowing coals sending her glorious hair into a glinting, deep scarlet blaze across his chest.

And he, the man who always had something to do, somewhere to be, didn't want to move. Naked, beginning to feel a bit chilled in the still room except for where her warm skin touched his, he felt . . . content. Him.

Then Sophia stirred. Adam quickly closed his eyes again, feigning sleep even as he decided that was a silly, childish thing to do. He felt her head lift, and then cold down his left side as she sat up. Evidently she didn't feel the same contentment that he did, though his was rapidly beginning to fade.

She returned, sitting beside him, and the cool sensation of a blanket draped over him up to his chest. A moment later she lay down against him again beneath the blanket, and her lips brushed feather-light against his cheek. Her head settled on his shoulder once more, and he pretended to stir so he could circle her waist with his hand.

Once her breathing softened and deepened into sleep, he opened his eyes again. What kind of life had he lived, that he couldn't recall moments like this? That he'd never experienced this . . . peace before now? Or that he'd never met anyone with whom he could simply relax before a dying fire? She'd covered him with a damned blanket, when he wouldn't know whether she'd spared him a thought or not.

She'd said he'd made Christmas for her. If he could

continue feeling like he did at this moment, he would gladly make Christmas for her every day. He would give her much more than that, if she would only allow him, if he could have some assurance that whatever drudgery awaited him in life, so would this . . . perfection.

Sometime after that he fell asleep again, and only awoke when a wet, snuffling nose stuck itself in his ear. "Damnation," he muttered, shoving Brutus away from him. Sophia was gone from his side, but a second later he heard her quiet chuckle. "That's a fine good morning," he said as he sat up.

Sophia was perched on the end of the couch closest to him, her bare legs tucked beneath her and only her man's shirt concealing the rest of her lovely form from him. "They were pawing at the door," she explained. "If I hadn't let them in, someone would have come to investigate."

"No, they wouldn't, if they valued their continued employment. Toss me my trousers, will you?" Once she did so, he pulled them on and stood. "You prefer tea in the morning, yes?"

"Yes, but—"

Before she could finish her protest he opened the door. "Udgell. A pot of tea." He closed the door again.

"But I'm mostly naked," she said, her voice squeaking, and shot to her feet.

"He won't come in." Adam crossed to her, putting his hands on her shoulders and kissing her.

She kissed him back, her mouth soft and surprising despite the occasional biting wit of her words. "So Udgell knows to leave the tea outside? You must do this often, then."

"Hm." Firming his grip on her shoulders, he pushed her back down onto the couch. "I'm occasionally moody, as you might have noticed," he said slowly. "When the door is latched, he leaves the tea outside."

"Oh." She frowned as he dropped down beside her. "I wasn't trying to say I was jealous. Because I'm not. Evidently I'm simply not witty before breakfast."

"Witty enough to have a dog sneeze in my ear."

That made her laugh. "That was a happy coincidence."

Jealous. Generally he detested that word. It had signaled the end of more than one arrangement with a mistress. At this moment, however, part of him wished she *was* jealous. This friendship, however, evidently didn't work that way. Aside from that, in a few short weeks she would be married, and to a vicar, of all things. Lucifer's balls, she would be miserable. And damn Hennessy for selecting a torture for her when he might just as easily have been kind. The fact that he would be in a nearly identical circumstance might have been ironic, but he didn't find it all that amusing.

"This moodiness of yours," she said abruptly, her jaw tightening a little, as though she wasn't certain of his reaction. "Is that why you have houseguests over Christmas? Not this Christmas, of course, but generally."

And just like that she figured him out. He had friends whom he'd known for years with less insight into his character. They saw precisely what he allowed them to see. He could dissemble, laugh away her suggestion, or attack in a different direction, but that would be doing both of them a disservice. "Yes. I don't like it here, but having a large number of people about makes it more tolerable. It gives me less time to myself, I suppose."

"If you don't like Greaves Park, why do you come?"

"It's the family seat." He shrugged. "If I avoided it, people would notice. I'm not about to advertise a weakness."

For a moment she studied his face, though he had no idea what he thought she saw. "I know you don't need my advice, but perhaps having Lady Wallace here makes the circumstance more . . . difficult than it needs to be. Especially this year."

This time he drew a breath, pushing back against the tendrils of annoyance that began climbing through him. He rarely required advice, and certainly not from a gaming room chit. On the other hand, she wasn't that easy to classify. "Not all of my guests are unconcerned with their reputations. As I'm unmarried, I require a female hostess. A family member. Especially this year."

The door handle rattled, and both Caesar and Brutus began barking. "Hush, boys," Sophia chastised, reaching out with both hands to scratch the mastiffs. Unlikely as it seemed that this petite woman could manage those massive dogs, they both melted into tail-wagging, leg-thumping heaps.

Clearly the lads adored her, Adam noted as he climbed to his feet and went to retrieve the pot of tea. And so did he. He paused midstep, then continued, glad he was facing away from her so she couldn't see his expression. He adored her.

It wasn't all that surprising, he supposed, considering that they'd been together almost constantly for ten days, and that she was pretty, exceedingly good-natured, and just as compassionate. More unexpected was the fact that the realization startled him. He did have friends in whom he confided, after all, and women with whom he had sex. He'd just never had both in one package before.

Shaking himself, and deciding that his sudden self-awareness was somewhat pitiful rather than earth-shaking, he pulled open the drawing room door and retrieved the tea tray set on the floor. If not for his looming thirtieth birthday and Eustace circling like a vulture and waiting for him to fail so she could dig her claws into his inheritance, he would have sent for the Jones brothers. It would have been a small matter to tell them he didn't like the bridge construction, and for them to begin the project over again. Then he could spend Christmas alone with Sophia. That would be a present he definitely appreciated, if the cost to him wouldn't have been more than he could tolerate.

EIGHT

The Greaves Park music room lay directly off the portrait gallery. Sophia paused at the top of the stairs, her gaze already drifting to the former Duke of Greaves's portrait despite her resolve never to spare that man another glance.

"It's just a painting," she muttered to herself, squaring her shoulders and stepping forward.

As she drew even with the portrait, though, she slowed. Not only had this man tormented his family in life, but he'd made arrangements to control his son's life even in death. In a sense, he'd tried to ensure that Adam would marry without love—or at the least merely to keep his properties—that the new Duke of Greaves would have as little reason to respect and honor his wife as he'd had himself.

With a deep breath she faced the painting. Those compelling gray eyes gazed back at her, unblinking. Because she knew a little bit more about him now, she could study his expression, his stance, for hints of that self-concerned cruelty, that sense of arrogant superiority he must have had.

Michael Arthur Baswich. The ninth Duke of Greaves. Evidently she would have been just his type. A shudder ran down her spine. If that man had invited her to a Christmas house party, she would have declined the invitation. She couldn't imagine wanting to spend time in his company, much less being intimate with him.

His son, though, was something else entirely. Yes, he could be arrogant and too sure of himself, but he actually listened when she spoke. He remained concerned over her comfort, and he didn't mind losing a hand or two of cards—even to a female.

Most telling, whether or not he would ever acknowledge it, he cared about the sort of man he was. And the sort of man he wasn't. How many dukes invited to their homes an illegitimate, employed female who wore trousers and oversized gowns? Not the one in that painting, she was certain.

"I don't like you," she said, and turned her back on him.

Adam stood at the end of the hallway, watching her. *Damnation.* She couldn't even have a one-sided conversation with a painting without someone seeing.

A moment passed before he walked forward. "I know now how you feel about him," he drawled, indicating the portrait behind her. "How do you feel about me?"

A smile curved her mouth, her insides heating at the mere notion that he'd bothered to ask her such a question. She reached up ostensibly to straighten his cravat, but mostly so she could touch him. "It's too early to tell."

"Oh it is, is it?" He leaned down and kissed her softly. "What are you doing in here? You didn't come by just to reprimand my father, I assume."

It took a moment for her to find her voice again after that kiss. "I used to play the pianoforte. I wanted to know if I still remembered."

He nodded, then released her to open a neighboring door where a maid cleaned windows. "Two mugs of hot cider in the music room," he said, and returned to her side. "Shall we?"

"I thought you were meeting with your bridge builders this afternoon."

"They aren't here yet." He took her hands and turned her in a circle, his deep gray eyes sparkling. "I'm almost disappointed you're not wearing trousers today."

She glanced down at her blue muslin. "Milly's washing them for me. This is actually *my* dress."

"I remember. It's the one you wore into the river. I'm glad it wasn't ruined."

"One sleeve was torn and the hem was ripped out, but Milly mended it for me." She sent him a sideways glance as they strolled into the music room. "Why did you order your head housekeeper to be my maid?"

"Because you had one gown and a godawful hat to your name, and every lady should have a maid at least once in her life."

"And you decided that even before you knew about my father's ultimatum," she returned with a soft sigh. And he doubted his own humanity, the lummox.

"I'm evidently very intuitive."

Sophia snorted. "It is nice having someone help me put up my hair. Lucille and I sometimes do each other's hair, but she digs the clips into my skull."

Adam chuckled. "I'm glad to spare you a little cranial scarring, then."

With a laugh she sat at the lovely pianoforte with its panel of inlaid mahogany and polished ivory keys. "It's almost too pretty to play."

"Nonsense. Show me what you can do."

Suddenly a little nervous, she paged through the music resting atop the instrument. The Nocturne no. 4 in A Major by John Field seemed vaguely familiar, and she experimentally played a few stanzas. Slowly her fingers began to remember the notes, and her confidence grew.

When a pair of long-fingered, masculine hands reached past her shoulder to turn the page she started, stumbling over a handful of notes until her mind caught up to her fingers again. "Sorry about that," he murmured.

"Don't be. My fault."

She finished the piece with an impromptu flourish of the keys, and Adam applauded. "You play well."

"It was barely passable, but thank you. I don't play nearly enough."

"Do you have a pianoforte at the club?"

"No. It would have been nice, but none of us could ever afford one, and Diane and Oliver already provide more generously than we ever expected."

"I'll purchase one for you."

Sophia looked up at him. A lock of his black hair had fallen across his forehead, and she brushed it away, lowering her fingers to touch his cheek. He was so handsome, and she wanted to ask how many women had fallen in love with him. "I won't be there to play it."

"I'll send it to Cornwall, then."

If he put his mind to it, he could make a great deal of trouble for her. "You cannot purchase a pianoforte for me. That's much worse than a horse. It's more . . . personal."

His eyes narrowed for just a breath. "Then I'll gift it anonymously to The Tantalus Club's employees in your name. I imagine quite a few of the ladies know how to play."

That sounded more reasonable, thank goodness. "Yes, they do. And since you're ridiculously wealthy and the girls will be thrilled, I won't argue with you."

His lips curved in a slow smile. "I'm all astonishment." His gaze holding hers, Adam kissed her again.

She pulled him onto the wooden seat beside her, sliding her arms around his neck and kissing him back. Mm, she liked this man. He kept saying she was unique, but she'd never met anyone like him—dark and dangerous at one moment, witty and good-humored the next. It would take years and years to decipher him, and she would have been exceedingly willing to take the time to do so.

The thought startled her, and she opened her eyes even as Adam lifted her onto his lap. The past fortnight had felt like a dream—that was why she could think such outlandish things. The larger, crueler world had stopped at the edge of the river, and part of her wished the Jones brothers would never repair that bridge, whatever the consequences to the Tantalus when she failed to appear for her own wedding.

Adam slowly slid his palm up her leg, drawing her skirt with it. Then the music room door opened.

"Hello, Adam," Keating Blackwood drawled, the tray of cider in his hands. "Get your hands off Sophia."

Sophia yelped, shoving down her rising skirt and leaping to her feet so fast she nearly knocked him off the bench. "Hello, Keating," Adam said in his coolest tone, considering he couldn't stand at the moment. He shifted his gaze past his tall, dark-haired friend. "Where's your wife? Or have you forgotten her?"

"Your butler's taking her up to our room. Once I heard that the two of you were in the music room, I thought I should be the advance scout." Suspicious brown eyes glanced over at Sophia. "Hello, my dear. You're well, I take it?"

So the blackguard thought he was doing something nefarious with the houseguest. Well, he was, but it was mutual. "Calm yourself, Blackwood."

Sophia strode forward and took the tray from Keating. She set it down on a chair, then gave Blackwood a sound hug. "I'm glad you came," she said feelingly, kissing him on the cheek. "I'm going to find Cammy." Without a backward glance she fled the room.

Once she was gone, Keating lifted an eyebrow. "I'm

awaiting an explanation that doesn't end with me punching you in the nose."

That was damned uncalled for, considering Keating's reputation. "I have—had—one guest in residence. Sophia and I frequently take tea or cider together. And we're both adults, so stand down or I'll take you up on the suggestion of fisticuffs."

With a quick glance around the room and another look at him, Keating relaxed his stance a little. "I'll accept that."

"Good."

"Thank you for inviting us to your home," Blackwood continued. "I'm attempting a life of propriety, but I haven't been able to convince anyone of that fact. We don't receive many invitations."

"You stole your bride from someone else's wedding, Keating. As your grand return to Society after that previous bit of scandal, it was certainly memorable but not very confidence-raising."

Keating picked up one of the cider mugs and took a drink, then retrieved the other one and walked over to Adam. "And yet it was utterly worth it."

"I'll admit that you've lately seemed more civilized."

"Just happier," his friend returned, handing over the second mug. "And I tried not to take it personally that the first year in seven that I decided to accept your invitation, the one bridge to your estate fell into the river."

Adam mustered a grin now that his mind, and his body, had mostly caught up to current events. If anyone had to arrive to interrupt this odd, peaceful interlude, he would rather it be Keating than nearly anyone else. "I'm glad you came."

Narrowing one eye, Keating took another drink of cider. "And you wished to see a dazzling parade of unattached chits as well, then?"

"Not so much wished as needed to see," he returned. "You do remember which birthday I'm nearing, don't you?"

Keating looked at him blankly for a moment before his brows lowered in a scowl. "You mean to marry one of them. Of course. I'd forgotten."

"So had I. Or rather, I ignored the inevitable until it arrived to gnaw on my ankle. This seemed the best setting to select someone appropriate."

"Do they know why they're here?"

"Not the details or the timing, but doesn't every young woman have matrimony on her mind at every given moment?" Even as he spoke he knew there was at least one young lady present who would have preferred *not* to be facing matrimony, but Sophia seemed an exception to every rule, anyway.

"Then explain Sophia," Keating said on the tail of that thought.

"I already did."

"Yes, two adults thrown together by circumstance. Bollocks."

Adam lifted an eyebrow. "You doubt my word?"

"Yes, I do. The letters Sophia's been sending across the river to Cammy have been very . . . affectionate toward you, and my wife was worried that you might be up to some game or other. So was I. And considering what I saw in here, I'm not reassured."

"I'm not leading Sophia astray, if that's what you're intimating. She has her own set of circumstances, but I'm not divulging them. You'll have to speak with her." Adam paused as the rest of what Keating had said struck him. "How affectionate were Sophia's letters toward me?"

"Ridiculously so, at least to someone who knows you as well as I do. She's a friend, Adam, and she helped me win Camille. So I hope you aren't doing something disreputable."

Adam took a swallow of warm cider. "I am not disreputable."

"And I'm not blind. I'll be speaking with Sophia just to verify your interpretation of this morning."

As if he could do something to Sophia against her will without receiving a kick to the groin, anyway. Adam ignored the slight to his honor and stood. His flock of brides was likely crossing the bridge at this very moment, but he wasn't heading for the foyer to greet them. Instead, he led the way to the upstairs room he'd given over to Sophia.

Her door stood open, and even from the stairway he could hear chatting and laughing. She must be relieved to have her friends finally there. Why wouldn't she be? Now she had Camille Blackwood with whom to discuss her troubles, and from whom she could borrow gowns and gloves. Adam frowned briefly. He liked providing her with pretty things. It would be difficult to stop.

"May we come in?" he asked, stopping in the doorway to see Sophia and Camille Blackwood laughing over the wreck of a hat that had survived the dunking in the river.

She looked up at him, her green eyes dancing. "Cammy doesn't like my new hat," she exclaimed.

"All her things were lost in the river, Keating," Camille said, rising from her seat on the bed to offer her hand to Adam. "I knew I should have brought more clothes."

"If you'd brought any more clothes, we would have collapsed the bridge again," her husband said dryly.

Adam took Camille's hand and bowed over it. "Sophia is very practical. She's found or borrowed a very . . . unique wardrobe."

Dimly from the front of the house he heard the sound of more voices, and he steeled himself against the abrupt wish to flee the inevitable. The pleasant part of this holiday had just ended. "I have more guests arriving," he said, attempting not to put any additional meaning into the words as he looked at Sophia. "I need to go greet them." He turned his gaze to Keating. "I've given you two the corner room, right next to this one."

With a slight inclination of his head, he left the room, pretending that he hadn't just seen the sliver of regret touch Sophia's pretty eyes. Did she regret the end of their interlude, or that it had begun at all? This was what would have happened a fortnight ago if the bridge hadn't fallen into the river. Simply because it abruptly seemed as if the past fortnight hadn't existed, that didn't mean it truly hadn't. Unless it did, and this had all been a perfect, snow-tinted daydream.

"You truly don't need to, Cammy," Sophia protested, as Camille dug into her just arrived trunk. "I have several gowns I've borrowed from servants."

"I've brought more than I can wear," Cammy returned. "Keating loves to purchase gowns for me."

"Another reason I shouldn't be wearing them."

"Sophia, you can't wear a servant's dress to a Society dinner." Straightening, Camille lifted a pretty blue gown in her hands. "This one should fit you."

The deep gray gown Mrs. Brooks had found in an old trunk was at least as fine as Camille's, Sophia decided, and she'd been wanting to wear it. Not to a large dinner, of course, but at least it did seem adequate for that occasion. More than adequate. "I'll be fine. You should wear that one. It'll look divine on you."

"We used to share clothes all the time at the Tantalus. Why are you so reluctant now?"

"It's not that." Sophia sighed. "You'll need to wear

those clothes. I don't want these people thinking you're wearing *my* gowns or something. I have no place in Society; you and Keating do."

"Perhaps on the very fringes. A killer and a runaway bride aren't precisely going to be invited to Almack's."

Snorting, Sophia took the gown and held it up in front of her friend. It no doubt looked very good on Camille, with her buttermilk blond hair and blue eyes. "Perhaps not this Season, but you're both interesting. I imagine in another year or two you'll be the toast of London once again. Definitely wear this one tonight. Say you will."

"Oh, very well. But you know you may borrow anything of mine you like. Whenever you like." Placing the dress on the bed, Camille sat beside it and folded her hands in her lap. "Now. The Duke of Greaves."

"What about him?"

"You said in your letters that he took you shoe shopping and riding and that you played several interesting games of billiards and piquet. You like him."

Sophia lowered her brows. "Of course I do. We've become friends." Friends who did some rather naughty things together, but that seemed beside the point.

"Is that all?" Camille asked skeptically. "Friends?"

"Close friends," Sophia conceded with a smile.

"Oh, you sly thing!" her friend exclaimed. "Did he seduce you?"

With a shrug, Sophia plunked herself down on the bed, as well. "It was mutual. We were trapped here, after all. One has to have something to do to pass the time."

Camille covered her mouth with her hands, her expression partly amused and partly dismayed. "You know he has mistresses. Did he offer you . . . that?"

"He mentioned it, but I just enjoy spending time with him. And I don't see anything wrong with that."

Perhaps she sounded defiant, but for heaven's sake. She lived a very different kind of life than most women who resided in Mayfair. Even Camille was the daughter of a lord and lady and had lived a privileged life until an arranged marriage changed everything and had sent her to The Tantalus Club.

"Very well," Camille commented thoughtfully. "Just please tell me you'll keep in mind that Adam Baswich is temporary. Don't let yourself be hurt."

She blinked. For a delightful set of moments she'd forgotten her future, and she'd forgotten that she needed to tell her friend about it. With a quick breath to steady herself she did so, beginning with the Duke of Hennessy's unexpected arrival at the Tantalus when she'd thought him long gone from London for the year. In her most matter-of-fact tone she told Cammy about his concisely stated disdain for her and his disgust with her circumstances and the gossip that he and his family had to contend with almost daily during the Season, and then about his decision to remove her from London and to give her over to the Reverend Loines in Cornwall. And what he would do to the Tantalus if she refused.

As she finished, Camille looked at her, white-faced. "I never liked that man," she said, her voice shaking, "but I honestly didn't think he would be so cruel."

A tear ran down her face, and Sophia reached over to wipe it away. "Adam says that from Hennessy's perspective he's taken care of a problem and seen me to a position where I will have a roof over my head, a proper husband, and respectability. And stop crying or you'll have me weeping again, when I've decided it's useless and makes my eyes swell."

"There must be something we can do, Sophia. Something."

"I've already considered and discarded a hundred

plots," Sophia returned, hugging her friend. "If I run, he'll set all his assets and his allies against Lord and Lady Haybury and the Tantalus. He's bested me, but at least he's also given me a few weeks—more than likely to ponder my fate and my scandalous life, but I'm using them to attend a house party with my dearest friend."

"And I'm very glad you did so," Cammy commented, with a clearly forced smile. "But you'll have to forgive me if I attempt to find a way for you to escape this idiocy."

"Oh, feel free to make the attempt. As we say at the faro tables, there's always a chance."

In truth she knew there wasn't, but if plotting gave Camille something to do and kept either of them from dwelling too much on the inevitable, she would consider it worthwhile. She squeezed her friend's hand. "Now. Let me dress, and we'll go down to dinner. I'll give all the pretty young ladies nightmares, which will be very amusing, don't you think? After that, I can dine in my room in peace."

"Why are there so many unmarried women here?" Camille asked, standing again.

"You'll have to ask Greaves about that. Or Keating, since he likely knows by now." With that, Sophia left her friend to go dress for dinner. Milly and the newly discovered gray gown waited for her in her bedchamber. "How in the world do you manage to keep finding these things?" Sophia asked as they pulled the charcoal-colored gown up over her hips and she threaded her arms through the lacy sleeves. "It's breathtaking."

"It's a large house, don't you know. Bits and bobs turn up everywhere. I think this might have belonged to a cousin or an aunt."

"Well, she had very good taste, whoever she was." Sophia twirled in front of the full-length mirror, then stopped as a dismaying thought occurred to her. "This cousin or aunt isn't one of the houseguests, is she? I don't wish to be accused of stealing her clothes."

"Oh, I'm certain she isn't," Milly said dismissively. "That was years and years ago. Now sit down and let me fix your hair."

Sophia almost declined, but she wanted a look at the bridal parade, those females Adam had deemed appropriate for marriage to a duke. "Something dramatic, I think."

"That is precisely what I intend. And if there is a lady you think would best do His Grace, you should tell him. He trusts your opinion, and I'd rather have someone you think is fine than someone Lady Wallace prefers."

Stifling a sigh, Sophia nodded. It certainly didn't matter who she thought would best suit Adam, and it mattered even less if for a bare moment here and there she'd imagined herself in that role. She already had a husband waiting for her, and even if she didn't, her parentage made her utterly unsuitable for a duke. For any aristocrat. "I'll do my utmost," she said aloud.

They decided on an intricate, braided knot coiled at the top of her head, with long, wispy strands at her temples and artfully escaping down the nape of her neck. If she said so herself, she'd never looked better even on her best nights at The Tantalus Club. When the ladies and gentlemen began sending her disdainful looks, it would be because of her parentage, and not her appearance. And if they could dismiss her for something in which she'd had no part, shame on them. In an odd way, it enabled her to look down on them the very same way they looked down on her. For tonight, annoyed as she was that their arrival had ruined her private, glorious holiday, it would have to be enough.

"I think you'll do," Milly said appraisingly. "Those

grand ladies will have to look their best if they want a hope of holding a candle to you."

Sophia grimaced. "Don't say that, Milly. I just want to make it difficult for them to ignore me for once."

"Well, His Grace won't be ignoring you. That's for certain."

"Adam and I are friends. Nothing more."

"Well, between you and me, all the servants know about that 'nothing more.' Not that we'd say anything. His Grace values his privacy, and so we see to it."

Oh, dear. "Thank you for that," she said. "But it's true. We're simply friends. I'm not attempting to do anything tonight but hold my head high. I don't have many opportunities to do so, and soon I won't have any at all."

The housekeeper gave her a hug, careful not to cause any wrinkles or out-of-place curls. "You're a brave girl, Sophia. I wouldn't have the nerve to live the way you do. And I'll be cheering for you, tonight."

"You are a very kind woman, Milly. Thank you."

By the time they finished fiddling with her hair, the guests had begun to gather in the drawing room to await the call to dinner. The feeling in the pit of her stomach reminded her of how she'd felt the night The Tantalus Club had opened—a certain dubious hope that everything would go well, accompanied by a very strong suspicion that she and her fellow employees would be run out of Town by morning. The Tantalus had been and continued to be a success, but the odds tonight seemed much less promising.

At the foot of the stairs she paused. She'd intentionally timed her arrival so that she wouldn't be either the first or the last person to arrive for dinner, but that meant a dozen people stood about chatting among themselves in the decorated drawing room. Well, she'd faced worse before, and hopefully Adam and her friends would be present already. Squaring her shoulders, she stepped through the doorway.

Her friends weren't there. Instead, twelve pairs of eyes turned in her direction. "Good evening," she said, inclining her head.

The two guests nearest her, females who looked enough alike to be like sisters, turned their backs on her and continued chatting. With a stifled sigh she continued forward, toward an empty chair beneath the window.

"You're from the Tantalus, ain't you?" a male voice asked from behind her, his voice loud enough that anyone who hadn't known that information previously, would now.

"Yes, I am," she answered, facing the voice's source. A short, rotund man with a thinning head of short brown hair stood beneath the twigs of mistletoe—though she doubted that was intentional. "Mr. Henning, isn't it?"

"That's me; Francis Henning. Lord Haybury had me at the club as a guest. Play's a bit too rich for my blood, though. Grandmama would shoot me if I lost my going-about-Town blunt to wagering."

Well, at least Mr. Henning gave away his own secrets as well as everyone else's. "You're a friend of His Grace's, then?"

"I think I was sitting at the table when he invited Haybury, but he was kind enough to include me."

That was interesting. She'd had no idea that Lord and Lady Haybury—her employers and the owners of The Tantalus Club—had been invited to Yorkshire. Given the rumors of the bad blood between Oliver and Adam she wasn't surprised they hadn't come, but Diane might have mentioned that they'd declined an invitation. A few more allies would have been nice.

The guests closest by the door stirred, and she turned as Adam Baswich strolled into the room. He'd dressed in black and gray, and looked both formidable and attractive all at the same time. Belatedly she curtsied as the rest of the guests sank before him. Odd that she'd done that on their previous meetings in London, but she'd never thought to do so at Greaves Park.

"Good evening," he said to the room at large. "Thank you for coming to my slightly delayed party." He nodded into the scattered applause. "Most of you are acquainted, and some of you have been here in previous years, so you know that the house and horses and staff are yours, and that we don't particularly stand on ceremony." He rubbed his hands together. "Now. Let's have some roast venison, shall we?"

Twelve, no fifteen more people appeared, at least eight of them females, and they all moved across the hallway to the main dining room. Sophia had never eaten in there, and the display of polished silver and crystal was nearly blinding in the chandelier light. Generally at a formal event the diners would have been arranged in an intricate combination of rank and sex, so that no one would have to chat with anyone too far below his or her station. Tonight, however, other than the rush to sit close to Greaves at the head of the table, everyone took a chair where they pleased.

Males were rather outnumbered, though she doubted their lack of presence had anything to do with the reason that no one pulled out the chair she'd selected—until Udgell appeared from nowhere to do so for her. She sent the butler a grateful smile. "Thank you," she whispered, and he inclined his head, setting the napkin across her lap before he vanished again.

It wasn't until nearly everyone was settled that she realized the chairs on either side of her were empty. If she'd needed any additional proof that the fairy tale of winter at Greaves Park was over, that answered it.

* * *

Adam seated himself at the head of the table. Immediately he noted that Eustace had joined the party and ensconced herself between Lord Timmerlane and her good friend Prudence, Lady Scoffield. He didn't like that she was present to spit her venom, but he supposed that, as she was the party's hostess, he couldn't very well keep her locked in her rooms.

The next moment he noticed Sophia seated two thirds of the way down the left side of the long table—and the empty seats around her. He drew in a breath, annoyed. Yes, he'd partly invited her because her presence would cause a stir, but he hadn't intended for her to be ostracized. Or rather, it had never occurred to him that her presence at Greaves Park might cause her pain. And as resigned as she was to the unalterable . . . stiffness of her fellows, even with the greater unkindness shoved upon her by her father, it did have to hurt.

As he was debating whether to order everyone to move closer and take up any empty seats, Keating appeared in the doorway, his blond-haired nymph of a wife on his arm. A low mutter traveled down the length of the table, which didn't surprise him in the least. With a quick glance about the room, Keating pulled out the chair to Sophia's right for Camille, then seated himself to her left—which clearly discomfited Miss Rebecca Hart on his other side.

Udgell and the footmen served a fine quail egg soup, and Adam attempted to relax into the conversation. Generally he wore this persona—the pleasant, charming, slightly standoffish one he showed to Society—like a second skin. Tonight, however, the fit seemed tight. Considering that he needed to choose one bride from among the dozen single females he'd invited, and considering that he was predisposed to dislike anyone who flung herself at him, he understood the reason for his own consternation. But it still needed to be done. At the same time, the chit who kept catching his eye was the least appropriate, most unique female in Yorkshire.

"So tell me, Greaves," the Marquis of Drymes said from immediately to his right, "the redhead, Hennessy's by-blow, she's been here for nearly a fortnight, hasn't she?"

"Miss White? Yes. Her coach went through the ice when the bridge collapsed. She nearly drowned."

"A pity she didn't," he heard Eustace say. From that distance he couldn't retaliate without alerting everyone in the room to the argument, so he ignored the faint comment. For the moment.

Drymes was chuckling. "You've outdone yourself this time, Greaves—a murderer, a runaway bride, a highborn whore, and the loveliest selection of marriageable young ladies in the country. Is Miss White yours, or may anyone imbibe?"

"I believe that's up to Miss White," he heard himself say.

By now she and Camille Blackwood were chatting like the close friends he knew them to be, and when she grinned several of the few gentlemen present looked in her direction. In that deep gray gown he'd had made for her, she positively dazzled. At the time he'd ordered it, he'd thought she would wear it to one of their private dinners. This—he wasn't certain he liked it, and he wasn't certain why that was.

"I had my eye on her at the Tantalus," Drymes continued, "but you know the blasted rules there. If the damned place wasn't so popular, Lady H would never get away with it, much less with her bloody 'hands off' shit."

"It ain't hands off," Aubrey Burroughs put in from two seats farther down the table. "You can't touch the chits without their permission, is all." He flashed a grin, an expression several women had deemed swoonworthy. "A bauble or two gains their permission. Trust me."

"You men and your fascinations." Lady Caroline Emery gave a mock scowl. "There are proper females here, you know. Chat about your scandalous liaisons over cigars and port; dinner is where we discuss legitimate matches, and we ask questions like whether His Grace has decided it's time to put the ladies of Mayfair out of their misery and finally marry."

He lifted an eyebrow. Despite the convenient turn of conversation, he was reluctant to begin the nonsense. If better than five hundred thousand pounds' worth of property and holdings hadn't been involved, he wouldn't have done it. Marrying was one thing that didn't require a deadline to make it even more troublesome. Adam took a slow, deep breath. "That is an interesting suggestion, Caroline. And there are certainly a goodly number of eligible and lovely young ladies present, if I should decide to do so."

The surrounding diners actually applauded, excited tittering and nervous laughter passing through the group in a growing wave. "Are you serious, Greaves?" Burroughs chortled. "Because you've just raised the hopes of a thousand pining women."

"I think the number present is more than adequate," he returned, and offered the room at large a toast.

Prudence Jones, the daughter of Viscount Halifax, fainted in her chair. Good God. And it would only get worse from here. As Miss Jones was revived and the plates of venison were brought in, Adam glanced about the table again. Not one of them stirred anything in him other than a mild disgust that they were so easily willing to be wooed by the likes of him. And their mommas had been all too happy to make the journey with them—whether they had pretended to be surprised by the news that he was spouse hunting or not, they'd already come to that conclusion. Otherwise, what was the damned point of a pinch-faced vulture like Lady Halifax and her ilk journeying all the way to Yorkshire? The viscountess loathed his lifestyle to his face and envied his position to his back. And most of them were precisely the same.

"Did you shoot the deer, Greaves?" Francis Henning asked from halfway down the table.

At least he had a few odd friends and hangers-on in the mix. "I did. A fine eight-point buck. There's still some good shooting to be done, if anyone's interested; the rumor is that half a dozen or so Christmas turkeys escaped drowning when the mail coach went into the Aire."

"Oh, that would be sterling!" Henning exclaimed, his opinion echoed by most of the men at the table.

"I'll arrange it, then," Adam said, nodding. "Tomorrow, if the weather's clear."

"Tell me you have raisins, Your Grace," Miss Sylvia Hart, Rebecca's younger sister, pleaded with a bright smile. "I do so look forward to playing snapdragon at Christmas."

Before he could respond to that, everyone began to chime in with their favorite games and activities at Christmastime. From Caroline's commentary it looked as if they would be singing carols again—Caroline delighted in showing off her skills at the pianoforte.

Adam risked a look down the length of the table again. Ignoring him and everyone else who seemed to ignore her, Sophia was evidently reenacting her ice fishing triumph for Keating and Camille. Even the cynical William Clint, Lord Lassiter, across the table from her offered the briefest, faintest of smiles—though Lassiter wasn't precisely known for upholding Society's highest standards.

As far as he was concerned, dismissing Sophia was Society's loss; he knew for a fact that she was a fine conversationalist and a keen wit. And no, he didn't want Drymes or anyone else going near her with their propositions and their baubles. Unless he laid claim to her, though, he wasn't certain how to prevent it. And as he was wife hunting and a well-respected, high-ranking member of the *ton* and she was not his mistress, he needed to be cautious in proclaiming any sort of public connection to her.

That was simply the way things were. In addition, Eustace wasn't the only one aware of the late Duke of Greaves's fondness for redheads. And the only thing worse than his sister proclaiming that he was living down to their father's reputation would be for anyone else to do so.

NINE

Sophia stood in the morning room, which looked out over the frozen garden and the riding path beyond. A quartet of riders trotted by, kicking up the loose snow and evidently on their way into Hanlith. Miss Rebecca Hart looked especially fetching in her dark green riding habit as she sat upon Copper.

"You look very nice," Camille commented, as she strolled into the room. "I can see why you haven't borrowed any of my clothes."

Sophia took a breath and turned away from the window. "Evidently generations of visitors here have left behind articles of clothing. Mrs. Brooks is exceptional at finding ones that fit me, or altering them so that they do."

"I'm surprised generations of visitors haven't gone missing, this house is so big." Cammy tugged at the sleeve of Sophia's green and burgundy riding habit. "If you're going riding, shouldn't you be outside?"

"I thought about it, but I changed my mind."

Camille favored her with an assessing look, then sat on the low couch and patted the cushion beside her. "Well, Keating's out shooting at things, so come and chat with me. I want to know everything that's been happening at the club, and any detail you might have left out about your father's visit. And please tell me that you aren't truly sharing a room with Lucille Hampton."

Sophia snorted. "I've—I had—made it into a game. Every time she said the word 'handsome' I put aside a shilling to spend on hats. I have a great many hats, now." Hats she'd left behind, because she couldn't imagine that Mr. Loines would see anything but frivolity in their purchase—and where she considered frivolousness to be the point, she didn't want to hear it called a sin.

With a laugh, Cammy put her head into her hands. "I remember when Lucille first arrived. She was so certain one of those handsome men who came to the club would sweep her away into a fairy-tale marriage."

"Oh, she still is. I can't decide whether to be amused, annoyed, or full of pity." She tucked her arm around Camille's. "And then right before I left, she said she felt sorry for me. That was excessively annoying."

"I missed you, you know," Camille commented, her blue eyes swimming again.

Sophia grimaced. "This holiday is for me to not have to think about what happens next. Talking about it certainly won't alter that, and neither will making you weep over it."

"It just isn't like you to surrender, Sophia."

Her grimace deepened to a frown. "I used to think that, too. But then I realized that I surrender all the time. I've simply learned to make the best of the situation. I've never attempted to alter the situation, mind you. I just laugh through it. And I'll do the same thing again, because I don't have any choice."

"You *could* flee."

"Yes, I suppose I could. After all, Lady Haybury's survived being poor and abandoned before, hasn't she? Would it be so bad to force her to face that once more? Surely the Duke of Hennessy and half the House of Lords couldn't do that much damage to a gentlemen's club, or the ladies who are employed there. They all have other places to go, anyway." She sent Camille a sideways glance.

"It isn't fair," her friend grated. "He's relied on your affection for your friends in order to ruin your life."

"My life was always ruined. He's just taken one last step to make it unbearably so."

"Oh, Sophia."

She shook herself. "Enough of this," she said briskly, standing up and shaking out her hands. "I'm not in Cornwall yet. And you will tell me all about Shropshire and Havard's Glen. It is as lovely as you described?"

With obvious effort Cammy began chatting about her life as Mrs. Blackwood. Thank goodness at least one of them had managed to alter fate. And thank goodness it had been Cammy. She deserved to be happy.

They sat talking for a good hour before Sophia felt the tension across her shoulders ease. A minute after that, her stomach began rumbling. "Are you hungry? Mrs. Beasel informed me that she was baking apple tarts to put out for luncheon."

Camille stood. "Have I mentioned that I'm becoming fond of Greaves Park?" she asked, pulling Sophia to her feet.

"Ah, listen to you. Bribed with an apple tart."

They were just short of the morning room doorway when Sophia heard Adam's voice approaching down the hallway. Considering that he'd barely glanced at her in two days, she certainly didn't want to look as though she was pouncing on him from the shadows. And then she heard another male voice mention her name. Moving quickly, she drew Cammy back against the wall beside the door.

"—want me to admit, Burroughs?" Adam's voice came.

"I want you to admit that you've made an arrangement with her. You lost Helena Brennan to wedded bliss.

You always have the prettiest chit in London, and now you're hunting for a proper wife. Ergo, Sophia White is your new mistress."

"I have no idea why my pulling a ruined chit out of a river and then keeping a roof over her head for the next fortnight or so means that I've made her my mistress."

The voices continued on in the direction of the billiards room. Sophia swallowed, her hand tightly gripping Camille's even though she wasn't certain what she wanted—or didn't want—to hear.

"Fourteen days, Greaves. That's why. She's employed at a damned gentlemen's club, and she's a duke's by-blow. She isn't here to enjoy the weather. I know you've been at her. I just want to know if she's available for me to bed, or if you have an agreement with her. I won't tread in your garden."

For a moment she heard only silence. "I'm admitting to nothing. I'll only advise you to be careful where you walk."

"Ha! I knew it."

Once she was certain that the men had gone into the billiards room, Sophia pulled Camille into the hallway and down the front stairs. On the surface, Adam had said precisely nothing. At the same time, he'd very strongly *implied* that she'd become his mistress. His woman, paid to be available for sex and evidently for holiday parties. Her last days of freedom, and he'd just turned her into a kept woman—at least as far as every one of his guests was concerned.

"Sophia, you're crushing my hand."

Starting, she released her grip on Camille. "I'm sorry."

"No permanent damage done. I understand; he's playing loose with your reputation. But you won't have to face these people ever again. What—"

"What's the harm?" she finished. "None," she lied, stomping down to the foyer. "But would it be so far beneath him to acknowledge that I'm here because we're friends? He and Lord Drymes are friends."

"You aren't friends like he and Drymes are friends," Cammy returned in a low voice. "For one thing, I doubt he's ever seen Drymes naked. You've seen Greaves naked, and that means pride is involved. And he's a man, so of course he'll say whatever protects his sense of self-worth."

Camille made sense. But she'd also hesitated—and Sophia knew why. Clearly for her own sanity she needed to put her feet firmly back on the ground before she found herself shackled there permanently. "You said 'for one thing.' What's your other point?"

Camille frowned. "Sophia."

"Don't try to spare my feelings now, Cammy. Just say it."

"Fine. I grew up in the middle of Mayfair. Friendships are based on common backgrounds and experiences. You and Greaves aren't equals. If he goes about saying you're friends, he'll look foolish." She took a breath. "There. And don't be mad at me, because you knew what I was going to say, and you made me say it anyway."

"I'm not mad at you. I'm mad at myself for being naïve despite what I grew up with. And I'm mad at Greaves for . . . humoring me, I suppose, in private, when he knew he would never do so in public."

There was more to it than that, but she wasn't ready to delve into it at the moment. But it did hurt. A great deal. With a glance around, she resumed their trek to the kitchen.

"You and I aren't equals, either, Cammy," she mused after a moment.

Camille took her shoulder, turning her around. "You

and I lost everything and still managed to survive and even be independent," she said, her light blue eyes serious. "We're both terribly scandalous, because we've done what was necessary. And we are friends. You are my dearest friend. Don't you dare ever think otherwise."

Well. That certainly helped ease the pain a little. "Thank you, Cammy." Sophia hugged her friend.

"What are you going to do?" her friend asked, straightening. "If you wish to leave now, Keating and I will go with you."

"You speak for Keating, do you?" she queried, mustering some amusement at Camille's matter-of-fact statement.

Cammy's lips twitched. "He's my husband. Of course I speak for him."

Sophia considered for a long moment. Yes, she could leave, go back to London and wait for her days of relative freedom to end, surrender once more to a circumstance not of her own making, and have to say her good-byes all over again.

Or with her remaining time at Greaves Park she could make this holiday the one she did want to remember, no matter who looked sideways at her or thought she needed to be more . . . whatever it was she wasn't. Adam had invited her because of who she was, and she could be that person. She happened to like that person.

She sent Cammy a slow smile. "I'm not going to leave. I'm going to stay and enjoy my first country house Christmas. My only country house Christmas."

"Oh, dear. You're going to cause trouble, aren't you?"

"Very likely."

"Oh, I wish it snowed like this in Kent," Sylvia Hart exclaimed. "I would drive everywhere in a sleigh."

Adam, seated between her and her sister on the rear-facing seat of the vehicle, sent Sylvia a sideways glance.

The younger Miss Hart was a pretty thing, but once the conversation traveled beyond fashion and the weather, she became somewhat vapid. Aside from that, she and her sister were not only desperate to find a wealthy husband, but they had a lamentable tendency to chase after the same man—and thereby destroy each other's chances. All he knew was that after one morning in their company, he would rather stab himself in the ears than marry one of them. He ran through his guest list. Perhaps he could put them onto Drymes's scent. That would at least be interesting to watch.

"I dearly love the snow, myself," Rebecca put in with the timing of a clock. "It's so refreshing."

Yes, definitely Lord Drymes. The viscount wouldn't know what to do with two pretty chits chasing after him. He would have selected Burroughs, but his gambling debts were common knowledge. Or Lassiter, but he only wanted a bit of amusement—not to put the Hart sisters in peril of becoming wives number four and five to a husband who seemed to grind his spouses into dust with alarming regularity.

"It's such a shame, Rebecca, that the cold turns your nose that ghastly shade of red. You know, the color it is right now."

"My nose is not red, Sylvia!"

It was, but Adam ignored the argument. Across from him Caroline and Burroughs were chatting about whether a woman could possibly be a good marksman. Considering that Caroline generally carried a small, single-shot pistol in her reticule, Adam wouldn't have cared to challenge her on that front. He tilted his head, assessing Lady Caroline Emery once more. She was one of the few ladies present whose acquaintance he'd already made, and while her father, the Marquis of Woling, had only a single small property well away from London, the family was well respected. She'd made several poor choices in her companions, but she had her wits about her, putting her several steps in front of the Hart sisters.

Abruptly Caroline sat forward, her gaze somewhere beyond Adam's shoulder. "Well, what do you think of that?" she asked, with a slight, quizzical smile.

Burroughs followed her gaze. "Speaking of being out in the weather."

Rebecca turned around. "Is that . . . *that* woman? What in heavens does she think she's about?"

Sylvia kneeled in her seat to look across the front of the sleigh. "I am scandalized!"

That was difficult to believe, but Adam had to look now. As the sleigh slowed and turned into the stable yard, he glanced toward the lake. At the near shore a single figure swung a large knotted rope and then threw it. His two dogs, barking and tails wagging, went charging after it.

Sophia had donned his old coat over her borrowed men's clothes, the floppy-brimmed groom's hat jammed over her scarlet hair. He narrowed his eyes, not scandalized, but . . . annoyed. She could dress as she pleased when he was the only one present, but she wasn't improving her reputation by doing so in front of everyone else. In fact, she was only making her father's decision about what to do with her seem more reasonable.

As he watched, Brutus reared up to plant his gigantic front paws on her shoulders. With a breathless laugh, Sophia went down flat onto her back, disappearing completely into a pile of snow. A moment later she sat up, wrapping her hands around the mastiff's neck as he licked her face.

Damnation. He stood, but before he could untangle himself from the clinging women seated on either side of him, Aubrey had stepped over Caroline and jumped to the ground, plowing his way over to Sophia. He held out his hand to her.

"Are you injured, Miss White?"

She gripped her hand around his and pulled herself to her feet. "Not in the least," she said, chuckling as she swiped her sleeve across her face. "Thank you, Mr. Burroughs."

"My pleasure. It wouldn't do to have you trampled."

"At least the snow is soft." For the first time she seemed to notice the sleigh and its passengers. "Good afternoon, Your Grace. Caesar and Brutus needed a bit of fresh air."

Her pale cheeks positively glowed, and in his opinion her red nose didn't look so much ghastly as healthy. Snow caked into her hat and the ends of her hair. There was no sense dissembling—Sophia White looked utterly stunning. "Miss White," he uttered.

"What in the world do you think you're wearing?" Rebecca demanded, no doubt noting that she'd lost the attention of both men present.

Sophia looked down at herself and brushed away more snow from her front. "A footman's uniform," she answered succinctly. "And a groom's hat and boots. Excuse me."

Turning her back on the group, she snatched the rope back from Caesar and led a mad scramble onto the ice. The dogs leaped and barked and slid about excitedly as she threw the knot for them again.

"What a disgraceful display," Sylvia snapped, stepping down from the sleigh. "I refuse to witness anything further. Do take me inside, Your Grace."

"And me," Rebecca seconded.

Adam blinked. *Splendid.* The only thing worse than staring at a chit was being caught at it. Resisting the urge to roll his shoulders, he stepped down from the vehicle and offered an arm to either Hart sister while Aubrey and Caroline fell in behind them. As they walked the short distance to the house they took turns regaling him with their dismay and shock at seeing such an unacceptable female behaving so scandalously. As for himself, his attention was now on Aubrey Burroughs, who kept glancing back in the direction of the lake. He recognized the predatory look on the rake's face, and he didn't like it. At all.

Once he managed to escape the Hart harpies, Adam made his way to the ground-level sitting room at the front of the house. If Sophia didn't wish to make a stir among his guests, she was certainly going about it the wrong way. On the other hand, she might very well not have considered that, and she was simply being herself. One way or the other, he needed to make certain she realized that she was further damaging her own reputation.

He stopped in the doorway and stifled a curse. Five men, including Burroughs, stood in front of the sitting room window. All of them had glasses of what smelled like whiskey, all of them were gazing toward the lake, and all of them were chatting about what they saw there.

"I never considered trousers to be arousing until now." Lord Lassiter chuckled at his own commentary.

"I want to be a dog," Burroughs said.

"You are a dog." Lord Patrick Alder elbowed Francis Henning beside him. "You chatted with her. Has she invited you to join her in her bedchamber yet?"

The fifth man, Peter Blense, the Earl of Aames, shook his head. "I'll wager she belongs to Greaves. Why else would she be here? Pretty as she is, I'm not about to cross him."

"It might be worth it." Burroughs tapped against the window. "Woof woof."

That was good to know. Adam slipped away from the room before anyone there could notice his presence. Anger and frustration edged through him, which made no sense. He'd had some of those same conversations himself, about different women.

Thus far everyone seemed to think he and Sophia were lovers—which, of course, they were. But everyone also seemed convinced that he'd purchased her favors. He supposed that made sense, considering her status in Society. Although in the past he had invited his mistresses to holiday along with gamblers and rakes of both sexes, they all tended to be blue bloods, members of Society. Even Keating, who likely had the worst reputation of anyone there, was a marquis's cousin and a marquis's grandson.

Sophia was different. He enjoyed that difference, or he had before the rest of his guests arrived and began asking questions he didn't care to answer. Even so, he couldn't quite wish that he'd never invited her at all. He *did* wish that he'd spoken to her before his fellows appeared. And he wished she didn't attract quite so much attention from everyone else. She couldn't like what was being said about her, even if she claimed to ignore most of it. And *he* definitely didn't like the way most of the males in his house looked at her.

As he reached the foyer, debating whether it would do more harm than good if he went out and dragged her into the house, Keating and Camille appeared, arm in arm, at the foot of the stairs. Adam blew out his breath. "You need to go speak with Sophia," he said in a low voice.

"Why?" Camille asked, putting a hand to her chest. "What's happened?"

"'What's happened?'" he repeated. "She's wearing those blasted trousers, and everyone's talking about her."

"Oh. I don't think she cares what they think of her. It couldn't be much worse than it is, anyway. Especially now."

Adam frowned. This was not helping one bloody bit. "There's a difference between being unconventional and putting yourself in the path of trouble. Go fetch her."

Keating stepped forward, putting himself between Adam and Camille. "I suggest you rephrase that."

Clearly they didn't understand the seriousness of the situation, if they were quibbling over his choice of phrase. Or if they were questioning him. "Very well. How about 'I saved your damned life and made it possible for the two of you to marry, so go get Sophia before you make me regret any of that'?"

For a long moment Keating gazed at him. "Go get her yourself, Greaves," he finally snapped, taking Camille's hand and striding back up the stairs with her.

Something was very wrong. He didn't misjudge circumstances, and he didn't overplay his hand. And people did not walk away from him. Clearly everyone around him was going mad, all at the same time. Uttering an expletive, he yanked open the front door and stalked outside.

Sophia and the dogs had returned to the near shore, so at least Adam didn't have to chase across the ice after her. If she hadn't been practically bent over with laughter, he would have thought she was making a spectacle of herself on purpose—though he had no idea why she would do such a thing.

She straightened from tugging on Caesar's ears as he approached. "Do these good boys ever tire?" she panted. "I'm about to drop dead from exhaustion."

"Then you should go inside before you do so," he returned, his jaw clenched.

With a frown she gave up possession of the mangled rope to the dogs. "What's amiss?"

"Half my guests are gawking at you from the sitting room, and you're wandering about in trousers and rollicking in the snow like a lunatic. That's what's amiss."

The dogs ran back up, jumping around her. With a sharp whistle he put them into an attentive sit. They continued to pant and look hopefully at Sophia, but they stayed where they were told.

"That was mean," she stated. "They didn't do anything wrong. And these are the clothes I've been wearing for a fortnight. You haven't taken the dogs for so much as a walk in two days, and I couldn't very well do so in one of my borrowed gowns."

They were her gowns; she merely didn't know it yet. This, however, was certainly not the time for that particular conversation. "The grooms can take the dogs for a walk. They aren't your responsibility. Stop behaving like a fool."

She blinked, her expression flashing from surprised to hurt and angry. "I see," she said slowly. "So if I were to throw a snowball at you now, you wouldn't find it amusing."

"Not in the least."

"Very well, then." Sophia bent down and picked up a clump of snow.

"Don't you bloody dare."

"I liked you better before I realized you cared so much for everyone else's opinion. What you need to realize is that I don't care what anyone else thinks of me. I know who I am. And I suppose, unless you ask me to leave Greaves Park, that I'll conduct myself in a manner that sees me with the most pleasant holiday possible." Pointedly she dropped the snowball from her fingers and stalked past him to the house.

Adam slowly let out his breath. Whether she thought that what she did now didn't matter, that she would never have to face its consequences in Cornwall, she needed to realize that Hennessy could always find a way to make things even worse for her. She didn't understand the nuances of Society; she'd always been on the outside, looking in. He, on the other hand, had lived his entire life at its center. The strong preyed on the weak. Whether she was angry with him or not, he'd just saved her a great deal of troub—

Something cold and wet slapped into the back of his head.

Shaking snow out of his hair, he whipped around just as Sophia disappeared through the front door. *That damned chit.* He wanted so badly to chase after her that the muscles across his shoulders creaked. He, however, did not lose control. Doing so in her presence once had clearly been a mistake; she didn't see him the same way everyone else did. He was the damned Duke of Greaves, for God's sake. People did not pelt him with snowballs or defy his orders.

Making himself walk at a normal pace back to the shallow steps and the front door, Adam whistled the dogs in and clenched his fists. Yes, he wanted to hunt Sophia down and wrap his hands around her neck. But it wasn't just anger pushing at him. The rest of the men present wanted her. He wanted her.

Out there, romping with the dogs, she'd seemed so . . . free. As if she truly didn't care what anyone else might think of her. And with that hair and those laughing eyes . . . Yes, he wanted to punish her, to make her understand what she couldn't do. And at the same time he wanted to bury himself in her and watch as she came around him.

For the devil's sake, she aggravated him no end. At the moment he had no idea what to do—and that never happened to him. Ever. Even in his worst moments when he drank too much and saw too much of his father when he looked into the mirror, he knew precisely what the trouble was, and he knew which steps to take to alter the situation. It was a simple task and an impossible one all at the same time.

Perhaps he and Sophia did have some things in common, both with their pasts and their futures. But now was neither of those things. And his next confrontation with her would be somewhere with no witnesses. And no ammunition to hand. He might have asked for the snowball to the skull, but he wasn't an idiot.

For the remainder of the day he pretended nothing had happened, playing a fair game of billiards and taking an afternoon ride around the lake with a half-dozen chits. No one dared mention anything about his encounter with Miss White, though he knew they'd all been gossiping about it behind his back.

Being a duke, being in the position to which all men secretly aspired and which all women secretly wished to share, was a two-edged sword, but he'd learned a long time ago how to keep hold of the hilt. Except, evidently, for the moments he spent in Sophia's company. Whatever else he felt, and particularly given his task for this Christmas, she was bad for him. And yet, at least half his thoughts had been about how he meant to meet with her again—in private.

He arrived downstairs for dinner before anyone else. That seemed the simplest and most direct way to keep the speculation and tongue-wagging to a minimum. And it would be a favor to Sophia, as well, since his guests would see him before they could begin—or resume, rather—gossiping about her. Four more guests had arrived today, all of them close friends of Eustace's. If she'd convinced her allies to lie in wait somewhere just on the other side of the river Aire until she sent for them, then she meant to make more trouble. Another problem added to his platter.

Lady Caroline Emery glided into the drawing room.

In a deep green silk gown trimmed with gold thread, she looked the very image of Christmas, expensive and impeccable. "Oh, I hate being early," she drawled, pouring two glasses of wine and walking up to hand him one of them. "At least I'm not the only one here."

He took a swallow, nodding his thanks. Half his attention remained on the open doorway, on the chance that Sophia would appear in one of her more outlandish outfits. He couldn't allow that; not when the prevailing rumor linked the two of them. And not, of course, when her unconventional behavior could cause her trouble.

"I have a wonder, Your Grace," Caroline said in her low, sweet voice.

"What are you wondering about?"

"You."

Ah. He'd been wondering when she would present her credentials for marriage. "Anything in particular?"

She took a deep breath, her low-cut gown showing her rising and falling bosom to best advantage. "I have a particular Christmas gift in mind for you," she went on with a slow smile. "But first I need to ask if you have a wish for such a gift."

With her tall, willowy frame and brunette hair, Lady Caroline Emery was lovely, and she had an elegant conversation and a fair wit. Her breeding, of course, was impeccable. And if Sophia hadn't whetted his appetite for a very particular and unique delicacy, he wouldn't have hesitated.

"Perhaps we could discuss that later," he said aloud, at the same time cursing himself silently for not simply putting the troublesome Sophia out of his thoughts and moving forward with plans he'd put in motion weeks ago.

"Whatever you wish, Your Grace." She sipped her wine, looking at him over the rim of the glass, not sparing a glance as the rest of the guests began to trickle into the room. "I will only say that I would never embarrass you. And I would certainly never throw anything at you."

Not even if he deserved it? "Duly noted."

"I—"

Sophia strolled into the room, and he missed whatever it was that Caroline said next. Miss White wasn't wearing trousers or her oversized yellow muslin, but his relief at that was tempered by a darker craving. She'd donned the dark green gown that ostensibly belonged to Susan Simmons, her hair swept up into an elegant tangle that made his hands ache with the desire to run his fingers through the lush waves. Only belatedly did it occur to him that she and Lady Caroline were wearing virtually the same gown—and that it showed better on Sophia. That wouldn't go over well.

Her light green eyes touched him, then moved on to the rest of the occupants in the slowly filling room. If she was worried that he would retaliate for the snowball, she certainly didn't show it. Not much, though, seemed to worry her. For Lucifer's sake, she was weeks away from a marriage that she had to dread even more than he did his own nuptials.

When she walked up to chat with Henning and Timmerlane, he excused himself from Caroline and went to find Keating, standing with Camille and James and Ivy Flanagan. Not for the first time, he wished that Oliver Warren, the Marquis of Haybury, had decided to come, so at least the Blackwoods and Sophia would have allies other than him. But Oliver Warren wasn't any better at forgiveness or forgetting than he was.

"A word, Keating?"

With a glance at his wife, Blackwood followed him to an empty corner. "I hope this is an apology for ordering my wife about—though in that case you should be speaking to her."

Adam lifted an eyebrow. "You're ferocious tonight, aren't you?"

"When it concerns dukes who think that snapping at ladies who've worked as hard as Cammy and Sophia have to earn their independence, yes, I'm bloody ferocious."

Considering that a year ago Keating Blackwood hadn't cared what anyone said or did about anything unless it concerned drink or brawling, perhaps Adam needed to approach this conversation differently than he'd originally intended. Camille had performed something of a miracle.

What Keating had said was interesting, too. Sophia hadn't given up a privileged life like Camille had, but she had chosen one where she could make her own decisions. The aggravation was that her decisions, which had originally been amusing and refreshing, were now driving him mad.

He drew a breath. "Then I'll apologize to your wife. Later."

"See that you do."

"Don't press me, Blackwood." Lucifer knew he'd been pushed near enough to the edge of his patience already today.

Keating folded his arms. "I owe you a great deal, Adam. I do not owe you my servitude. No one here does. You can't control everything."

Adam gazed at him for a moment. He'd been about to ask a favor, for one of the Blackwoods to speak to Sophia about the impression she was making. Now he clearly couldn't do that without proving Keating correct. Anger bit at him again. "Go back to your pretty wife. And don't cross me. *I* owe *you* nothing."

With a stiff nod, Keating turned his back and walked away. Despite himself, Adam was impressed. Seven or eight months ago, Keating would have swung at him. And that would have been an interesting brawl—and one he wasn't entirely certain he would have won.

Drawing his thoughts and his temper back in, he handed his half-empty glass of wine to a footman. Considering his mood, he would not be drinking anything more this evening. If he went too far tonight, he would be facing nearly forty witnesses.

"Greaves," Timmerlane called, "how many decks of cards do you have here? Sophia has agreed to deal vingt-et-un for us tonight."

"Oh, please, Lord Timmerlane," his sister put in with a high-pitched laugh, "this is a respectable home, not a gambling establishment."

That was it. The chit was trying to give him an apoplexy. He sent Sophia a glare, but she was laughing at something Henning said and didn't even notice him walking up behind her. "Miss White."

Starting, she turned around. The smile on her face faltered a little at his expression but didn't vanish completely. "Good evening, Your Grace. Care to join us for cards?"

He could practically feel the heat coming off her, making him want to close on her and kiss her and shake some sense into her all at the same time. "Play cards tomorrow, if you like. Tonight I've arranged for an orchestra to come up from Hanlith."

Sylvia Hart materialized at his side. "Oh, is there to be dancing? Please say there will be dancing!"

"Yes, there will be dancing."

"Waltzes, I hope," her sister chimed in. "At least two."

"Three," he decided, still glaring at Sophia.

That chit, though, merely sighed. "That sounds wonderful. I'm afraid I twisted my ankle romping with the dogs earlier, but I would love to watch the rest of you."

And so however much he'd contemplated it, however well he thought he'd plotted it, with one sentence she'd managed to evade him yet again. For the moment. For the damned moment.

TEN

At three minutes past midnight Sophia excused herself from the festivities and followed Camille upstairs in the direction of their respective bedchambers.

"I like Ivy Flanagan," she said, wrapping her arm around her friend's. "Are you going to visit her and James as they asked?"

"We may," Cammy conceded with a tired smile. "I hadn't realized that James knew Keating at Cambridge. Keating says he's a good man, even if he is Irish."

Sophia chuckled. "I think you should go. You need to meet people who don't give a fig about Society gossip."

"It's been . . . interesting, deciphering former friends and deciding whether I can trust new ones. And you and Mr. Loines will always be welcome at Havard's Glen, you know."

"I don't think that will ever happen, but it's very nice of you to say." They stopped outside Cammy's door. "I'm so glad you've found a happy life, Cammy."

"I am happy. I'm happier than I've ever been in my entire life."

"I do like hearing you say that, my love." Keating's low drawl came from down the hallway. He stopped on Cammy's other side and put his arm across her shoulders, leaning in to kiss his wife.

"I thought you were going to stay downstairs and smoke all of Greaves's cigars."

Keating shook his head. "I decided it would be more fun up here."

As Cammy blushed, Sophia laughed again. "I certainly can't compete with that. I'll see you in the morning."

Before she could walk down the hallway to her own room, Keating took her arm. "Greaves is angry," he muttered. "He's not particularly nice when he's angry. Be wary."

"I will be." She shrugged free. "Good night, Blackwoods."

Once she slipped into her quiet, firelit room, she leaned back against the closed door and blew out her breath. So Adam was angry, was he? Well, he was the one who'd decided that everything that had happened before his silly guests arrived was unacceptable now. That she was an embarrassment. That the only reason she could possibly be there was to be his mistress. And now that he had a wife to choose, she was supposed to be ignored or ridiculed until she went away. That was fine for him, but she wasn't about to stop living simply because he had better things to do and better people with whom to chat.

"Arrogant man," she muttered, straightening again to unbutton her gown and pull on her comfortable, oversized night rail.

Blowing out the candle set beside her bed, she slipped beneath the warm covers. Generally she had very little trouble falling asleep—but not tonight. She turned over, pounding her pillow into a comfortable shape, then rolled back the other way. If everyone thought she was Adam's mistress, then once the bridal competition narrowed down a bit more, she would find herself more directly disliked. A duke might not marry her, but no duchess wanted to see her husband flirting about with the likes of her. Not even for a few days, not even before she went to marry the vicar of Gulval.

Sophia threw off the covers and stood up. She didn't care about these people—most of them, anyway—any more than they cared about her. All she'd ever wanted was to be left alone to live her life as she chose, but they couldn't even let her do that.

Stalking to the window, she pushed aside the heavy curtains. Tonight moonlight glinted silvery blue across the snow, still and silent and stark. Cold radiated from the glass, but it served to cool her temper a little. All things considered, she was there because she still wanted to be.

The question remained, was it better or worse to experience a few moments to treasure in her memory, when those same moments could be a dagger of might-have-beens in her heart? For now the answer was simple, in that she would much rather be here in the company of a few dear friends than moping about the Tantalus. But when she no longer had access to these friends, she wasn't certain she would feel the same.

Air moved around her legs, and she turned. Silently her door inched open, so slowly and carefully that if she'd been covered up in bed, she never would have noticed. The hallway beyond was dark and quiet, and all she could make out was the edge of a shadow blacker than its surroundings.

So now someone was trying to spy on her? Scowling, Sophia rushed forward, grabbed the door handle, and yanked the door open.

Adam Baswich stood there, his expression for once easy to decipher. Her abrupt appearance had plainly stunned him.

Sophia opened her mouth to demand an explanation for his presence. Before she could do more than draw a breath, though, he clamped a hand over her mouth and barged into the room.

He swung the door closed, half carrying her into the middle of the room. Once she had her feet back under her, she pushed away from him. "What do you think you're doing?" she snapped, yanking the sagging sleeve of her night rail back onto her shoulder. "You think I'm a fool, remember?"

"Keep your voice down," he warned in a low tone. "You said you twisted your ankle. I was assisting you into the room."

"Well, assist yourself out of the room."

Adam narrowed his eyes. "I'm not going anywhere until you come to your senses."

Now, wasn't that just like a man? Putting her hands on her hips, Sophia glowered at him. "I'm not the one sneaking into people's bedchambers."

"I thought you might not be alone, with the way Burroughs kept looking at you all evening."

That stopped her for a moment, considering she'd been thinking the same thing about Adam and Lady Caroline. "Oh, please. He's a rake and a braggart."

"Someone impressed you sometime or other. You weren't a virgin when we met."

Momentarily ignoring the hypocrisy of that statement, she stalked to the hearth, digging an iron poker into the fire to stir up the dying flames and brighten the room a little. "Actually, I was, when we first met. But that was nearly two years ago. And they were interesting men, not people so enamored of the sound of their own voices that your own conversation doesn't even signify."

He closed the distance she'd put between them. " 'They'? How many were there?"

"You answer that question, and I will."

After a moment spent glaring at her, he walked over

to look out her window. "I'm not here to discuss your string of lovers."

It didn't seem likely that two previous lovers equaled a string, but she set aside the poker and straightened. "Ah, yes. You mentioned something about my lost senses. But I'm still behaving in precisely the same manner I was a fortnight ago."

"This is nothing to jest about, Sophia. You can't go about in trousers or throwing things at people."

She expected to hear it, but it still hurt. "Evidently I can."

His shoulders tensed. "You did it deliberately," he said, his voice a low growl.

"Of course I did," she returned. "No one throws a snowball by accident. And you deserved it."

"You went rolling about in the snow on purpose." Slowly he drew the curtains closed again, the room dimming with the absence of the moonlight. "The question is, did you do it to aggravate me, or because you know what those damned trousers do to me?"

A low shiver went through her. So even if he'd decided she was *too* unconventional, he still desired her. But she hadn't been the one ignoring him; it was the other way around. "I am what the world and circumstance have made me," she said after a moment, trying to shake herself free of the distraction of having him in her room. "Surely you're aware of that by now. Don't expect me to be embarrassed just because you would be, and don't give me orders."

"You feel comfortable talking back to me, do you?" he murmured.

Not so much comfortable as . . . electrified, but that didn't leave her any more inclined to give in to his wish for her to be like everyone else. "I'm having the holiday *I* want. If that's not acceptable, then I'll leave. I offered to do that the day I arrived, if you'll recall."

"I recall." His jaw clenched. "It would be easier if you left."

Stunned surprise sucked all the air out of her lungs. He knew how much this holiday meant to her, and he knew why that was so. Well. At least it would be easier now to look back on these weeks without the keen longing she feared would leave Greaves Park with her. "I'll be gone before breakfast, then." Her voice shook a little, but she didn't particularly care.

"I said it would be easier. You set everything on its ear. With you running loose here, someone's going to get hurt. More than likely me. But I didn't say you should go."

Sophia snatched one of her drying boots set before the fire and threw it at him. He must have expected it, because he caught the thing just before it could smack him in the chest. Lifting an eyebrow, he dropped it back to the floor.

"You are no gentleman, sir," she ground out. "You say I should leave, then offer me a very nice compliment, and then tell me you were only jesting about having me go? Was that to make me feel grateful? I have enough troubles awaiting me without you adding to them."

His expression darkened. "That's enough, Sophia."

"It certainly is. You and Caroline Emery can laugh all about it after I go. She's the one you've settled on, isn't she?"

He stalked directly in front of her. "You aren't leaving," he stated.

"Go to the dev—"

Adam caught her by the back of her night rail as she stalked past him toward the door. Evidently she intended to walk to Hanlith barefoot and in her night clothes. Before she could lift a hand to hit him, he spun her around, caught both her hands in one of his, and closed his mouth over hers.

Good-natured Sophia evidently had a temper at the end of her long fuse, and he'd finally lit it. That seemed only fair. He shouldn't have to be the only one driven mad in this little scramble. In her opinion he'd clearly done something wrong, and he understood that even though he tended to think just the opposite. But by God she gave as good as she got, and he had to admire that about her. Almost as much as he admired the way her enormous slip fell down from her shoulders. He'd been bloody patient enough.

Only when she began kissing him back did he release his grip on her hands. Sophia slid her arms around his shoulders, but thankfully didn't then attempt to strangle him. Instead she shoved. Reluctantly he gave way, straightening. "No more arguing," he cut in, before she could begin something else. "Not tonight, at least."

She looked him squarely in the eye. "I'm not your mistress. I happen to want you, and that's all this is."

If she had been his mistress, she wouldn't have been nearly as much trouble. "I want you as well," he agreed, then closed on her again.

Perhaps she'd acted as she had today to declare her . . . defiance of Society in general. As part of that Society, he found it both dismaying and arousing. One swift tug reduced her night rail to a puddle around her feet. Her hair was already loose, and he tangled his fingers into the heavy mass and gently pulled back, exposing her throat to his kisses.

Sophia moaned, and sharp arousal speared through him, decimating the frustration that had dogged his heels all day. Bending, he scooped her into his arms and carried her to her bed.

Women pursued him all the time, and for the past three days he'd felt rather like the last grain seed in a meadow full of geese. And he still found her the most interesting chit in the house. Sophia, who didn't follow the rules, who embarrassed him and hurled snowballs and boots at him. Sliding onto the bed beside her, he took one of her breasts into his mouth.

Gasping again, she reached up to push off his jacket. With his mouth occupied, Adam unfastened his waist-coat and cravat and cast them aside. When he sat on the edge of the bed to pull off his boots, she moved up behind him, pressing her warm breasts against his back. Sophia kissed the nape of his neck, then reached around his shoulders to unfasten his trousers.

"Come here," she said, chuckling, and pulled him backward to lie flat on the bed.

He wasn't in the mood to wait there for her to torture him, however. Not after she'd already done so—knowingly or not—all day. Before she could straddle his hips, Adam yanked the French condom, which he'd been fingering for the past two hours, from his pocket and kicked out of his trousers. Turning onto his hands and knees, he pursued her across the bed as she grinned and scooted backward.

"Oh, let me," she breathed, taking the condom from his hand.

"Don't play about with it," he cautioned, unable to help his grin at her aroused excitement.

Running her tongue across her lips, Sophia took his cock in her hand. As he gritted his teeth and concentrated on anything other than the exceedingly desirable and very naked young woman touching him so intimately, she slid the goat intestine up over him and tied the red ribbon to hold it in place.

"There," she said, straightening the bow a little.

"That's enough of that," he rumbled. Tugging on her legs, he pulled her beneath him. Delivering another deep kiss, he took a moment to brace his hands on either side of her shoulders before he pushed forward, entering her.

With a breathless smile Sophia wrapped her arms and ankles around him, throwing back her head as he rocked into her again and again. When her muscles began to tense he slowed his pace, deepening his thrusts until with a muffled cry she climaxed.

The sensation was . . . exquisite. There was no other word for it. And he couldn't resist it. With a deep groan he followed her over the edge, holding himself hard and deep inside her.

When he could breathe again, he put an arm around her back and flopped them over. Panting, Sophia draped herself across his chest. The pulse of her fast-beating heart drummed from her into him. Adam held his breath to feel her more closely.

After a moment Sophia lifted her head. "I haven't killed you, have I?" she asked.

Adam let his breath out in a low laugh. "Not yet." Brushing her hair out of her face, he leaned up to kiss her again. "There's no reason you can't make an attempt not to scandalize everyone, is there?" Impressively worded, if he said so himself. Not an order or a demand in earshot.

She put both hands on his chest and levered herself up to look down at him. "The more you want me to be someone else, the less inclined I am to listen to you. I'm anticipating a lifetime of being frowned at, and I don't intend to begin changing my ways before I absolutely have to."

Stubborn, stubborn chit. And she made a damned fine argument, as well. "Being unconventional is what caused you this trouble in the first place. Perhaps if you . . . made an attempt to fit in, your father wouldn't have felt the need to send you so far away," he said cautiously.

With a short laugh she rolled to the edge of the bed and stood. "Being unconventional has been a matter of survival for me, Adam. And if you'll recall, all I ever did was attempt to survive without selling my body. I'm not accepting the blame for my father's . . . lack of compassion," she said, picking up her night rail and pulling it on over her head. "You have a great deal of nerve, attempting to hand me advice."

There were times that control and patience were overrated. "People fall over themselves to receive my advice," he snapped.

"Aha. I think you're far too accustomed to people falling over themselves to please you. For most of us, things just don't bend to our whim."

"That's what you've come up with after a fortnight?" he retorted. "That I'm accustomed to getting what I want? Of course I am. I'm a duke. And we were discussing you."

To his surprise, she returned to the bed and slipped under the covers beside him. "And I am—I was—a card dealer in a gentlemen's club. Perhaps I should have said that things just don't bend to *my* whim."

"And?" he prompted, turning onto his side to gaze at her, and finding himself genuinely curious about where this conversation was going. No one else had ever spoken to him the way she did, and for some damned reason he found it endlessly fascinating.

"And I'm not like anyone else. At least not anyone else you know. I never will be. I don't want to be. Whatever Hennessy or Mr. Loines say or think, and whatever I may have to . . . pretend in order to survive, I know who I am. I like who I am. Can you say the same thing?"

He could say that of course he was perfectly happy with himself, but they would both know it was a lie. She'd seen him behaving like a lunatic out on the ice. Happy persons, he was fairly certain, didn't act in that manner. Neither of them happened to be particularly enthused about their impending nuptials, and neither of them had much of a choice in the matter. The only difference was that she was acquiescing in order to help her friends. He was doing it to help himself.

"Don't be angry," she said after a moment, thudding a hand against his chest. "I've seen you help your friends thanks to who you are. You're a good man, and there's nothing wrong with wishing to keep hold of what you have. If I could manage it, I would do the same."

"Don't humor me, chit."

"Then don't say insulting things to me, boy."

He lifted an eyebrow. " 'Boy'?"

Sophia scowled. "I couldn't think of an insulting term for you. Everyone knows 'chit,' or 'hoyden,' or 'minx.' There aren't any good insults for dukes."

"Yes, well, we arranged it that way." Stifling a laugh, he tucked her against his side. "Go to sleep, chit." Relaxing, he closed his eyes.

"Of course there is 'scoundrel,' " she mused into the silence, and he opened one eye.

"Beg pardon?"

"And rogue. And rapscallion."

Sighing, he shut his eye again. "Don't forget 'devil.' "

"Oh, that's a good one. Or 'devilish rogue.' Is 'picaroon' still appropriate?"

"Very old-fashioned of you."

He heard the soft catch of her breath as she chuckled. "I have to agree," she said thoughtfully. "Hm. 'Scaly bounder.' "

"I am not scaly. And if you call me a blackguard, I'm going to throw you out the window."

"Damnation. I hadn't thought of that one."

Adam smiled. "Good."

As he felt her slowly fall into sleep, he decided that he would do something to help her. He was a damned duke, after all, and if a duke couldn't arrange to do a good deed for a . . . for a dear friend, then he wasn't anything but a scaly bounder. Just what the something was, he didn't know yet, but he hadn't earned a reputation for deviousness by being stupid. All he needed was a plan. And a little more time.

The sky at the edges of the curtains had already grayed when Adam awoke. Sophia lay beside him, one hand across his abdomen and her wild hair half obscuring her face and tickling his nose. While under other circumstances he would have been perfectly content to remain there, this morning he didn't have time for sentiment.

He lifted her hand and gently deposited it beside him, then slid to the edge of the bed and stood. All he—they—needed was for someone to see him stepping out of her bedchamber at nearly six o'clock in the morning. All the rumors would be confirmed, and no one would believe anything other than the gossip that Sophia was his mistress. Only secondary was whatever fit his future bride might choose to throw; whoever she was, if she didn't know about his reputation then he had little sympathy for her.

Why would Sophia simply wish to be his lover, when she could do so in exchange for money or whatever else it was he usually doled out? And why would the Duke of Greaves choose to spend the night with such an eccentric chit without some assurance that he had her loyalty and her silence? Her leash, as it were? That was what they all would think. He could almost hear the gossip already. They had no idea of her true character. And thanks to Hennessy, they would likely have forgotten all about her before the beginning of the Season. That was her father's aim, after all.

She sat up, brushing hair out of her face. "It's morning."

"Very nearly." Swiftly he buttoned his trousers and pulled on his shirt. "Some of us are going for a ride around the lake after breakfast. You're welcome to join us."

"Do you have enough horses?"

"I do, but regardless of that, you have your own mount."

"Oh."

Adam frowned as he buttoned up his waistcoat. "What does that mean?"

"I believe it to be a mild exclamation of surprise or affirmation."

"It's too early for you to be taxing my wits, Sophia. Just speak plainly, will you?"

She tilted her head. "I don't wish to sound petulant or complaining." Scooting to the edge of the bed, she turned onto her stomach and placed her chin in her hands over her bent elbows.

"I've never seen you petulant," he returned. "Go on."

"Very well. It irritated me yesterday when I saw Sylvia Hart riding Copper. But then I realized that when you originally planned this party you of course intended for all the horses—except for Zeus—to be at everyone's disposal. Selling me Copper for three pence was a jest, and I shouldn't have taken it seriously now that circumstances have changed. I'll hardly have a use for her after this holiday, anyway." •

Damnation. He was going to have a word with his stable staff. "If Sylvia rode Copper yesterday, that was a mistake," he said succinctly. "You purchased Copper, and she is yours. Here, or London, or Cornwall. It won't happen again." He sat in the chair by the hearth to pull on his boots, but settled for draping his wrinkled cravat over his shoulders rather than attempting to knot it into anything resembling its former grandeur.

"I might go riding," she said slowly. "I'll have to see what Cammy is up to this morning. And I said I would deal faro."

Adam stood again. So she still insisted on reminding everyone who—what—she was. He stopped his protest, however; he could already hear her response that she was merely *being* who she was and he should keep his snobbery to himself and let her have her fun. Instead he nodded. "I'll have the faro table set up. But don't feel obligated if there's something else you'd rather be doing. You're on holiday, after all."

That earned him a smile, thank God. Swiftly he walked over, knelt beside the bed, and kissed her. Desire tugged through him at her warm response, but he stood again anyway. If he didn't leave now, how he felt toward Sophia White would be obvious to anyone he encountered between there and his own bedchamber.

"Good morning," he said, and walked to her door.

"Good morning."

He cracked open the door and peered into the hallway. It stood silent, dim, and empty. Stepping out, he silently shut her door behind him and made his way to the corridor that connected the east wing of the house to his rooms in the west wing.

A few of his servants were about, lighting hallway sconces and opening curtains, but other than acknowledging their hushed greetings, he ignored them. There likely wasn't one of them who didn't already know with whom he'd been spending his nights and sharing his baths. *His* servants kept his secrets. It was everyone else's he had to worry about.

Once he made it back inside his dark, chilly bedchamber, he stopped, resting his forehead against the closed door. He needed to stop delaying his own search. Yes, he wanted to help Sophia, but he couldn't very well do that if he lost half his properties and became the jester of London because of it. His wife was there, at Greaves Park. He merely needed to point at one of the chits and say, "Her. She'll do." Because at this point the who of it didn't matter. If there had been a particular female he wanted to marry, he would have done so by now. All he needed, then, was a spouse. Any spouse. And spending time with Sophia, though eminently more pleasant, wasn't helping either one of them.

"I don't think 'later' has the same meaning for you that it does for me," a soft, silky voice said from the direction of his bed.

Shit. "Caroline," he said, turning around.

She lay on her side beneath his covers, her head propped up on one elbow. Given the emerald evening gown neatly folded over the back of a chair, she was naked beneath the sheets. And from her half-asleep expression, she'd been there for some time. Likely all night.

"I thought you wished a better acquaintance, Your Grace. But it seems you had someone else's acquaintance to make."

"Blackwood plays a relentless game of piquet," he stated, sliding off his loose cravat and dropping it onto his writing table. "And yes, evidently we do have different interpretations of the word 'later.' My apologies."

She uncoiled and sat up, catlike. The sheets dropped to her waist, revealing a large, inviting pair of breasts. "No harm done," she purred with a slow, seductive smile. "What is your interpretation of the word 'now'?"

She likely didn't want to hear his interpretation of anything at this moment, because it involved a great deal of cursing. Nothing he or Sophia had ever said to each other had implied anything exclusive or even more than casual, but she was the first place his thoughts went. Even when the woman he was most likely to marry sat, attractive and naked, five feet away from him.

With Caroline on his arm during the Season, he would have a companion for soirees and dinners and nights at the theater, and he would have a mother for his heirs. But whatever his conversations with Sophia had or hadn't touched on, whatever he knew with as much certainty as he knew his own face, stating his intentions to Caroline would mean ending something with Sophia. And he wasn't prepared to do that.

He took a deep breath. "Unfortunately, my interpretation of 'now' is when I need to change my clothes and go downstairs for breakfast."

Dark brown eyes, black in the dimness of the room, regarded him levelly. "Should we discuss 'later' on another occasion, then? Or should I assume that I altogether misinterpreted my invitation to Greaves Park?"

God, she was so civilized. So . . . bloodless. Precisely what he wanted in a wife—someone who would show well and not put up a fuss if or when he decided to take up with some mistress or other. No arguing for Lady Caroline, no throwing things—and no supreme joy or passion or laughter.

Distinctly feeling the need to sit down for a moment, instead he collected her gown and walked over to place it on the bed. "You didn't misinterpret. I misspoke. Unintentionally, but there you have it. My . . . reason for inviting you here this holiday hasn't altered."

"Well. I am pleased to see that we both remain on the same page, so to speak."

"As am I. For the moment, however, I prefer not to begin other female tongues wagging. The din is deafening."

With a smile, she nodded. "I understand."

"I'll be back in twenty minutes," he said, returning to the door.

"I'll be gone in fifteen, then."

* * *

Sophia walked down the short hallway and into the breakfast room. Her friends stood at the sideboard, Cammy nudging Keating out from in front of the sliced ham. A dozen other guests were already seated, chatting over their own breakfasts. "Good morning," she said to no one in particular, and went to select her own fare.

Cammy kissed her on the cheek. "Good morning, my dear. Do you fancy a drive into Hanlith this morning?"

"I thought I might make another attempt at going riding. His Grace says several of them are venturing around the lake, and I've been wanting a closer look at the temple of Athena over on the far side." She put an arm around her friend's shoulders. "You and Keating should go into the village, though. The bakery there has the most delicious cinnamon biscuits I have ever eaten. Ever."

"You're certain?" Camille asked with a grin, shrugging off Keating's poking finger and emphatic nodding.

"Of course I am."

"Very well, then. We'll be back in the afternoon, if you'd like a coze."

"I don't know when I'll be back, so take your time."

She left them for the stables directly after breakfast to find Adam, Timmerlane, Francis Henning, the Hart sisters, Miss Prentiss, Prudence Jones, and Aubrey Burroughs selecting mounts for their ride. "Ah, there you are, Miss White," Adam drawled. "I took the liberty of having your mare saddled. You have a fine eye for horseflesh, I have to say. I almost regret selling her to you."

Well, that was well and diplomatically done. Sophia sent him a smile, making every attempt to ignore the disdainful looks the other females sent her. She actually preferred when they turned their backs, so she wouldn't have to look at their faces. "It's far too late for seller's remorse, Your Grace. You may envy Copper from a distance."

Adam checked what might have been an approach, and instead swung into big Zeus's saddle. "You're a heartless woman, Miss White."

It was Aubrey Burroughs who offered her a hand up into the saddle before he mounted a pretty bay gelding. "Thank you, Mr. Burroughs," she said, favoring him with a smile.

"Always happy to help a lovely lady," he returned, tipping his hat.

The Hart sisters rode past her, both with their noses in the air, but other than noting that, she made every attempt to forget they even existed. Adam had spoken civilly to her in public, and compared to yesterday, she had to count that as a definite improvement.

The wind had swept most of the snow covering the lake into several large drifts against the east shore, while it had left a thin layer of ice coating the bare twigs and branches of the trees. The sight was exquisitely lovely. She understood why Adam didn't like being at Greaves Park, but she found its stark beauty enchanting. In the spring it was no doubt doubly so.

"You're being very quiet, Sophia," Aubrey commented, leaving Miss Jones's side and kneeing his bay up even with Copper.

"I was just admiring the scenery. Where do you call home, Mr. Burroughs?"

"I've a small estate just outside Bath," he said. "It's pretty, but nothing to compare with Greaves's sprawl."

"I'm certain it's lovely. I've driven through the Cotswolds, though I've never stayed there. I've never seen a greener countryside or fatter sheep."

"Well, you're welcome to visit Farling any time you wish. My fat sheep would be happy to be complimented."

She laughed. "I'm certain your sheep don't care a fig for my opinion, but thank you."

"I know *I* don't care a fig for her opinion," she heard Miss Rebecca mutter to her sister, and Miss Sylvia laughed behind her hand. In front of them, Helena Prentiss sent her a glance one generally reserved for stinging flies and then went back to her conversation with Lord Timmerlane.

Sophia didn't know how he managed it, but somehow Adam gracefully maneuvered big Zeus between the sisters' mounts. "I've noticed the snow has cleared from the lake," he commented, his voice sounding just the slightest bit brusque. "And I happen to own several pairs of skates."

"Oh, ice skating! I haven't skated since the Thames froze over four years ago," Rebecca exclaimed, reaching over to clutch his left sleeve. "We must do it! Say we shall, Your Grace."

"That's why I mentioned it. I suggest this afternoon. I have a suspicion we'll see more snow tomorrow."

While the Hart sisters loudly declared how much fun they were going to have and asked everyone but her if they would care to join in the festivities, Adam reined Zeus back until Sophia and Aubrey drew even with him. "And you, Miss White?" he asked, smiling. "Care to make an attempt at ice skating?"

"An attempt?" she countered, grinning back at him. "I'm a sterling ice skater."

"Oh, really? Care to wager on that?"

"Definitely."

ELEVEN

"You know," Keating Blackwood said as he glided by with his laughing wife clinging to his arm, "if you didn't want us here you might have just not repaired the bridge. Murder seems somewhat extreme."

"I don't know what you're complaining about," Adam returned with a short grin. "You look very graceful."

"Bastard" floated back to him on the air.

Hiding most of his amusement at the profound lack of skill and coordination before him, Adam made a leisurely circle around the gaggle of skaters. Lassiter was the only one who lived as far north as he did, but the viscount wasn't out on the ice.

Sylvia Hart flailed up to him, and he shifted a little to the side to avoid a collision. The gaggle had annoyed him from the moment he'd invited them. Now that he'd very nearly settled on one of the geese, the rest of them were nearly intolerable. "This is splendid, Your Grace," she panted, nearly losing her footing when he failed to catch her and then finding her balance again. "I shall come here every year and skate!"

He nodded, reflecting that she and her sister were not going to be asked back again. Ever. His tolerance for nonsense had its limits. "You're quite skilled."

"Oh, I know. It's always been like that. I attempt something, and suddenly everyone's complimenting me."

"Henning!" he called, glancing past her. "Let Miss Sylvia show you how it's done."

"Ah, thank you, Greaves," Francis said, stumbling up to them. "This ain't as easy as it looks."

Once a bewildered-looking Sylvia, Henning in tow, headed back into the crowd of skaters, Adam returned his attention to Sophia. She was even worse at ice skating than Sylvia Hart, but at least she had no delusions about that. The grin on her face would have put the sun to shame if it had been shining, but despite that he wasn't nearly as amused as she clearly was.

Circling around her and freely offering both advice and his arm, was Burroughs. Either Aubrey believed his rumor-quashing about Sophia not being his mistress, or Burroughs didn't care.

"You're scowling," Keating said as he crossed by again.

"No I'm not."

"Well, you have that look about you," his friend amended. "As if you intend to do someone harm."

Adam shook himself. Keating knew him better than most, but if he couldn't disguise his temper from everyone, he was doing something wrong. "It's going to snow tomorrow. I find that annoying," he settled on.

"Mm-hm." The Blackwoods came to a stop behind him. "This is an amusing outing," Keating offered in a low voice. "To my surprise, you know how to have fun. It's your own fault you have a dozen fluttery chits chasing after you, so I suggest you make the best of it. At least laugh at the severe lack of coordination."

"I have been," he returned in the same tone. "And I know whose fault this is." His, of course, and now he could partly blame Sophia. She had no right to be more interesting than any other female present, and to cause him to make comparisons that would have her blushing and the other women in question mortified that he held them up to a Tantalus girl's reflection and found them lacking. "Now give me your wife, and I'll show her how skating is supposed to be done."

"Just give her back," Keating said with a short smile, cautiously moving closer as Adam offered his arm to Camille.

She transferred her grip to Adam, clutching his arm with both hands. "Thank you," she said, her grin deepening. "I'd begun to worry that Keating would fall on me, but I didn't want to make him more self-conscious."

"I heard that," Keating commented from behind them.

Letting Camille continue to lean on him, Adam made a slow circuit around the snow-cleared edges of the ice. Slowly she began to relax a little, and loosened her grip to stand more upright. "You're doing quite well," he complimented, "now that Keating's not holding you back."

She chuckled. "I didn't imagine you as an ice skater," she said. "But clearly you've done it often enough to do it well."

"It's mostly a memory from my youth," he returned, refusing to let his mind drift back beyond that statement, to staying out on the lake until his fingers and toes were numb just to avoid going back into the house. "Like riding a horse, I suppose, it's difficult to forget."

With little effort they outdistanced Keating, and Adam steered them farther out onto the lake. Camille's grip on his arm clenched as she skated over a dusting of snow, then lightened again. "What did you want to discuss then, Your Grace?" she asked.

Clearly Sophia didn't have stupid friends. "You shared a room with Miss White when you both worked at the Tantalus, did you not?"

"Yes, I did."

"Why?"

She frowned briefly. "Why? Because there were two beds in each room. We all shared."

"I mean, why you and Miss White? You're a marquis's daughter. Before that . . . incident, you were the toast of the *ton*."

"And after that 'incident,' as you call it, my parents turned me out, and none of my dear friends would look at me unless it was to deliver an insult. The Tantalus Club saved my life. It's saved the life of nearly every female who works there."

"I wasn't making a commentary about the club. Merely about the reasoning behind your friendship."

Camille took a breath. "To answer your question more directly, then, I was a bit . . . cautious of Sophia when we first met. She was born notorious, after all. But I think that, in a sense, gave her an advantage."

That was quite possibly the last thing he'd expected to hear. "Explain."

"She's not . . . obligated to anyone. As long as Hennessy doesn't acknowledge her, which he will never do, she will always be on the outside. Her situation is fixed. Or it was, anyway." She frowned. "The Duke of Hennessy should have let her be; she certainly wasn't harming anyone."

"I would agree with that. In fact, I've been considering whether there's a way to help her . . . situation."

She sent him a sideways glance that nearly set her off balance again. "If you have an idea, please enlighten me. Because I haven't been able to conjure anything practical at all."

So much for his vague hope that Sophia's clever friend would have discovered a crack or a crevasse that he'd overlooked. "Hennessy's a difficult man to dissuade," he said reluctantly. "He doesn't require money, and there's nothing nefarious in his past other than Sophia."

Camille nodded. "He wants her to disappear, and to

take any blows to his pride along with her. In my experience, a man will spend a great deal of time and money to protect his pride. Haybury has the money to challenge him, but Oliver is part of the club, and just as notorious, really. Hennessy would win that battle. I don't think Sophia even told Diane and Oliver the details of her marriage."

Behind them Keating had given up the chase and was circling in a very ungainly manner back to where the bulk of the skaters cavorted. Adam took a breath. "I generally deal with persons in one of three ways: blackmail, threats, or bribery. At least two of those would seem to be inappropriate for this situation. I attempted to encourage Sophia simply to run, but she won't stand for seeing The Tantalus Club attacked."

"Neither will I." She looked down at her feet, which sent her stumbling again until he caught her shoulder to steady her. "I'm so angry," she finally muttered, sending a swift look in Sophia's direction. "She's always managed, and I imagine she thinks that she'll simply have to figure out how to manage Vicar Loines. But she won't ever be able to escape, and he won't ever have anything but a frown and a switch for her—if not something even worse. It's . . . untenable, but I don't know what to do about it."

He could claim that he had his own troubles, but in truth Sophia's plight concerned him at least as much as his own. After all, he could ask for Caroline's hand this afternoon and be married tomorrow. Problem, such as it was, solved. Neither of them would likely be . . . happy, but that was hardly the point. He would keep his money and his properties, and that was what mattered. Sophia marrying the damned vicar would gain her nothing— not for herself, anyway. "I feel outflanked," he said after a moment, wondering if Mrs. Blackwood would know how rarely he admitted to such a thing.

Slowing, she glanced up at him again. "She likes you, you know. Not your lineage, not your income, not how you make your way in the world. You. And I hope you value that."

"I do."

"Then save her."

For a long moment he gazed at the ragged tree line. "That's a fine thing to ask, the moment after you declare that you don't have a clue how to perform that particular miracle."

"You're a duke, and you have money, and people in general are terrified of you. That has to count for something."

He snorted. "I certainly hope it does."

"I suppose we'll find out."

Their circle had brought them back to the bulk of the skaters, and Keating stumbled over to intercept them. "Are you finished now, or should I send for tea?"

"You skate like a rhinoceros, you know," Adam said mildly, handing Camille back. "Don't trample her. I believe marrying that woman to be the most intelligent thing you've ever done."

"I agree." Keating gave a smile. "So hands off."

Because no one had ever won an argument with a jealous man, Adam simply glided backward until he was out of reach. Across from him damned Burroughs was still smothering Sophia. He could at least save her from that. Digging the toe of one skate into the ice, Adam pushed off toward them.

"I heard a rumor that you were a sterling skater, Miss White," he drawled.

"I may have exaggerated," she said, chuckling. "I thought we would be using Norwegian skates, with which of course I am well versed."

"Mm-hm." Moving directly in front of her, he held out both his gloved hands.

"I'm assisting her, Greaves," Burroughs said, moving in again. "Don't trouble yourself."

Adam shifted his weight a little, ready to drop Burroughs to the ice. "It's no trouble. You've been attempting to render her seaworthy for nearly an hour. I've decided to step in before spring thaw."

Sophia put her hands in his. "Certainly I need all the instruction I can get."

While Burroughs continued to glare at them, Adam began moving slowly backward, holding Sophia's hands to draw her forward. Her toes turned in and out, nearly colliding and then nearly going completely out from under her.

"Don't watch your feet," he instructed.

"If I don't watch them, there's no telling where they'll go," she returned with a breathless grin.

"Look at my face. Trust me."

Immediately she lifted her head, her eyes meeting his. Clearly she did trust him, then. The notion was . . . heartwarming. "When I say right, push your right toe down and back. Just a little. When I say left, do the same thing with your other foot. I won't let you fall."

Sophia nodded. "If I do fall, I'm going to do my damnedest to land on you."

He smiled; it was impossible not to. "Fair enough. Ready? Right."

She stuttered and jolted, and he gave her a moment to recover her balance. Once her grip on his hands loosened a little, he pushed off with his right foot. "Left." Pause. "Good. Right." Pause. "Better. Left."

For a few minutes she looked like a kitten trying to climb on glass, but then she began to steady, making deeper cuts into the ice with each push. Her back straightened, and he moved in closer, matching her forward strokes with reverse ones of his own.

"It's like dancing," she exclaimed, laughing in obvious delight. "And flying, all at the same time."

"Very like."

"Can I look at my feet now?"

"No. A bird never looks at its wings while it's flying. If it did, it would realize it's doing something utterly impossible, and fall to the ground."

Her smile softened. "That's beautiful."

Wonderful. Now he was being poetical. "It just seemed like sound advice," he returned, shrugging.

"I think I might be a bird." She closed her eyes.

In response, he sped their pace, until they were nearly flying across the ice. Perhaps she *was* a bird. She flew through her life with more grace than he could imagine. And damned Hennessy was trying to—had succeeded in—clipping her wings. He couldn't allow it to happen. He couldn't.

Along with all her clothes and most of her worldly possessions, two small boxes had been lost in the river Aire. An onyx cravat pin for Keating, and a deep blue pair of ear bobs with matching hair ribbon for Camille. Sophia had the money to replace the items; it sat in a small bank account the Marquis of Haybury had opened in her name. In London, where she couldn't get to it.

She could have borrowed something from Adam; he'd been trying to purchase things for her for weeks, now. But borrowing money for a gift seemed . . . wrong. Particularly when she now had three Christmas gifts she wished to give.

"What do you think of this?" Milly asked, pulling half a skein of deep blue yarn from her sewing basket. "Udgell's wife had it left over from mittens she made last year."

"Udgell is married?"

Milly snorted. "I know. I always thought his leg would snap off if he sank down on one knee. Mary's in York now, visiting her sister. But Udgell said the yarn's yours if you want it."

Sophia took the yarn, turning it over in her hands. "It's a lovely color. I can use it for trim." Leaning sideways, she picked up the half-finished scarf she'd been knitting for Adam. Grays and blacks and now the deep blue all seemed colors that fit him, but it had been a very long time since she'd knitted anything.

"Oh, Sophia, that blue will finish it off just perfectly, I think."

She smiled. "Thank you, Milly. Have you had any luck finding a green yarn for Keating's scarf?"

"I know Mrs. Orling in the village has some, but she's wily. I'll get the green from her, though, don't you fret. I have a yellow hair ribbon she's been admiring."

This was beginning to sound dismaying. "You can't trade your own things for me." Sophia rose, going to the mostly empty wardrobe. "What about a peach ribbon? You said this was from a box in the attic. No one will miss it."

Milly furrowed her brow. "But it goes so well with your blue walking dress. I couldn't—"

"Of course you can. I insist." All the servants at Greaves Park—and Milly in particular—had been so generous to her already that it was almost overwhelming. If they'd found something for her to use that belonged to no one, of course she would give it up. "I like bartering. It's fun."

The housekeeper dropped the ribbon into her basket. "I don't think Mrs. Orling will be able to resist it. I'll have that yarn for you by dinner."

"Excellent. Just don't remind me that it's only three days before Christmas." And if she tried very hard, she could almost pretend that nothing lay beyond that day but snow and . . . and watching Adam finally declare for Lady Caroline. That would be nearly as painful as the moment she took her own vows. Perhaps she could leave before that happened.

Milly stood, hefting her sewing basket over her arm. "Oh, that's a world of time, Sophia," she said. "A few late nights and you'll be finished."

Sophia watched Milly out the bedchamber door, took a sip of her cooling tea, and picked up the knitting needles, also borrowed. *A world of time.* That was what she truly wanted as a Christmas gift. But not even the Duke of Greaves would be able to manage such a thing. Best to concentrate on what she *could* manage—and that was finishing a trio of scarves for a trio of friends.

As usual now when she thought of Adam, a smile touched her mouth. He'd spent every night with her lately. Oh, she would miss his solid, warm presence, both in her bed and in her life. All she could do at the moment, though, was knit.

After nearly an hour Sophia stood to stretch her back. The moment she leaned against the window frame to catch a glimpse of the sledders below, though, someone knocked at her door.

"Drat," she muttered, and grabbed a spare blanket off the bed to throw over her pile of yarn and knitting. "Come in," she called, sitting in her just-vacated chair and pulling a book onto her lap.

Aubrey Burroughs leaned through the doorway, then stepped into her room. "I hope I'm not intruding," he said with a warm smile.

"Of course not. I'm just doing some reading."

As he approached, he bent down to read the title of the book she held. "*Robinson Crusoe*. That seems fitting, to escape to tropical adventures while we're all trapped in the deep snow."

"I don't feel trapped," she returned. "It's beautiful here."

Light brown eyes traveled from the book to her face. "It is, indeed." Without being asked, he dropped into the chair nearest to hers.

Sophia had lost count several years ago of the number of men who had given her that look. It generally occurred shortly before the suggestion that as a pretty chit with no prospects, she would be better off under the protection of someone with blunt and a taste for fine things. Lately, though, those particular conversations had taken place across a gaming table at the Tantalus, where she'd had the rules and several Helpful Men to underscore her polite refusal. This afternoon she had a husband waiting for a marriage, and every reason to meet him at the church.

"Is there an arrangement between you and Greaves?" Burroughs asked after a moment. "He is one of those men it simply isn't wise to cross."

Thunder boomed low over the valley. The poor weather had been coming more frequently, which Adam had said was typical. As he described it, anyone there by the tenth of January would be staying through February. She meant to leave by the fourth, at the latest. "No," she said, "I don't have an arrangement with anyone."

Aubrey smiled. "I didn't think so. It would be like Prinny taking up with a fishmonger's wife. You couldn't take her to dinner without everyone noticing the smell."

"I beg your pardon," Sophia commented, closing the book, "but is that the method you mean to use to win my affections?"

"What about this method?" he asked, pulling a pretty pearl necklace from his jacket pocket. "And this would only be the beginning."

For a moment she stayed silent, gazing at him. What

was it about men, that made them so certain they were irresistible, despite all evidence to the contrary? "You neglected to consider the fishmonger's wife's viewpoint in your analogy. Where would she wear her pearls and pretty baubles?"

A muscle beneath his right eye jumped. "You can't be serious. She could sell them to purchase food and clothing."

"But she already has the fishmonger." *Or a vicar, in her case.* "And fish, presumably. And she would still have that smell about her."

With a click he set the pearls on the table between them. "I didn't intend to insult you, Sophia. You're a beautiful chit, and you could do better than sitting at a gaming table and using your bosom to entice men to wager more deeply."

"My bosom is perfectly content with its employment," she returned, beginning to wonder if he would say anything to her that wasn't insulting.

"This is ridiculous," he stated, his voice clipped. "Name your price."

"My price, Mr. Burroughs, is that I need to like you. Now if you'll excuse me, I would like to finish this chapter before dinner."

He sat forward, his lips tightening. "*You* need to like *me*?" he retorted. "You should be grateful that *I* found *you* attractive. Otherwise you would have no use at all."

And she'd heard that before, too. "Evidently you believe I have some worth, or you wouldn't have come in here to bargain with me over it. I'm simply not selling myself to you."

Aubrey Burroughs stood, picking up the pearls and shoving them back into his pocket. "In five or ten years, when you aren't pretty enough or young enough to work at the Tantalus any longer, you'll be begging on the streets for what I just offered you. I imagine you'll have men paying your price three times a night. Four, if you're lucky."

With that, he strode out of her room.

Almost on his heels, Milly hurried in. "Don't you listen to that awful man, Sophia," she growled, hugging Sophia to her bosom and nearly smothering her in the process. "You pricked his pride, and he only wanted to hurt you in return."

As gently as she could given the fact that she couldn't breathe, Sophia set the housekeeper back a step. "It's nothing I haven't heard before," she stated, attempting to keep her voice level. "And he knows nothing of my circumstances."

Even before Hennessy had stepped in to alter her life, she'd been quite aware that she couldn't work at The Tantalus Club indefinitely; the average age of the girls there was twenty-one, and she was already past her twenty-third birthday.

But she had that bank account where she put every bit of money she'd saved each month, and she'd had a plan. Once she'd decided it was time to go and once she'd had enough money, she would have purchased a small shop in some village far enough away from London that no one would recognize her. It would have been her timing, her terms, and her choice. And she certainly never would have chosen a man like the Reverend Loines with whom to share her life. Nor would she have cut herself off from the friends she'd made, or from buying silly hats and far too much lace.

"Sophia."

She shook herself. "I'm fine, Milly. Truly."

"No you aren't. You listened to him. He's just a worthless man with a gnat's cock, trying to buy your silence so you won't laugh at him in bed."

That caught her attention. A laugh burst from her chest. "Mrs. Brooks! I'm shocked."

Milly narrowed one eye. "You promise me you'll pay no heed to what he said. It was just . . . bluster. Promise me, Sophia."

What Milly didn't understand was that she'd already imagined her future, more times than she cared to recall, and that Aubrey Burroughs's version was less painful to her than her reality. All he'd done was remind her of it at a time when she'd been trying to forget, to sink into the happiness of this moment and let it wash over her. "I promise, Milly. Of course."

"Good. Then I have something for you." Milly produced a ball of deep, forest-colored green yarn from a bulging pocket of her pelisse. "Mrs. Orling says to thank you for the ribbon. It's just the thing she wanted to give her granddaughter for Christmas."

"Oh, it's perfect. Thank you so much. And not just for getting the yarn."

The housekeeper actually wiped a tear from one cheek. "You might have been *my* daughter, you know, if Adam Baswich's father had fancied northern women of solid stock."

So Milly had served the household during the former duke's tenure. That explained a few things about the servant's interest and compassion for her own circumstances, Sophia realized. "You knew the duke?"

"Well. Not *knew* him, thank heavens." Milly put both hands over her heart. "That man had a way of looking at you that just . . ." She trailed off, then visibly shook herself. "Even those who never believed in God, believed in the devil after meeting the ninth Duke of Greaves."

"And what of the tenth Duke of Greaves?"

Milly's expression cleared. "Oh, he has a temper,

and a way of knowing things that sometimes gives me the shivers, but from when he was a lad till now, I have never felt afraid to be in a room with him." The servant smiled, patting Sophia on the shoulder. "Now I don't gossip about my employers, or there are some tales I could tell you."

For someone who didn't carry tales, Milly was certainly generous with her information. Sophia smiled back at her. "I am grateful for your discretion."

And she needed to find a way to broach the subject of Christmas gifts for his very loyal servants with Adam. She had more than a hunch that the man who noticed everything had no idea how much he was appreciated here. As for her, she knew her fate. It was just a matter of putting off thinking about it for as long as possible. And Adam was very good at distracting her from that.

Adam looked at the list he'd compiled. Thirteen names of thirteen young ladies. All of them were between eighteen and twenty-five years of age, all of impeccable lineage, and all considered to be somewhere in the range of pretty to stunningly lovely. And all of them eager to be the next Duchess of Greaves.

One by one he gazed at the names, considered the various ladies in question, and then drew a thick black line of ink across the letters. Sylvia Hart's voice cut through him like a nail across glass. Lady Julia Greyson of the much praised blue eyes had the wits of a pigeon. Rebecca Hart was petty and grasping.

Finally only two names remained. Helena Prentiss had a calm demeanor and was known to be a superb hostess. And Lady Caroline Emery was lovely and had a firm grasp on both what would be expected of a duchess and what sort of husband he was likely to be. He preferred that no one have any illusions when this was nothing more than a business agreement. Slowly he drew a line through Miss Prentiss's name, as well.

At the sound of a quiet knock, he lifted his head. "Who is it?"

"Mrs. Brooks, Your Grace."

"Come in. And shut the door behind you."

The housekeeper complied, standing nearly at attention in front of his desk. Beginning to fear that she wasn't breathing, he gestured for her to sit in one of the pair of chairs facing him across the polished mahogany.

"You gave away the ribbon?" he asked, when she continued to sit in silence.

"I did, Your Grace. Miss Sophia is a generous-hearted young lady."

He'd noticed days ago that Sophia had won over his servants, but the extent to which she'd earned their loyalty continued to surprise him. "And you still aren't going to tell me why she was set on giving it away?"

"Not unless you order me to do so, Your Grace. I'll say it's about Christmas, but no more."

"Very well. Thank you." He lowered his head and went back to do a last assessment of his matrimonial choice. After all the time he'd spent delaying the inevitable, he'd expected the decision to be more difficult. As it was, he mostly wanted to put the paper into a drawer and go find Sophia for a game of cards.

Mrs. Brooks didn't move.

Stifling a sigh, Adam put down his quill. "Is there something else?"

"Yes, Your Grace. I—if it pleases you, I don't want to be like that fellow they killed when he ran from Marathon."

"The messenger?" he supplied. "No one killed him. He dropped dead after running for twenty or so miles."

An edge of uneasiness brushed him. "As the messenger, you are perfectly safe, Mrs. Brooks. What did you wish to tell me?"

"Oh, dear," she muttered, looking down at her hands as she twisted them in her lap. "You wanted to be notified if anyone spoke . . . ill to Miss Sophia, or if—"

"What happened?" he asked, all humor fleeing.

When the housekeeper looked up at him again, she swallowed hard. "Mr. Burroughs went to see her in her room, and—"

Adam shot to his feet. If Burroughs had charmed his way into Sophia's bed, he was a dead man. If he'd touched her, he was a dead man. The anger curling into him was hot, clean, and palpable.

Abruptly he caught sight of the white-faced servant cowering in the chair across the desk from him. Choking back his fury, he very slowly seated himself again. Considering that he'd just promised the blasted woman that nothing would happen to the messenger, he needed to calm the devil down. "You were saying?" he managed.

She cleared her throat. Twice. He could practically count the number of his heartbeats that stretched between when he'd spoken and when she opened her mouth again.

"He—Burroughs—asked if Sophia wouldn't like to be kept by him. When she refused, he said she would end up on the streets as a whore. Not in those exact words, but I heard it all, and it wasn't pleasant, Your Grace. I would have gone in and stopped him, but until that last venom he spat at her, she was giving better than she got. I got . . . caught up in listening to her."

That, he understood. For a moment Adam concentrated on the last sentence or two his housekeeper had uttered. Sophia's past and the nature of men told him that she'd been propositioned before, and *her* nature told him that she would no doubt have some very direct responses to those same men. But Burroughs had a nasty streak. He'd on occasion appreciated its bite.

"Thank you, Mrs. Brooks. I'll see to it."

She put out a hand. "But Your Grace! Sophia will know I've been talking to you, and she'll never trust me again." Tears began streaming down her plump cheeks. "That poor girl! I would never—"

Slamming the flat of his hands on the surface of his desk, he stood again. "I'll see to it, Mrs. Brooks," he repeated more forcefully. "You needn't worry about you and Miss White."

"Oh. Oh. Thank you, Your Grace. I do apologize, Your Grace. It's just that—"

"That will be all, Mrs. Brooks. Go down to the kitchen and have some tea. Calm yourself."

Moving with more speed than he'd thought she could manage, the housekeeper stood and darted out his door, slamming it shut again with more force than he would generally have found tolerable in a servant. Adam bowed his head, staying where he was for a long moment while he weighed what he wanted to do against the wisest course of action.

Things had definitely changed, if he was hesitating to act out of consideration for a housekeeper and a redheaded slip of a girl who'd been promised to a vicar. What he wanted to do was simple: he wanted to beat Aubrey Burroughs into a bloody pulp. Of course he also wanted to beat Mr. Loines into a bloody pulp, and he'd never even met the man. What he *should* do, however, was more difficult to discern.

He stalked to the door and yanked on the bellpull hanging on the wall there. Half a minute later, Udgell knocked at the door, and he pulled it open. "Find Keating Blackwood and bring him here," Adam said, and closed the door again before the butler could acknowledge the order.

Burroughs and he were friends. They had been for years. Eight years or so earlier, the two of them and Oliver Warren had been the closest of friends. Shortly after the debacle with Oliver, Adam and Burroughs had begun drifting apart, as well. In a sense, Aubrey Burroughs was a remnant of an old life that Adam had mostly discarded once he'd realized it wasn't going in the direction he wanted. Once he'd realized how closely he'd begun following in his unlamented father's footsteps.

"What?" Keating said, pushing open the door and stepping inside.

"I need a word with you," Adam returned stiffly, closing the door before he stalked to the office window and back again.

"Get on with it, then. Camille and Sophia are eating all the roasted chestnuts."

Adam faced him. "Sophia is with you?"

Lifting an eyebrow, Keating dropped into a chair. "They're nearly inseparable, if you haven't noticed. Not that I mind; I owe Sophia a great deal, and Cammy's suffered a scarcity of friends." His expression cooling, he sat forward a little. "What's wrong? You look like you want to hit something again."

Though he would rather have kept pacing, that wasn't helping anything. Adam sat on the arm of the chair beside Keating. "Did Sophia look upset about anything?"

"Now that you've made me consider it, I suppose she was a little . . . subdued, but with what she has coming in her direction, I'd be subdued, as well."

She was subdued. Burroughs *had* hurt her. Adam therefore meant to hurt him. "Was Burroughs present?" he pressed, unable to help the growl in his voice when he said his former friend's name.

Rather than answering, Keating folded his arms over his chest. "I'm not saying anything else until you tell me why you're holding this unpleasant little inquisition."

Including anyone else in his plans, in his decisions, had never appealed to Adam. But whether he wanted to acknowledge it or not, he'd called in Keating for a reason. He trusted Blackwood. "I need your silence about what I'm about to say."

Keating nodded. "You have it."

His friend hadn't hesitated. No conditions, no favors to be collected at a later date. Blackwood had his own demons to contend with, but there was a forthright honesty about him and what he'd done that Adam had always admired. Those were some of the same qualities he admired about Sophia, now that he considered it.

"Secondhand, I just learned that Burroughs asked Sophia to be his mistress. When she declined, he said some rather nasty things to her, the gist of which was that she would die whoring herself in the street. The fact that her actual future is only marginally more tolerable is, I believe, beside the point."

For a long moment Keating sat very still. That gave Adam time to remember that until he'd met Camille, Keating had spent much of the past six years drinking and brawling. That could be useful, except that if anyone was going to hit Burroughs, it was going to be him.

"I have a question," Keating finally said in a low voice.

"I'm listening."

"What is Sophia to you?"

That stopped him. "What? What kind of question is that? I just told you that someone insulted your wife's dearest friend."

"And I'd like to know whether you've done the same thing."

That old, molten heat began rising deep in his gut. "Explain yourself," he murmured.

"No. You explain *your*self."

Evidently unconditional support only went so far. "I may have mentioned that I could remove any monetary burdens she might ever have," he conceded grudgingly. "When she declined, she also told me her circumstances. I did not call her names because of her background. I did not insult her over her choice of livelihood. When I *did* insult her, she cracked me in the head with a snowball."

As he spoke, that roiling rage subsided a little. Even thoughts of Sophia had the effect of lighting his soul just a little.

"You invited her to sell herself to you."

He might have found some balance, but if anything Keating sounded even angrier. "I wouldn't have put it quite that way, and it was more of a suggestion than an invitation, but yes. It's nothing new, Keating. And for some women it offers them a way to keep their nice homes and their nice jewels and their nice dress—"

Keating hit him. Sitting on the arm of the chair as he was, Adam went backward into the seat. With a growl he rolled onto his feet. His first instinct was to strike back. Hard. Again, though, he needed Keating. If Blackwood was dead, he couldn't help. So instead of swinging, Adam clenched his fist into the back of the chair. "I'll excuse that," he said very evenly, tasting blood from a cut lip, "because I'm glad she has a protector. Do it again, and I won't be so generous."

"Do whatever the hell you like. Camille and Sophia and I are leaving."

"No you're not."

"You expect me to remain here while you proposition my friend and allow other men to do the same? She wanted a pleasant damned holiday, Greaves. Not to have her host make things even worse for her. You're a bastard, and I'm done with you."

With a curse Adam strode up to block the door. "I did it once, Keating. Weeks ago. Since then, Sophia and I have been . . . We're friends."

"Ha."

"Don't 'ha' at me. I've been spending the nights in her room for the past week. Whatever is between us, we're in agreement about." More or less, anyway. Precisely what was between them, he couldn't define. He wasn't certain he wanted to; that would dredge up more questions he couldn't possibly answer. "We both know what Hennessy has set out for her, but she still has a few weeks to do as she pleases."

"Oh, so now you've ruined her, which I'm certain will make her life in Cornwall much easier. You had to know that no good could possibly come of you gadding about. Isn't there someone closer to your own rank you could play with?"

That was enough of that. "Excuse me, but didn't you steal your cousin's fiancée from a church? In the middle of the wedding? Don't you dare lecture me about my behavior. If Sophia is content with this, then so am I."

Keating paced back and forth in front of the desk. "Very well. If I can't hit you, then I'm going to hit Burroughs."

"No, you can't hit Burroughs. If Sophia realizes that I know what transpired, she'll know that someone told me. I . . . gave my word that I would keep that person's confidence."

Oh, good God. What the devil was wrong with him? Everyone knew that when he wanted something accomplished, he saw to it. The means and method were secondary. And yet he'd assured Mrs. Brooks that the messenger wouldn't be punished. Beyond that, he was quite aware that Sophia liked the housekeeper, and he wasn't going to be the reason she lost another member of her small, odd circle of friends.

"Then why am I here?"

"To keep *me* from hitting Burroughs. And to favor me with some advice about how I can be rid of him without making Sophia suspicious."

Keating narrowed his eyes. "A shame Burroughs wasn't the one to fall into the river."

"It's early days yet. Anything could happen."

TWELVE

Adam took his customary seat at the head of the dining room table, noting that Sophia sat between Keating and the mostly harmless Francis Henning. Good. Burroughs, on the other hand, had moved to the far end of the table close by Eustace. Whether he'd moved simply to distance himself from Sophia, or to signal some sort of alliance with the pointy-nosed brigade, Adam didn't know. But he meant to discover the answer.

"If I may say so, Miss Sophia, you look stunning tonight," Henning said, offering her a toast.

Several other men, all unmarried, Adam noticed, raised their own glasses to her and muttered their agreement. Adam wanted to toast her, as well, since stroking his hands along her curves was momentarily out of the question. She'd donned the deep crimson gown he'd ordered for her, the one he'd demanded to see fabric samples for to be certain it would perfectly complement her hair. Now she looked like flame and fire, vibrant and laughing and the most alive person in the room.

To keep from staring, he bent his head and concentrated on his roast turkey. Henning, Timmerlane, and Lassiter had found four of the surviving gobblers and brought them down, though he'd been halfway to hoping that they would successfully escape their fate.

Someone tapped a glass, the sound cutting through the conversation and laughter, and Adam looked up again. And narrowed his eyes as Aubrey Burroughs stood, his wineglass in hand.

"A toast," Burroughs said with a broad smile as everyone quieted. "To our host, His Grace, the Duke of Greaves, for so generously sharing his bounty."

"His Grace," the guests affirmed, lifting their own glasses in his direction and then drinking.

Burroughs was a clever bastard. Adam couldn't attack him now without looking petty—and jealous. It would appear precisely as Aubrey likely intended, that something he didn't want to share had been taken.

Swearing silently, Adam glanced at Sophia, to find her fair cheeks even whiter than usual. His anger deepened. Sophia didn't know that he'd been informed about her conversation with Burroughs. What did she make of the toast, then? That Aubrey was attempting to leave clues about her sharing her own bounty with his male guests? That seemed the most likely explanation.

Distressing Sophia was not allowed. He stood.

Before he could charge around the table to plow into Burroughs, Camille Blackwood gave a small, surprised yelp and shot to her feet. "I have a toast, as well," she said in an unsteady voice, sparing a quick, annoyed glare at her husband still seated beside her.

Because a female had risen, every man present was then obligated to do the same. Burroughs wasn't the only clever fellow at the table. And Keating was proving to be a better friend than Aubrey had ever managed to be.

"What is your toast, Mrs. Blackwood?" Lassiter asked with a lazy smile, as everyone lifted their glasses.

She looked at Keating again, and he put an arm around her. "May I, my love?" he asked.

"Certainly. In fact, I insist."

He grinned. "To good friends. A growing circle of good friends."

The echo of his words was drowned out by Sophia's delighted shriek. "*Your* growing circle?" she demanded, grabbing Camille's free hand and bringing it to her chest.

Camille nodded, finally smiling. "Yes."

Sophia hugged her friend. The Hart sisters, to their credit, began applauding, offering their own good wishes, as did Lady Caroline. Though Eustace's end of the table for the most part remained subdued, he was likely the only one to notice that in the general wave of congratulations.

With a grin of his own, he walked around the table to clap Keating on the shoulder. "Well done, Blackwood."

"Thank you." Keating grabbed him by the arm, pulling him closer. "Calm down," he murmured. "I don't have any more surprises up my sleeve."

"He wasn't supposed to mention this one until I had a chance to tell Sophia privately," his wife chimed in sweetly.

Still smiling, her joy obvious, Sophia leaned up to kiss Keating on one cheek. "Never mind that. I am so happy f—"

"Dash it! You clumsy oaf!"

Adam looked beyond Sophia. Burroughs backed away from the table, his impeccably tailored brown jacket and black and brown waistcoat covered with the remains of a turkey dinner. Beside him, Udgell held an empty plate and swatted a napkin at the mess, smearing it in further.

"I beg your pardon, Mr. Burroughs," he rumbled, his face as impassive as usual. "An unforgivable mistake."

"Yes, it is unforgivable!" Aubrey snapped around to pin Adam with a glare. "You should do better than hire apes to serve you."

In the entire fifteen years of Udgell's service, Adam

had never known the butler to drop anything. Ever. "To the kitchen, Udgell," he said mildly, hiding an abrupt urge to smile. "Go and change your clothes, Burroughs. It's not the fall of Rome."

Evidently the affection and loyalty his servants felt for Sophia went even deeper than he'd realized. And Udgell was getting a damned Christmas bonus.

"What says everyone to a game of snapdragon?" Adam asked, strolling into the drawing room with the rest of his male guests on his heels. The faint scent of cigars and port touched Sophia a moment later.

Camille, seated on the couch beside her, clapped her hands. "I haven't played snapdragon in ages!"

Sophia had heard of the game, of course, but she'd never played it herself. Rising, she pulled Cammy to her feet as two footmen moved furniture out of the middle of the room and set a plain wooden table in the cleared area. A third footman arrived with a large, shallow porcelain bowl in his hands, while a fourth carried a smaller bowl of raisins and a decanter of warmed brandy.

Adam took the bowl of raisins, then produced a small black button from his pocket. "Whoever finds this button," he said, showing it off, "will receive a boon from me."

"An estate?" Drymes asked with a grin.

"Your damned horse," someone whose name she didn't know stated.

As everyone began suggesting outrageous gifts, laughing and talking over each other, Adam lifted his hand. Without him having to say a word, the room quieted. For a moment Sophia wondered what it would be like to have everyone hanging on her every word and commanding everyone's attention with a single gesture. Adam did it effortlessly. Even when he was sitting or standing or skating on ice, he drew everyone's attention. He certainly drew her attention.

"I see that I need to be more specific," he drawled. "Whoever finds the button," he repeated, "will receive *this* boon."

Another footman approached, a small mahogany box held carefully in both hands. When he stopped in front of his master, Adam opened the box's lid, reached in, and withdrew a delicate silver chain. At the end of the chain, sparkling in the chandelier light, hung a splendid, perfect diamond. It spun slowly, as large as a chestnut and worth more than she could earn in three years at the Tantalus. In five years, even.

Adam put the diamond back and shut the box lid again. "Do you accept the challenge?"

In response to the chorus of "yes," he ceremoniously dropped the button into the bowl of raisins and swirled his finger through it. "Queue up, one line to each side of the table. You get two attempts, and then move to the back of the line for your next go-round."

The footman with the brandy poured it into the shallow bowl, and Adam liberally sprinkled the hundreds of raisins all across the flat bottom. The same footman lit a touchwood in the fireplace, while the others went about putting out all the candles in the large room. In the near total darkness, Adam took the touchwood.

"Best of luck," he said, and lit the brandy.

Blue flames poured out over the top of the bowl, eerie and beautiful in the darkness. The faces immediately around the bowl took on a blue cast, like Christmas ghosts in the stories she'd read as a child.

And then, one by one, their owners giggling and challenging each other, hands darted into the bowl, emerged covered with blue flame, and popped the burning raisins into their mouths. "Oh, my goodness," she breathed.

"It ain't as hot as it looks," Mr. Henning supplied from behind her. "The trick is to get the fire out before the brandy burns off."

Ahead of them Sylvia Hart yelped, covering her mouth with one hand. "That stung," she exclaimed, lowering her hand again and laughing.

Well, if Sylvia Hart could withstand it, then so could she. With someone chanting "Button, button, who'll get the button?," her line swiftly advanced. With the lights out, it was difficult to distinguish countesses from Tantalus girls until they were directly in front of the bowl, and that felt . . . nice. She could join in the laughter and playful taunts without being cut or ignored or glared at for presuming to mingle with her betters.

Then it was her turn. She'd been watching the others, so she took a breath and slipped her hand into the bowl. Heat crackled along her fingers, noticeable, but not painful. She grabbed a raisin, lifted out her flaming, brandy-covered hand, and popped it into her mouth.

Hard and smooth landed on her tongue. *The button.* She half choked, stunned, and spat it out surreptitiously under the pretense of coughing. Damnation. This would never do. Taking a towel, she wiped off her hand while keeping the button hidden between two fingers.

Thinking fast, Sophia dipped her hand back into the bowl for her second attempt. She opened her fingers, dropping the button. In the same motion she scooped up a raisin and closed her mouth around the blue flame. Then, forcing a laugh, she moved around to the rear of the queue.

A hand closed over her mouth, another around her shoulders, and pulled her backward.

"Shh," Adam breathed before she could muster enough breath for a squawk, and she relaxed a little as he towed her out the drawing room door.

"You frightened me half to death," she whispered, smacking him on the arm when he released her.

"What were you doing in there?" he murmured back. She couldn't see his face, but his voice had a flatness to it that didn't sound at all amused.

"Playing snapdragon. I've never done so before."

"You found the button."

Blast it all. "I did not."

"I was watching, my dear. You may be adept at sleight-of-hand, but so am I. Explain yourself."

How in the world was she supposed to explain this to someone like him? For a moment she occupied herself with wiping the remains of the brandy off her fingers. "I weighed the value of the diamond against what everyone else here would say and think and expect, the suspicions about my honesty and my relationship to you, and the question of how I would explain such a thing to my vicar of a spouse. The diamond weighed less, so I put it back."

Her eyes began slowly to adjust, so that she could just make out the deep scowl on his face and the way he loomed over her. He would not, however, make her feel like a naughty schoolgirl caught knotting a rival's hair ribbons. Sophia lifted her chin.

"I thought you didn't care about my other guests' opinions," he said almost soundlessly.

"I don't. I *do* care what trouble they can make for me, now and later. If gossip turns me into a thief, that could hurt the reputation of The Tantalus Club. I did not agree to Hennessy's terms for leaving in order to injure the club by my own actions."

Someone in the drawing room began cheering, the sound swiftly followed by groans and a few irritated-sounding whistles. He turned his head to listen, then looked back at her again. "This is not acceptable."

"It's the way it is. Now go give the prize to the winner."

Adam cupped her face in his hands and kissed her, openmouthed. "Don't tell me what to do," he breathed, and vanished back into the drawing room.

Sophia sagged against the wall in the darkness. Until she heard him deliver the diamond to whoever had found the button, she wasn't going back in there. If he began some nonsense about who the boon truly belonged to, she was running.

Yes, it would have been a lovely bauble, and she could have sold it and put the money in her account. An additional wardrobe or a carriage, or something else she would never be able to make use of in Cornwall, paid for. It simply wasn't worth it.

"Ah, Lady Caroline. Your boon," Adam's voice came, and she relaxed, pushing upright again. Thank goodness. And the diamond was going to the woman Adam would select for marriage, as it should. She could almost ignore the uncomfortable, heated jealousy at the mere thought of it, if she tried very hard.

As the servants lit the candles again, she slipped back into the room. Someone proposed a game of charades, which she sat and watched. She'd attempted charades once at school, only to have her supposed teammates refuse to guess what her motions signified. It would only be worse here. And with Mr. Burroughs in the room, she didn't care to make herself the center of attention, even for a game. Not tonight, anyway.

Lady Caroline pranced about the room, the diamond hanging from her throat. When Camille took a seat and made a face behind her hand, Sophia laughed. "She's pleased with herself. There's nothing wrong with that."

"It was purely chance. Someone had to win. I thought ladies knew how to be gracious in loss or in victory."

"Oh, let her dance about. *You* have the better news, Cammy."

Camille grinned. "I'm so sorry Keating blurted it out like that. I wanted to tell you on Christmas Eve, when I asked you to be the child's godmother."

Her breath stopped. "Me?" she whispered, a chill running down to her toes. "I can't. I can't even imagine what the vicar would make of taking in the child of Camille and Keating Blackwood." She shuddered. What if she should have a child of her own? Would the Reverend Loines punish it for being hers? For her sins?

"You would manage, if necessary. Given my parents' reaction to me and to Keating, I don't want them responsible for a son or daughter of mine if something should happen to us. I trust you, Sophia." She sighed. "Consider it, will you, my dear? Please?"

The idea of it sent her heart into her throat. At the same time, she knew what it was like to be raised in a household that felt inconvenienced and ashamed merely because of her presence. Slowly, Sophia nodded. For his own sake, the vicar had best keep his hands and his words to himself where a child was concerned. Any child. "I will do it. Just promise me that nothing will happen to you and Keating."

Cammy hugged her arm. "That is my intention. Thank you. I feel better now."

"And I need a breath of air." Kissing her friend on the cheek, Sophia stood. "You should go to bed, too."

"Oh, don't start fussing over me. Keating's already been driving me mad."

"Mm-hm. Good night."

"Good night, Sophia."

A few of the other guests were also making their way upstairs, and she feigned adjusting her shoe for a moment until she wouldn't have to pretend not to notice that no one was speaking to her. Even with her caution, though, a trio of women remained in the hallway as she topped the stairs. Considering how poorly her day had gone, with the notable exception of a rather splendid kiss and the terror of being named a godmother, she wasn't even surprised.

"That's a lovely gown," one of them said, looking over at her.

"Thank you, Lady Fiona," she answered, inclining her head.

"It's a bit pretentious of you, though, don't you think, to wear such a scandalous color simply because it complements your hair?"

"Not that that garish hair is worth celebrating," one of the others commented.

Sophia kept the faint smile on her face. "I appreciate your concern, but as my hair came from my mother and I borrowed this gown from the late Duchess of Greaves's wardrobe, I can only assume you meant to insult them." She curtsied. "Good evening."

The third woman, Claire, the Marchioness of Hayforth, furrowed her brow. "Wherever you acquired that gown, it wasn't from Juliana Baswich. She detested red. Everyone knows that, dear. You need to compose better lies."

Given what Sophia knew of the late duchess, that made sense. Where in the world had Milly found it, then? If she hadn't been so taken with the color and the way it so perfectly went with her hair, she would have realized that. Milly would have some explaining to do in the morning.

Sophia stifled a sigh as she reached her bedchamber and opened the door. The dress could have come from an actress and she wouldn't have cared; she would have been grateful, as she remained, to have the use of it. But if she owed someone a favor—and her thanks—she needed to know it.

Her box of knitting sat at the back of the wardrobe, and she brought it out to set by the chair closest to the fireplace. A woolen scarf had seemed a good idea at the time, but that had been before the Duke of Greaves began handing out diamonds as party favors.

With a curse she'd learned from the Marquis of St. Aubyn after a particularly unlucky hand of faro, she pulled out Adam's scarf and resumed her knitting. Whether he would appreciate it or not, she wanted to make this effort to give him a gift.

After only half an hour and subsequent to pulling out her third row of loops to begin it over again, she set the scarf aside. She hated feeling melancholy, and with nothing to do but stare at yarn, she couldn't escape it. Her borrowed boots had been cleaned and stood beside the wardrobe, and she slipped out of her simple brown mules to step into them.

Adam's boyhood jacket was warm and heavy, and she shrugged into it over her lovely and scandalous scarlet gown. Depending on who this dress actually belonged to, perhaps she could arrange to purchase it. She would only be able to wear it in private, when her husband was out calling on his parishioners or some such thing, but she felt so . . . fiery and alive with it draped about her.

Her hair was still up in its pins, so she settled for tying an old scarf over her ears to protect them from the cold. Then she opened her door—and nearly ran into Adam.

He stood with his hand raised to knock, his expression going from slightly amused to quizzical as he took in her attire. "Where are you going?" he asked in a low voice.

"I needed some fresh air. Just a short walk in the garden."

With a quick glance at the warm room behind her, he frowned. "You do know it's nearly one o'clock in the morning."

"I'll borrow a lantern."

Most of the time she couldn't tell what Adam Baswich might be thinking, but this time she wasn't surprised when he held out his arm. "I'll go with you."

Sophia shook her head. "You don't have a coat."

He smiled, his lips curving in a way that made her want to kiss them. "Stop arguing, will you?" he murmured, taking her hand and placing it over his dark brown sleeve.

Giving in, she stepped the rest of the way into the hallway and shut her door behind her. There was certainly no need to alert anyone that she wasn't in bed. A few candles were still lit here and there, and she thought she heard male voices coming from the billiards room. Abruptly she wondered if one of them was Aubrey Burrough's voice, and what tale he might be spinning about her.

The servants' stairs at the rear of the east wing were empty, and she put her free hand on one wall to guide herself down. At the far end of the quiet kitchen, Adam took down what looked like a footman's overcoat from the rack by the door and pulled it on. His shoulders were broader than whoever owned the garment and he couldn't fasten it, but at least it would provide some protection for him. All she needed was to cause the Duke of Greaves to catch a chill.

"I don't think we need a lantern," he noted as they stepped outside. A three-quarters moon glinted through a thin layer of clouds, turning the snow silver.

Somewhere out beyond the trees a fox yelped. It was an old, lonely sound, and Sophia moved in closer to

Adam. She couldn't help herself. He'd become honey, and she the bee. Whatever this had begun as—a novelty, a friendship, a protest against a lonely future—being in his company now seemed . . . vital. Necessary to her continued happiness and her sanity.

If for no other reason than that, she should likely stop it. If she'd learned anything during the course of her life, it was to seize happiness where she could find it, and be just as ready to see it gone again. When she couldn't imagine seeing it gone, she was clearly stepping into a great deal of trouble and heartbreak. At the same time, she'd never known a bee to voluntarily swear off honey. Trouble was for later. Adam was for now.

"Well, this is refreshing," Adam noted, his breath fogging in the air.

That made her grin. "You volunteered to come out here. Stop complaining."

He lifted an eyebrow, amusement making his gray eyes dance. "And you have such a reputation for being good-natured and sunny. People have no idea, do they?"

This moment was perfect. She gazed up at his face, wanting to memorize everything about it—the cold, the warmth of his sleeve, the silver moonlight tipping his black hair, the crunch of their boots in the snow. "No, they don't," she said aloud.

"And are you going to tell me now why you so desperately needed a breath of fresh air?"

"All the usual reasons," she returned, shifting her grip to his hand and doing half a dance step around him. He pulled her back in, drawing her up against his chest and bending his head to kiss her.

Desire stirred through her, hot and welcome. But unless she was very much mistaken, she was nearly treading on another woman's toes. If nothing else could manage to turn her toward reality, that should do it. It was one thing to see herself hurt. It was quite another to cause someone else pain. "I have a query," she said, meeting his gaze as he straightened.

"That can't be good." Taking her hand again, he led her along the dark path between bare sticks and snow-covered shrubbery to the empty fountain at the center of the garden. He sat on the bench facing the wild sea crea-tures fleeing from the frozen, trident-wielding Poseidon at the center of the fountain, and pulled her down beside him. "I have a question or two for you, as well, but ladies first."

Their two hands, his fingers twining and untwining with hers, fascinated her. "Lady Caroline Emery," she said.

His expression didn't change, but his eyes cooled just a little, enough to remind her that people generally didn't question him. "I know who she is, but that isn't a question," he murmured.

"Being direct isn't a great difficulty for me, Adam, if you're merely attempting to delay answering me."

"Perhaps I only wish to hear you ask the question," the duke returned.

"Very well." She drew in a slow breath. It *was* a difficult thing to say, mostly because she preferred that the circumstance of his marriage, of her marriage, didn't exist in the first place. Then she could simply remain at Greaves Park with him forever. "Have you or have you not settled on Lady Caroline to be your duchess?"

A gust of wind shook ice out of the tree in front of them, and it tinkled like glass as it hit the branches and fell to the snow below. "I have lately begun to think that Caroline Emery would be the most suited to that posi-tion," he finally said, his tone clearly reluctant. "Very insightful of you."

"She's pretty. I knew it couldn't be either one of the Hart sisters: They make my head ache. And most of the others are far too flighty and nervous for you."

"I concur." He kept his gaze on the house as lights went out one by one. "However, I haven't asked her yet."

She pulled her hand free, fighting against the sensation that the ground had begun spinning beneath her feet. "What's the delay? You need to become better acquainted with her, Adam."

"Why? Evidently I'll have a lifetime to do so. And I have a good idea that I know all I need to about her, anyway." He stood again.

Sophia rose as well. Perfect moments were short-lived. "You're going to be changing her life. And yours. You owe it to both of you to at least become friends."

"I have enough friends." He reached over and brushed a strand of hair from her face.

"But t—"

"If you begin advising me on the merits of knowing a future spouse, I will do the same thing to you." He stepped closer. "I mean, have you ever spoken a word with your vicar? Do you even know his Christian name?"

Sophia retreated the same two steps that he advanced. "No, I don't. I do know that Hennessy chose him, with the idea of keeping me away from London and anyone with a wagging tongue. And I know that Hennessy told me how very seriously the Reverend Loines views sin and sinners. I don't need to know any more than that."

Adam closed on her again. "Then stop telling me to proceed any differently."

Well, he had a point. But it wasn't the same. He had the opportunity to choose the most tolerable of spouses, while she'd had the least tolerable of all chosen for her.

"Then don't become acquainted with her. Either way, there is now an obligation between the two of you. And I am not stepping into that kind of mess."

He reached out for her hand again, but she moved out of the way. His expression darkening, he stopped. "I am not married yet. And neither are you. And this is still our last, best holiday to do as we please. Now come here."

This time she let him catch her hand and tug her closer. "I can't help noticing that the end of the holiday keeps approaching. Running forward, in fact. And I don't want to hurt her."

"She's already acquainted with several of my former . . . companions. I daresay she already knows I'm spending my evenings with someone else."

Shaking her head, she tucked herself against him, inside his borrowed coat. "I do not understand aristocrats," she muttered. "I can't even wear a red gown without being accused of impropriety and lying, I can't even be left to live a simple life above a gentlemen's club, and a woman whose parents happen to be married can win a diamond, marry a duke, smile at his mistresses, and have tea with bishops."

"There are no bishops here. Trust me on that."

She sent him a glare. "You know what I mean."

"You could have won the diamond, so I don't actually think you can put that on her head."

Glowering, she circled the silent fountain. "No, I couldn't have won the diamond." She rubbed her chilled hands together. "I'm finished complaining now. Shall we go inside?"

Adam held out his hand and she took it, twining her fingers again with his. "How are you a liar for wearing a red dress?" he asked, starting back up the path beside her.

Oh, she probably shouldn't have mentioned that, dash

it all. The last thing she wanted was to bring his parents into what was finally becoming a pleasant evening. "It was nothing. Just some of the ladies making certain I know my place."

Her hand still caught in his, Adam stopped. "Not good enough. Who said what to you? Precisely."

"Adam."

He shook his head. "I'll keep you out here until we both freeze, or you can answer my question. I leave the choice to you."

That wasn't much of a choice. There were drawbacks to having as a dear, dear friend a man who demanded to know all the facts of everything. "For heaven's sake. Milly found this gown for me, and said it came from your mother's old wardrobe. When I mentioned where I'd acquired it, Lady Hayforth merely pointed out that Juliana Baswich would never wear red. So Milly must have been mistaken over whose old wardrobe she was pilfering. That's all."

"I'll accept that. And no, I don't believe my mother would ever wear red. Wherever that dress came from, however, you wear it well. Exceptionally well."

Sophia grinned. "Thank you, Your Grace."

"You also look exceptionally nice wearing nothing at all. Or so I recall. I'll have to see you naked again to be certain."

That made her laugh, and she put her free hand across her mouth to try to muffle the sound. Whatever happened tomorrow or the next day, wherever or with whomever they were forced to be, at this moment she was exactly where she wanted to be, and with whom she *wanted* to be.

She shifted closer to him, and he tucked her in against his shoulder, kissing her hair as he did so. Because out there alone in the frozen garden beneath the moonlight she felt that magic again, that sensation of not quite being part of the world, and she could admit to one more thing.

Just to herself she could admit that she loved Adam Baswich, the Duke of Greaves. And she knew that was a disaster, for every possible reason imaginable.

THIRTEEN

At the door to Sophia's bedchamber, she abruptly lurched forward ahead of him into her room. Whipping around to face him, she caught hold of the door. "Wait here," she whispered, and closed the door on him.

With anyone else, Adam would have been annoyed. Supremely annoyed. No one kept him waiting, and no one shut a door on his face. With Sophia, however, he was mostly curious about what the deuce she was doing in there. And so he waited outside her door, wondering who was most likely to stumble across him standing there, and what he would say to shut them up.

The door opened again. When he didn't move, she eyed him. "Well? Come in before someone sees you."

He walked into the room, and she swiftly closed the door behind him. Nothing looked different, up to and including her clothing; whatever she'd been doing in there, it hadn't been redecorating. Or pulling off that dress, for which he was grateful. He wanted to do that himself.

His borrowed footman's greatcoat had been left behind in the kitchen, so he sat in one of the chairs before the fireplace as Sophia divested herself of her coat and boots. Mrs. Orling the seamstress had outdone herself. If this all hadn't been a secret, he could likely have half the chits in London purchasing her skills.

Finally Sophia padded over to him in her bare feet

and gracefully draped herself onto his lap. "If we're ignoring the inevitable, I think you should kiss me," she said, her light green eyes glinting emerald in the firelight.

"I would be amenable to that," he returned, sliding an arm around her waist as he lowered his mouth over hers. His sprite, who refused diamonds because the bauble would bring her attention and more trouble than its sale would alleviate. His heart, who wore trousers with the same joy she did the most elegant and expensive gowns in the north of England. His peace, who'd soothed his soul as no one else had ever been able to do.

One by one he pulled the pins from her hair, until the heavy waves fell in a glorious scarlet cascade through his fingers and down her back. The fire added bronze and gold to the color, alive and lush and mesmerizing. Fisting his hand in the waves, he gently pulled her head back, baring her throat to his kisses.

She untied his cravat and dropped it to the floor, then leaned in to run her tongue along the curve of his ear. Just the lemon scent of her intoxicated him. It was ridiculous that he couldn't simply claim her in public and order every other male who looked in her direction to keep their distance because she belonged to him.

Except that she didn't. She belonged to some faceless vicar who would only try to kill everything joyous about her. Adam placed a palm on her ankle and slid it slowly up her leg, drawing her skirt with him as he ascended. If Hennessy hadn't specified that anything other than a wedding would spell both her ruin and that of The Tantalus Club, the Reverend Loines might well find himself in the Royal Navy and on his way to the Orient. It couldn't be wrong simply to want to protect her, and to make certain no one else but him ever touched her.

Sophia wiggled her bottom, grinding across his

aroused, constricted member, then grinned. "This is a very comfortable chair, isn't it?" she asked, her breath hitching.

"I'm glad you think so, because we aren't going anywhere."

He lifted her, and she swung her left leg over, straddling him. Catching her mouth in another deep, tongue-tangling kiss, at the same time he slid his hand between her legs and pressed a finger up inside her. She was damp and hot and doing the most exquisite wriggling, and it took him a moment to brace himself against her soft assault.

While she unbuttoned his waistcoat, he went to work on the buttons at the back of her gown. "Lift your arms," he ordered once he had that done. She complied, and he drew the silk and lace over her head and dropped it to the floor.

Immediately he pulled her forward, taking her left breast into his mouth and sucking. With a gasp she dug her fingers into his scalp, and in response to that he flicked his tongue across her nipple.

"You are a very naughty man," she groaned, gasping as his fingers entered her again.

Adam grinned up at her, and moved his attention to her right breast, shifting his fingers at the same time. "Should I stop?"

"Oh! Oh, definitely not. In fact . . ." She reached between her legs, pushing his hand out of the way and opening the fastenings of his trousers.

When he lifted his hips a little, she pushed his pants down to his thighs. Because she clearly knew by now that he tended to arrive at her door prepared, she reached into his pocket for a French condom and tied it in place. "Very impressive," he noted, his jaw clenched against the tugging and pulling on his cock. "You didn't even look."

"I have you memorized," she breathed, sinking down on him until he was deeply inside her.

That seemed a profoundly resplendent thing to say—not about his body, but about her regard for him. His ability to think about it logically, however, was severely impaired at the moment. She lifted half off him, and he pushed up with his hips as she lowered herself again.

"Mm," she chuckled breathlessly, and grabbed his open waistcoat to shove it in bumps and starts off his shoulders.

When she sat forward to kiss him, he shut his eyes, reveling in the sensation of her. Then her warm hands slid up under his shirt, caressing his shoulders and running down his chest to pinch his nipples. *Sweet Lucifer.* Adam groaned, moving his own hands to her hips. Increasing his pace, he pulled her down over his rising hips again and again.

With a loud moan, she caught his mouth again. As he felt her come, he shoved up hard into her, bringing himself to climax and joining her.

Sophia sagged against his chest, sliding her arms over his shoulders and lowering her head against his neck. He held still, taking her weight, and wishing he could take on all her burdens so easily. While he appreciated irony, he didn't find the way he held no sway over what he most cherished in life terribly amusing.

Finally she took a deep breath and straightened. "Are you in a pleasant mood?"

"I am now."

She kissed him. "Good. I need to ask you something."

His heart skittered, but he kept his expression carefully neutral. "I'm listening."

"Don't be angry."

That didn't sound very promising. "I'll make an attempt," he hedged.

Making a face, she climbed off him and picked up her pretty dress. Carefully she folded it and set it across the opposite chair. "Your servants," she said, walking naked and lovely to climb beneath the covers of her bed.

Adam pulled off his boots and shrugged the rest of the way out of his trousers. "What about my servants?" he asked, disposing of the condom and sending his shirt after his trousers.

"They adore you."

He crossed the room and slid beneath the blankets beside her. "I pay them. I pay for their loyalty."

"Don't be so cynical. Everyone at least attempts to pay their servants enough to be assured of their discretion. Loyalty is different." She snuggled up against him, her back to his front.

"Why are we discussing loyalty, then?" he murmured, putting an arm around her waist and tucking her hand into his. He liked holding her hand; it was actually a new experience for him. Previously he'd never cared for the sensation. It made him feel trapped. With her, however, it gave him a sense of connection. Of not being alone.

"I think you should reward their loyalty by giving them a very nice bonus for Christmas," she said, her voice sleepy.

After he'd seen Udgell dump food all over Aubrey Burroughs earlier, he'd been thinking the same thing himself. And yet, he didn't need—didn't like—other people telling him what to do. Last year when Eustace had suggested he sack one of his grooms for some offense or other, he'd told her in no uncertain terms to stay out of his bloody business.

"How much do you recommend?" he asked, mostly to hear what she would say.

"Ten pounds each," she returned promptly, and yawned.

"That's quite a bonus." If he gave out that amount and any other households learned of it, there was likely to be a riot across Mayfair. Hm. That could actually be amusing. "I'll see to it. With something additional for Udgell."

"And for Milly Brooks."

"And for Mrs. Brooks," he echoed. Clearly she was nearly asleep, and he took a breath, mentally crossing his fingers. If she told him what had transpired with Aubrey, he could openly take action. "It was a shame Burroughs's nice jacket was ruined at dinner," he ventured.

"And his trousers," she put in, and snorted. "It's a shame no one dropped the snapdragon bowl on his lap."

"Did his lap offend you, then?"

Sophia sighed. "He's very full of appreciation for himself. It's tiresome." With that, her breathing slowly deepened and leveled out.

Damnation. Even when someone injured her, she shrugged it off her shoulders. It was exasperating, and at the same time he felt . . . proud to know her. Proud that she considered him not just a lover, but a friend.

All he needed to do now was figure out how to be rid of Mr. Loines, save the Tantalus, and remove her from her father's influence—and somehow keep her in his life while he planned his own bloody wedding.

Cornwall in the winter would be at least three days there and three days back—a week, at least, once he'd hunted down this Loines fellow. He would miss Christmas, he would miss days with Sophia, and he would be taking a chance on offending not only Caroline, but all the other chits he'd invited to attempt to win his hand. Damnation.

He could send Keating, but there was half a chance that Blackwood would refuse to leave his wife on their first Christmas together, and he wasn't about to risk a pregnant woman—or losing Sophia's main allies here in an increasingly unfriendly house. Sliding carefully from beneath Sophia, Adam sat on the edge of the bed.

The list of men he trusted to meet with the vicar, to determine whether he could be kinder than Hennessy had portrayed him, whether he would be someone worthy of Sophia's warmth and wit or could be . . . persuaded toward the light, as it were, was very short. Nonexistent, in fact. Or rather, almost nonexistent.

Swearing beneath his breath, Adam rose, pulled a spare blanket from the back of a chair and shrugged it over his shoulders, and padded barefoot to the room's small writing desk. Finding paper and ink, he moved over to the table beneath the window and cracked the curtains to make use of the moonlight.

There was a time when he'd considered Oliver Warren, the Marquis of Haybury, his closest, dearest friend. And then because of his own inflated sense of importance and a large degree of shortsightedness, he'd destroyed the friendship and nearly destroyed the man, himself. But Oliver was one of Sophia's employers now, the co-owner of The Tantalus Club. And because he knew Sophia, he would have to care what happened to her. It was impossible not to.

Swiftly he wrote out the note, emphasizing the importance to Sophia rather than to himself, hoping Haybury would do a favor for one if not for the other of them. Then he pulled the bell for a servant, handed the missive and his instruction over at the quiet scratch on the door, and returned to the warm bed. If he couldn't outright save her, perhaps he could at least make her path easier. It didn't seem adequate, but at the moment all he owned was hope and a rapidly spinning pocket watch. Time was running out—for both of them.

* * *

Sometime later he awoke to the sound of curtains opening. "Good morning, Soph— Oh, good gracious! Your
Grace!"

Adam snapped his eyes open. Mrs. Brooks, his
housekeeper and Sophia's maid, stood at the edge of the
bed, her hands in the midst of stripping off the blankets.
At the same moment Sophia lurched upright beside him.

"Release the sheets and step back, Mrs. Brooks," he
stated.

She squawked a few more times, but belatedly backed
away from the bed. "I apologize, Your Grace. I certainly
didn't intend—Oh, heavens. And Sophia. Miss White.
You're well, yes? I could—I—"

"I'm perfectly fine, Milly," Sophia answered, the
stirrings of amusement in her voice. "Thank you for
your concern." Then she thwacked him on the arm.
"Say something reassuring."

Inwardly shaking his head at the abuse she heaped
on his shoulders and that he continued to tolerate, Adam
made certain the blankets remained tucked around his
hips, and then sat up straighter. Evidently he was about
to test the loyalty Sophia claimed his servants felt for
him. "Please give us twenty minutes, Mrs. Brooks," he
said in his mildest tone. "And I shall trust to your discretion."

The housekeeper curtsied so deeply that for a moment he wondered whether she would be able to return
upright. "You may rely on me, Your Grace. I shan't
breathe a word." She backed toward the door. "I brought
you a cup of tea, Soph— Miss White, just as you like it."
With a last squawk she vanished through the door and
closed it behind her.

"I thought you locked that," he commented, lying
back again.

Sophia flopped across his chest to kiss him. "So did
I. What time is it?"

Nudging her head aside, he lifted up a little to look at the small clock on the mantel. With the curtains open, he could just make out the hands against the white background. "Damnation. It's past nine o'clock."

They were going to be seen. *He* was going to be seen, still wearing his evening clothes and leaving her bedchamber. Swearing again, Adam slid to the edge of the bed and stood, striding over to grab up his trousers.

"You can't allow Lady Caroline to see you here."

Still fastening the front of his breeches, he looked over at her. Sophia sat on the edge of the bed, her disheveled hair covering her breasts and making her look very like a lithe version of Botticelli's painting of Venus rising from the clamshell. "I told you that she knows I'm not a virgin."

"It's one thing to know a thing, and a very different one to actually see the evidence of it." She stood, going to her wardrobe and pulling on a shift. "And we need to stop doing this."

"I have no idea why Lady Caroline's feelings concern you," he retorted, beginning to be bothered that she couldn't even be stirred enough to be jealous. They were discussing his future with another woman, after all.

"Because they do."

She actually approached to button his waistcoat and tie a loose knot in his wilted cravat, which he accepted as proof that she wasn't angry. Even so, he caught hold of her arm and pulled her up against his front to kiss her. "Will you go ice fishing with us today?"

"I have a few things to see to."

He frowned. Whatever might be best for any and all concerned, he had no intention of giving her up. Not yet. "Which things?"

"It's two days before Christmas. Don't ask so many questions."

When she smiled, he finally relaxed a little. "Don't tell me what to do," he responded, kissing her again.

The door rattled and then inched open. "May I come in?" Mrs. Brooks whispered, only the tip of her nose visible.

"Of course," Sophia answered, as though she was surprised that any servant would stop to ask permission to enter their employer's private rooms.

The housekeeper slipped through the narrow opening, no small feat for a woman of her breadth, and closed the door again. "Your Grace, Udgell and Evans just began a very loud disagreement in the foyer. Everyone's hurried to the front stairs to see. The hallway and back stairs are presently empty."

"I asked for your discretion, Mrs. Brooks."

Milly flushed, straightened to her full height. "I didn't mention your name, Your Grace. All I said was that Sophia needed a distraction and the back steps cleared."

Hm. With a slight grin, Adam walked forward, pausing to catch Sophia's arm as he did so. "Evidently *you* have my servants' loyalty," he murmured, and released her again. "Thank you, Mrs. Brooks."

"Of course, Your Grace."

The moment Adam left the room, Sophia sat down at her dressing table. "Thank heaven for you, Milly," she said feelingly. "I do *not* want any of those other women thinking I stole Adam from them or something. Especially Lady Caroline."

The housekeeper plunked herself down onto a chair by the fire. "Oh, mercy. I thought for certain he would sack me."

Alarmed, Sophia rose again and hurried over to hug Milly. "I would never allow someone to be let go because of me. Don't fret. I should have warned you to be cautious when you came into my room."

Milly patted her arm. "You're the brightest soul to

be under this roof in a very long time, my dear. Perhaps that's why the duke favors you. This has never been a happy place, until now."

Well, that was a very nice thing to say. And even though pushing him away was the wiser thing to do, she was very content to have him disagree with that. Any time she could spend with Adam was welcome. It wouldn't last forever, after all.

That last thought hurt even more keenly than it usually did, but she tried to set it aside as something over which she had no control. Rolling her shoulders, she sat at her dressing table. "Thank you for saying so, Milly. By the by, where did you truly get that scarlet gown I wore last night?"

"The red one? I told you. I found it in an old wardrobe of Her Grace's."

"You couldn't have, because the duchess never wore red."

Milly dropped the hairbrush and bent to pick it up again. "Perhaps it belonged to Lady Wallace, then."

Sophia turned around to face her. "Both you and I know that Eustace Landen would never wear that gown, much less purchase it. And if it did belong to her, she certainly would have said something if she saw me wearing it." She glanced over at the pretty thing, still folded over the back of a chair. "And it's not matronly at all, now that I consider it. Aside from its being the very height of current fashion."

The housekeeper pushed on her shoulders to get her to sit again. "Is it? I hadn't noticed."

"Milly. Tell me the truth. You didn't purchase this gown for me, did you?"

"Yes," the servant blurted. "I bought it for you. As a Christmas gift."

"Milly! You must take it back, then! It must have been so expensive." Shock ran through her. That sensation, though, was swiftly followed by suspicion as she looked at the half-open wardrobe, filled—for the most part—with dresses that fit her to perfection. None of them were out of fashion, and all of them were sewn by an expert hand with a very keen sense of style.

"I will not take it back," the maid stated. "It doesn't fit me."

Sophia pulled away, standing to face the maid again. When Milly reached for a ribbon, she batted it out of the servant's fingers. Then, taking both of Milly's hands in hers, Sophia looked the stout woman in the eye. "The truth this time, Milly. Where did all these dresses come from? I won't be angry with you."

"Do you promise?"

"I promise."

The maid seemed to deflate. "They came from His Grace. When you needed that first gown, the green one, he sent word to Mrs. Simmons to have it made by Mrs. Orling, the seamstress in Hanlith. Once we knew it fit you, he kept ordering gowns and had me stash them about the house for us to find. Then when all the guests came I didn't want them finding any of the dresses and claiming them because they are *so* lovely, so I had to hide them in my room and invent where they were from. And I forgot the old duchess hated red."

It took a moment for Sophia to decipher and comprehend the torrent of words that tumbled from the housekeeper's mouth. "It was Adam? The entire time?"

"Yes. Oh, you promised you wouldn't be angry with me. It was all his idea. I'm only a housekeeper. And the way he fussed over getting the exact color he wanted for that red dress, I thought it would never get finished."

Goodness. She should be angry, she supposed, but not with Milly. After all, he'd asked to purchase a gown for her, and she'd refused. *And* she'd told him precisely why she didn't want him buying things for her. He'd gone behind her back and done it anyway. For heaven's sake, he'd even asked her where in the world she'd found some of the creations. And yet . . .

And yet.

If she made a fuss about it now, either to yell at him for deceiving her or to thank him for some of the loveliest things she'd ever owned, everyone would know—and that was precisely what she'd wanted to avoid all along. Clever, deceitful man. Generous, underhanded man. Wonderful, maddening man.

"Sophia?"

She sighed. "Mrs. Orling is very talented, despite her unnatural attachment to green yarn."

Milly chuckled. "That she is. It's a shame she's never been able to see you in any of them. It's always been her dream to dress a lady."

"I'm hardly a lady."

"Look at those dresses. She sees you as one."

That stopped her. Generally she wouldn't have viewed anyone erroneously elevating her above her station as complimenting her. But Milly clearly meant it as a compliment. And so did Mrs. Orling, evidently. For a long moment she looked at her reflection in the dressing mirror: oversized night rail sliding down one shoulder, and her hair in an artful tangle. "You know what, Milly?" she said aloud.

"What?"

"I think I should put on that lovely riding habit and ride into Hanlith to thank Mrs. Orling for working so swiftly and so well."

The housekeeper blanched. "But then His Grace will know that I told you!"

"He'll know that I figured it out—but only if he realizes where I'm going. I'm certainly not going to tell him."

Milly sighed, then went to pull the habit out of the wardrobe. "Well, I can't very well stop you, can I?"

"No. I run faster than you do."

The housekeeper laughed. "An original. That's what you are."

Yes, she was an original, Sophia decided. In whatever she chose to wear, and in whomever she chose to love. And no matter what became of that.

When she arrived downstairs for breakfast, the room smelled deliciously of chicken soup and fresh bread. Only Francis Henning was present, just finishing a bowl, and she took the seat beside him. Whatever people thought of Mr. Henning—and she knew that both his intellect and his wagering skills were frequently belittled—he'd never been anything but polite and kind to her.

"Ah, good morning, Miss Sophia," he said around a mouthful of bread.

"Mr. Henning. I thought I was the only one who overslept this morning."

"Damned Burroughs kept me up till nearly three o'clock playing billiards. I lost twenty blasted quid to him for the aggravation."

She smiled. "Well, I'm sorry for that, but I'm happy to have the company for breakfast."

He beamed. "So am I. Lucifer take him, anyway."

"Indeed," she returned, trying not to put too much feeling into the word.

Abruptly Francis scowled. "You ain't going riding this morning, are you? It's snowing, you know. And it's devilish cold."

The weather had come in quickly, then, after the pretty moon of last night. "I just need to make a quick trip into the village."

"Everyone was going ice fishing, or the men, anyway, but now they've all gone into the music room to sing carols. My grandmama says I've a splendid baritone, but I wouldn't be any kind of a gentleman if I let you ride into the village alone."

Sophia stifled a grin. "Mr. Henning, you must go and sing. Think of what your grandmama will say when you tell her you sang carols at Greaves Park."

"She'd be near to bursting just knowing I was invited here. That she would. But you still can't go alone."

"I'll take a groom with me. Don't trouble yourself."

"Very well. You talked me into it."

Once she finished eating, she was tempted to go listen to the caroling if for no other reason than to determine whether Francis Henning's baritone was as fine as his grandmother claimed. If it was indeed snowing, however, the sooner she went and returned, the better.

At her request Evans had already saddled Copper and another mount for himself. "Thank you for joining me," she said with a smile. "I know you have other duties with all these people here."

"With all respect, Miss Sophia, I'd rather ride to Hanlith with you than pitch hay for the horses," he returned, grinning.

"Well, I can't argue with that." As they trotted off across the well-trampled ground of the stable yard, she sent him a sideways glance. "Speaking of arguing, I heard you had a bit of a row with Udgell this morning. Thank you."

Chuckling, he tipped his hat at her. "At first I didn't know what the devil was afoot when Udgell called me in and then started yelling at me for putting mud on the floor. Then he gives me a wink that nearly frightened me to death, but I figured something had happened. He told me later that you needed to make a quick escape from somewhere without being seen."

That wasn't quite what had happened, but that hardly mattered. "That was quick thinking from both of you."

"It was unexpected, for certain. Udgell almost never yells. It's his whisper that's generally terrifying."

At Hanlith it only took a few moments to find the small shop with the hanging sign depicting a sewing needle and thread above the door. Evans helped Sophia down from her mare, then took the leads to keep the animals walking while she pulled open the shop door.

A little bell attached to the door handle jingled. "One moment," a female voice came through the door at the rear of the tiny shop.

"No hurry," she returned, running her finger through the hair ribbons hanging over a display stand.

A moment later a tiny woman emerged from the back, a pile of blue-dyed lace in her hands. With her dark hair pulled so tightly into a bun at the back of her head that Sophia was surprised she could blink, the seamstress looked more like a shoe-making gnome than a dressmaker.

"May I help you?"

Sophia offered her a smile. "Are you Mrs. Orling?"

"I am. What do you . . ." Her voice trailed off as she took in Sophia from her head to the skirt of her very fine, dark green and burgundy riding habit. "Oh. Oh! I— Excuse me!" Whirling around, she vanished back through the rear door and closed it.

At nearly the same moment the front door of the shop banged open and Adam skidded in, snow falling from his greatcoat onto the floor. "Sophia," he panted, brushing more snow from his shoulders as he gazed around the shop.

"What are you doing here?" she asked, folding her arms across her chest.

"What are *you* doing here?" he countered.

So he meant to bluff until he discovered how much she knew. She debated torturing him, but the dresses were an impressive gift, whether she'd asked for them or not. "I came to thank my dressmaker." Sophia took a step closer and lowered her voice. "And what did you say to her? Mrs. Orling took one look at me in this dress and locked herself in the back room."

She would have started in that direction, but he caught her arm. "Does this mean you're not angry with me?" His gray eyes caught hers, his expression unreadable.

"Did you charge out here just to ask if I'm angry? What about your guests?"

"When I left they were in the midst of 'O Come, O Come, Emmanuel,'" he returned shortly. "And you had no clothes. I made certain no one knew where the gowns came from, and I paid the seamstress to keep her mouth shut about it. You said that was your objection."

For a moment he looked like a boy who'd been caught putting a frog in his nanny's cap. It was so incongruent that one of the most powerful men in England was worried about making her—*her*—angry. Slowly she leaned up and touched her lips to his. "They're very pretty dresses," she murmured.

He smiled back at her. "I think I'm thankful you're a good-tempered chit," he said quietly, kissing her back.

"Yes, because my wrath is terrible." Sophia laughed. "Now go in there with me and apologize for whatever you said to frighten Mrs. Orling."

Morning rides in Yorkshire were more interesting than he'd expected, Aubrey Burroughs reflected.

Crossing his arms over the saddle's low cantle, he gazed down the hill into the quaint village of Hanlith. From there he had a nice view of the front of a shop boasting a needle and thread over the door, though the place's function didn't concern him as much as had the two people who'd entered it.

Sophia White patronizing the shop of a seamstress had barely rated a glance. That, however, was before

Greaves had come galloping down the lane, snow flying from beneath Zeus's hooves. And then he'd vaulted off the animal and literally run through the door.

The Duke of Greaves, running. The man with so many spies and threads of information spinning through Mayfair and all of England that he might have been a spider, hurrying somewhere. Somewhere a supremely scandalous young lady happened to be.

If the day had been clear, he might have been able to see through the shop's front windows, but luck had evidently not crossed the river Aire to join him at Greaves Park. That much had become clear when Hennessy's by-blow had turned him away. Then the oaf of a butler had dropped dinner on him. Unconscionable as that was, this morning a half-witted footman had poured old, soured milk into his tea. His stomach still hadn't settled. Greaves needed to hand half his staff their papers.

The shop door below opened, and he straightened again. The scarlet-haired Tantalus girl emerged first, Greaves on her heels. Whatever the urgency had been, he didn't seem to be in any sort of hurry any longer. Rather, he walked the chit to her red horse and lifted her into the saddle. As she settled, she grabbed the lapel of Greaves's coat, leaned down, and kissed him. And he took her face in his hands to kiss her back.

Well.

No wonder the chit had turned him away, Aubrey thought, whether she admitted to having made an arrangement with Greaves or not. Adam Baswich was a clever bastard, and a cagey one. He'd let just enough of the rumors fly to leave doubt, and to keep him from being called a hypocrite if the truth should come out.

And she was a redhead, too. Given the old duke's penchant for the ginger-headed sect, Aubrey understood why Greaves might not have wanted to advertise the identity of his latest mistress. The apple and the tree definitely shared some common tastes. By God, the man was here to choose a wife. Perhaps he meant to keep Sophia White from his duchess. And if Adam could be embarrassed or bothered by any of that, well, this could be fun.

As the pair of riders and the accompanying groom rode out of the village, Aubrey kicked the chestnut gelding he'd borrowed in the ribs. Considering what he'd seen, it would be best to return to the house before Greaves did. And then he could decide how much mischief he wished to make with what he knew.

FOURTEEN

Adam strolled into the orangerie, his gaze immediately falling on his sister at the center of the dozen or so people who'd taken over the large, warm room for their afternoon tea. It all looked very civilized, if one ignored the undercurrent of malice lurking in the corners. Whatever else happened, he meant to make certain Sophia enjoyed the rest of her holiday. And that began here.

"There you are, Eustace," he said with a smile. "Might I have a word with you?"

The marchioness looked up at him, hesitating a moment before she rose. "Of course, brother. By the fire, perhaps? I'm a bit chilled."

The request didn't surprise him at all. Of course she wanted to remain in the room, where she would have allies and he would be distinctly outnumbered. He nodded. "Certainly." Phillip Jennering leaned against the mantel like a heavy-browed gargoyle, and Adam looked at him very levelly. "Give us a moment, Jennering."

The viscount's brother actually swallowed as he straightened. "Of course, Greaves."

"Why aren't Wallace and your offspring here?" he asked. "I thought with such a prize resting on the outcome of this holiday, you'd want my heir presumptive close to hand."

The question seemed to surprise her, as he'd hoped it would. "They aren't here because whatever you may think of me, I do not want my children exposed to the spectacle you've made of this Christmas, with women chasing after you and that . . . thing remaining under your roof. An illegitimate, employed female who spends every evening with multitudes of randy men playing cards and drinking and doing God knows what else."

"And yet you have even more of your pack here than you usually manage. To begin controlling the rumors should I fail to net a bride?"

"In the perhaps vain hope that a greater number of respectable people would balance your carnival and give this house at least the appearance of decency."

As well as he knew her, the deep venom in her voice unsettled him. It wasn't for show. She meant every word she said. "What would you have done, if you'd been born of some duke and a servant?" he asked quietly. "And don't say you'd drown yourself, because we both know you have a very keen sense of self-preservation."

"I would join a nunnery, or take myself off somewhere I could quietly live out my shameful life doing good works. I would not make even more of a spectacle of myself by seeking employment in the middle of Mayfair at the most scandalous establishment possible."

Interesting that she'd chosen nearly the same path that Hennessy had selected for his daughter. Eustace had obviously had that response prepared. But he'd been considering a few things, as well—not the least of which was that all Sophia had truly wanted of this holiday was a handful of fond memories. She would have that, even if it killed him. Or everyone else.

"Now that we know what you *would* do in her place, this is what you *will* do in yours. You will inform those venomous harpies of yours that if they make one more disparaging remark about any of my guests, I will hear about it and I will make it my business to disgrace, embarrass, or ruin them in the most public manner possible.

And you know I'll do it, because I've done it before. Do you understand?"

Her face had paled, though whether that was from anger or well-suppressed righteous indignation, he had no idea. "Yes," she ground out.

"Good. You will also lead your hyenas in friendly, polite conversation and greetings to everyone your paths cross. You will all smile and nod and be the gentlemen and ladies you were supposedly born to be. One sideways glance or turned back or behind-hand whisper, and I will—"

"Disgrace them. I heard you before. You don't need to repeat it."

She did seem to understand that she wasn't the only one who meant every word of their conversation, because she'd tensed all her muscles so tightly that she would likely break if he pushed her over. The warning would suffice, then, but only until she realized that he hadn't mentioned her, specifically. He couldn't disgrace her, after all, without doing the same to himself. Or so she likely thought. "One more thing," he continued.

"What, then? More threats? I told you; I understand."

Adam took a step closer. "One more thing," he repeated, his voice even lower. "You. You will show the same kindness and consideration to everyone under this roof. If you don't, I will cut you off. And I will marry the least respectable chit possible just to be able to do so."

Eustace gasped, color leaving her face completely. "You wouldn't dare."

"Perhaps you haven't realized it yet, sister, but I have had enough of you and your vitriol over every damned thing. Yes, you were born first, and yes, you are female. I have control over neither of those things. What I do have control over—and what I will keep control over—is this title and everything that goes with it." He drew a hard breath. "I'm finished with you now. You may go."

She turned as crisply as any soldier, and walked two steps. Then she faced him again. "One question."

"I suggest you word it very carefully, then."

His sister lifted her chin and walked those two steps back up to him. "I can guarantee that . . . woman's reception here. But I have no say in how the rest of London views her, or in what anyone will say when the Season begins. Do you mean to show her at the theater? At soirees?"

"Enough," he interrupted.

"No. I will speak. What am I to say when I hear the gossip? When Lady Jersey giggles and says 'like father, like son,' and everyone snickers? At you, or at our name? You may have kept people from sneering at her in your sight and on your property, but you're ruining what little is left of your own name and reputation by dragging that trouser-wearing woman about and making as much of a spectacle of yourself as she does. I certainly hope your interest in bedding her lasts long enough to justify your own destruction."

He should never have let her speak. Molten fury tore at his insides until he was surprised that his ears weren't bleeding. "I know you like to have the last word," he snarled, and she backed away a step. "But this time I will. Shut up."

With that he turned and left the room. If no one else had been there to see, he would have gone directly to the nearest liquor tantalus, but guests littered his house like yapping, tail-wagging dogs. He couldn't make a scene, couldn't yell until his throat bled, couldn't go stalking out into the snow until his fury cooled. All he could do was walk the house and hope no one stopped him for conversation.

It didn't matter that Eustace was wrong both about Sophia and about her future, because even if he would have been perfectly content to take her about London to everywhere she wanted to go, she wouldn't be in London. She wouldn't be anywhere near him, and she certainly wouldn't be happy about any of it. And neither would he.

A voice slid in through the cracks of his boiling mind, and he slowed outside the billiards room. His hand shaking so hard he could barely grasp the handle, he opened the door an inch.

Sophia leaned over the billiards table explaining her shooting technique to Francis Henning. Across from them, Keating leaned on a cue stick while his wife sat chatting with Ivy Flanagan. James Flanagan stood on the far side of Henning and offered his own pointers. To his surprise Lady Caroline was also present, seated by the window with a book in her lap and chuckling at the conversation.

A potential bride, a renowned muddlehead, a killer, a banker's brother and his wife, and two Tantalus girls. He could almost touch the humor and peace in the room. He wanted to join them. At the same time, he was fairly certain that if he stepped inside there with the roiling, putrid center of him clawing to get out, the windows would shatter and he would simply obliterate every ounce of . . . easy affection in the room. If he shut the door on it, though, he knew he would never find that moment again.

At that second Sophia looked up and saw him. Her grin deepened, lighting her green eyes. "Your Grace. Thank heavens. Do come and explain ball spin to Francis. We're going to turn him into a crack billiards player."

Adam pulled in a breath, and then a second one. And then, keeping his gaze on Sophia, he pushed the door wide open and stepped inside. The room didn't explode, the table didn't burst into flame, and the walls didn't crack.

Her expression altering a little, Sophia handed the cue to Henning and walked up to him. For a long moment she searched his gaze, then put her hand on his arm. "I heard you saying you had a sour stomach earlier," she announced, half pulling him toward a window. "For heaven's sake. Take a breath of fresh air. Why is it that men have to act so manly all the time?"

"Because we are manly," Keating put in, stepping past her to shove open the window. "And if you're going to cast up your accounts, do it out there. In a manly way, of course."

Cold air rushed against his face, and Adam took another breath. Behind him he heard someone jiggle the bellpull, and then Camille's voice requested a pot of peppermint tea, followed by Udgell's lower-toned response. The discussion of the part mathematics played in billiards resumed. And his insides slowly began to cool.

Sophia had taken a seat directly beside him to join in the chat about hats with Camille and Caroline and Mrs. Flanagan, but after a moment he felt her hand brush the edge of his jacket. "Are you well?" she breathed almost soundlessly.

He nodded, taking a last cool breath and shutting the window before everyone else in the room froze. What did he mean to do with Sophia? He had no idea, other than knowing that he needed her to be in his life. Somehow, somewhere in the past weeks, Sophia White had become his one, very unlikely, saving grace. He couldn't lose her. And certainly not to a man who would only disdain the very things about her that he loved.

* * *

"Oliver, there's a letter for you," Diane Warren, Lady Haybury, said, as her husband walked past the sitting room.

He backtracked, leaning into the doorway. "Since when do you announce my mail?" he asked, walking up beside her. Gently he pulled back a lock of her hair and kissed her on the cheek. "Unless it was a ruse to get me alone with you."

She chuckled. "I rarely resort to ruses. Not any longer, anyway." She handed the letter to him. "Kiss me before you open it, because you'll be in a foul mood afterward."

Without looking at the missive in his fingers, he settled his hands on her shoulders, leaned down, and took her mouth in a slow, deep kiss. "You taste like strawberries," he murmured, kissing her again.

"And you taste like sin," she returned in the same tone, smiling against his mouth. "My favorite flavor."

With a short laugh he backed away from her and flipped the missive so he could read the address. Immediately his smile vanished. "It's from Greaves," he said flatly, and glanced up at her. "But you knew that."

"I recognized the address."

Swiftly he unfolded the paper and glanced through the single page. Then he sank down into a chair.

"Is something wrong with Sophia?" she asked, taking the seat beside his. "I knew we should have stopped her from going."

"We might have stopped that, but she seems fairly assured that we won't be able to stop Hennessy." He spoke absently, his gaze following the lines of the letter as he read it again.

"Oliver?"

Finally he glanced up at her. "Listen to this: 'You owe me nothing, but I find myself in need of assistance.

Go to Cornwall, and meet with the vicar of Gulval. If you find Mr. Loines to be acceptable, or at least malleable, leave him be. If you find him to be otherwise, inform me at once. I ask this not for myself, but for someone of our mutual acquaintance. As you know, time is of the essence. I know your stake in this, and I do not ask you lightly. Greaves.' "

Diane studied her husband's expression for a moment. "I would suggest you tell him to bugger off, but I believe this Mr. Loines is the man Sophia wouldn't tell us about." She frowned. "I can't believe Hennessy actually thought a vicar would be appropriate for her." Standing, she took the letter from Oliver's hand and read it again herself. "What are the odds that Hennessy would choose someone of acceptable character for Sophia?"

"Very slim. He's a self-important toad."

Slowly she handed the missive back. "Greaves says we have a stake in this. In your opinion, could Hennessy shut the club down? We've had people speaking against us before, but he has his fingers in a great many pies."

Silently Oliver rose to join her by the window that overlooked the club's garden. Even with the roses cut back and the trees bare, it still looked inviting. And she was beginning to feel in need of a breath of fresh air.

"In a pitched fight," Oliver said in a low voice, "and taking into account his friendship with the prime minister and his influence over the House of Lords, yes. I think he could have our doors closed."

"Then the wisest course of action would be to let him have his way," Diane commented. "All he wants is Sophia gone from here, after all."

"And he's found her a husband. It isn't as if he's ordering us to do anything, nor is he turning her out onto the street," Lord Haybury agreed. "And as Greaves said, I certainly owe him nothing—other than a bloody nose, that is."

She had begun this club to provide for her own future. To make wagering pay her back a little for the trouble it had caused her life. The Tantalus girls, as the club's members had begun calling them, were employees, pretty things to entice the high and mighty to come calling and lose their money. This was not a home for lost women or a refuge for the scandalous and ruined.

Or it hadn't begun as one, anyway. Diane nodded, her gaze still on the garden. "I won't see Sophia given away to someone unworthy simply to save us some trouble."

Oliver drew his arms around her waist, pulling her back against his chest. "I'm not giving you your Christmas gift until I return, I'll have you know."

Twisting, she faced him. Sliding her arms around his shoulders, she lifted onto her toes and kissed him again. "If you find yourself face-to-face with the Duke of Greaves, make an effort not to kill him. I have no desire to be widowed a second time when they hang you for it. I've become accustomed to having you about."

She felt him smile against her mouth. "I love you, too, Diane."

The Hanlith church had clearly been built with the idea that it would on occasion house more than just the village's residents. The entire wing, set at a right angle to the main part of the church and out of the line of sight of all but the first pew of villagers, boasted more comfortable benches, the Duke of Greaves, and his entire retinue.

Sophia sat at the end of one pew at the back of the nobleman's wing, Camille beside her. At the front, the Reverend Gibbs droned on and on. When they'd all filed into the church, the rector's wife, introduced only as Mrs. Gibbs, had been standing beside him. Presumably she currently sat somewhere in the main wing, listening to her husband discuss the wages of sin and the sacrifices of the worthy. What had Mrs. Gibbs sacrificed? she wondered. Was she happy being married to a man who spent his time preaching to and advising others about how to live their lives? Was he a good husband to her? As a young woman, had she envisioned a life of romance and adventure for herself?

At least she could sit in the back of the church here, Sophia thought. Adam in the front pew had to pay attention and sit straight. Christmas Day. As much as she'd looked forward to the celebration at a grand country estate, she also dreaded it. In less than a fortnight, guests would begin leaving, going home to spend at least a short time before the lords, at least, had to journey to London for the winter session of Parliament.

She'd anticipated misery, but in a sense knowing that Adam was embarking on married life himself would be even worse. If her father had only bothered to acknowledge her, things could have been so different. Perhaps marrying a duke would still be beyond her reach, but it would at least have been worth a daydream or two. People wouldn't have turned their backs on her from the moment of her earliest memories. She would have been able to attend the occasional Society soiree and evenings at the theater. But as she still wouldn't have had Adam, perhaps a more acceptable life didn't matter all that much, after all.

Oh, for heaven's sake. She'd learned long ago that the world didn't alter just because she wished for it. And if her heart felt broken at the mere thought of leaving Greaves Park, that was only because she'd wished for something she knew perfectly well she couldn't have.

Even so, these few weeks marked the first time she could recall wishing she'd been born someone else, wishing her circumstances had been different.

Finally the sermon ended, and the Greaves Park group began filing out of the church and back to the plethora of vehicles waiting for them. As she moved to one side, Lady Scoffield stepped on her toe.

The woman glanced at her, then looked away—and then stopped. "I beg your pardon, Miss White," she said, turning around and smiling. "Please forgive me."

Sophia blinked. "Of course. No harm done."

"Thank you, my dear. And Happy Christmas."

"Happy Christmas to you, my lady."

"What was that?" Cammy asked from directly behind her.

She shrugged. "I have no idea."

That wasn't even the first time one of the members of Lady Wallace's frowny band had surprised her. Over the past two or three days, several of them had said hello to her. Phillip Jennering had even stood when she'd walked into the breakfast room yesterday. It all seemed suspiciously like something Adam would have arranged. She would have confronted him about it, except that whatever his last encounter with Eustace had been, it didn't seem to be anything he'd won.

She rode back to Greaves Park in the Blackwoods' coach, accompanied by the Blackwoods and Lady Caroline Emery. At first Lady Caroline's presence in their little group of misfits had made her suspicious. Then Francis Henning had told her about a rumored familial connection to an opera singer, and the good *ton*'s reticence around her made more sense—especially once it became clear that Adam preferred her over the rest of the bridal parade. And she'd seemed genuinely pleased to be welcomed into their band.

Once back at the manor she hurried upstairs to collect her paper-wrapped gifts and carry them down to the drawing room. As Milly had explained it, gift giving at Greaves Park was a very informal affair, everyone sitting where they pleased and handing presents to their recipients with no rhyme or order.

When she arrived in the drawing room, it was filled with guests and gift-carrying servants and boxes and ribbons and white paper. Sophia stopped in the doorway just to look. So this was what Christmas looked like in high Society. It was very colorful, and loud, and full of the smell of peppermint tea and warm, liquid chocolate.

"Sophia!" Camille waved at her from a grouping of chairs brought in from another room and set beneath the large windows in the east wall.

Grinning, she made her way through the crowd, accepting and returning at least a dozen more greetings than she'd expected. Selecting the correct package for each of her friends, she handed them over before she plunked herself down in a facing chair. "I originally had other gifts for you, but I suppose now some fisherman downriver will make someone in his family very happy with an onyx cravat pin and blue ear bobs."

Camille chuckled. "You didn't need to get us anything, Sophia. And certainly not a replacement gift."

"I wanted to. And forgive the workmanship."

Camille untied the ribbon and opened the paper. "Oh, it's lovely!" she exclaimed, holding up the blue and white knitted scarf. "You did this?"

"Don't sound so surprised. Knitting is a grand way to spend the evenings at boarding school."

Keating opened his, revealing the darker blue and green of his own wrap. "Well done, Sophia," he said, sitting forward to kiss her on the cheek. "And very useful."

"Yes, one season a year at least," she returned with a smile.

"For you, Miss White."

Startled, she looked up to see Lady Stanley holding out a small box tied with a pretty red ribbon. "I . . . Thank you."

Sophia sent a quizzical frown to Cammy. Her friend shrugged, which wasn't helpful at all. With a tight smile at Lady Stanley, Sophia pulled off the ribbon. Inside the box lay a very pretty blue fan ribbed with ivory and featuring a delicate painting of a white dove.

"Oh, it's lovely," she said, looking up. "Thank you so much."

"You're quite welcome." The woman stood there for a moment, looking at her expectantly.

With a sinking feeling, Sophia forced another smile. "I'm afraid I don't have a gift to give you in return, my lady."

Lady Stanley smiled again, the expression not reaching her eyes. "I didn't expect one. Happy Christmas."

"Happy Christmas to you, Lady Stanley."

When she walked away, Sophia sat back. "That was . . . curious."

"Has she ever even spoken to you before?" Cammy whispered, her expression quizzical.

"Mostly just to insult me."

"A discussion for later," Keating broke in, producing a small box from his pocket and handing it to Camille. "Happy Christmas, my love."

With a glance at her husband that Sophia couldn't even begin to decipher, Camille grinned and opened the box. From inside she drew out a stunning necklace of pearls and a matching pair of ear bobs. "Oh, Keating, it's lovely," she whispered, handing him the necklace and leaning forward so he could fasten it around her throat.

"As are you."

Camille moved to the edge of her chair and kissed her husband. It was terribly scandalous to do such a thing in public, but Sophia didn't mind. She looked down, studying her fan, until the two separated again. That was what she wanted. That moment when no one in the world existed but that single, vital person.

"Here you are, Sophia." At Camille's gesture, Keating reached behind his chair and produced a large hat box, which he handed over to Sophia.

She took it, pulling off the lid, and lifted a very pretty straw hat trimmed with a sprinkling of green and yellow straw flowers and matching ribbons. "It looks like springtime," she said, and hugged her friends. "Thank you so much."

"Happy Christmas, Miss White," another voice came, and she looked up once more.

This time it was Eustace, Lady Wallace, and she tensed. "Happy Christmas, my lady," she said cautiously.

"I purchased you a gift."

What is it, a poisonous viper? Sophia wondered, but took the object wrapped in neat white paper. Because Lady Wallace seemed to want to watch, she swiftly opened it—and pulled out a beautiful pair of white kid gloves edged with pearl buttons.

"My lady, this is too much," she protested, looking up again.

"Just a small token," the marchioness returned, and was gone into the crowd again.

"Be certain they aren't poisoned," Keating advised in a low voice.

"That was my first thought, as well," she returned, setting them atop the hat box.

Within the next ten minutes she'd received eight additional gifts, all from people she knew despised her: a pewter ring box, a necklace with a single faux emerald on a silver chain, another fan, a warm fur muff for her hands, a porcelain vase decorated in the Japanese style, a pair of diamond ear bobs, a silver calling card holder actually engraved with her initials, and a set of lovely blue teacups. Each one was more than she could afford to spend on herself, and each gift-giver waited to watch her open the present—and until she had to say that she had nothing to give in return.

Evidently Lady Wallace's new plan was to kill her—or at least terribly embarrass her—with kindness. No one else had as many gifts as she did, and no one else received more attention. It was certainly a unique way to be cruel.

Adam finally made his way from the other side of the room to their group. Udgell and two footmen trailed behind him, the butler bearing unopened gifts, and the footmen with boxes and sacks of presents clearly meant for the duke. Very nice presents. Sophia glanced at the small paper package still by one foot. A gift not fit for a duke.

"Happy Christmas, Blackwells, Miss White," he drawled, shaking Keating's hand and kissing first Camille's knuckles, and then hers. He squeezed her fingers for just a heartbeat, and then released her again. "I come bearing gifts. Or rather, I come with people bearing gifts."

Udgell handed him a large bag, which he in turn gave over to Keating. From inside Keating removed a finely crafted leather bridle, the fastenings covered with highly polished silver. At the same time, Keating motioned at yet another footman, who approached with a silver-trimmed hunting saddle for Adam. "Evidently we had the same thought," he said, grinning.

"Well done," Adam returned, running his hand along the saddle. "Walsall made?"

"I wouldn't have bothered bringing it if it wasn't,"

Keating said dryly. "We're not even for everything you've done for me, but this makes us closer."

"I'll accept that." Adam took another package and handed it to Camille. "And for you, my dear. I have faith in your good taste despite your choice of husband."

"And now we're even closer to being even," Keating rumbled.

Laughing, Camille opened the small box, to reveal a very pretty pearl pin. "Pearls! It's perfect."

"Keating said something about you liking pearls, and anything but a necklace. I hope this suffices."

"It does. Quite well." She stood up and kissed him on the cheek.

Adam glanced at Sophia, then took another package from Udgell and handed it over to her. "And a little something for you, Miss White. Happy Christmas."

"The same to you, Your Grace." Before she lost her nerve, Sophia reached down for the last present and handed it to him. "And something for you."

"Thank you," he said, his voice quieting as he took the gift.

She wondered if he was worried it would be something to show their connection, and if he would open it or not for that reason. But then he pulled off the bow and opened the paper. An intricate weave of blacks and grays and browns crisscrossed one another along the length of the scarf. It had nearly left her crippled and blind, but she'd finished it.

"You made this, didn't you?"

Sophia nodded, waiting for the knowing snickers from somewhere behind her, saying that of course she'd made it. Why else would it look like that? But the timbre of conversation didn't alter. Hm. That was at least as odd as the tremendous number of valuable gifts she'd received.

He draped it around his shoulders. "Thank you. I shall treasure it."

Whether he meant something additional or not, she decided that attempting to decipher any of his comments now would be a very poor idea. And so, trying not to let her fingers shake with anticipation, she opened the box he'd given her. Moving the paper aside, she revealed a lovely green and yellow scarf that matched her new hat. *A scarf.*

"It's a scarf," he said helpfully. "Camille showed me the hat, and I thought something to match would be nice."

A scarf. In terms of value, it was likely the least expensive of the gifts she'd received today. In terms of importance, she couldn't remember ever mentioning scarves in his presence, or him in hers. In other words, it meant nothing to either one of them. Of course she'd also given him a scarf, but at least she'd made it herself.

"It's lovely," she heard herself say. After all, he'd already given her dresses and saved her life. What the devil had she expected? A wedding ring? Diamonds? Those were the things she would never receive from him, because firstly she was to be married to someone else, and secondly because she couldn't be purchased.

With his toe, he nudged the stack of other gifts she'd received. "Where did these come from?"

"From Lady Wallace, and Lady Hayforth, and oh, everyone.. They were very kind to me. I feel terrible that I didn't purchase something for them in return."

Something very dark crossed his face and then was gone again. He lifted an eyebrow. "Purchase something for them with what? Everything you brought with you washed down the river, as I recall," he stated in a carrying voice. "The fact that you managed to find the materials and then knit a scarf"—he glanced at Keating who was making some sort of motion—"three scarves, is extremely impressive. As is the craftsmanship."

Whether he was attempting to explain her circumstance or thank her too vehemently for a knit scarf, she didn't know, but she didn't particularly like either conclusion. "Thank you again, Your Grace," she said, standing. "Udgell, would you mind helping me bring my new possessions up to my bedchamber?"

The butler immediately squatted down and picked up a stack of gifts. "Of course, Miss Sophia."

Though Cammy sent her an uncertain look, Sophia smiled and kissed her on the cheek. "Are you staying in for luncheon?"

"I believe so."

"Then I'll see you in a bit."

She curtsied at the room in general and walked out. On the one hand she'd gotten some very nice, if impractical, gifts that she could sell to put a little more money in the bank. On the other hand, the man she adored, the man she couldn't wait to see every night and hated to part from every morning, had given her a present that was only slightly more meaningful than a doorknob.

If he'd given Lady Caroline something as stupid as a scarf, she would eat it. No, she couldn't have him, and no, they didn't have anything close to a lasting relationship, but he might have found . . . something that meant something special. Just between the two of them. Happy Christmas, indeed.

"Really, Greaves? A scarf?"

Adam stiffened and turned around. Aubrey Burroughs stood close to the center of the room, where of course everyone couldn't help noticing him. "Are you complaining that you received a pocket watch,

Burroughs?" he asked. "I can more than likely find you a scarf, if you wish one."

"Actually what I mean is you couldn't have found a gift to more obviously show your disinterest in the chit if you wanted to. Trying a bit too hard, aren't you?"

Aubrey Burroughs was a dead man. "I have no idea what you're talking about. Have you been drinking again?"

"I'll admit, she isn't your usual sort, but for Christ's sake, Greaves. She wouldn't be here if she wasn't your mistress. We all know that. So why bother with the cheap and cheerful gifts?" He gestured at Eustace, who sat with a smile absolutely pasted on her otherwise still face. "Your sister and her friends know the truth, or they wouldn't have showered her with so many pretty trinkets. Why haven't you bothered to tell your own friends, so we'll know to keep our hands off? I nearly went after her myself, you know."

Damnation. Adam had evidently fallen into a hole made by his own cleverness. And now, there they were. But how much did Burroughs actually know, or was it all bluster and supposition? Grateful now that Sophia had left the room, he kept his relaxed stance, though he felt anything but easy on the inside. "I did invite *you* here, Burroughs, and we both know I had no ulterior motive for that. She's a friend, as I've said before. Just as you are." Or were, anyway.

"You see?" Burroughs returned, clearly playing to his rapt audience. "The more you dissemble, the more we want to know why. You never hid Lady Helena Brennan. In fact, you took her to Almack's with you."

Eustace shot to her feet. "Come, gentlemen. It's Christmas. You—John—bring champagne for everyone."

So there was a good side to his sister's obsession with propriety. He hadn't expected that she would ally herself with him, whatever her reasons for doing so. "And the fig pudding," he added, as the footman hurried out of the room.

"I saw you, Greaves." Burroughs seated himself, crossing one leg over the other and looking every inch a gentleman at leisure. "You met her at that dressmaker's shop—where I presume you've been having all those pretty gowns made—and you kissed her. I hate to carry tales, but I fail to see an alternate explanation for your attention."

"Hear, hear," Lassiter seconded from across the room. "Is the chit your mistress, or isn't she? We have wagers to settle, here."

They all looked at him. What was the alternative? He'd been seen kissing her. In the eyes of Society, a duke and . . . whatever Sophia was, kissed for one reason: he'd arranged for her care and support in exchange for exclusive sexual favors. A duke didn't lose his heart to an unredeemable by-blow got on a maid. On the other hand, the Duke of Greaves—both the ninth and the tenth—did favor redheads. If he admitted that he cared for her, he would look like a fool.

"If it looks like a duck," he snapped, leaving his supposed friends to finish the proverb by themselves.

"Greaves," Keating hissed in a very low voice behind him.

Ignoring Blackwood, Adam sketched a lazy bow. "Now if you'll excuse me for a moment, I need to go soothe a wounded bird."

Cursing under his breath, he stomped up the stairs and along the familiar path to Sophia's room. She would be furious. But she wouldn't be returning to London, anyway. And this little lie would serve to keep everyone and their opinions polite until she left Yorkshire. No other man would proposition her, and he could spend his time with her as he pleased.

He pushed open the closed door without knocking. "Sophia."

She looked up from her seat by the window, the scarf he'd given her in her hands. "You shouldn't have given me this," she said.

Truer words were never spoken. "Yes, I know. It was just for show. I do have another gift for you, however."

"I mean, you saved my life. And all these dresses you've bought for me. It's too much." She narrowed one eye. "And you don't have to wear that scarf. I just wanted to give you . . . something. It was silly."

"It was not silly. You made this." He fingered the warm wrap still hanging about his neck. "With your time and your hands. It's the nicest gift I received."

Her expression softened a little, and finally she offered him a crooked smile. "I don't quite believe you, but that was well said." She jabbed a finger in his direction. "And I had to hide it every time you came in here. For a time I thought I was going to have to crawl under the bed to finish it."

Sending up a quick prayer that she would listen to reason despite the fact that he'd just done the one thing she'd asked him not to, he pulled the oblong box from an inner pocket. A gift first would hopefully soften her objections to what he needed to explain to her.

"Your actual Christmas gift," he said, and handed it to her.

Dividing her attention between him and the box, she took it from him, brushing his fingers with hers as she did so. Her shoulders rising and falling with her breath, she opened the lid.

Firelight caught the strands of delicate gold chain, and sent wildly glinting reflections off the hundred tiny diamonds set around the length of the twisting, twining necklace. The thing was absurdly delicate looking, and the Hanlith jeweler might never recover from its creation, but the beautiful asymmetry of it reminded him of Sophia.

"Do you like it?" he asked after a moment, when she continued to sit there wordlessly.

"It's the most beautiful thing I've ever seen," she whispered, lifting it and letting it drip through her fingers.

"I had it made for you."

She looked up at him, a tear running down one cheek. "Thank you. Truly, Adam. But you know I can't accept this. I could never wear it without everyone asking where it came from. Without . . . my husband asking why I would ever receive such a gift."

Adam took a stiff breath. It was now or never, he knew. And nothing in his life had ever made him quite as nervous as this moment. "You can accept it, you know."

"Of course I can't. And it's too dear to sell, as I'm going to do with all these baubles." She gestured at the pile of gifts on her bed. The ones Eustace had undoubtedly orchestrated.

He took her hand. "Why do you want to make your life so difficult, when I could make it so easy for you? At least the next few weeks of it. This isn't a fairy tale, Sophia. This is the world. I can make you so much more comfortable. You wanted a happy holiday. I can certainly give that to you, no matter who is here, or for what reason."

Her face had paled, but at least she seemed to be listening. She needed to understand. He needed her to understand.

"I know you've fought for everything you have. I congratulate you for that. But you don't need to keep fighting. Not here. If I could, I would give you an apartment and servants and jewels for every day of the week. You won't take that from me, I know. But take this

necklace, and take what I can offer you. For God's
sake, you could hide it away from your husband and
have the blunt to run if you ever felt the need. And you
could run to me. In fact, after a year or two, how would
Hennessy be able to blame your flight on the club? Especially if he had no idea where you were."

"But you would be married."

"As would you be. I don't care."

Her tears had stopped. She turned to look out the
window, at the slow, lazy drift of snow that had begun
on the return drive from church. He'd already memorized her profile, but he didn't think he would ever tire
of looking at her.

Finally she looked up at him, her light green eyes
deep and endless and very, very serious. "May I think
about it?" she whispered.

Adam scowled. "What the devil is there to think
about? I'm offering you the world."

"A very large world, and a very different one, and
I'd like to consider what you've said," she countered, a
touch of color returning to her cheeks. "Give me until
luncheon at least, will you?"

If he gave her a minute, she might refuse him. If he
pressed her, though, she definitely would refuse. Unclenching his jaw, he nodded. "Until one o'clock." To
underscore everything his offer entailed, he took the
necklace and stood to fasten it around her throat. Then
he moved around in front of her, catching her mouth
with his in a deep, hot kiss.

She slipped her hands around his shoulders as she
sank into his embrace. How could she do anything but
accept his offer, when the alternative would be a life
with a man who would never appreciate who she was?
Who would keep her prisoner in a tiny village and heap
guilt on her until she broke from the weight? And once
she fled Cornwall for London, she would never leave

him. He would never have to part from the serenity and the joy she gave him.

He lifted his head. "One o'clock," he repeated for emphasis. "Consider everything, Sophia. Everything I will give you."

She nodded, running her fingers down his cheek. "I will."

FIFTEEN

Sophia watched as Adam left her room. Then she stood and went to the bellpull to summon Milly.

That done, she reached up to carefully remove her beautiful necklace and gently place it back in its velvet-lined box. Just as carefully she kept her mind on the present, on the exact moment before her. The walk to the wardrobe. The ugly old hat she dropped to the floor. The hat box she carried to the bed. The pretty, hurtful gifts she could fit inside.

Adam had offered her nothing but a few more weeks of what she already wanted—him. He'd merely attached a monetary worth to her presence, made her a thing. And then he'd made it even worse, by suggesting a way she could escape her fate, when they both knew she could never do such a thing. Or he should have known that about her, anyway.

She'd agreed to marry Mr. Loines to save the Tantalus. Why, then, would she run the moment she thought she could get away with it, when that would ruin her husband, herself, and the woman whom Adam would have married by then? He hadn't even suggested that she find her freedom, but only that she trade a wedding band for a mistress's chains.

And for a bare, awful moment she'd been tempted. "No, no, no," she muttered to herself. Whatever people thought of her, whatever stigma had been placed on her from the moment of her birth, she meant to do the right thing. Even if it broke her heart.

Setting eyes on Adam again would shatter her into a million pieces. Yes, she was disappointed in him, but she certainly understood his dilemma and his frustration. She shared them. If he couldn't force himself to make the correct, difficult decision of walking away, she would do it for both of them. Better to plunge the dagger into her chest all at once and be done with it.

Her door opened again. "Did His Grace like the scarf?" Milly asked, then stopped. Abruptly she closed the door behind her and latched it. "What's happened, my dear? You look like death!"

That made sense, because she *was* dead. "I need to ask you two very large favors, Milly," she said, surprised that her voice was steady.

"Of course. What do you need?"

The swift answer nearly sent her over the edge into tears, and she fought for calm again. "I need for you to quietly ask Evans to saddle Copper and take me into Hanlith, and I need you to ask Udgell to see that His Grace doesn't notice my departure at least until one o'clock."

The housekeeper began to look very alarmed. "I . . . can do that. But what's happened? Did you and His Grace quarrel over something? Surely it's not so serious you need to flee."

"It is precisely that serious." She turned her purse over into her hand, and her few remaining coins tumbled into her hand. One pound, two shillings. Not enough to get her to Cornwall and purchase meals along the way. *Damnation.* "I also need you to find Camille Blackwood and ask her to lend me five pounds. Tell her I will repay the money, but I needed to send someone into the village to make a purchase."

Milly nodded despite the wringing of her hands. "Shall I bring her up here?"

Alarm skittered through Sophia. She would much rather remember Cammy and Keating as they smiled over their Christmas gifts—not as Camille watched her drive off to Cornwall and misery. "No. No one is to know."

"Oh, dear. Very well."

"And please hurry."

"Oh, dear, oh, dear."

The housekeeper hurried from the room, and Sophia locked the door again. By the mantel clock it was nearly eleven, and the mail stage left Hanlith at noon. It would take her to Cornwall within four days. Once there she would find the vicar and inform him that there was no sense in delaying their nuptials until January fifteenth. Then any temptations or thoughts of escape could simply wither and die.

Swiftly she removed her pretty gray gown and pulled on her blue muslin traveling dress. Her new walking shoes went into a sack; she would return Evans's boots to him in Hanlith. She hesitated over Adam's old caped greatcoat. Her own coat had been ruined, and she hadn't replaced it. Finally she pulled it on. She needed it, and so she would take it. The remainder of her unasked-for dresses she left in the wardrobe. She didn't want to explain to the vicar where she'd gotten them.

Finally she returned to the writing desk. She'd promised Adam a definitive answer, if not an explanation, and she kept her word. It was done in a moment, and she folded the missive, addressed his name on it, and sealed it with wax. Then she placed it beneath the oblong box on the center of the bed where he would be certain to notice it.

When Milly returned she was ready, her old hat box

full and heavy in one hand, and her new one with her spring hat in the other. Her coins were in the pocket of her greatcoat. Tears in her eyes, the housekeeper handed over five pounds, which Sophia added to her own money.

"You're certain of this?" Milly asked, wiping at her eyes. "You want to leave? I thought you didn't need to be in Cornwall until after the beginning of the year."

She never wanted to leave, which was why she needed to go. "I'm certain. No sense in chancing the weather."

"Down the back stairs, then. Udgell and the other servants are assembling in the drawing room to sing carols for the pleasure of His Grace and his guests."

She almost hated to miss that—but then she would miss nearly everything about this place. Together they hurried down the servants' stairs and through the kitchen, where Mrs. Beasel studiously ignored them. Evans waited just outside with Copper and his own horse, and Sophia handed up both hat boxes before she turned to give Milly a tight hug.

"Go and join the choir, so you won't be blamed for helping me."

Milly rubbed at her eyes again. "I will miss you, child. You warmed this cold, old house."

"I will miss you, Milly," Sophia returned, still refusing to cry. Not yet. Not until she was safely away.

Evans handed her up, and they circled around the back of the stable to stay out of view of the house. The snow had begun falling more heavily, but Sophia pulled her borrowed hat down lower on her head and otherwise ignored the weather.

In twenty minutes they'd reached Hanlith, and Evans stopped just outside the Trout's Mouth Inn. The mail stage was already there, standing while the horses were changed. The groom helped her to the ground and she gave him a hug, as well. "And this is for Udgell," she said, planting a kiss on his cheek.

"I'm sorry to see you go, Miss Sophia," he said gruffly, handing her the hat boxes.

"I'm sorry to leave." She set a box down to grip his sleeve. "I don't know how to keep Greaves from knowing you aided me. If he sacks you, go to The Tantalus Club in London. I swear there will be employment waiting for you at the stable if you should need it."

He nodded, then doffed his hat, waiting as she sat on a bench to pull off the boots and hat and return them to him. Once she stepped into her walking shoes, he moved back to the horses. "Best of luck to you, Miss Sophia."

"And to you, Evans."

With that she walked into the warm, crowded inn and purchased a seat on the mail coach going all the way south to Cornwall. Fifteen minutes later she sat on the rear-facing seat beside someone's grandmother and opposite Rector Gibbs and his wife, headed south to Rotherham. The irony of her companions might once have struck her as amusing, but at the moment it felt like the first chime of the bells of doom.

As Mr. Gibbs immediately began lecturing about a life of sin and finding redemption through charitable works, she looked out the coach's window. She'd had one last kiss with Adam, at least. And she would always remember it, because she would never see him or touch him again.

The only servants who didn't seem to be present for the unexpected recital were the lads from the stable and part of the kitchen staff. Adam hadn't known Udgell could sing, but the butler had a surprisingly good bass voice. As for why his servants were serenading his rather amused guests, he had something of an idea; everyone in the house had seemed more . . . animated since

Sophia's arrival. She should be there in fact, because she would certainly enjoy this spectacle.

According to his pocket watch, however, he had twenty more minutes to wait. He remained uncertain about what she might be contemplating, precisely, except for the damage to her own pride. Sophia was eminently practical, though, so she would realize his plan was the only one worth following.

The couch settled beside him. "You're a bastard," Keating murmured, keeping his gaze on the servant choir.

Splendid. "Sophia knows what I can provide her. And she knows I can certainly offer her a more pleasant life than she'll find with the Reverend Loines."

"Aside from the fact that you don't know anything about this pastor, Sophia had a reason for agreeing to marry him."

"Yes, well, she needs to have more care over her own well-being."

"Then where the deuce is she? Shouldn't she be sitting in your lap and feeding you grapes if she agreed with you?"

Finally Adam glanced sideways at his friend. "She wanted time to think. I'll bring her down with me in a few minutes." And then he wouldn't have to hide his interest any longer. He could smile at her in front of everyone, because she would have taken an ordered place in his well-ordered world. And once he offered for Lady Caroline, he wouldn't even have to explain his attachment to Sophia. Such things were understood in their world, after all.

"She's thinking about it?" Keating repeated, furrowing his brow. "Then she hasn't agreed to anything, despite what you told everyone in here. I was wrong; you aren't a bastard."

"Thank you for realizing that."

"You're a villain."

So he'd been called before, but not lately. This was beginning to be irritating. "I offered her everything, Keating. And she can still marry the damned vicar. Long enough to fulfill her obligations, anyway."

"As a married man, I find that very offensive."

"I'm not attempting to convince you."

Keating shook his head. "You're assuming she wants what you want."

Adam had no idea when Blackwood thought he'd become such an expert. "Of course she does. Do you think for a moment that I would treat her poorly?"

Blackwood continued to eye him. "You insulted her, and you're continuing to do so. But believe what you will. And I wonder if you've considered that you also insulted your future potential wife. I do hope she doesn't decide that marrying a fiend isn't worth the wealth she'll receive."

"Then you don't know as much about women as you think."

The rousing rendition of "Adeste Fideles" drew to a ragged end, and Adam stood, applauding. A breath later and his guests joined him in the ovation. His servants bowed, then with a nod from Udgell, scattered to resume their duties.

"What I think is that I don't actually want to look at you any longer." Keating stood and strolled over to rejoin his wife.

Well, wasn't that hilarious? Keating Blackwood, who'd once killed a lover's husband, wanted nothing to do with him. Adam knew the nature of people. He knew how to find their weaknesses, and he generally knew precisely what someone would do in any given situation. He knew what Sophia would do. He needed her in his life, and she wouldn't refuse him.

"Your Grace," Udgell said, as the butler walked up to him. "You asked to be informed of a particular piece of mail." The servant held up the silver salver, a single folded piece of paper resting on it.

At least Oliver still had splendid timing. With a nod, Adam took the paper and retreated to his office. As he broke the wax seal and unfolded the single page, he shut his eyes. He *knew* the Reverend Loines would be unsuitable for Sophia, because otherwise her father wouldn't have chosen him.

But what if Hennessy had found a drop of kindness in his soul? What if Mr. Loines was a perfectly kind, understanding young man who would accept Sophia without question? Was he a monster, a villain, for hoping otherwise? For wanting to be correct in his assessment of the situation, and wanting Sophia to accept that he'd found the only reasonable solution to her troubles?

He opened his eyes again. "'Greaves,'" he read to himself, remembering at the last moment to be surprised and thankful that Oliver had bothered to help him at all, "'I spoke with the Reverend Loines this morning. He is well educated, well spoken, and eager to marry.'"

That stopped him for a moment. By now in his imaginings the vicar had become a drooling, mouth-breathing ape with damp hands and bulging eyes. Narrowing his own eyes, he resumed the letter.

"'In fact, I believe he sees marrying and reforming Sophia as the reason he was called to the Church,'" Haybury went on, and Adam's consternation began to deepen toward anger. "'If he were in a more powerful position, I would call him dangerous rather than simply close-minded and tending toward cruelty.

"'I have no idea why you've involved yourself, Greaves, but from what I've been able to decipher, Hennessy has made The Tantalus Club the hostage in this predicament. That makes me rather angry. Do something to resolve the situation, or *I will*. I intend to remain in Cornwall until the fifth of January. Haybury.'"

Adam sat back in his chair. The intelligent zealots were the dangerous ones, and he wondered how much sly preaching and criticism it would take to convince Sophia that she deserved to be trodden beneath the feet of her betters. Could he even risk her staying in Loines's company for the year or so it would take for her agreement with Hennessy to be fulfilled?

The better question was whether he could stand to see her gone from him for that year. He pulled out his pocket watch and flipped it open. Five minutes of one o'clock—close énough.

Sophia's door was closed, and this time he knocked. Silence.

"Sophia," he said, and opened the door.

The gray gown she'd worn earlier was on the floor, and automatically his gaze went to her bed. She wasn't in it, however. Her half-drowned hat lay on the floor as well, but he was more interested in the jewelry box he spied in the middle of her quilted bedspread.

A cold chill ran up his spine and out to his fingertips as he picked up the box and opened it. Her new necklace lay inside. Setting it aside again, pushing against the cold that was seeping now into his chest, he turned his attention to the folded missive that lay beneath the box.

She'd written "Adam" on the outside, which at least sounded friendly. At the same time, in the back of his thoughts he knew that if the letter had been truly good news, she would have been in her room to deliver it instead of lurking somewhere else while he read it.

Adam broke the seal and unfolded the note. "'My answer is No,'" he read. "'I know my duty and value my friendships, even if you do not. Sophia.'"

For what felt like a very long time he stood there,

studying the practiced curve of the letters and the elegant swirl of the *S* in her name. The meaning of the words seeped into him, cold and hopeless. He'd offered her everything, and she'd turned him down and gone to hide somewhere.

So. Where had she gone? She preferred the orangerie or the library, but if she was attempting to avoid talking to him, she could very well have slipped away to find the Blackwoods. If so, he would be having that confrontation with Keating after all. No one would keep him from Sophia. He had to convince her, because he couldn't imagine spending the remainder of his life without her.

Stuffing the note and the necklace into his pocket, he left the room again. Most of his company was at luncheon, but other than looking into the dining room to note that Sophia wasn't there, he didn't spare them a thought. Neither Keating nor Camille were present, either, which meant he'd likely been correct and Sophia was somewhere barricaded with them.

Next he strode into the orangerie, but it stood silent. In the library Lord Hayforth sat snoring in a chair, which meant that Sophia would be nowhere in the vicinity. Agitation began to pull at him. He'd been damned patient in all this, but searching a very large house on Christmas Day, of all things, wasn't improving his mood. It wasn't like her to hide, anyway.

The door to the Blackwoods' bedchamber stood partly open, and he leaned inside. Keating closed a portmanteau and carried it toward the door, while Camille folded one of her dresses and dropped it into another valise. "What are you doing?" he asked, shoving the door open the rest of the way.

"We're going," Keating answered.

"Keating. No brawling," Camille said absently, opening a drawer and removing another piece of clothing.

His aggravation increased by another notch. "She refused my offer, if that makes a difference."

"Of course she refused you, idiot." Keating didn't move forward, but he didn't retreat, either.

Because he'd clearly made a mistake in the way he approached Sophia, he let the insult pass. "Has she been in to see you?"

Camille looked up when Keating remained silent. "No. But if you made her cry, Your Grace, I'm going to tell my husband to thrash you."

And he'd asked them here to keep him from being outnumbered by sycophants and hangers-on. "She actually left me a note," he said grudgingly. "I've been looking for her, but haven't had any luck."

"If she said no, then perhaps you should leave her alone, Greaves."

Tilting his head at Keating, Adam took a slow step forward. "I don't want to leave her alone. I have additional information about her vicar that she needs to know. And I've reached the end of my patience with your growling. Do it again. I dare you."

"Oh, heavens." Moving quickly, Camille dropped the clothes she'd been carrying and moved in between him and her husband. "Stop it. And you," she said, pointing a finger at Adam, "go look in the library or the orangerie. She likes it in there."

"I did."

Clearly the Blackwoods truly had no idea where Sophia might be. And the old hat on the floor in her bedchamber abruptly became more significant. That hat had been in a hat box. With a curse he turned on his heel and strode back down to the empty room. The hat box was gone. And so were the gifts she'd received, with the notable exception of the necklace. Her blue dress was missing as well, as were her borrowed groom's boots and his old greatcoat.

"What are you doing?" Keating demanded from the doorway.

Adam straightened from digging through Sophia's wardrobe. "She's gone."

"Well, she isn't in the wardrobe. What—"

"No," he barked, turning again and shoving past Blackwood. "She's *gone*. To damned Cornwall. Udgell!"

The butler appeared almost immediately. "Yes, Your Grace?"

"You know the comings and goings of everyone in this house. Tell me what you know of Miss White."

"I don't understand, Your Grace."

Clenching his jaw, Adam closed the distance between them. "You heard me. When did Sophia White leave this house? Answer me now, or I will sack anyone involved. Everyone involved."

A muscle beneath the butler's left eye jumped. "As a point of clarification, Your Grace, does this mean that if I did know something and told you about it, no one's employment would be in danger?"

Sophia would kill him if he fired one of his servants because of her. And angry as he was, as small as his chances of even seeing her again, he didn't feel prepared to put another brick in the wall that he and circumstance had built between them. "That is correct," he said stiffly. "*If* you tell me immediately."

"Miss Sophia left Greaves Park at approximately eleven o'clock this morning. She rode into Hanlith and boarded the southbound mail stage, which departed at noon."

A sharp, grinding pain speared through his chest, as if someone had stabbed him. She'd truly left. She'd gone away and hadn't said a word to him first. And if she'd been gone since eleven, she'd known from the moment they'd spoken that she was going to leave. For a moment he felt like a boy whose one favorite toy had been taken away, but that wasn't it. Her absence left him . . . empty. Truthfully he couldn't even be angry with her, because he'd caused this. He'd found something precious, and he'd trod all over it and now she'd decided that misery in Cornwall was better than being insulted by him.

"Adam, I hope you're not contemplating something stupid," Keating said in a low voice, his tone actually cautious.

"What? Of course not. I've parted company from women before." The words tasted sour in his mouth, but what the deuce was he supposed to say, that more than anything he wanted to ride through the storm after her, drag her back, and lock her in a room with him until she saw reason? "And I have an engagement to announce." After he informed Lady Caroline that he'd settled on her, that was. At least he could do *that* in the correct order.

"So all this over the past weeks was just playing? You could have fooled me."

"Evidently I did." Adam sketched a shallow bow and made his way to his private rooms.

The moment he opened his door Caesar and Brutus came forward, snuffling into his hands and demanding scratches. Sophia had turned his guard dogs into wagging house pets in a matter of weeks. He complied, more to keep them from leaping on him than anything else. Otherwise he wasn't feeling particularly friendly.

What the devil had he done? He walked to the window and pushed open the glass. The light snow of earlier had become a heavy blanket that curtained the trees and the hills beyond, leaving Greaves Park alone in a sea of white nothingness.

Any sane woman of her limited means would have agreed to his terms. Why, then, had she not only refused, but fled? The answer was somewhere directly in front of him. He knew it was something he'd done. Something he was.

Snow began to drift through the window into the room, and he pushed the glass closed again. Then he sat on the floor beneath the sill. As badly as he wanted a drink, he didn't dare. This time if he gave in to the molten blackness inside him, he didn't think he would be able to climb out of the pit again.

A knock came at his door. The dogs began barking, but he stayed where he was. Until he figured out what to do next, how to make this right, he wasn't going anywhere.

His door opened. "Greaves?" Keating walked into the room. "What— Christ. You—dogs—out." He shoved the mastiffs out into the hallway and closed the door again, locking it behind them.

Adam noted it all dully but didn't particularly care. The ice inside him continued to spread, chilling him to the bone. Everyone said he had no heart. Clearly he'd just proven them correct.

"Greaves," Keating repeated, and squatted down in front of him. "Adam."

"If you're here for another round of 'I told you so,' keep it to yourself," Adam finally said.

"Very well." Blackwood took a breath. "Six months ago you said something to me. I remember the exact wording. 'There is no one so blind as he who thinks he doesn't deserve to see.' I'm repeating it to you now because of what I owe you, which is every moment of happiness I've experienced since then."

Finally Adam met his friend's gaze. "What is it that I think I don't deserve, then? I made a bid for Sophia, and she refused me. She's content to do her duty by her friends, and I shall do my duty to keep my inheritance.

It's merely been a long day. I'll be fine tomorrow." He would never be fine, but no one else was allowed to know that.

"I think you hit on the difficulty rather precisely just now. You made a 'bid' for Sophia. Even I know that she isn't for sale. She wouldn't have been, even if she didn't know she needed to martyr herself for the sake of the Tantalus." Keating caught sight of the note on the desk, and without ceremony he opened it. "You're corresponding with Haybury? When did that happen?"

"Today. A few days ago. It doesn't matter."

"Hm. I think it does. He says she'll be miserable. That vicar will break her, you know. We've both seen it happen."

"How the bloody hell am I supposed to do anything about it?" Adam burst out, pain tearing through his chest again. "She chose. Him, and misery, over me."

"I can't tell how or what to do. You're a duke, and she's an unacknowledged by-blow of a duke, and she's promised to another man. Figure out what you truly want, but—"

"That's what I'm attempting to do," Adam snapped. "Get the hell out of here."

"But I'm not certain you can manage it," Keating finished, standing again. "Not even the Duke of Greaves can perform miracles."

The door closed again. " 'Not even Greaves can perform miracles,' " Adam repeated, mimicking Keating's low drawl. "Very helpful, Blackwood."

He pushed to his feet so he could pace as questions pelted through his mind like gunfire. How many times had he teased Sophia by announcing that he was a duke and could therefore do anything? She'd very effectively just proven him wrong about that. And in a few days she would prove him wrong again. She would prove that he couldn't protect her, couldn't keep her safe or happy.

No damned amount of blunt in the world, no pretty baubles or gowns, could save her.

What had Keating said? That he should figure out what he truly wanted. Well, that was simple. He wanted Sophia. He wanted to chat with her and tease with her and hold her and not have to hide how very much he'd come to love her.

Adam stopped in the middle of the room, stunned not by the thought, because he knew it already, but by the way it felt. He loved the sound of her laugh, and her wit, and the courage that had enabled her to be so warm despite the chill of her life. She warmed him, when he'd been so cold for so long.

He cursed again, long and loud. So he knew what he wanted. How, though, to achieve it? Keating didn't seem to think he would be able to do so. Very well, then. He could work backward, begin with the answer and figure out the steps he needed to make to reach it. He'd done it before, though never when the stakes had been this high, this . . . necessary to his continued existence.

And the best, most perfect answer to what he wanted was marriage. To Sophia White. The idea made his heart scamper about like a nervous puppy. The only way he could own her was if she owned him to the same degree. Taking a breath, he resumed pacing. Pacing helped.

Marrying Sophia. His mother would spin in her grave. His sister would likely drop dead of mortification and end in a grave. His father . . . his father would be baffled that he cared for a chit enough to go to the trouble. And he—he, as powerful as he was, would face censure. The loss of friendships, such as they'd turned out to be. The loss of business partnerships and alliances. But he would keep his properties and his income.

In fact, the only obligation marrying her would fulfill was the actual decree that he marry. As clever and cruel as his father might have thought he was being, the ninth duke had never specified the pedigree of this nameless bride—only that his son marry by his thirtieth year.

That realization stopped him again. His friends, his sister, could moan and cry and tear out their hair, but they couldn't actually *do* anything. Not to him, and not to Sophia. The next fence blocking his way was, therefore, what Hennessy could do to her, to him, and to the Tantalus if he swooped in and stole the bride for himself.

The Duke of Hennessy, if he used every ounce of his influence, called in every favor, and played on every drop of pride owned by the aristocracy, could crush The Tantalus Club. He could make being a member ridiculous, and worse, he could make certain that those who visited the club faced public and monetary censure. If that happened, it would be closed within a year.

What the Duke of Hennessy wouldn't have bargained on, what he couldn't possibly have anticipated, however, was another duke becoming involved. And not just any duke, but one with a reputation for getting what he wanted, by whatever means necessary. One who could take a man's spine-stiffening pride and twist it until it snapped.

A slow, grim smile touched his mouth, new determination heated his chilled insides. All he had to do was not make a single misstep. And not fail. It seemed he would be journeying to Cornwall, after all. He had one or two matters to see to, first, however. If he was attempting to make things right, he wasn't doing it halfway. And it was about damned time, if he said so himself.

"Ah, there you are, Greaves," Burroughs said with a slight smile, leaning an elbow on the pianoforte in the crowded music room. "I heard a rumor that someone is missing. Do you need any help looking for h—"

Adam punched him. With a grunt Aubrey went down on his backside, his feet kicking up in the air. "God Rest Ye Merry, Gentlemen" clanked to a halt, and Sylvia Hart fainted. Before Burroughs could regain his feet Adam hauled him up by the lapel and shoved him into a chair.

"Blackwoods, please move over there," he said, noting belatedly that Keating and Camille had evidently changed their minds about abandoning him. Either that, or they wanted to make certain he didn't go charging after Sophia. He *was* going after her, but he was going prepared.

With a lifted eyebrow, Keating took his wife's arm and they moved back by the window where he indicated. "Mr. and Mrs. Flanagan," he continued, "over by the Blackwoods. Now."

"Greaves," Keating rumbled.

"Later. Henning. With the Blackwoods. And you as well, Lady Caroline." He sent a glance at Drymes. The marquis had asked about his relationship to Sophia, but he hadn't taken part in the gift giving or the taunts or wagering. And he was a scoundrel, which today counted in his favor. "Drymes. You, too."

The marquis shrugged and moved to stand beside Caroline. "Very well."

"This is unacceptable, brother," Eustace chirped, not doing a very good job at concealing the affront on her pretty face. "You cannot order your guests about like . . . like servants."

He turned his back on the small group he'd gathered. "Everyone whose name I did not just call, I want you out of this house by nightfall."

Sylvia miraculously lifted her head as she lay in Lord Lassiter's arms. "But you invited us here! You mean to say you've chosen Lady Caroline? Oh, that's unfair!"

"And it's Christmas!" her sister chimed in, plump tears rolling down her cheeks and turning her nose that ghastly red color again.

"I don't care which day it is. Out. Now."

"You cannot!" Eustace wailed.

"I just did." He folded his arms across his chest, resisting the urge to begin grabbing people and shoving them out of the music room. "I suggest you also make certain that anyone who wasn't in here also be informed that they are to leave."

With indignant looks and sour-sounding muttering, twenty aristocrats filed out of the room and began clomping loudly down the portrait gallery. He could even make out a word or two comparing him to his wildly erratic father, and he didn't give a damn. Instead, he walked over to Lady Caroline and took her aside. "I need to explain something to you, Caroline. I'm not going to offer for you," he said in a low voice. "Th—"

She put up a hand. "Your Grace, if you *had* asked me to marry you, I would have declined."

Slowly Adam closed his mouth again. "Not to complain, but why, precisely, would you have turned me down?"

"Because I have some pride, and I cannot see myself being second to a duke's unacknowledged by-blow. A legitimate daughter, yes. But—and please don't take this wrong, because I actually happen to like Miss White—I would not care to hear the gossip about the affair." She put a hand on his arm. "I hope you're able to make an arrangement that sees both of you happy, but I'm glad you understand that it cannot include me." She leaned in closer. "And between you and me, your sister is a terror."

"I . . . agree," he said slowly, looking at her with a

great deal more insight than he'd possessed a handful of minutes ago.

"I shall pack my things and leave with the others, then."

"You may do so if you wish, but considering that you wished me well, wished Sophia well, and insulted my sister all in the same breath, I would just as soon you remain here."

She smiled. "I would like that."

Another chit he could consider an ally. Either Sophia had set the world on its ear, or she'd set him on his ear.

When he turned around, Eustace remained in her seat by the window. "Adam," she said in a low voice, sending an annoyed glance past him at the remaining seven people in the room. "Do you have any idea what you've just done? You have embarrassed yourself, and me, and the Baswich name."

"I'm not interested in your opinion, Eustace. If you wish to complain about how I'm shaming the family, you may do so in a letter. I suggest you wait a month or two before writing me, however, because I won't yet have returned from my honeymoon before then."

His sister shook her head. "Caroline Emry. A marquis's daughter, at least, but did you have to choose one who has an Italian opera singer for a cousin? You are determined to disgrace the Baswich name, aren't you?"

Adam gazed at his sister. "I'm not going to marry Caroline Emry," he said in a low voice. "I'm after a duke's daughter."

"A . . ." Her mouth snapped shut. "What does that mean?" she asked, her voice even more shrill. "I insist that you state precisely your intentions. No games, Adam. Your future—and mine—rests on this."

He smiled. "And I insist that you use your imagination. Conjure the worst thing you can possibly imagine happening to the Baswich family name. Combine that with the realization that dear young Jonathan is not going to claim my fortune. Ever." Adam waited, watching his sister's already fair face turn almost gray as she blanched. "*That* is what I'm going to do. Exactly what you're thinking."

"Adam, for God's sake! You can't m—"

"You're still here. Leave."

"You can't set me out of this house," she protested, her voice shaking. "I am your sister."

"What you are is a hateful vulture who's been picking at me since I was born, and who just spent weeks doing everything possible to make a holiday miserable for a woman who only wanted to experience a pleasant Christmas for once in her life. Get your damned luggage and get out of my house. And be glad I'm not doing anything further."

With a rage-filled squawk, she fled the room. When Adam turned around, the remaining occupants looked decidedly uneasy, with the exception of Keating. Blackwood looked rather amused. "You lot," Adam said, straightening his arms and flexing his fingers. "I'm going to be leaving in the next day or so, but you're welcome to stay. In addition, my holiday party next year is going to be much smaller. I would be pleased if you would agree to join me."

"Is it going to be this exciting next year?" Lady Caroline asked, a smile touching her brown eyes.

"Anything is possible."

"I say, that's good of you, Greaves," Henning put in. "I'm honored."

Adam nodded. "No. *I* am honored. One would think I'm a bit old to be making self-discoveries, but evidently I still have some lessons to learn. Now if you'll excuse me, I have to go set footmen in the hallways and tell the cook we'll have fewer guests for dinner."

He had some other arrangements to make as well, but for the moment he would keep those to himself. And he needed to figure out how to convince Sophia to trust him enough to agree to wed him rather than marry a vicar and simply . . . surrender.

SIXTEEN

By the time the snow of Yorkshire reached Cornwall, it had lowered into a stiff, blowing rain. Hefting a hat box in each hand and burying her cheeks into her stolen greatcoat, Sophia walked down the mud and stone main street of Gulval, her gaze on the old church at the end of the pathway.

Old gray stones with patches of moss around the north-facing window looked unblinkingly back at her. Black slate roof tiles glistened in the heavy rain, and a scattering of headstones leaned amid the winter-bare sticks and flattened grass. If she'd been visiting, she might have found it . . . quaint. Possibly. Knowing that she would be spending the rest of her life in the equally stony house located two dozen feet from the rear of the church, however, all she could do was stifle a shiver. The weather might have been colder in Yorkshire, but her insides had never felt as chill as they did now.

The woman at the inn, where she'd left the mail stage, had informed her that the vicar would be in the church all afternoon, preparing Sunday's sermon. She wouldn't be expected for a fortnight, but if she'd delayed somewhere else that might have given her a moment or two of hope again—and that seemed a cruel thing to do to herself.

In the same vein, she might have attempted to convince herself that Gulval, in the Penwith district of Cornwall, would have been less gloomy in better weather, that if she'd arrived with the sun shining and the birds singing she might have felt more optimistic about her future. But the weather truly didn't signify. It was inside that she felt cold and lifeless and moss-covered.

Traveling to Yorkshire and Greaves Park had been a stupid mistake to begin with. No, she hadn't expected to fall in love, much less with the least likely man in the country, but she'd been looking for more of that blasted hope. For fond memories. All that meant now, though, was that she had more regrets. And one maddening, amazing man she both wished she could forget and wanted to keep inside her heart always.

With Adam, she'd charmed a man most people were afraid even to speak to. Could the Reverend Loines possibly be as difficult as the Duke of Greaves? With measured footsteps, shoving hard against the feeling that she was walking to her own funeral, she pushed open the church door and stepped inside. Silently she moved up the center aisle, between rows of black-painted pews and toward the altar draped in white cloth and topped by a pair of candles.

"Hello?" she called, not seeing anyone within the main room.

A wooden door to the left side of the altar creaked open. A young man, hair brown and neatly combed, stepped inside. "May I help you?" he asked, brown eyes taking in her drenched greatcoat and the rivulets of water running down her face from her ruined blue bonnet.

Well, he didn't look like Frankenstein's monster, anyway. She mustered a smile. "Mr. Loines?"

"Yes." His eyes narrowed, then widened. "Miss White."

"Yes. I'm several weeks early, but—"

He backed into the side room and shut the door on

her sentence. For a moment Sophia stood there, dripping. As that wasn't even the rudest thing ever done to her, she set down her boxes again and made for the doorway. As she reached it, though, it opened again.

"You are to wait here," the Reverend Loines said, as he pulled a heavy coat and wide-brimmed hat on over his simple black and brown attire. "I will fetch Mother, who will be your companion until our marriage."

"Your moth—"

"I cannot be alone with you," he interrupted, "as we are unmarried." Moving past her, he hurried up the length of the church and vanished out the main door.

"Well."

She couldn't even remember the last time a man had decided he couldn't be in a room alone with her. With a scowl, she sat in the front pew and practiced folding her hands in her lap. The bench was hard and far too straight-backed to be comfortable, though they had likely been so for years before Mr. Loines was even born. A few cushions, however, would do wonders.

For some reason she'd thought he would be older, someone Hennessy had deemed capable of keeping her in check. But he'd barely looked older than she was, herself. If he was merely four- or five-and-twenty, he couldn't have been in this position for long. Perhaps he wasn't as set in his ways as she'd feared.

The idea of Mr. Loines had haunted her for weeks. And whichever conclusions she wished to leap to now about his youth and his character had no more validity than her nightmares. She was here. The good or bad of it wouldn't matter, except it would determine how she could best make do.

Nearly ten minutes passed before the church door opened again. A tall, round woman stepped inside and pulled a scarf from over her white-peppered dark hair. "Mrs. Loines, I presume?" Sophia asked, standing again.

"I am."

"I'm pleased to m—"

"You surprised the vicar. Have a seat while I fetch some tea, and he'll return momentarily."

Sophia sat again. "Where did he go, if I might ask?"

The vicar's mother vanished into the side room, then emerged a moment later with a pot and three cups. "To the house. He has some notes, he said." The woman eyed her. "You're going to behave, I hope. Gulval is a God-fearing village, and we won't stand for a woman leading our men astray."

"Please, Mother," the vicar's voice came from behind them. "You're speaking to my betrothed. Miss White is not going to lead anyone astray."

Well, that was nice—and unexpected. "Thank you, Vicar. I—"

"She is the example from which we all shall learn how better to serve our Lord and savior," he continued. "Christ walked among lepers, and we shall follow his example."

"I'm not a leper," Sophia stated, frowning.

"Of course not," he said, dragging a chair from one side of the room to sit directly in front of her. "You are Mary Magdalene, a fallen woman waiting to be raised to grace. And I shall raise you."

"I didn't fall anywhere," Sophia retorted, the gleam in his eye somehow more troubling than if he had been a drooling, arm-swinging monster. "My parents are unmarried, which is no fault of mine."

He smiled. "Yes, of course. And your employment at a den of sin? Your life in a house full of Jezebels? Is that no fault of yours? And your fraternization with men? You must acknowledge your faults in order to learn from them. And you must be the example for other women who teeter on the edge of damnation."

Sophia sent a glance at Mrs. Loines, who'd taken a

seat on the opposite pew and nodded. "Is there no woman in Gulval who's caught your eye, Mr. Loines?" she asked. "You seem to view me as a poor choice for matrimony."

"A vicar should marry so that he may more completely serve as an example to his congregation. You are a perfect choice for me to demonstrate the effects of faith and charity and repentance."

Ice coursing down her spine, Sophia scooted back as far into the pew as she could. The degree of . . . hate the Duke of Hennessy must have had for her—and why? Because she'd been born? Every muscle, every sinew in her body tensed up, ready for her to run. She *wanted* to run. But she couldn't. The Tantalus Club, the three dozen women who'd sought employment there for the same reasons she had—because they had nowhere else to go but the streets—would suffer if she fled.

"You seem very certain of my place in all this," she ventured, attempting to keep her voice steady. In the back of her mind she could abruptly hear Adam's voice, telling her that she was an unusual, extraordinary woman. She concentrated on that, drawing strength from the idea that someone else in the world found her worthwhile. "And yet, I don't even know your Christian name."

He nodded, folding his hands together. "Peter. But we must be proper in all things. I am to be addressed as Vicar, the Reverend Loines, or Mr. Loines at all times. Just as you will be Mrs. Loines."

"But your mother is Mrs. Loines."

His mother sat forward. "I have agreed to go by Mother Loines," she said.

"Oh."

The vicar rested his elbows on his knees. "I know a vicarage is frequently a . . . gift, given to an aristocrat's younger son merely to provide him an income. That is not so with me. Mother says I was born for this. It is precisely where I'm meant to be."

Sophia forced a smile. "It's rare for someone to find their perfect place in the world."

He tilted his head at her. "This is your perfect place as well, Miss White. Here you will join me in church every Sunday, sitting right where you are now, and twice a week when portions of the congregation gather you will confess your sins and we will pray for you. You will do good works, tending the poor and reading the Bible for the uneducated and the infirm. And of course you will contemplate your sins wh—"

The door at the back of the church creaked open. "There you are, Sophia," came the familiar voice of the Marquis of Haybury.

Jumping, she whipped her head around. "What? What are y—"

"I'm glad I arrived early," he cut in, striding forward to her side. "It isn't every day I'm invited to give the bride away, after all."

The vicar stood when she did. "My lord, I hadn't realized you were still in Gulval. And I was under the impression that you didn't care for the idea of this wedding."

The marquis offered a smile that didn't touch his eyes. "Suffice it to say that when Miss White marries, I mean to be there."

That sounded rather ominous, even to her. And considering that she hadn't expected to see anyone she knew ever again, Sophia was quite proud of herself for not bursting into tears. But she hadn't told Lord and Lady Haybury the details of this match. All she'd told them was that Hennessy had found her a husband, and that she had agreed to marry.

Lord Haybury took her hand and tucked it around

his arm. "Have you settled on a date yet?" he asked, briefly squeezing her fingers. "I hadn't expected to see you until just before the fifteenth of the month."

"Neither did I," Mr. Loines returned, a scowl knitting his brows together. "Nor did I expect that anyone from your previous . . . life would be in attendance. You are to begin a new life here."

"Yes, I know," Sophia said, far too flippantly. Considering that she was near to having an apoplexy, though, it would have to do. "But Lord Haybury is family."

"I'm like a father to her," Haybury seconded, clearly ignoring the fact that he was only six years her senior.

"I see." The vicar looked from one to the other of them. "This is to be a small, simple ceremony, presided over by the vicar from Newmill. As you're here, I see no reason to wait. The Reverend Matthews can marry us by Thursday afternoon."

"Aren't you going to have the banns read?" Oliver asked, frowning in turn. "It would be somewhat improper to ignore the custom under the circumstances, would it not?"

"I have been reading the banns," the Reverend Loines returned. "Sunday will be the third occasion. I didn't wish to have the wedding delayed after Miss White's arrival. An unmarried female of her character roaming about the village would be . . . unfitting."

"You've been thorough," the marquis returned. "We will wait, of course, until after the third reading of the banns. I suggest a week from Saturday. That will give you ten days, Miss White, to find an appropriate gown to wear. Most of her things were lost in a carriage accident, you know. They went into the river. She nearly drowned."

Mother Loines snorted. "You aren't suggesting she wear white, are you, my lord?"

"Mother, please. Saturday next would be acceptable. And I shall use the metaphor of lost belongings to equate with the wages of sin being washed away." He tapped a long forefinger against his chin in a gesture no doubt meant to look thoughtful. "There remains the matter of where to place you until we are safely wed. I suppose you could remain at my home, sharing Mother Loines's bed, until the wedding. That would halt any talk of impropriety."

There had been some lovely cliffs on the road down from London. Perhaps she could find one of them now and simply leap off. It would be less painful than a lifetime of this. How could she manage it? How could she manage not to run when that was all she wanted to do? When Adam had already given her a place to hide if she could stand this for a year or so?

"I've rented out the Oyster Shell," Haybury countered. "There are four empty rooms there, and a staff. Surely that would suffice just as well."

"I don't believe th—"

"Yes, that will be lovely," she heard herself say. "Do you think we might go there now, my lord? I find that four days in a mail coach has tired me terribly."

"Of course." Haybury nodded at the vicar and his mother, who looked at the moment like frowning mirrors of each other. "Perhaps Mr. Loines will call on us there at breakfast."

"I . . . certainly will. There are rules you must learn before the wedding. And vows I've written for you to recite."

Clutching the marquis's arm, she dipped down to pick up one of her hat boxes, while he took the other. Then, before someone could lock the church door and prevent them from leaving, she made her exit. Haybury, of course, had an umbrella waiting outside, and he handed her the second box before he put an arm across her shoulders and lifted the umbrella to shelter both of them.

"The inn's just over here," he said, guiding her across the street.

Sophia nodded, not trusting herself to speak until they were safely inside. Safe—she doubted she would ever feel safe or secure again. Every moment of the rest of her life, with the exception of the next ten days, would be spent either in the company of her husband or his mother. And she would have to listen to every bit of her past being criticized, the act of a fallen woman, while they preached over her moldering carcass.

"Sit," Haybury said, nudging her toward a table set beside a large stone hearth. He said something to the thin man who'd followed them inside the common room, and with a nod the fellow fled again. A moment later the marquis took the seat opposite her and poured them each a glass of whiskey. "Drink."

She downed it all at once. The heat bit into her throat, sending her shuddering into life again. "What are you doing here?" she rasped.

Gray eyes assessed her. They were a shade or two lighter than Adam's stormy gaze, she noticed, and though the two men shared a jaded cynicism, she would never confuse one for the other. The Duke of Greaves's gaze lifted her heart, warmed her insides, filled her spirit, even when he was angry.

"I think the better question is, why are *you* here?" he finally returned, refilling her glass. "You neglected to mention a few details about your nuptials, I believe."

Deliberately draining the glass again, Sophia shook her head. "Oh, no, you don't. You knew about the coach falling in the river. And you're here, when you have no reason to be. You need to tell me."

"You know, my employees don't generally attempt to order me about."

"I don't work for you. I worked for Diane."

"Semantics," he countered easily. "I received a letter. Two of them actually."

"From whom?" It couldn't have been from Adam, because the two men didn't speak. Keating? Or more likely, Camille. But why? Cammy would have known that nothing could help the situation, and she knew quite well that Lord and Lady Haybury were not to know the details of this arrangement.

"That's my business," he answered.

"I need to know," she stated, thumping her fist on the tabletop. "If Greaves has been corresponding with you, and told you to be here, then I have to be suspicious that he means to make trouble for me."

He eyed her. "The days when Adam Baswich orders me to do anything are long gone. No, that's not true. Those days never existed."

That had the ring of truth to it. "When did these letters arrive, then?"

"Persistent, aren't you? The first one arrived a week or so ago, directing me to travel here and meet your betrothed, and asking for my . . . assessment of his character. The second one arrived by courier this morning. That lad nearly dropped dead from exhaustion the moment he handed it off to me. And that's all I'm saying about them."

It must have been Camille, or her and Keating together. They, at least, would be worried over her vicar-to-be. "Very well, then."

The marquis took a sip of his whiskey and then set his elbows on the table, resting his chin on his folded hands. "You made an agreement with Hennessy that day he came calling at the club. And it wasn't merely about a marriage. I assume it was 'Marry Mr. Loines, or I'll destroy the Tantalus,' or something equally naughty."

"My reasons for marrying the vicar are my own. What did the second letter say?"

"Several very interesting things. Tell me about your holiday. How did you find Greaves Park?"

Though she attempted not to think about what he'd just said, the moment he uttered the words her mind conjured the snowy hills, the crackling cold of the air, and holly and mistletoe and ribbons in the drawing room. And Adam, smiling at her. A tear ran down her cheek before she could stop it. "It was very nice," she said, wishing now that she hadn't drunk so much whiskey on an empty stomach. Sophia squared her shoulders. "And you shouldn't have delayed the wedding. Ten days? I just want to have it done with."

"Because you're so looking forward to being that zealot's wife, I assume. Yes, I can see how very compatible the two of you are."

"I agreed to marry him. I am a woman of my word. You're only making things worse."

"I do enjoy trouble." He rolled his shoulders in his dark gray jacket. "Even so, a person generally only marries once. You should do it well."

"I don't have any money with me. And you can't purchase me a dress." Her heart broke a little bit more as she remembered having a very similar conversation just over four weeks ago. Heavens, had it only been a month? It seemed a lifetime ago.

"You have money in your account in London. I will lend you a sum against it. Because you cannot marry in that." He gestured at her dripping wet blue walking dress, still half covered by Adam's greatcoat. "And I would not suggest you walk into the church garbed in one of your Tantalus gowns."

Sophia glanced down at her dress. The poor garment had survived her dunking in the river, four days in a mail coach, and now another soaking in the rain. The Reverend Loines would more than likely be delighted to see a bedraggled, drooping, heartsick bride, and he would use her appearance as proof that she was a sorry, broken soul. At this moment, she felt like one.

"I have a question for you," Haybury asked, then paused as a servant hurried in with a pile of blankets. As the man left again, the marquis stood and walked around behind her to wrap one of the blankets around her shoulders. "Greaves." He took his seat again.

She closed her eyes for just a moment, but that only made the images in her mind more vivid. "What about him?"

"He's a cracking bad sort, a meddler, a game player, and a heartless fiend. But that's merely my opinion of his character. What's yours?"

Sophia huddled into the blanket, wishing she could disappear into it. "I don't know what those letters said, but it doesn't matter. I went to York for a . . . a new experience, a different sort of holiday. And it was lovely. Now I'm marrying Mr. Loines. In ten days, evidently." She stood. "Where is my room? I'd like to change out of my wet clothes."

"Up the stairs, first door on the right," he returned, not moving. "I'm surprised you're surrendering; it's not like you, Sophia."

"It's very like me. You simply don't know me as well as you thought you did."

Oliver watched her up the stairs and through the door into her small, rented room. Then he downed the rest of the whiskey in his glass and refilled it. If he didn't know her as well as he thought he did, and more importantly, if Greaves didn't know her as well as he thought *he* did, they were all about to be in for a great deal of trouble. Well, they were in for a great deal of trouble, anyway. The only question was whether it would be worth it or not.

Regardless, at the moment he was a damned nanny. One who found himself in the dullest village in Cornwall, on the rainiest day of the year, and with the chore for the next ten days of keeping a duke's illegitimate daughter from somehow finding a way to marry a man who would drain the life from her like a bloody leech. Greaves had owed him a great deal before. Now, well, he'd always admired the duke's Thoroughbred. Zeus would do well—as a start.

If Adam hadn't already been aware that the Duke of Hennessy wasn't entertaining, the butler's startled expression when a coach and four arrived at the front door of Hennessy House in Hampshire would have led him to the same conclusion. Aside from the fact that he couldn't recall more than two or three soirees ever being held at Reynolds House, Hennessy's London home, he doubted many people would voluntarily spend their holiday being constantly frowned at.

In this instance "House" was something of a misnomer; the estate wasn't as large as Greaves Park—few homes were—but it was impressive. And cold and stifling, but then he'd thought the same thing about his own estate until Sophia had arrived there bringing sunshine where none had ever shone before.

"May I help you?" the butler asked, resuming a more disdainful expression.

"Is Hennessy in residence?" Adam returned, pushing back at his brimming frustration. The events of the past few days had sharpened his temper to a degree that even he found troubling, but the anger and frustration were also the only things that kept his mind focused on the task at hand rather than on the impossible one that still lay before him in Cornwall.

"And who may I say is calling? The household is presently abed and cannot be disturbed."

Abed—what the devil time was it? He'd been measuring by days rather than hours, because all that mattered was that he hadn't seen Sophia in six days. It felt longer, and shorter; he could conjure their last kiss—though at the time he hadn't known it was the last—with no effort at all.

"The Duke of Greaves," he said aloud, though he would have thought the large coat of arms painted on the large black coach would have supplied his pedigree just as well.

The butler blinked. "Please come inside and make yourself comfortable, Your Grace," he said crisply, backing out of the doorway and leading the way to a rather formal-looking sitting room. Adam didn't sit, however. Nothing about him had been able to relax for days.

He would have left Greaves Park sooner, but that would have meant shirking duties as both a duke and a landowner. The gifts of food to the poor the day after Christmas, the gifts and obligations to his servants, and a hundred other tasks that he traditionally saw to at this time of year. If he'd left without seeing to his people, he wouldn't have felt . . . worthy of pursuing Sophia. Not after she'd reminded him that he was human.

Nearly forty minutes of silent, building annoyance passed before the sitting room door opened again. "Greaves," a low voice rumbled. "What in the world brings you to Hampshire at this time of year? And at this hour?"

The Duke of Hennessy was a large man, stout and barrel-chested, with a gut that had expanded at approximately the same rate that his straight gray hair had receded toward the top of his head. He looked nothing at all like Sophia, thankfully, except perhaps for the slightly curved eyebrows and something he couldn't quite name about the eyes.

"I need to speak to you about your daughter," Adam replied, not in the mood for idle chitchat.

Hennessy frowned. "Katherine? She's here with Marshall and the children. What about her?"

"I'm here about Sophia White."

The duke's eyes narrowed a fraction. "Then we have nothing to discuss. I'm sorry you came all this way for no reason."

"You threatened her, bullied her into agreeing to a marriage for which she is utterly unsuited. I don't like that."

"I'm pleased to have you stay for breakfast," Hennessy stated levelly, "but I am finished discussing this topic."

Adam frowned, the days of frustration and tension edging into fine, sharp-tipped fury. "You made her. Why the devil won't you take responsibility for her well-being?"

"I continue to be baffled by this conversation. In theory, however, I have seen her into a proper circumstance."

"You've seen her to Cornwall, where you can attempt to forget that she exists."

A mottled red began seeping into Hennessy's jowls. "Given your own lineage, I find you unqualified to preach morality to me."

The Adam of several weeks ago would have felt that comment cut. This Adam had another, greater concern. "When the devil faults your reasoning, you should pay attention," he snapped.

"I have done nothing wrong. And this conversation is over."

Christ. At least *he* admitted to the mistakes he made, Adam thought. Or most of them, anyway. Did denial make Hennessy the sober, religious, propriety-minded man he so loudly proclaimed himself to be? The duke would likely think so, but Adam had already decided he liked Hennessy even less than he had previously. And he needed to win this argument. Sophia's future—and his own—rested on it, because now that he'd realized what he could have, settling for anything else would be impossible, whatever the consequences.

"You paid for her schooling," he pushed again, beginning to lose the badly fraying reins of his temper.

"I don't believe in charity. It only gives false hope to those who haven't earned their way."

"You're a damned dog," Adam finally snapped. "If you're man enough to fuck someone, be man enough to take responsibility for the results."

The duke drew himself up to his full height, still nearly a head shorter than Adam. "I have seen to her future, when I was under no obligation to do so. It's none of your affair, Greaves. I've done right by this person. Now leave."

"I'm not finished with you yet. You threatened The Tantalus Club if she refused the future you shoved at her. I have a different future in mind."

"Oh, really?" Hennessy asked skeptically.

"Yes. You will leave Sophia White alone, and you will leave that club alone. I have taken a particular interest in the woman and in the place, and I will fiercely—and tirelessly—defend their right to exist in the manner of their own choosing."

"That den of iniquity is a blight on all of London," Hennessy retorted, the red blotching his skin deepening. "It needs to go away."

Adam took a slow step closer. "I am not some crusader for women's rights. Neither am I a shiny-eyed youth with large ideas and small means. I have no use for propriety or manners or your good graces, and I have no use for you. I will not be fair, and I will be brutal. Are you prepared to cross me in this?"

For a moment he thought the duke might drop dead in his own stuffy morning room. "That is a great deal of bluster over what, a mistress?"

And that would be the last time anyone called her that. "I mean to marry Sophia White. In order to do so, I will insure the safety of The Tant—"

"Marry her?" Hennessy repeated, his brows drawing together. "You're a duke, boy. You can't marry some commoner. Less than a commoner, even. It's absurd! Not even your father would *marry* a whore, for God's sake."

"I'm not my father," Adam bit out, for one of the few times in his life knowing that he spoke the truth. Because his father would never have fallen in love, much less risked his reputation for anyone other than himself. Sophia had evidently made him a better man, even against his own will. "And if you had bothered to become acquainted with your daughter, you would have found the time spent to be worthwhile. She is . . . remarkable."

"Y—"

"I'm taking care of your so-called problem, Hennessy. I'm removing her from the Tantalus. The Tantalus will remain. The gossip that will accompany her will be solely *your* fault, for fathering her and then failing to acknowledge her even when she becomes the Duchess of Greaves." For a long moment he gazed directly at the duke. "Are we perfectly clear?" he finally murmured.

"If I discover that Haybury or his wife put you up to this, I will—"

"Say it. The Tantalus remains."

Hennessy actually growled. "The Tantalus remains," he repeated stiffly. "Now y—"

"I'm finished with you now," Adam said, cutting into Hennessy's bluster once more. "The Tantalus, Sophia, left alone. If I hear any differently, I'll see you destroyed. If you think I'm lying about that, you're free to test me." With a stiff nod, he turned his back and made for the door.

"You're making a mistake, Greaves. Marrying a whore will bring you down; not raise her up. You're the one who'll pay for your foolishness."

"And I'll be happy to have the opportunity to do so." In fact, he prayed he would have the opportunity to make amends to her.

Out in the hallway, a petite form blocked his path. "Greaves," the gray-haired Duchess of Hennessy said, regarding him.

"Your Grace," he returned, inclining his head. "If you'll excuse me, I'm late to stop one wedding and arrange for a second one." And if Haybury hadn't done his part, it might already be too late. Ice gripped his heart. It couldn't be too late. Losing her now . . . He couldn't contemplate it.

"Carlton did not pay for Miss White's education," the duchess said in a low voice, taking his arm as he made his way to the foyer. "I did."

That surprised him to his bones. "Your husband took a lover, and you paid for the resulting child's education?" he commented. "I'm thankful, but why?"

"Because I don't believe in leaving messes lying about. My husband is a weak man who clings to religion in the vain hope that others will see him as better than he is. I wanted her to have the opportunity to be more than a blight upon humanity."

Adam slowed. "I need to begin speaking with more women," he said. "I'm finding you're all full of surprises."

"Not all of us. Just the good ones." She took a breath. "Carlton is correct about one thing; if you pursue this path you seem to have chosen, you will encounter ridicule and censure. I know this, because I faced something similar when the gossip began about my maid being with child. You won't like it, Greaves. You're not accustomed to it."

"I love her, Your Grace." There was more to it than that, of course, but that was between Sophia and him.

"Well, then. I've given you my counsel. Do with it what you will."

He extracted his arm as the butler opened the front door for him. This side trip had cost him a day, but it had been utterly necessary. Unless he could guarantee the well-being of the Tantalus, Sophia would never alter from the path her father had forced her on. And that would never do.

SEVENTEEN

The weather had improved in Gulval, but Sophia's mood hadn't. For a week she'd puttered about the village, spending money to purchase two new dresses in addition to a high-necked gray one she'd deemed more suitable for a wedding to a member of the church.

Generous spending had gained her if not friendship, then a certain warm tolerance from London's shopkeepers. In Gulval, though, men seemed to run away at the sight of her, and women turned their backs to avoid talking with her. Whatever the vicar had told his congregation, she seemed to be the closest thing to Delilah or Jezebel this part of Cornwall had ever encountered.

For the first two or three days, she'd told herself that it would all change once she became Mrs. Loines. But how could it? How could someone detest her, and then like her the next day simply because she'd put a ring on her finger? Particularly when she'd done so under duress? She was to be the ugly thing everyone wanted to point at to make themselves feel superior.

And then there were the luncheons. She lifted the cloth napkin from her lap and wiped at the corner of her mouth. The roast chicken before her was edible enough, if she'd had any appetite. Mostly she attempted to avoid vomiting on the woman seated across from her at the small table at Mrs. Jones's Meat Pies shop.

"It will be lovely, I must say, to have someone to assist

me," Mother Loines said, taking a sip of Madeira. "There are days when I simply don't have time to call on all of the parish's unfortunates."

While aiding "the unfortunates"—the only way she'd heard the vicar's mother refer to the poor and destitute of Gulval—actually sounded like something worthy, Sophia had already realized that her idea of helping and Mother Loines's idea were two very different things. And her way, of course, was wrong.

Calling on someone didn't entail bringing food or clothing. Rather, Mother Loines called early in the morning on her first unfortunate and read aloud for an hour or so from the Bible several appropriate passages regarding the wretched or the unworthy. Having dispensed her daily doom and gloom, she continued on to her next unfortunate—and so on, for at least ten hours every day. Except for Sunday, of course, when she spent the entire day in the church.

"I still don't see the harm in providing bread or blankets to those in need," Sophia finally said, interrupting the detailed description of Wednesdays, the day the congregation met to jointly pray over the past week's greatest sinner.

"Because once an unfortunate is provided with goods, they lose the will to see to themselves," Mother Loines returned, annoyance touching her honeyed voice. "Why should they find employment when they are simply given food to eat or clothes to wear? You would only make matters worse, Miss White. You have a great deal to learn." The woman offered Sophia a brief smile. "I shall call on you in the morning, at seven o'clock, and I will provide you with some appropriate Scriptures that suit your present circumstance and will prepare you for being a vicar's wife."

"Once I am married to your son, how will you spend

your days?" Sophia asked, though she had a very good idea already of the answer to that. Mother Loines did not seem like someone who would willingly relinquish her place or her status in the community. "Because as the vicar's wife, *I* will be the one making the rounds, will I not?"

"Oh, dear, I couldn't possibly leave the reputation of the vicar and the church in your hands. Not for years."

Another pound of metaphorical bricks settled onto Sophia's shoulders. By the time of the marriage, she wouldn't even be able to stand upright. She could tell herself that these were the cruelest kind people she'd ever encountered, but knowing that didn't do her any good at all. It didn't alter the fact that she had to— *had to*—marry the Reverend Loines. That she had to live in a house dominated by Mother Loines, that she would never be able to do right because neither of them considered a sinner such as she capable of such a thing.

Mentally cursing the Duke of Hennessy, she settled for nodding and then drank down the remainder of the Madeira in her own glass. Until she'd met the vicar and his mother, she'd loved people, loved learning new things and experiencing new things, even when those same people didn't know how to address her or were leery of being in her company.

Even dreams of Adam Baswich, while they improved her nights, only made her days worse by comparison. She already hated this new life, and she wanted to flee. Only two things kept her in Cornwall; she would render the Tantalus safely available for the other young ladies who so desperately needed its haven, and she wouldn't become so pitiful as to be Adam's mistress, to sit in a little house on the edge of London and waste her life waiting for those moments when he had time to spare for her. As that was the only way she could have him, she would do without. Even if it killed her. And if it *was* going to kill her, she'd begun to hope that that would happen sooner rather than later.

Adam rode into an empty village. Shops stood closed, and no one lingered about the public stable yard. The entire place consisted of fifty or so buildings at most, the majority of them tiny, ramshackle cottages edged by tiny gardens of vegetables and overrun by chickens and ducks.

Where the devil was everyone? At approximately the same moment he caught sight of the Oyster Shell inn, where Haybury was staying, he heard a church bell peal. Alarm threaded ice-cold through his veins. He'd told Haybury to get him ten days. Eight had passed. Had the marquis been unable to prevent the marriage? Had he lost Sophia, after all?

His hands shaking, he dismounted. *Think, damn it all.* It was Sunday morning. Everyone would of course be in church. That was the explanation. It had to be. Firmly hanging on to that thought, he pushed open the inn's front door and walked inside. Empty.

"Haybury!" he yelled.

Dimly he heard a door open and then close again. "Greaves."

He turned around, then stopped. The Marquis of Haybury stood at the top of the narrow stairs leading into the public room. "Hello, Oliver. Is she still unmarried?"

"Still unmarried."

Adam let out the breath he'd been holding for what felt like a week. "Thank God. Is she here?"

"At the church. Sunday services last several hours."

"Good. I'll need the time to prepare things."

Oliver didn't move. "I think you need to settle things, first," he said after a moment, his voice flat.

"That's what I—"

"With me, Greaves."

Splendid. "I think Sophia is in a more dire situation than you are," he retorted. "You can wait."

"No I can't. Because I don't trust you. I don't trust that you aren't simply playing another game. I've been here for thirteen days, kicking my heels, and trying to decipher what the devil you're about. Sophia may love you, but I don't. And you're not getting near her until you convince me that you will improve her circumstance rather than making an even greater muck of it than Hennessy has managed."

Adam clenched his fists, every ounce of the past days' frustration pushing him to flatten the marquis. Slowly, though, taking deep breaths, he forced his fists to uncurl. If today was the day for him to pay for all of his prior sins, he wanted to get on with it so he could have a damned conversation with the woman he loved. The man before him seemed a rather appropriate place to begin cleaning his slate. "What do you want me to say, Oliver?" he asked, keeping his voice as level and reasonable as he could manage. "Do you want a confession of my sins? The ones committed against her, or against you?"

"That's a start," the marquis returned, folding his arms over his chest.

"You're no angel, either."

"I'm not trying to stop a vicar's wedding. Or play with an unfortunate young lady's life. So explain yourself. To my satisfaction, or I'll put every roadblock in front of you that I can manage."

"So you want her to marry the Reverend Loines?"

"No, I don't. I don't want to see her facing worse

than that from you, either. You wanted her to be your mistress. She told me that. That might be handy for you, but Sophia has a roof over her head and a means to earn an income all without you."

"Not if Hennessy closes you down," Adam retorted, deciding against admitting—for the moment, anyway—that he'd seen to that part of the problem.

"I'm willing to risk that, as is Diane." Haybury leaned against the door frame, the very image of an immovable, and formidable, rival.

"But Sophia isn't willing to risk the club. She knows how much it means to you and her friends." Adam blew out his breath. "What do you want from me, Oliver? A confession? Very well. Yes. I cheated you that night at faro. I bribed the dealer to change the banker's cards in order to ensure that you would lose."

Oliver stalked down the stairs, his lean face pale and the line of his jaw hard. "I am supremely aware of that. But do you have any idea what you did to me that night? My uncle had cut me off, and I was attempting to win enough blunt to live off of. Thanks to you, I had to leave England for Vienna."

"Where you met Diane Benchley, I believe."

"Beside the point," Oliver said brusquely. "We were damned friends. Or I thought we were. And you didn't need the bloody money. Why? Why would you do that to me?"

For a long moment Adam looked down at the floor. Even after nearly six years, he could still hear the anger in Haybury's voice. He'd done that. And he'd done a great many other things that were less than heroic. Oliver was correct: he needed to make amends for his ill deeds before he could be allowed a . . . a happy ending. "You won't believe me, but I was trying to help."

" 'Trying to help'?" the marquis repeated, his voice a growl. "By ruining me?"

"No. You were . . . so damned arrogant, Oliver. I thought if I removed the choice, you would have to reconcile with your uncle. I thought I was helping." He blew out his breath. "I had no blasted idea that you would choose to leave England rather than apologize for being an ass. And by the time I realized you were gone . . . well, you wouldn't have taken money from me anyway, after that night."

"Unbelievable," Haybury muttered, glaring at him. "Did I somewhere go mad and ask for your intervention? Did you ask if you could help?"

"No. That's why I thought it was a good deed." Adam shrugged. "I know what I did. All I can do now is apologize. You knew I wasn't a nice man. I saw something, and I took action. Evidently that was more significant to me than the actual results."

For a moment he reflected that he might have been using this same dialogue to speak with Sophia. For Lucifer's sake, he'd been a blind, arrogant fool. And for years he'd been so. It had taken a slip of a scandalous chit to make him finally look at himself. And he hoped to God it wasn't too late for him to be a . . . a better man.

For a long moment Oliver looked at him. "Evidently we're both stubborn, arrogant bastards," he finally muttered. "Sophia. Explain."

"Thank you," Adam said, actually surprised that he was being given the chance to continue.

"Don't thank me yet. All I know is that you suggested she become your mistress, and she turned you down. What are you doing here, then? And what am I doing here? Surely you've been rejected at least once prior to this."

"Actually, no, I haven't been. But I'd prefer to have that discussion with Sophia."

"Me first."

Damnation. Did Haybury want to see his exposed, shriveled heart, as well? "I wanted her with me, and asking her to be my mistress seemed the most expedient way to accomplish that."

"Ah. So it was all about efficiency. A shame you didn't take into account the fact that she doesn't want anyone else to be responsible for her life or her safety. And a shame you thought you could charm her into doing what you wanted."

Adam frowned. "I didn't try to charm her into anything. We became friends. I like her company. I didn't want her to leave at the end of the holiday. I'm required to marry by my thirtieth birthday—which is barely a month away, you may recall—and so I chose what seemed like the most logical way to keep her about."

"If I theoretically accept this explanation of yours, why should I let you see her now? So you can ask her again? As atrocious as I consider this match with Loines to be, it does give her a measure of respectability. Being your mistress would not."

"Because I have . . ."—the scent of lemons touched his nostrils, and his heart stumbled—"a different offer for her. But I'm not discussing that with you." It took every ounce of self-discipline he owned to keep from turning around, but he stayed precisely where he was. "I will give you my word that if she turns me away or rejects my plan, I'll go. Without protest. And she can do whatever she feels is necessary to make her way in the world."

Oliver glanced beyond his shoulder, then nodded. "You have five minutes. In this room. And I'll be directly outside the door. I might even be listening to your conversation." Haybury turned around, then paused and looked back again. "And I want your horse. Zeus. Then I might begin to forgive you."

"You . . . Very well. He's yours."

Still not turning around, Adam watched the Marquis of Haybury retreat up the narrow stairs again and shut the door. Then, closing his eyes for just a moment and sending up a quick prayer that he hadn't ruined things so thoroughly that she would never listen to him or trust anything he said, he turned around.

Sophia gazed at the Duke of Greaves. Even though Haybury had never told her who'd written him the pair of notes, she'd had her suspicions. But then the preparations for the wedding kept proceeding, and while the marquis had been sympathetic, he hadn't done anything to stand in her way. She'd begun to think that perhaps it had been Cammy who'd sent the letters, and that Oliver Warren was there only to be certain that she was going into this marriage without any illusions as to what she faced.

But now Adam was standing five feet away from her, his gray eyes gazing at her squarely, his fingers clenching and unclenching as if he wanted to grab her. And he looked tired, she decided, his lean face taut and serious. She likely looked very much the same.

"Sophia," he murmured, taking a step toward her.

"No. Stop," she ordered, backing away. If they touched, she wouldn't be able to stand it. Resolving to do the right things was killing her as it was. Adding him into the mix would tear her to pieces. Just seeing him again was too much.

He froze, lowering the hand he'd raised. "Very well. May I speak?"

"About what?"

Adam cleared his throat. "First of all, I spoke with Hennessy. Whatever you may decide today, The Tantalus Club is safe. I swear it. You do not *have* to marry . . . anyone."

The world seemed to turn white and misty. Dimly she felt Adam's arms go around her, then the dizzy sensation of being lifted. A moment later color and sound began to return, and she blinked. Somehow he'd carried her to one of the two large chairs in front of the fireplace and set her gently down. He squatted by one arm, looking up at her.

"I don't have to marry him," she stammered, putting her hands over her face. "I can go back to the Tantalus?"

He stood again, a muscle in his jaw jumping. "Yes, you can. Or you could take a third path."

Everything had begun moving too fast for her to keep up. But if he hadn't accepted the answer she'd left for him at Greaves Park, if he truly didn't understand how badly he'd insulted her, she would explain it to him. "I don't want to hear you reargue your same points again," she stated, lowering her hands again to clench them in her lap.

"I don't mean to do so."

"If you're here, then I think you do. I told you that I fought for my entire life to make a place for myself, and firstly you wanted me to turn my back on all my friends—my family—at the club, and secondly you wanted for me to . . . run away from a husband and live hidden and in scandal somewhere. Thank you for saving me from this. Truly. But for the last time, I do not wish to be your mistress, Adam. I don't want part of you. I don't want to give up what I have, what I am, in exchange for . . . nothing."

"I know that."

She slammed her fist into her thigh, though that was a poor substitute for wanting to hit him or a wall or something. Anything, because physical pain couldn't be any worse than the ache in her chest. "Then why could you ever ask me such a thing?"

"Because I couldn't see any other way to keep you in my life." He scowled. "No one could see any other reason why you and I would be together, and I . . . couldn't explain what I wanted, even to myself. It was wrong and selfish."

"Thank you. I accept your apology." A tear ran down her cheek, but she ignored it. "I wish we could have ended this on better terms. Now, I need to go pack my things so I can return to London with Haybury. Good day." Standing, she turned her back on him.

"I need to marry, Sophia. You know that."

"Of course I do. And I wish you well, Adam. But please don't come see me again. Don't visit the Tantalus. I don't . . . I wish I'd never met you."

He made a sound, deep in his chest. It wrenched at her, but for heaven's sake, how much was she supposed to stand there and take from him? She grabbed onto the stair railing and climbed the first step.

"Give me another minute, Sophia. Please."

Please. She didn't think she'd ever heard him use that word before. Despite the fact that she knew better, somewhere deep inside what was left of her heart she wanted to hear him say something that restored her faith in him, that proved she hadn't just been an idiot to fall in love with him. Slowly she lowered her hand. "This is not a children's tale. We had a lovely holiday, and now it's over with. Stop making it worse."

"Look at me."

Even more reluctantly she turned around and descended into the room again. "Don't make me yell and throw things, Adam," she whispered. "And don't make me hate you."

He swallowed visibly, actually looking nervous for the first time. It struck her forcefully; this powerful, wealthy man whom everyone respected and most people feared, standing in a ramshackle inn's public room and hesitating to speak to her, of all people. Slowly he took one step forward.

"You are quite possibly the best person I have ever

met, Sophia White. All the nonsense that's been thrown at you simply for being born, and you've stood on your own two feet and laughed at the world. I . . . adore you for that. And I should have told you so long before now."

The door opened above and behind her. "Your five minutes are—"

Sophia whipped her head around. "Five more minutes," she stated, glaring at her employer's husband until he nodded and shut the door again. Hopefully he wouldn't hold it against her later. She certainly needed her job at The Tantalus Club, now more than ever. But she wasn't about to allow Adam to stop speaking now. "Go on. You adore me."

His lips twitched. "I fiercely adore you. But this is about me, too." Adam cleared his throat. "You know I worry that I'm becoming more and more like my father. Eustace made me so damned angry with her gifts to you and the assumptions everyone had, and so I think I just . . . surrendered. If they all considered me to be just like him, then at least I would have you. At least a little."

"I understand." She shook herself, trying to escape the sensation of being warm and surrounded and safe again. "And I think you just saved my life. But I can't be your friend. Not knowing that you have a wife and will have a family. I just can't, Adam."

"This is *my* confession," he stated, tilting his head. "So listen. When you refused me and left, something dawned on me. I didn't need those people around me reminding me of who I was or what I wasn't. I didn't need a party to save me from keeping my own company. All I needed was a friend to remind me of who I wanted to be."

"You only have a few weeks left, Adam," she returned, attempting to be reasonable. "If you did something rash, you need to go apologize to Lady Caroline, not to me. I know you liked her. She'll do well for you. Please tell me you didn't just leave them all at Greaves Park and ride all the way to Cornwall when you have your own future to save."

"No, I didn't leave them all behind. I kicked them all out on their collective fat arses."

Sophia blinked. "But Camille! And Keating. You didn't—"

"I made an exception for seven of them. Drymes, and the ones who were with you in the billiards room. You liked them. I let them stay. And they'll be the only ones I invite back next year."

Oh, goodness. She certainly hadn't expected that, of all things. "Then at least you didn't destroy things with Caroline. What of your sister?" None of it was her concern any longer, but she couldn't help wanting to know. Wanting to hear his voice, to see him so close by her.

"I won't be seeing Eustace again. She can be consumed with a family name she doesn't even bear anymore somewhere far away from me."

"I'm sorry you've lost your family," she returned, "but I'm glad she won't be about to hurt you any longer. All the more reason for you to set your attention on marrying Caroline."

"I'm not marrying Caroline!" he said forcefully, then drew a breath. "I apologize. I didn't mean to yell, but you're driving me mad." He took another step closer. "I've never been as happy as I was when I was with you, you know. I would like that again. Very much."

"But—"

"Quiet."

"Don't tell me what to do."

"Likewise." With a brief smile, he took two steps forward this time and stopped directly in front of her. And then he sank down on one knee.

Sophia froze. She couldn't have moved if her life

depended on it—and she thought it might. "What are you doing?" she squeaked, all the blood leaving her face.

"I've spent every second since you left trying to come up with a solution that addresses all of your concerns, and all of mine."

Reaching out, he took her left hand in both of his. A shock went through her at the contact, and she stopped breathing. "You can't do th—"

"Hush. Yes, we could argue that you're a duke's daughter and then a maid's daughter, and all the messy details about your birth. But I don't care about that, other than it made you who you are. I want you to be a part of my life, and I would like to be a part of yours. I want to live my life with you, and I want to have children with you, and I want them to be good-humored and strong like you are. I love . . . I love you, Sophia. I think I have since you wore that silly yellow dress. If you think perhaps you could care for me the way I c—"

"I love you, too, Adam," she whispered, more tears running down her face.

He closed his eyes for a moment, then opened them again to look up at her face. "Then marry me, Sophia. Be my wife. Be my duchess. Be anything you want, but do it with me. Save me. Save us both."

Her breath returned in a heart-rattling rasp. "But the scandal! Don't you realize what everyone will say?"

"I realize that very well. I don't care. I believe I've mentioned before that I'm a duke. I do as I please. I've never needed anyone's permission for anything. But I ask for yours. Will you marry me?"

How could he even ask the question? People like him didn't marry people like her. This wasn't a fairy tale.

And yet he continued to kneel before her, his hands shaking just a little as he held hers. His fingers were warm and gentle. His gray eyes gazed at her, hope and worry and a little bit of amusement lighting them from the inside. A duke. Her duke, if she wanted him. And she did, so very, very much.

"Yes," she said. "You're utterly mad, but yes."

He stood again, drawing her into his arms. "Then I advise you to kiss me, for God's sake, before I begin weeping."

Sophia laughed as his mouth met hers. He had saved them both. Or perhaps, she decided as he swung her in a slow, delightful circle, they had saved each other.